Elizabeth Chadwick lives in Nottingham with her husband and two sons. Much of her research is carried out as a member of Regia Anglorum, an early mediaeval re-enactment society with the emphasis on accurately recreating the past. She also tutors in the skill of writing historical and romantic fiction. She won a Betty Trask Award for *The Wild Hunt* her first novel, and was short-listed for the Romantic Novelists' Award in 1998 for *The Champion*, in 2001 for *Lords of the White Castle*, in 2002 for *The Winter Mantle* and in 2003 for *The Falcons of Montabard*.

For more details on Elizabeth Chadwick and her books, visit www.elizabethchadwick.com

Praise for Elizabeth Chadwick

'Blends authentic period details with modern convention for emotional drama'
Elizabeth Buchan, *Mail on Sunday*

'One of Elizabeth Chadwick's strengths is her stunning grasp of historical detail . . . her characters are beguiling, and the story intriguing and very enjoyable'
Barbara Erskine

'Prepare to be dazzled'
Nottingham Evening Post

'The best writer of medieval fiction currently around'
Historical Novel Review

'Elizabeth Chadwick knows exactly how to write convincing and compelling historical fiction'
Marina

SHIELDS OF PRIDE

Elizabeth Chadwick

SPHERE

First published in Great Britain in 1994 by Michael Joseph Ltd
This paperback edition published in 2007 by Sphere

A CIP catalogue record for this book
is available from the British Library.

ISBN 978-0-7515-4027-7

Papers used by Sphere are natural, recyclable products made from
wood grown in sustainable forests and certified in accordance with
the rules of the Forest Stewardship Council.

Typeset in Baskerville by Palimpsest Book Production Limited
Printed and bound in Great Britain by Clays Ltd, St Ives plc
Paper supplied by Hellefoss AS, Norway

Sphere
An imprint of
Little, Brown Book Group
100 Victoria Embankment
London EC4Y 0DY

An Hachette Livre UK Company

www.littlebrown.co.uk

Author's Note and Acknowledgement

Shields of Pride was published in hardcover in the UK in 1994 but due to various complications, not least the demise of the Maxwell empire, it was never followed up in paperback and thus has had very limited availability until now. I am delighted that Little, Brown has republished this long-out-of-print novel. I am also delighted to have had the opportunity to re-edit it with a fresh eye and I hope readers will enjoy this twelfth-century tale of adventure and romance.

I would like to say thank you to my editor Barbara Daniel at Little, Brown for giving me the chance to refurbish this novel for a second debut to a wider audience and, as always, the advice, friendship and tireless endeavour of my agent, Carole Blake, has been a solid foundation-stone.

A very special thank you goes to the members of Regia Anglorum, the early-medieval re-enactment society, who have taught me so much more than I could ever glean from research books alone. Down the years, being a part of Regia has proved an invaluable part of my research and my novels would be very different without the expertise of its members past and present.

My protagonists are imaginary but their circumstances are taken from lives that were lived. Indeed, readers familiar with a later novel of mine, *Shadows and Strongholds*, will know that another Joscelin, a mercenary captain, actually lived in the mid-twelfth century and was given custody of Ludlow Castle together with the rich widow Sybilla FitzJohn and her two daughters.

Rushcliffe and Arnsby are imaginary castles but the former is the name of a constituency in South Nottinghamshire and while it has no castle to its name, it deserves one!

Nottingham itself is riddled with underground cave systems and I have been down several of them in the course of my research. There is an excellent one open to the public in the Broad Marsh shopping centre in the city centre, once the site of the foulsome tanneries mentioned in passing in *Shields of Pride*.

1

Summer 1173

Swearing through his teeth, Joscelin de Gael drew rein at the head of his mercenary troop and scowled at the covered baggage wain that was slewed across the Clerkenwell road, blocking the way. He had been in the saddle since dawn. It was late afternoon now, had been raining all day, and the comfort of his father's London house was still five miles away on the other side of the obstruction.

An assortment of knights and men-at-arms surrounded the wain like witnesses clustering around a fresh corpse while a crouched man examined a damaged wheel. His cloak was trimmed with sable, his boots were of red leather and the horse his squire held was clean-limbed and glossy. A handful of women huddled together, anonymous in mantles and hoods, and watched the men from beneath the dubious shelter of an ash tree overhanging the road.

Dismounting, Joscelin tossed his reins to his own squire and approached the crippled wain. The soldiers stiffened, hands descending to sword-hilts and fingers tightening upon spear-shafts. The crouching man stood up and his gaze narrowed as he recognized Joscelin.

Joscelin eyed Giles de Montsorrel with similar disfavour.

The baron was distantly related to the Earl of Leicester and thus considered himself a man of high standing. He viewed Joscelin, the bastard of a warrior who had carved his own nobility by the sword, as dung beneath his boots. They had encountered each other occasionally on the French tourney circuits but no amity had sprung from these meetings, Montsorrel not being the kind to forgive being bowled from the saddle on the end of a blunted jousting lance.

Forced by circumstance to be civil, Montsorrel gave Joscelin an icy nod which Joscelin returned in the same spirit before fixing his attention on the broken wheel. Not just broken, he could see now, but with a hopelessly shattered rim. 'You haven't a chance in hell of cobbling a repair here,' he said. 'You'll have to hire another cart from the nearest village.' He walked slowly around the stricken wain, examining it from all angles before halting in front of the three sturdy cobs still harnessed in line between the shafts. 'How much weight do you carry?'

'None of your business!' Montsorrel snapped.

'Oh, but it is,' Joscelin said. 'I cannot bring my own wain past while yours is obstructing the road. If it's not too heavy, I'd be more than willing to help you drag it to one side.'

Montsorrel glared. 'You think I'm going to stand aside for hired scum like you?'

Joscelin thumbed the side of his jaw. Suddenly he was very aware of the pressure of his sword-hilt against his hip. 'Hired scum?' he repeated softly.

One of the women murmured to her companions and, detaching herself from their group, stepped forward to place herself between the two men. She faced Joscelin, forcing him to divert his attention from Montsorrel. She had delicate features and unfathomable grey-blue eyes that held his for a moment before she turned to indicate the broken wain.

'Messire, by the time we have found a wheelwright or hired another cart, the city gates will have closed for the night.' She hesitated. 'Forgive me, but I notice your own wain is larger than ours and but lightly laden. I am sure if you lent it to us of a kindness, my husband would compensate you for your inconvenience.'

Joscelin stared at her in surprise. He was accustomed to being propositioned by women but in different social circumstances and for different reasons, it had to be said, and never in front of their husbands. She looked down, a flush brightening her cheekbones. The rain continued to fall in a steady, cloth-soaking drizzle.

'Linnet!' Montsorrel's anger diverted from Joscelin to his wife. 'Do you dare to interfere?'

She flinched, but her voice was steady as she turned to him. 'I was thinking of your son, my lord. He must not catch a chill.'

Montsorrel cast an irritated glare in the direction of the other women. Joscelin looked, too. One of the bundled figures under the tree was a small child. A little hand was held in the grasp of a nursemaid and Joscelin received the impression of wide, frightened eyes and a snub nose set in a small, wan face. Amid anger at finding himself trapped because he could not for shame refuse the woman, he felt a thread of pity for the infant.

Montsorrel said stiffly to Joscelin, 'Very well, you're a mercenary. I'll pay you the rate to deliver the goods to my house.'

Joscelin bit back the urge to retort that he was not so much of a mercenary that he would allow the likes of Giles de Montsorrel to buy his obedience. 'I'll not serve you,' he said derisively, 'but your lady did speak of compensation. Perhaps we can reach an agreement.'

Montsorrel clenched his fists and looked as if he might burst.

'No?' Shrugging, Joscelin started to turn away.

'Christ's wounds, just get on with it!' Montsorrel snarled.

Joscelin gave a sarcastic flourish and sauntered away to instruct his men to strip and reload his own sound wain.

Linnet de Montsorrel rejoined the women. Her stomach was queasy with fear. Everything had its price and she knew she would have to pay hers later when she and Giles were alone.

'I'm cold, Mama,' her son whimpered, and abandoned his nurse to cling to Linnet's damp skirts.

She stooped to chafe his hands, noting with concern that his eyes were heavy and his complexion pale with exhaustion. 'It won't be long now, sweetheart,' she comforted. She folded him beneath the protection of her cloak like a mother hen spreading her wing over a chick.

'Madam, I know that man.' Ella, her personal maid, jutted her chin towards the mercenary whom Linnet had just shamed into helping them. 'It's Joscelin de Gael, son of William Ironheart.'

'Oh?' Linnet knew of William Ironheart by reputation. They said he was so hard he pissed nails, that he was stubborn, embittered and dangerous to cross. Linnet studied his son. 'How do you come to be acquainted with such a one?'

Ella blushed. 'I only know him by sight, madam. He was at my sister's wedding in the spring as a friend of the groom. They were both garrison soldiers at Nottingham Castle.'

4

Linnet assessed de Gael thoughtfully. She judged him to be in his late twenties. 'What is he doing in the mercenary trade if he's Ironheart's son?'

'He's only Lord William's bastard. His mother was a common camp-follower, so rumour says.' Ella folded her arms, hugging her shawl against her body. 'Apparently when de Gael's mother died in childbed, Lord William went mad with grief and tried to kill himself, but his sword shattered and he was only wounded. After that, men started calling him Ironheart because his breast was stronger than the steel. I'd say Brokenheart was more appropriate.' Ella's gaze returned to their reluctant rescuer, who was now standing back from the wain, one hand on his sword-hilt, the other pushing his rain-soaked hair off his forehead.

Linnet, all romantic notions literally knocked out of her head by six years of marriage to Giles, said nothing, her feeling one of irritation rather than pity. She knew what it was like to be usurped by another woman in your own hall and how much that other woman's status also depended on arrogant masculine whim.

Two panting men-at-arms struggled out of the broken wain carrying a large, ironbound chest between them.

'Make haste!' Giles snapped, and Linnet saw him scowl at de Gael, who was eyeing the chest with open speculation.

'I see now the kind of weight you carry,' de Gael remarked. 'Small wonder that your wheel broke.' In his own good time he withdrew his scrutiny and approached the women.

Linnet retreated behind downcast lids, knowing she would be the one to suffer if de Gael chose to take his impertinence further. Giles might think twice about assaulting a man of the mercenary's undoubted ability, but no such restraint would prevent him from beating her. She heard the men puffing and swearing as their strongbox was manoeuvred into de Gael's wain. Giles's voice was querulous with impatience and bad temper, and inwardly she quailed.

De Gael crouched on his heels and gently peeled aside a wet fold of her cloak. 'And who have we here?' he asked.

'My son, Robert.' She flashed a rapid glance at her husband. He was still occupied in ranting at his guards but in a moment he would turn round.

De Gael did not miss her look. 'You have a high courage, my lady,' he murmured. 'I won't make it harder for you than it already is.' Plucking the child from beneath her cloak, he swept him up in his arms. 'Come, my young soldier, there's a dry corner prepared especially for you in my cart.'

Linnet stretched her arms towards her son with an involuntary sound of protest. Robert peered at his mother over de Gael's shoulder, his eyes wide with shock, but the move had been so sudden that he had no time to cry and by the time he belatedly found his voice, he was being placed on a dry blanket in the good wain with a lambskin rug tucked up to his chin.

Linnet, following hard on de Gael's heels, found herself taken by the elbow and helped up beside her son. Robert stopped crying and began to knead the lamb's wool like a nursing kitten. Linnet stroked his brow and looked at de Gael. 'You have my gratitude,' she said. 'Thank you.'

The mercenary shrugged. 'No sense in keeping him out in that downpour when he can be warm in here. I expect your husband's compensation to reflect my care of his goods.' He started to withdraw. 'There is room for your women, too, my lady. I'll tell them, shall I?'

Rain pattered on the roof of the wain. She looked out

6

through a canvas arch on a tableau of hazy green and brown. The smell of her wet garments clogged her nostrils. De Gael walked across to her maids. He moved with a wolf's ungainly elegance and she did not think that the similarity stopped there. And yet he had been considerate beyond the bounds of most men of her acquaintance.

Linnet eyed her husband and felt queasy at the sight of his fists clenched around his belt. She had tried to be a good wife to him but he was difficult to please and she dwelt in a constant state of trepidation, wondering from which angle of his nature the next small cruelty would come. He always found a scapegoat to blame; nothing was ever his fault, and in the household that scapegoat was usually her.

Behind her, at the other end of the wain, their soldiers were depositing the clothing coffers with much bumping and cursing. Robert's eyelids drooped and closed. Linnet leaned her head against her son's, her arm around him, and wearily shut her own eyes.

2

'Joscelin, you rogue!' Maude de Montsart swamped her nephew in an embrace he remembered from childhood. His nostrils were overpowered by mingled scents of lavender, sweat and the sweet almond marchpane she adored. For the last five years she had been a widow and dwelling in the de Rocher household as a companion and housekeeper to the lady Agnes, his father's wife. 'What brings you to London?'

He returned her hug and smiled. 'I'm here for the horse fair. I have to replace some war gear, and I need a new palfrey.'

'I thought you'd be in France by now, doing the round of the tourneys.' She handed his saturated cloak to a servant and drew him down the hall to the dais where there stood a wine flagon and some fine glazed cups. Filling one from the other, she watched him drink. He took four rapid, deep swallows, and then breathed out hard. His shoulders relaxed and his smile this time was less perfunctory.

'Not this season. I've a contract to serve the justiciar until Michaelmas at least. He may send me and the men to Normandy to join the king but we're more likely to be used for garrison duty.' He refilled the cup and gazed around the hall. Two servants were lighting the candles and closing the shutters on a thickening but calm dusk. The rain had stopped an hour since and the sun had glimmered through the clouds in time to set. Another woman stirred a pot of soup over the central hearth and the smoke rising from the fire was savoury with the aroma of garlic and onions. There were some hangings on the wall he had not seen before and he noticed that his father had finally bought a new box chair for himself. The old one, through a combination of splinters and woodworm, had been lethal. The cups were new also. He recognized Maude's taste in the cheerful horse-and-rider scenes painted in thick white slip on the red background.

'It's a bad business, the king's own sons turning against him.' Maude folded her arms beneath her ample bosom and clucked her tongue. 'I'm old enough to remember how it was before Henry sat on the throne, and I never want to live through the like again. What was he thinking to have his eldest son anointed? Bound to give the boy ideas beyond himself.'

'He already had ideas beyond himself before that, feck-less whelp.' Joscelin took another long swallow of wine and felt it glide smoothly down his throat with a slight after-sting in his nostrils. 'When his father had him crowned he thought that by confirming the succession in so strong a manner he was creating stability. Little did he know.' He shook his head. 'I do not suppose he expected the discord to come from the very son he has anointed, but he was always going to store up trouble. The boy's realized that for all the frippery and promises he's no closer to power than he was as a swaddled infant. As far as his father's concerned, he can be a king all he wants

9

as long as it's king of nothing. I'm inclined to agree.' Grimacing, Joscelin twitched his shoulders. The rain had soaked through his cloak and there was an uncomfortable clamminess across the back of his neck. 'At least it keeps me employed. What does my father say?'

'The same as you, but he's less polite.'

Joscelin's hazel eyes brightened with amusement. 'Where is the old wolf anyway? I'd have expected him to have bellowed my backside off by now.'

'He's dining with the justiciar.'

'Is he now?' Joscelin looked thoughtful as he sat down in his father's new chair. Richard de Luci was the nominal ruler of England while the king was absent in Normandy. Fiercely loyal to Henry, he was a skilled administrator and warrior. Joscelin's father and Richard de Luci were friends of long standing and similar interests, but their socializing was usually a matter of business as well as pleasure.

'Apparently the Earl of Leicester and others are in London for the purpose of asking de Luci's permission to leave England with troops and money for King Henry's army.' Maude ordered a servant to bring food.

Joscelin raised his brows. Robert of Leicester was self-seeking and arrogant, without an honest bone in his body. If he was going to war, it was to feather his own nest at the expense of weaker men. King Henry was certainly not weak – but his son was. 'I saw some of that money today,' he told his aunt. 'Indeed, I helped bring it into the city. It was in the custody of one of young Henry's lick-boots and if I have not walked in here with Giles de Montsorrel's blood all over my hands, it is one of God's miracles.'

Maude sat down beside him, leaned her elbows on the trestle and gave him her full attention as he told her about

10

his encounter on the Clerkenwell road, his tone growing vehement with disgust as the tale progressed. 'De Montsorrel looked at me as if he had a stink beneath his nose that he was too highbred to mention. I tell you, if it were not for the women and the little boy, I'd have struck him in the teeth and withdrawn my aid. You should have seen his men struggling with his strongbox. There was more in it than a few shillings to buy himself a couple of nags at Smithfield and trinkets for his wife.'

'He's lately come into an inheritance.' Maude screwed up her face as she strove to remember. 'His father died of a seizure at Eastertide, although he'd been having falling fits for almost a year.'

Joscelin nodded. 'So I'd heard.' He did not add that Raymond's final seizure on Easter Sunday, immediately before Mass, had taken place between the thighs of a servant's daughter at the moment of supreme pleasure. The incident had been the source of much ribald comment in alehouse and barracks. Giles de Montsorrel had either a family reputation to keep up or one he was never going to live down. That thought reminded him of his own half-brothers and he grimaced.

'Are Ralf and Ivo here?'

A servant mounted the dais and set a steaming bowl of the soup before Joscelin, and a simnel loaf with a cross cut in the top.

'I'm afraid they are.' The pleated wrinkles around Maude's mouth deepened. 'Not that we often see them, the amount of time they spend carousing in the stews. Your father says they're just sowing wild oats and that they'll tire soon enough.'

'But you are not as convinced.'

'Would you be?'

Joscelin cut a chunk from the bread and dipped it into

the soup. 'You know how matters stand between my half-brothers and me,' he said. 'I'm the bastard, Ralf's the heir, and he rams it down my throat at every opportunity.' His expression was suddenly grim. 'And Ivo's like a sheep – follows Ralf's lead even if it happens to be off the edge of a cliff. Thank Christ I won't be here much above a week.'

'You've only just arrived!' Maude protested.

'I've a bad memory,' he said ruefully. 'It's not until I come home that I remember the reasons why I left in the first place and by then it's too late.'

3

Linnet de Montsorrel stared at a cobweb veiling an oak roof-beam. A spider was sucking the life from a fly that was still twitching feebly in the vampire embrace. Giles bit the soft skin between her throat and shoulder. His fingers gouged her buttocks, drawing her up to meet the crisis of his thrusting body. Clinging sweat, raw, stabbing pain. He groaned, stiffened and jammed into her as he climaxed. Linnet arched in silent agony. His arms relaxed and he collapsed on her with a gasp, flattening her into the mattress. On the web above her the fly no longer twitched, a mercy not permitted herself. She remained Giles's victim, to be unwrapped, impaled, and used repeatedly at his whim. Her ribs hurt and small spots of colour fluctuated before her eyes. 'Please!' she gasped. 'Please, you're crushing me!'

Still panting, he raised his head and glowered at her. 'God's eyes, don't you ever do anything but complain?' He slid out of her and rolled to one side. She averted her eyes from his genitals and closed her aching thighs. Her neck was sore where he had bitten her.

'Don't just lie there, fetch me a clean tunic!' he snapped. 'I've a rendezvous at Leicester's house tonight.'

Sitting up, Linnet drew on her chemise and went to the clothing pole. Crumpled on the floor were his discarded shirt and tunic, the latter torn in his haste to bed her. He would expect it mended by morning but at least if he was going out she had some time to herself.

'If you don't like it, you should hurry up and quicken with a babe,' Giles growled as he snatched the fresh garments from her hands. 'The only child you've borne to me in six years of marriage is that milksop weakling out there and you know what I think about him!'

Swallowing, Linnet turned away to fetch his belt. Bearing Robert had almost killed her, for she had not reached her full growth then and her hips had still been narrow. Giles had told the midwives to save the infant – he could always take another wife and what use was a bad breeder anyway? But she had survived and one of the midwives had advised her how to avoid quickening again too soon. It involved vinegar douches and small pieces of trimmed sponge or moss soaked in the same. Of late she had stopped using them in the hopes of conceiving again but thus far there had been no interruption to her monthly bleeds.

Giles donned his braies and tied the drawstring. 'You think I enjoy ploughing a corpse?' He flayed her with a look. 'I might as well spread the legs of an effigy for all the response I get from you!'

She risked a single frightened glance at his lean, tense frame, then looked at the floor. When he touched her, she did indeed wish to be dead or turned to stone.

'Mayhap you dream elsewhere,' he said as he plunged into his shirt and tunic. 'You must know that I was displeased with your boldness this afternoon.'

'I'm sorry, my lord; I was only thinking of Robert's welfare.'

14

'Were you indeed? I saw the way de Gael looked at you after you spoke to him. A man of his ilk needs little encouragement.'

'I swear I gave him none, my lord.' Cold fear rippled up Linnet's spine. She knew what he was capable of when riled. 'On my soul I swear it.'

Giles snatched the belt out of her hands and she flinched. 'On your soul?' he enquired softly. 'Shall we not say rather "on your hide"?' He ran the leather through his fingers until they stopped against the dragon's-head buckle.

'On my hide, I swear it,' Linnet said, looking at the intricate curlicues of English workmanship on the cold, solid bronze and knowing how much their impact hurt. 'I swear it.'

Giles drew out the moment, letting her suffer. 'I might have trusted you once,' he said huskily and a shadow of pain tensed the corners of his eyes. 'Then I discovered that any bitch in heat will run to be serviced by the nearest dog!' He jerked the belt around his lean waist and latched the buckle. 'If you give me cause to reprimand you again, you know the consequences.'

Linnet lowered her eyes and stared at the floor. She could see his legs, the right one thrusting belligerently forward, encased in soft red leather. 'Yes, my lord,' she whispered, feeling cold and sick.

He pivoted on his heel and headed to the door. 'Hurry up and get dressed, you've a household to order. Make yourself useful for something at least!' He flung out the door and she heard him descend the stairs, yelling at one of his squires to summon a boatman to row him down-river to Leicester's house.

After a moment Linnet gathered herself sufficiently to take a comb from her coffer to tidy her hair. She did not

15

want to summon her maid; she needed a moment of solitude to compose herself, to fix in position the calm facade she would present to her household. Hair smoothed, she picked up a small clay jar of marigold salve to anoint the mark on her throat.

It was not the first time that Giles had bitten her, nor the most painful, but as she broke the beeswax seal and took a daub of ointment on her fingertip, her eyes stung with tears. Jesu, how she hated being at his mercy, trapped like a fly in a web.

Vision blurring, she sat down on the strongbox, which stood beside Giles's clothing chest. The studs on the iron reinforcing bands dug into the backs of her thighs, which were still tender from the grip of his fingers. Beneath the strongbox's twin locks lay the coin from the sale of their entire wool clip and all the rents and toll monies from their villages. So did all the silver plate from the keep at Rushcliffe. The latter was part of her dowry and Giles had no right to bestow it upon Robert of Leicester for some dubious scheme in Normandy. Giles needed this coin to keep the moneylenders at bay. Promises did not put bread on the board and her husband had already taxed the villagers to the limit of their means. If there was a bad harvest this year, some of their people would starve for the cause of an adolescent youth with delusions of grandeur.

Giles was supposedly accompanying Leicester across the Narrow Sea to offer support to King Henry's efforts to crush his rebellious sons, but Linnet suspected that treachery was intended. Giles disliked the controls that King Henry had imposed on baronial rights and would certainly not beggar himself to go to the King's aid. To her husband, the prospect of an untried youth on the throne held endless possibilities, especially for the men who helped to place him there. It was a gamble, it was treason, and she had never seen Giles so excited – irritable and exhilarated at the same time. And it was she who bore the brunt of his mood swings.

Rising from the coffer, Linnet wiped away her tears on the heel of her hand. They were a release, nothing more. Giles was not softened by them and she would have dismissed them from her armoury long ago had she not discovered that others were less impervious to their effect.

She set her jaw and summoned Ella with a stony composure that did not falter even when the woman's eyes flickered over the ugly, blood-filled bruise on her neck with knowing, unspoken pity.

'You'll be wanting warm water and a towel first,' Ella said practically and went to fetch them.

Linnet lit a taper from the night candle and crossed the room to the small, portable screen at the end. Behind it, exhausted by the long, fraught journey, her son slept in his small truckle bed. Against the pillow, his hair stood up in waifish blond spikes. He was fine-boned and fragile, light as thistledown, and she loved him with a fierce and guilty desperation. Frail children so often died in infancy and she would find herself watching him intently, waiting for the first cough or sneeze or sign of fever to have him swaddled up and dosed with all manner of nostrums. And if he did live to adulthood, what kind of man would he make? Never such a one as his father, she vowed, although God alone knew the ways in which he would be twisted when he left the safety of her skirts for the masculine world beyond the bower.

'Never,' she vowed, hand cupped around the candle flame, protecting her child from the hot drip of the wax. If only it were as easy to protect him from his future.

4

Richard de Luci, chief custodian of the realm during King Henry's absence across the Narrow Sea, reclined in his pelt-spread chair, goblet resting comfortably on the neat curve of his belly, and regarded his guest. 'What do you think about the latest news from Normandy?'

William de Rocher, nicknamed Ironheart, stroked his chin. In his youth his hawkish features had been striking but advancing age and the effects of a life hard-lived had imbued his visage with an unsettling cadaverous quality.

'You mean about Queen Eleanor being caught defecting to Paris disguised as a man, to join her sons in rebellion? Nothing would surprise me about that wanton.' He cast a dark look at his own wife. Dumpy and plain, she sat like a lump of proving dough beside de Luci's elegant wife. At least Agnes knew her place, and if she ever approached the borderline of his tolerance, a bellow and a raised fist sent her scuttling back to her corner with downcast eyes and a trembling mouth. But some women, brought up without benefit of discipline, were wont to snarl and bite the hand that fed them. 'I trust she's well under lock and key now?'

'Indeed so, but it doesn't make the rebellion any less dangerous.'

Ironheart grunted and considered de Luci from beneath untidy silver brows. 'I hear the Earl of Leicester has approached you for permission to cross to Normandy and offer his support to the king. Rumour has it, too, that he has amassed no small amount of treasure to fund his expedition.'

De Luci stared at him, then laughed and shook his head. 'I swear to God, William, you know more than I do half the time!'

'I listen at the right keyholes,' Ironheart replied with a dour grin. 'Besides, Leicester's not exactly been making a secret of the fact, has he?'

'You've never approved of Robert of Leicester, have you?'

The grin faded. 'His father was as solid as granite; you could trust him with your life, but I wouldn't trust his heir further than I could hurl a fistful of fluff. And, before you ask, I've no evidence to prove him unworthy. It's a feeling inside here, a soldier's gut.' He struck the area between heart and belt.

'Then it's not jealousy because your sons spend more time in his company than they do in yours?'

Ironheart looked insulted. 'Why should I be jealous?' he scoffed. 'I am their father, he is just a turd clad in cloth of gold. Let them have their flirtation. Once they've unwrapped Earl Robert's bindings, they'll back away.'

De Luci pursed his lips, not so sure. 'I'm willing to give Leicester a chance,' he said and, with a rueful smile, patted his own paunch. 'A diplomat's gut, William.'

Ironheart snorted rudely and held out his wine cup to be refilled. 'I know which I'd rather trust.'

De Luci chose to ignore the remark and changed the

direction of the conversation. 'Did you know I'd commissioned Joscelin for the rest of the summer?'

'No, but I thought you might, the situation being what it is.'

'If the opportunity arises, I'd like to give him more responsibility – perhaps a seneschal's post. He's proven his abilities in my service time and again this last year and a half.'

William stared down at his war-scarred hands. 'I forget how old the boy is,' he said, 'and how old I am growing.' Then he gave a laugh that held more snarl than amusement. 'He'll make you a good seneschal if you give him the chance – one of the best.'

An atmosphere, rather than anything said, caused de Luci to glance at the women. Behind her doughy impassivity, he could tell that Agnes de Rocher was furious. Her fists were clenched and there were hectic red blotches on her throat and face. But then, he and William had been discussing Joscelin's advancement, which was tantamount in Agnes' presence to drawing a sword.

'Rohese, why don't you take Agnes above and show her those bolts of silk that arrived yesterday from Italy,' he said to his wife, hoping to rectify the lapse of his diplomat's gut.

'By your leave, my lord,' murmured Rohese de Luci, giving him a look compounded of irritation and sympathy as she signalled for the finger bowl.

De Luci returned her look with one of apologetic gratitude and knew that he would now have to purchase the bolt of peacock-coloured damask she had been angling after.

As the women curtseyed and left the hall, William's breath eased out on a long sigh of relief. 'When Martin enters your household next year to be a squire, I'm going to buy her a pension in a nunnery,' he said, eyes upon his wife's disappearing rump.

De Luci quirked an eyebrow. 'Does Agnes know?'

'Not yet.' Ironheart shrugged. 'I can't see her objecting. We live separate lives most of the time as it is.'

De Luci said nothing, although he gave his friend a wry glance. If Agnes de Rocher was scarcely the ideal wife, William de Rocher was certainly not the perfect husband. De Luci had been a groomsman at their wedding almost thirty years ago and had watched them labour under the yoke, mismatched and tugging in opposite directions. And after Joscelin's mother had left her mark on their lives, any chance of marital harmony had been utterly destroyed.

Ironheart took a long swallow of his wine. 'To future freedom,' he toasted. 'Let's talk of other matters.'

Ironheart's squire handed Agnes from her litter and set her down in the courtyard at the rear of the house. William dismounted from his palfrey. The perfume of rain-wet grass and leaves drifted from the orchards beyond the stables and warred with the smell of the saturated dung and straw underfoot. At the end of the garden the Thames glinted in the last green glow of twilight. A groom and his apprentice emerged from the depths of the stables, the latter bearing a candle-lantern on a pole. By its light, William saw that the stalls were crowded with horseflesh, little of it his own.

Bestowing his mount's reins upon the lad, he stooped under the lintel and, hands on hips, regarded the additions. A handsome liver-chestnut with distinctive white markings swung its head from the manger and regarded him with a liquid, intelligent eye. He knew Whitesocks well, for he had bred him from his own stud herd and gifted him to Joscelin four years ago as a leggy, untrained colt.

Agnes sniffed furiously. 'How long are these animals going to eat us out of house and home?' she demanded, goaded by resentment to a boldness that she would not usually have dared.

'It will only be for a couple of days. He'll be stabling them at the Crown's expense after that,' William answered in a preoccupied voice.

The mildness of his response encouraged Agnes to press harder. 'You know that Ralf and Joscelin hate the sight of each other. This is just asking for a confrontation.'

'And I am master in this house. There will be no trouble.' He stroked the satin liver-chestnut hide. 'Besides, Ralf's not here. He's out wasting his substance in some den of fools.'

Agnes glared at her husband's long, straight spine and mane of unkempt, badger-grey hair. As a bride of sixteen, she had loved him so hard that even to look at him had made her queasy with joy. And in those first months he had been kind enough for her to imagine that he at least returned a measure of her affection. She had borne him four daughters in as many years and became pregnant again within three months of Adele's birth. Exhausted, sick and miserable, she had watched William ride away to war and every day she had prayed for him, callousing her knees on the cold chapel floor.

Her pleas to God had been answered after a fashion, for three months later he had returned unscathed, bringing with him a contingent of Breton mercenaries to garrison their castle. He had also brought a woman, the sister of one of the mercenaries. The glow of early pregnancy had been upon her, making her shine like a candle among

22

common rush dips. She had been dark-haired, green-eyed and regal of bearing, and she had given William his first son to replace Agnes's own stillborn baby boy. It was then, seeing the blaze of joy, triumph and naked love in William's eyes, that Agnes had begun to learn hatred.

Three sons she had given him since then but her success was tarnished. The shadow of Morwenna and her bastard had made all her own efforts dross. 'There is always trouble when Joscelin shows his face,' she said bitterly.

William rounded on her with angry eyes. 'Watch your tongue or you'll be wearing a scold's bridle to curb it,' he growled.

Compressing her lips, she turned from him and marched angrily across the yard and up the exterior stairs to the upper floor of the house. She would not go into the hall, for that would have meant acknowledging Joscelin. A maid opened the door for her but it was Agnes who slammed it shut, the sound reverberating across the soft summer dusk.

William's eyelids tensed. He knew he was not being fair but he didn't care enough to change his attitude. When he entered the hall, Joscelin was lounging on a bench before the central hearth. His squire sat on a footstool nearby, fair head bent over a dagger grip he was rebinding with new strips of hide. A different dagger twisted in William's heart as he approached the fire and his eldest son raised his head. God's life, he was so much like his mother. The green-hazel eyes and the expression in them were all hers and flooded Ironheart with unbearable bittersweet memories.

Joscelin sprang to his feet and engulfed his father in a bone-crunching embrace. They were of a height and similar build, for William still had a tough, muscular body on which no softness had been allowed to encroach.

'I swear you grow more like a plough ox every time I see you!' Ironheart gasped and, thrusting his son aside, prowled to the hearth. The squire scrambled to his feet in deference, blue eyes wary.

'Fetch wine,' William commanded, 'two cups.' He glanced at the cloak spread upon the chair and spilling to the floor. 'I trust you'll stay to drink a measure with your old father?'

Joscelin's colour heightened. 'Of course, sir. I was waiting for you.'

William grunted and gave him an eloquent stare but said nothing. If Joscelin intended going out into the city at night it was none of his business but, nevertheless, he was curious. Joscelin was not usually one for the vices that were to be found in the alehouses and stews on the wrong side of curfew.

The squire returned with the wine.

'Was your journey free of hazard?'

Joscelin looked at the floor for a moment before raising laughter-bright eyes. 'How do you always know where to strike a nut to crack the shell and come to the meat?'

'Call it grim experience.'

For the second time that evening Joscelin related the tale of his encounter with Giles de Montsorrel. 'It stinks like a barrel of rotten fish,' he concluded. 'Why should he want to bring his worldly wealth all the way to London?'

From the upper floor came the muffled sound of women's voices and the loud thud of a coffer lid opening and slamming. William flickered an irritated glance aloft. 'He's related to Robert of Leicester, is he not? And Leicester has obtained de Luci's permission to sail for Normandy in the next week or so with men and money to succour King Henry, or so Leicester would have us believe. Myself, I've heard more truth in a minstrel's lay.'

Joscelin nodded thoughtfully. 'And Montsorrel is contributing his bit to Leicester's endeavor. From what I know of Giles, if he was going to take sides I would say that he would choose young Henry's.'

Ironheart gave a disparaging shake of his head. 'I certainly wouldn't chance my all on an untried youth of sixteen with a reputation for being as fickle as a Southwark whore, both on the battlefield and off. Mind you, it's easier to manipulate a vain, spoiled boy than it is to obtain satisfaction from a man well versed in statecraft who's had his backside on the throne for the past twenty years.' William took a swallow of wine. 'Giles de Montsorrel is a fool.'

'A wealthy fool with the Rushcliffe inheritance new in his purse,' Joscelin said.

'Hah, not for long,' Ironheart said. 'He's already squandered most of the money his wife brought to their marriage bed. I knew her father, Robert de Courcelles – too soft for his own good, but decent enough.' He gave his son a shrewd look and changed the subject. 'De Luci informs me he's keeping you on through the summer.'

Joscelin shrugged. 'The rewards are greater on the tourney circuits, but so are the risks. Garrison duty's usually boring but if there's food in my belly and money in my pouch, I won't grumble.'

William winced. There was no rancour in Joscelin's tone, no intent to complain, but still the older man was struck by guilt. This was his firstborn son, the only child Morwenna had given him, and because he was bastard born debarred from inheriting any of the de Rocher lands. Joscelin had had to make his own way in the world and that meant either by the priesthood or by the sword. William had done his best, educated Joscelin for both vocations and furnished him with the tools of his chosen trade, but it would never be enough for his bleeding conscience.

'I doubt you'll have time for boredom to be a hazard,' he said as Joscelin drained his cup and reached for his cloak. 'De Luci didn't say much but I gather he's got more in mind for you than just garrison duty.'

Joscelin forced his cloak pin through the good woollen cloth. 'Such as?'

'That's for de Luci to tell you.'

Joscelin's brows arched. 'I'd best make the most of my freedom, then,' he said, and gestured round. 'As you've noticed by the emptiness in the hall, my men are already about it with gusto.'

Ironheart could sense the undercurrent of turbulence in Joscelin's manner – probably a residue of the meeting with Montsorrel and his wife that afternoon. A night in an alehouse might settle it, or a woman who knew her trade, but it was a dangerous burden to bear into London after curfew. 'Have a care, my son,' he said with a warning stare.

'As always.' Joscelin dismissed the caution far too lightly for his father's liking and, with a casual salute, disappeared into the night.

William heaved a sigh. Gesturing the wide-eyed squire away to his pallet, he sat down before the banked hearth to finish his wine. His thoughts, of their own volition, strayed to Joscelin's mother. Morwenna. Even now, the mere thought of her name twisted his vitals.

She had been a mercenary's sister whose favours he had bought one spring evening in 1144 while on campaign. Until Morwenna, he thought he had women in perspective but she had broken all rules and moulds and finally his heart. Five years it had lasted, from the night she unbound her hair for him at an army campfire to the night they combed it down over the cold breast of her corpse, a swaddled stillborn daughter in the crook of her arm. Nothing of her existence had remained except a bewildered little boy and an even more bewildered man of four-and-thirty.

Dear Christ, how he had hated Agnes in the months following Morwenna's death. All the tolerance in his nature had died, all the gentleness too. He should have been delighted at how swiftly his wife quickened with child, at how easily she was delivered, but he had felt nothing but cursed. He knew he treated his dogs better than he did Agnes but it was ingrained now. Every time he looked at her, he saw Morwenna's lifeless body and grieved anew. They said that it was a tragic accident, that fall downstairs so late into her pregnancy. The afterbirth came away, she started to bleed, and she and the baby had died. He hadn't reached her in time even to have the grace of a last farewell.

The candle on the pricket near him sputtered and he emerged from his dismal reverie with a start. In the shadows beyond the light, the servants were asleep on straw mattresses. Normally they would have drawn nearer to the fire, but no one dared to encroach on his solitude. Ironheart heaved himself to his feet, tossed the wine dregs into the flames where they hissed into vapour, and wearily sought his bed.

Farther along the Strand, the Earl of Leicester's house stood open to the last of the gloaming. It was a new dwelling, constructed of traditional plaster and timber with a red-tiled roof. Tiles were more expensive than thatch but a symbol of status and far less of a fire hazard. Both indoors and out, torches blazed in high wall-brackets, illuminating the revellers who either sat at long trestles in the puddle-filled courtyard or crowded into the main room, jostling one another for elbow room. Herb-seasoned mutton, shiny with grease, hissed over fire pits in the garth, tended by a spit-boy half-drunk on cider. He wavered erratically between the carcasses, a cup in one hand, basting ladle in the other.

Joscelin hesitated. He could see some of the justiciar's men at one of the trestles – soldiers of his acquaintance who would welcome him among their number. The light and laughter beckoned. So did a girl with slumberous dark eyes and the slender body of a weasel. She smiled at Joscelin and lounged on one hip in blatant invitation. Against his better judgement but susceptible to the lure tonight, he stepped across the threshold and entered the crowded room.

The tables lining the walls were packed with Leicester's knights and retainers. He saw a Flemish mercenary captain he knew from the tourney circuits and two renowned jousters who had been overwintering at the earl's board. On the dais at the far end of the room, beneath crisscrossed gilded banners, sat Leicester himself. He was a fleshy man in his early thirties, handsome in an overblown, florid way that did not bode well for his looks and health in his later years. An arm was draped in camaraderie across the shoulders of his guest Giles de Montsorrel and the latter was well on the way to being drunk if his exaggerated gestures and overloud voice were any indication. At his other side, hunched forward listening to the conversation, sat another distant relative of Leicester's, Hubert de Beaumont. Joscelin knew him vaguely – a disreputable roisterer who would cling like a leech to any lord prepared to sponsor him in the tourneys, although he'd had precious little success on the circuit.

Deciding that the girl was not worth the discomfort of drinking in such a rancid den of rebels, even with a leavening of de Luci's men present, Joscelin turned to leave.

'Ho, peasant!' crowed a mocking voice he knew only too well and his shoulder was thumped with bruising force. 'Come scrounging like the rest, have you?'

Joscelin turned slowly to face his half-brother.

'Aelflin, fetch wine for our exalted guest!' commanded Ralf de Rocher with a sarcastic flourish.

The dark-eyed girl fluttered her eyelashes and swayed off to do his bidding. Ralf reseated himself and made room for Joscelin on the crowded bench but the gesture held more challenge than generosity. At the same table among other young knights and squires sat Ivo, younger than Ralf by two years and a shadowy replica of his copper-haired brother.

'Have you come to hire out your sword?' Ralf asked. 'Leicester's paying good rates and you look as if you need the coin.' His light-brown stare disparaged Joscelin's garments which, although of good-quality wool, showed evidence of hard wear and were devoid of embroidery or embellishment.

'I already have a commission,' Joscelin replied. 'I'm not so poor that I cannot choose a decent paymaster.'

'Oh ho!' Ralf gave a mocking grin. 'Living on principles, are we?'

Ivo laughed nervously. 'Have you ever known a mercenary with principles?' His glance sidled between Ralf and Joscelin and anticipation gleamed through his sandy lashes.

'You wouldn't know a principle, Ivo, if it walked up to you and bit you on the backside,' Joscelin said with disdain.

The girl returned with a pitcher and refilled the empty cups at the trestle with rough red wine. Ralf caught her wrist and swung her round on to his lap. She squealed but did not resist as his arm encircled her waist and his hand took liberties upwards.

'So you're already commissioned?' Ralf asked.

'To the justiciar until Michaelmas.' Joscelin took a gulp of the wine.

Ralf fondled the girl's breasts. 'You reckon you're going to live that long?'

'Longer than you.' Joscelin swept a contemptuous gaze around the crowded trestles. 'If you think this expedition to Normandy is the easy way to glory, then your brains must dwell in your arse.'

Ivo sniggered.

'Don't judge me by your own baseborn abilities,' Ralf growled. 'What would you know of brains?' Ralf's focus suddenly altered and fixed on the heavily set man easing past their trestle. 'Hubert.' He set a detaining arm on the man's sleeve. 'Have you met my brother Joscelin?'

Hubert de Beaumont paused to give Joscelin a brusque nod of acknowledgement. 'Your face looks familiar,' he said. 'Didn't I see you in Paris at Easter?'

'Try the midsummer joust at Anet last year.'

Beaumont frowned. His lips moved, repeating Joscelin's words, and his expression suddenly changed. 'Yes, I remember.' His tone was not altogether complimentary. He turned back to Ralf. 'He's your brother, you say?'

'Only my half-brother,' Ralf replied and added with malicious delight, relishing each word, 'He's my father's bastard out of a tourney whore who'd had more lances in her target than an old quintain shield by the time she came to his bed.'

The serving girl screamed as she was sent flying and the brothers hit the trestle, Joscelin uppermost, fist raised. Cups flew in all directions, their contents splattering far and wide. The pitcher crashed on its side, bleeding a lake of wine across the scrubbed oak. The brothers rocked for a moment on the board, the red Anjou soaking like a huge bloodstain into Ralf's tunic, and then they crashed to the floor, rolling amid the rushes.

Open-mouthed, Hubert de Beaumont stared. Ivo brushed wine from his tunic with the palm of one hand and shifted his position the better to watch the brawl, his complexion flushed with glee.

Ralf came uppermost, his hand flashing to his dagger-hilt. Nine inches of greased steel sparkled free. Joscelin brought up his knee and kicked hard, hurling Ralf back towards the fire pit. Ralf sprawled his head, almost striking a hearthstone, but he recovered swiftly, regained his feet and attacked. Joscelin wove under the slashing assault and again thrust Ralf backward. His own hand streaked to his dagger, closed on the leather grip, then stopped, holding hard, for Ralf lay where he had landed and a soldier was crushing a booted foot down upon Ralf's wrist.

Joscelin recognized Brien FitzRenard of Ravenstow, one of de Luci's retainers – a knight skilled in both reconnaisance and diplomacy. He was tall and powerfully built with exquisitely barbered blond hair and shrewd grey eyes surrounded by fine weather-lines.

'Enough,' FitzRenard said and stooped to remove the offending weapon from Ralf's hand. He looked at Joscelin, his gaze irritated, but not unfriendly. 'Best if you leave now before anything uglier develops.' His voice, like his movements, was measured without being in the least slow.

Joscelin glanced round the room. A low hum of conversation had started again. He was aware of being scrutinized with a mixture of hostility, contempt and curiosity. On the dais, Leicester's expression was one of cold anger. Giles had succumbed to the wine, his head flat on the board, his mop of fair hair trailing its edges in the finger bowl.

FitzRenard lifted his boot and permitted Ralf to regain his feet but displayed no inclination to return the dagger. Ralf was breathing heavily. His expensive tunic was ruined by the wine stain and stubbled with bits of floor straw.

'One day I'll kill you, I swear it!' Ralf gasped at Joscelin. He was white and shaking with rage.

'Then I'll make sure to guard my back,' Joscelin retorted. 'It's the only direction from which I fear your attack.' Wiping a thin trickle of blood from the corner of his mouth, he stormed out into the humid summer evening. His breath came unevenly and tears of fury and humiliation stung his eyes. He was aware of having failed himself, of not wanting to care and of caring too damned much.

5

The mouse sat on its haunches, industriously manipulating an ear of grain in its forepaws, sharp teeth nibbling through the husk to reach the sweet, starchy kernel. Sunlight wove through the crack in the stable door, patterning the straw, splashing up the wattle-and-daub walls and gilding the hide of a dozing liver-chestnut stallion.

Joscelin watched the busy rodent with the myopic gaze of the newly awakened. His head was throbbing and his mouth was dry and tasted of kennel sweepings – payment for last night's sins of which, after the fight with Ralf, he remembered very little – nor wished to.

A blur of rust and gold suddenly shot past the tip of his nose and pounced in a flurry of straw. Startled, Joscelin jerked upright, heart thrusting vigorously against his ribs. The tabby stable cat regarded him, a mixture of wariness and disdain in its agate-green eyes, a mouse dangling from its jaws like a moustache. Then, keeping him in view, it slunk across the stable and undulated through the narrowly open door into the courtyard.

Joscelin exhaled with a soft groan and put his head down between his parted knees. Outside he could hear the sounds of his father's house coming to life in the bright summer morning – two maids gossiping at the trough, the cheeky wolf-whistle of a soldier and the good-natured riposte. Hens crooned and scratched in the dust. Feet scuffled immediately outside the stable door, voices consulted in low tones, one adolescent, the other mature.

'I have to tend the horses, sir, but he's still asleep in there.'

'Not surprising, the state he returned in last night,' commented the older voice. 'All right, go and break your fast. I'll see if I can rouse him up.'

'No need,' Joscelin pushed open the stable door to the full light of morning and squinted blearily at the groom and his wide-eyed lad. He raked his hand through his rumpled hair and plucked out a stalk of straw. 'I would have made my way to bed in the hall but the stables were closer and I wasn't sure my feet would carry me the extra distance.'

A grin widened the groom's weather-brown face. 'You were a trifle unsteady, Messire Joscelin,' he agreed.

'I was gilded to the eyeballs,' Joscelin replied, 'and I've a head to prove it this morning.'

The apprentice sidled away to get his food before the groom had a chance to press him to his duty now that there was no longer an obstacle.

Joscelin loosened the drawstring of his braies and relieved himself in the waste channel that ran the length of the stable block.

'Messire Ralf didn't come home at all,' the groom volunteered and, picking up the dung fork, looked round in exasperation for his lad. 'Your lord father's not best pleased.'

Joscelin adjusted his garments and went to wash his hands and face in the rain butt against the gutter pipe.

His cut lip stung and his ribs ached. His lord father was going to be even less pleased when he heard about the fight. Perhaps he already knew; Ivo excelled at carrying tales.

'What about Ivo?'

'Sick as a dog,' said the groom with a gleam of satisfaction.

Joscelin's lips twitched. It might be possible to avoid the reckoning until he was fit to cope with it, after all.

'Joscelin!' A freckle-faced boy came sprinting across the yard and launched himself at Joscelin, clambering his body as if it were a tree and swarming aloft to sit on his shoulders. 'Will you take me to see the dancing bear at Smithfield?' He peered down into Joscelin's face at an angle that made focusing for Joscelin a nauseous pain. Raising his arms, he grabbed the child and somersaulted him to the ground, setting him on his feet.

His youngest half-brother, Martin, gazed up at him, an urchin grin polishing his face. At eight years old, he was soon to fledge the nest for a page's position in de Luci's household. He possessed his full share of the de Rocher self-assurance, although at the moment it was innocent rather than arrogant.

'Why in the world should I take you anywhere?' Joscelin demanded.

Chuckling, the groom departed in search of his wily apprentice.

'I'll be good, I promise!'

'I've heard that one before, too!'

'Please,' Martin beseeched with eyes as soulful as a hound's so that, despite his aching head, Joscelin had to bite his lip on his amusement.

'Let me settle my wits and my gut first and I'll see,' he said, and started towards the house. Martin skipped beside

35

him like a spring lamb and chattered about the dubious fairground delights offered on Smithfield's perimeter.

'There's a real mermaid!' he enthused as they entered the hall together. 'All bare up here but it costs a whole penny to see her.'

Joscelin knew the 'mermaid' well since fairgrounds and tourneys frequently travelled sword-in-sheath. The nearest she had ever come to being a fish was servicing herring men in a Southampton brothel. Her long blonde hair was a wig and her 'tail' was made of cunningly stitched snake-skins. He supposed that she had good breasts if that was the only opportunity you ever got to see a pair, but hardly a full penny's worth. 'Gingerbread's better value,' he advised gravely and halted, his expression becoming blank, as Lady Agnes descended upon them, her face puckered in temper.

'Where have you been?' she snapped at Martin and grabbed his arm in a pincer grip. 'Go and change your tunic, hurry. We're due at the justiciar's hall within the hour. You look like something disreputable in a merce-nary's baggage train!' She released him with a push.

Self-assured Martin might be, but not stupid, and he obeyed her command at a run, grimacing over his shoulder at Joscelin as he reached the end of the hall.

Her insult had been all for Joscelin. Last night he had responded to Ralf's baiting with violence. Now he offered the lady Agnes a stony courtesy. She might claim that he had been bred in the gutter but she was the one who stooped to it to sling mud.

He sat down at a trestle and took a small loaf from the bread basket in the centre of the table. Then he poured himself a mug of ale. He could have insisted on taking his place at the high table and commandeering white bread and good wine, but he could not be both-ered with that sort of battle this morning.

'Where's my father?' he asked, a glance round the hall showing him a suffering, bleary handful of his own men, the steward and servants, but few of the de Rocher retainers. For a moment he thought that she was not going to reply. Her eyes narrowed and her lips tightened. *None of your business*, her expression said, but the submission to male dominance was so ingrained that she did not openly defy him. 'He's gone to fetch Ralf from Leicester's house,' she said frostily and turned her back on him to chivvy the servants.

Joscelin broke the bread and began to eat. Small joy his father would have of Ralf, he thought. At four-and-twenty, brimful of anger and resentment, his half-brother was too old and dangerous to be whipped to heel like a raw adolescent. He regarded the skinned knuckles of his own right hand, flexed them and winced.

Agnes stalked away from the trestle with a stony face. The servants suffered. Joscelin thought about holding his ground and decided that it wasn't worth the aggravation. Cramming a final piece of bread into his mouth, he took his cup outside to finish his ale in peace. It was a mistake. As he sauntered into the warm morning air his father arrived, Ralf riding behind and both of them obviously in filthy tempers.

Ironheart dismounted, cuffed the groom's apprentice across the ear for being a fraction too slow at the bridle, and stamped towards the hall. His pace checked for an instant when he saw Joscelin and a muscle ticked beneath his cheekbone. Then he came on, his body stiff with anger.

'Leicester's house!' he snarled at Joscelin as he came level. 'You couldn't have chosen a more public place to brawl had you scoured all of London! You shame me and you shame your blood!'

Joscelin looked beyond his father's mottled fury to where Ralf still sat on his horse. 'I had good reason,' he said quietly. His fist tightened around the cup.

'Leicester says you were drunk,' Ironheart snapped. 'He was only too pleased to furnish me with the details while I dragged Ralf off some strumpet he'd fallen asleep on. I'd have done better to take a vow of celibacy than beget the brood of half-wit sons collaring me now!'

'I wasn't drunk, I was angry,' Joscelin said.

'And spoiling for a fight before you left me last night. A dozen eyewitnesses say that you started it. If you can't control that anger then you're not fit to lead men!'

Joscelin's shoulders went back as if he had taken a blow, but he said nothing. Not for the world would he repeat the insult that had goaded him to strike.

'Oh, get out of my way!' Ironheart snapped. 'Let me swallow a drink before I choke!' Thrusting past Joscelin into the house, he bellowed at his wife like a wounded bear.

Ralf rode over to Joscelin, deliberately fretting the horse, making it prance. 'I thought for the good of your hide you'd be long gone by now,' he said.

'As usual, you thought wrong,' Joscelin retorted.

Ralf's complexion was pale and sweaty. An ugly bruise marred his left eye socket where Joscelin's fist had connected the night before. Reddish beard stubble framed the compressed line of his mouth. 'One day I'll be lord of all my father owns and you'll be nothing,' he said, each word edged with bitterness. The horse stamped and sidled. The swish of its tail clipped the cup in Joscelin's hands.

Joscelin refused to be intimidated. 'You really don't know the difference, Ralf, between having nothing and being nothing,' he said and poured the dregs from his cup onto the ground. The dust lumped and glistened. 'I might sell my sword for money but never my integrity.'

For a moment, the prospect of another brawl hung imminent but the sound of Ironheart's choler-choked voice barking through the open hall doors held the brothers to caution. Ralf bestowed a single, glittering look on Joscelin that spoke more eloquently than words and snatched the horse around towards the waiting groom. In the course of its turn, his mount's glossy shoulder brushed Joscelin, forcing him to step back. A hoofprint bit into the dark stain in the dust where the drink had spilled. Joscelin stared at it and then at his brother's back. It was long and broad and the amount of fine Flemish cloth required to make his tunic must have cost Lady Agnes's domestic budget several shillings.

Ralf did not know the privation of lying down at a roadside because there was nowhere better to sleep. He had never had to fight for each mouthful of food or gather firewood in freezing, sleety rain when you were so weary you wanted to give up and die, but couldn't because people were depending on you. Ralf did not know what real hunger was.

Ralf moved restlessly around his mother's chamber, touching this and that without any real purpose. Agnes watched his progress with troubled eyes. She could still feel the dry imprint of his kiss on her cheek. He stank of wine, sweat and the cheap scent of whores. She was disappointed but not surprised; nor did she blame him. It was all William's fault.

'Shall I find you some salve for your eye, my love?'

Ralf shook his head and fiddled with a piece of braid lying on top of her work basket. 'It doesn't hurt,' he muttered. He dropped the braid and moved to the window.

Agnes admired his spare, angular grace and the gleam of his sun-bright hair. She was so proud of his golden fierceness and the fact that she had given him life.

'I need money,' he said. 'I don't want to ask my father and, even if I did, he would not give it to me.'

'How much?'

'Enough to see me comfortable while I'm in Normandy with Leicester's troops.'

Her heart plummeted. 'You are truly going?'

He said nothing but, after a moment, turned his head and fixed her with a stare that held a world of discontent and frustration. His eyes were light brown like her own. With the sun striking them obliquely, they held flecks of suspended gold. The swollen bruise was an affront to his beauty.

'Have you told your father?'

'Not in so many words, but he knows.'

And would do nothing to help him, Agnes thought, because he thoroughly disapproved of Robert of Leicester. If she herself disapproved it was because of the danger to Ralf's safety, but she knew she could no more hold him or persuade him to do her bidding than she could handle William's great Norway hawk. To her mind, it thus made eminent sense to ensure that Ralf had everything he needed to survive.

'How much?' she asked again and went to her jewel casket. Every penny she spent had to be accounted for to William but she still had her jewellery which was hers to dispose of as she wished. William never noticed whether she wore trinkets or not and she seldom felt the need to deck herself in finery. If she could spare Ralf even a moment of hardship, she would give up every last piece.

He left the window niche and crossed the room to stand at her shoulder as she raised the lid. There were rings and brooches, ornate belts, clasps and a braid girdle that her waist had outgrown in the course of numerous pregnancies. Ralf ignored all these and pounced upon a reliquary cross on a thick gold chain.

'This will do,' he said and held it up to the light. Amethyst and moonstone, sapphire and beryl flashed amid a fire of sun-caught gold. 'Thank you, Mother, I can always count on you for an ally.' He rewarded her with another kiss, less perfunctory this time, and, ducking the cross around his neck, headed for the door.

On the threshold he encountered his aunt Maude, a dish of marchpane-covered dates in her hand. He kissed her, too, snatched several of the sweetmeats off the tray and, whistling loudly, pounded away down the stairs.

Maude looked curiously at Agnes, who, pink-faced, was closing and locking her jewel casket.

'Ralf's uncommonly cocky to say that William almost flayed him alive earlier,' Maude remarked, setting the dish on the coffer. 'Have you been helping him out again?'

'If I have, it's none of your business,' Agnes sniffed. She considered her sister-in-law to be a greedy, interfering sow and a spy in the household.

'Just be careful. I don't think William would approve.'

Agnes gave her a hostile stare. 'Are you going to tell him?'

Maude shrugged and reached for one of the sweet-meats. 'It's none of my business, is it?' she said, returning Agnes' look impassively.

41

6

Linnet watched the dancing bear shamble in slow circles to the tune its owner was playing on a bone flute. A tarnished silver brooch pinned a moth-eaten bearskin at the man's shoulder and around his throat was a necklace of bear teeth interspersed with wicked curved claws. She had no doubt that they were the remains of the showman's former animal.

She eyed the stout chain that attached the bear to its stake and hoped there were no weak links. The beast itself looked weary to death. Its coat was scabby with mange, its eyes listless and the stench emanating from its body caused her to draw her wimple across her face. Poor creature, she thought, for she knew what it was to be trapped and forced to dance at another's will until nothing of self remained.

Glancing around, she watched her husband and some knights from Leicester's mesnie trying out the paces of the war-horses at a coper's booth nearby. Strange how there was money for what he wanted but never sufficient for her own requests. She had almost had to beg him that morning for the coin to purchase needles and thread and linen for summer tunics. It made her feel bitter when she thought of all that silver in their strongbox going to finance a stupid war.

Robert hid behind her skirts and peeped out at the bear, his grey eyes enormous with wonder and fear. He was clutching a honeyed fig in his little hand and Linnet was well aware that her gown would be covered in sticky fingerprints before the morning was out.

'Joscelin, look, here's the bear, I told you!' a child's voice shrilled.

Turning, Linnet saw an excited boy of about eight years old pointing towards the bear with one hand and dragging a laughing, resigned man with the other. Today Joscelin de Gael had discarded his mail for a tunic of russet wool, the sleeve-ends banded with tawny braid to match the undertunic and chausses. The excellence of the cloth was only emphasized by its lack of embellishment and the slightly worn but good-quality belt slanting between waist and hip, drawn down by the weight of a serviceable dagger. He and the child bore a resemblance to each other in the shape of their faces, the way they smiled and the manner of their walk.

Fascinated by the bear, too young to see the tarnish of its moth-eaten plight, the boy stared. De Gael shook his head and looked indulgent. Then he saw her and his expression became one of surprised pleasure.

'Lady de Montsorrel!'

Linnet's maid moved defensively to her side, and the two soldiers whom her husband had set over her as escort and guard eyed de Gael with sour disfavour and took closer order.

'Messire,' she murmured and lowered her gaze, knowing that Giles would blame her for any familiarity. And yet de Gael was owed a courteous response. 'I must thank you again for yesterday.'

'I didn't have much choice, did I?' he asked with amusement.

Linnet knew that she was blushing because her face felt hot. She dared not look up in reply to his teasing gambit. Joscelin de Gael rode the tourney circuits and she had to assume that flirting with women was just another accoutrement of his trade. His very presence at her side was a danger to her reputation, especially after yesterday.

He crouched on his heels, hands dangling in the space between his bent knees. 'And you look much brighter, young man,' he said to Robert. 'Do you like the bear?'

Robert clutched his mother's hand for reassurance and pressed himself against her. But he managed a silent nod of reply.

De Gael wrinkled his nose. 'I confess I don't, but I've been dragged to see it nonetheless.' He spoke softly to the little boy but his words were directed at Linnet.

She nodded towards the older child. 'Is this your son?'

'My half-brother Martin. The kind of existence I lead is no recommendation for marriage and children.' A shadow briefly crossed his face and when his smile resumed it was cynical. 'The fortune-teller yonder informs me I am going to wed a beautiful heiress and die in my dotage a rich and fulfilled man, but I have a feeling she had more of an eye on my purse than my future. If I married an heiress, beautiful or not, I'd spend all my time defending my new-found fortune by writ and by sword.'

Linnet warmed to his rueful candour despite herself. 'Instead, you defend other men's fortunes.'

'Oh yes, strongboxes full of them, for whatever purpose.' He slanted her a knowing look.

Sensing danger, Linnet grasped Robert's small sticky hand. 'Come, sweetheart,' she said, 'it is time to leave.' She inclined her head to de Gael in a perfunctory, formal farewell. He unfolded from his crouch and returned her salute, his gravity marred by a spark of humour that deepened the creases at the corners of his eyes

As Linnet hurried away from the danger of his proximity, she heard de Gael's small brother asking if he could have some gingerbread and the mercenary's good-natured response. Risking a look over her shoulder, she discovered that de Gael was staring after her in speculation. Her throat closed with fear.

'What did he want with you?'

Linnet halted abruptly as her husband blocked her path. He sat astride a fancy red-chestnut destrier whose paces he was trying. The beast had a rolling, wicked eye and Giles was barely in control, his fists clenched on the reins. 'Nothing,' she croaked and had to swallow before she could speak again. 'He was just passing the time of day.'

'Then why are you blushing? What did he say to you?'

'Nothing, I swear it; he was talking to Robert.'

'To a whey-faced brat?' The horse plunged and she had to step quickly aside to avoid being barged by its powerful shoulder. 'You expect me to believe that?'

'He has his own younger brother with him. Please, my lord, everyone is watching us. You will make a scandal out of nothing.'

Scowling, Giles stared around. Hubert de Beaumont and Ralf de Rocher were watching the scene with open relish. Richard de Luci, who was also inspecting the warhorses, had courteously turned the other way but William Ironheart, who was with him, had no such delicacy and his stare was direct.

'I hope for your sake that it is nothing,' Giles hissed, lowering his voice. 'Is it any wonder that I am loath to bring you anywhere when you shame me thus. You are no better than a whore!'

45

Linnet gasped at the final word and felt as if he had struck her with his whip. Hating him, sick with fear, she stood submissively before him, knowing she had no defence. Robert, frightened by the atmosphere, by the sidlings of the huge horse and the thunderous expression on his father's face, began to sniffle into her skirts.

'Go home and wait for me,' Giles snapped. He wrenched the chestnut horse around and pranced him back to his audience. She could tell from the looks on their faces and Giles's strutting manner that her humiliation sat well with them. Summoning the tatters of her dignity, she lifted Robert in her arms and went towards her waiting horse litter on the side of the field.

Joscelin indulged Martin with a square of gilded gingerbread from the booth adjacent to Melusine the Mermaid and, with that bribe, removed the child from the dubious attractions of the fairground to the more sober business of the selection and purchase of an all-purpose riding mount from the dozens offered for sale.

Taught first by his father and then by his uncle Conan upon the battlefields of Brittany, Normandy, Anjou and Aquitaine, Joscelin was an excellent judge of horseflesh. Sometimes a good mount was all that had stood between himself and death in the thick of the fray. He examined with a critical eye the various animals paraded before him, discarding several high-mettled beasts with the most perfunctory of glances despite the horse coper's assurances of their breeding and quality.

Martin was very taken with a dainty white mare but Joscelin shook his head. 'She'd do well enough on good roads in summertime but she hasn't got the heart-room for hard work and her legs are too spindly. Also, she'd never ford a stream without baulking. See how nervous she is?'

Martin pursed his lips. 'She's still very pretty.'

Joscelin chuckled. 'So are many women, but that's no recommendation to buy.'

'Lady de Montsorrel's pretty.'

Joscelin busied himself examining the teeth of a stocky bay cob. 'So she is,' he agreed, half his mind on the horse, the other half dwelling upon the memory of Linnet de Montsorrel's fine grey eyes and delicate features. His usual preference was for large-boned, buxom women – they adapted best to the vagaries of mercenary baggage trains – but occasionally he found himself drawn to more graceful fare. Breaca had been bird-boned and delicate, quick of movement, dark-eyed and quiet, but with a wild fire inside. He still thought of her sometimes on freezing winter nights when his own body heat was not enough to keep him warm. And of Juhel, too. Of him, he thought constantly.

With an abrupt gesture, he commanded the horse coper to trot the cob up and down so that he could study its gait with a critical eye.

Martin nibbled on the gingerbread and stared around the enormous field, which was bursting at the seams with colour and life. The market was held every sixth day of the week and Martin loved to visit if his family was in London. The atmosphere was exhilarating. Everyone was here – rich, poor, lord, merchant, soldier and farmer – all drawn by their common interest in livestock. Here you could buy anything from a plough-horse to a palfrey, from a child's first pony to a fully trained war-horse costing tens of marks. You could wager on the races between swift, thin-legged coursers and see hot-blooded Arab and Barb bloodstock from the deserts of Outremer. And if you became tired of looking at the horses, there were cattle and sheep, there were pigs and fowl of every variety.

There were farm implements to be purchased and crafts-men to watch at their work. And, best of all, there was the fairground.

'A knight's riding over from the destriers,' he told Joscelin. 'I think he wants you.' The coper hastily led the cob to one side, his expression anxious. Turning, Joscelin saw Giles de Montsorrel riding towards him upon a sweating chestnut destrier that was fighting the bit and side-stepping. The saddle was ill-fitting and the stirrups far too short. Giles himself was wattle-red in the face.

'If I see you near my wife again, I'll garter my hose with strips of your flayed hide!' Giles growled.

Joscelin stared up into Giles's temper-filled eyes. 'We but exchanged courtesies. Should I have turned the other way and slighted her?'

'You're a common mercenary. I know only too well what was in your mind.'

'Not having a mind of your own above the belt that you so freely use,' Joscelin retorted, his first astonishment rapidly turning to anger.

'Joscelin . . .' Martin whispered in a frightened voice.

Giles pricked his spurs into the destrier's flanks and it plunged towards boy and man, forehooves performing a deadly dance. Martin shrieked as the horse's shoulder struck him a sidelong blow and sent him flying. He hit the ground hard, the gingerbread flying from his fingers. Giles leaned over the saddle to strike Joscelin with his whip. The blow slashed across Joscelin's face, narrowly missing his eye and raising an immediate welt. Giles pursued, whip raised in his right fist, his left clamped upon the reins.

Martin scrambled to his feet and dashed for safety. Joscelin, about to be ridden down by a metal-shod fury, grabbed the horse coper's three-legged stool and swung it hard at the destrier's head. The stool shattered across rolling eye and temple and the stallion went mad. Giles, fighting to keep his seat, snatched at the right rein and hauled hard but it was too late for that kind of control. Half-blinded, wild with terror and rage, the stallion reared, came down on all fours, and bucked. Then, before the horrified gaze of a gathering crowd, it lay down and deliberately rolled upon its rider.

Giles screamed and screamed again. There was a sickening sound of snapping bones and still he screamed. Joscelin flung aside the remnants of the stool and ran to lay hold of the stallion's bridle. Others hurried forward to help restrain the horse and prevent it from rolling again while the coper and another merchant dragged Giles clear. Someone else brought a rope to bind the destrier.

Leaving the horse to others, Joscelin turned and dropped to his knees beside Giles. The latter was still alive but for how long was a moot point. Blood bubbled out of his mouth with each released breath, a sign that one or more of his broken ribs had punctured a lung.

'Let me pass!' cried a woman's voice, imperative with fear. 'In God's name, let me pass. I am his wife!'

Linnet de Montsorrel fought her way through the crowd, many of whom had diverted from the fairground to view this far more interesting spectacle. Reaching her husband, she knelt at his side. 'Giles . . .' She touched his hair with her fingertips, a look of disbelief on her face. Then she raised her eyes to Joscelin.

He shook his head. 'His ribs have broken inward. Someone has gone for a priest. I am sorry, my lady.'

She shuddered. 'I saw you arguing.'

'I had to strike the horse. He was going to ride Martin and me down.' He looked rapidly around the crowd and

49

breathed a sigh of relief when he saw Martin standing with Ironheart. The child was pale, more eyes than face, and his tunic was stained and torn but he looked otherwise unscathed.

'I wished myself free of him yesterday,' Linnet whispered. 'But not now, not like this.'

Joscelin turned back to her. The expression on her face filled him with an uncomfortable mixture of pity and guilt. His father had warned him about Giles de Montsorrel's jealousy and he had chosen not to heed. 'It is not your fault, my lady,' he said, laying his hand over hers.

She shook her head and removed her self from his touch. 'But it is,' she replied. 'You do not understand.'

The crowd was being encouraged to disperse by the justiciar's serjeants and a moment later Richard de Luci himself stooped over Giles. He grimaced at the signs of internal damage. 'I saw that horse earlier and thought he was a rogue,' he said. He gave Joscelin a brief piercing look but said nothing aloud about the human conflict that had played its part in the tragedy.

De Luci stood aside to permit a priest to take his place. 'My personal chaplain,' he identified, as he assisted Linnet to her feet. 'My lady, I will ensure your husband has the comfort of God in his extremity and that you are seen safely to your lodgings.'

'Thank you, my lord, I am grateful,' Linnet's response was flat with shock. Two dusty brown patches smeared her gown where she had been kneeling.

De Luci patted her hand and began making arrangements to bear Giles home delegating Joscelin to provide escort.

'My lord?' Joscelin looked at de Luci askance and touched the angry weal traversing the left side of his face.

The chaplain was shriving Giles lest he should die on the way home. Linnet de Montsorrel had taken her son from her maid and, ashen-faced, was hugging him tightly in her arms. 'Are you sure you want me for this duty?'

Again de Luci gave him that piercing look. 'You're the best man I have. I could send FitzRenard but I really need him elsewhere.' He gnawed on his thumb knuckle, briefly pondering. 'I'll send someone over to relieve you before vespers. With Montsorrel stricken like this, it will be prudent, I think, to have royal troops keep a friendly eye on his household.'

7

In the bedchamber above the hall, Linnet listened to her husband's breathing. The sound was akin to a dull-bladed saw dragging through wood. Mad, she thought, I will go mad, and turned away to pace the floor before she was tempted to seize a pillow and press it over Giles's face. She clenched her fists and halted as she reached the wall of whitewashed dung and plaster. Outside, the shutters rattled as a storm wind tried to gain entry, while within herself a storm fought to escape. 'Jesu,' she whispered, closing her eyes.

Giles groaned her name and she returned quickly to his bedside. He tossed his head, moaning softly in the grip of a dream induced by the poppy in wine she had given him. She laid a calming hand across his forehead but his eyes jerked wide open and fixed on her, the pupils black pinpoints in the fogged blue irises.

'The strongbox!' he bubbled, and seized her wrist in a grip that was still frighteningly strong.

'Lie still, my lord,' she soothed. 'You must conserve your strength.'

His grip tightened painfully. 'The strongbox . . .' he

repeated through bloodstained teeth. 'Give it . . . to Leicester.' He fell back against the pillows, breath rasping. His grip slackened. She snatched back her wrist and rubbed it, her own breathing loud with distress. If she permitted Leicester to take their coin, she would beggar her son's inheritance for another man's glory. She could not do it and yet, if young Henry's rebellion was successful, she would face terrible repercussions for denying his cause valuable funds.

'How does he fare, madam?'

Stifling a cry she spun to face Hubert de Beaumont. Her knees almost buckled with terror. Beaumont was squat, but powerful. His ugly tenacity had always reminded her of a bull-baiting dog. 'My husband needs rest,' she managed to say and leaned against the wall for support.

Beaumont considered her closely and clicked his tongue against the roof of his mouth. 'A bad business. The horse coper's in the stocks and he'll be lucky to escape the gibbet, selling a killer like that. He must have known the brute had that trick.' Advancing to the bed, he leaned over the dying man.

Linnet struggled for composure. 'I beg you not to disturb him,' she said.

Beaumont straightened and looked at her. 'As soon as I have possession of the silver your husband promised to Lord Leicester for his Normandy expedition, I'll leave you both in peace.' He removed a sealed parchment from the pouch on his belt. 'Here's my writ of authorization.'

The Earl of Leicester's seal dangled on a plaited cord, heavy with the weight of authority and obligation – far too heavy for her to accept into her own hands. 'My husband said nothing to me of such a promise. I cannot give you what you ask.'

Hubert's brows drew together across the bridge of his nose. 'Why should Giles have told you?' he dismissed. 'This is men's business. You would do well to obey.'

Linnet clasped her hands. Her eyes widened with innocent distress. 'You are right, this is men's business and I am unable to deal with it. Perhaps when Giles has improved—'

'Improved, my arse, he's as good as a corpse!' Beaumont scoffed. 'Lord Leicester wants the silver.' His glance flickered to the money chest beside the bed.

Linnet set her jaw. 'My lord Leicester will have to wait on the justiciar's yeasay,' she said, and going to the chest sat down upon it.

Giles made a strangling sound as he strove to sit up. Beaumont's eyes bulged. In two strides he had reached the strongbox, seized her arm and flung her aside. 'Where's the key?' he snarled.

'I don't know.' She rubbed her bruised arm.

Beaumont turned to the bed. 'Key?' he demanded of the choking Giles, who garbled his wife's name and pointed an accusing finger.

Linnet slowly backed away from Beaumont until her spine struck the wall and she could retreat no farther.

Beaumont's arm flashed out and he seized her round the neck. 'Where is it, you whore?' His thumb pressed against her windpipe.

Her breath crowing in her throat, Linnet struggled but his grip was too strong.

Ella, who had gone to fetch her mistress a hot posset of milk and nutmeg, halted in the doorway, taking in the scene with horror. Uttering a gasp, she cast the drink aside and fled back down the stairs to fetch help.

'Tell me!' Beaumont roared, his fingers tightening. Linnet kicked and struggled and did not answer but

Beaumont had noticed a leather cord around her neck, beneath his squeezing fingers, and that it disappeared beneath her undergown and tunic, concealing whatever was strung upon it. Panting with exertion and triumph, he set his fist around the cord and twisted.

Joscelin heard the church bells striking the hour of vespers as he unburdened his bladder in the latrine pit at the foot of the garth. The sky over Westminster was darkly overcast, closing hard on a thin, silver rim of setting light over the Tyburn.

Readjusting his braies, Joscelin started back towards the house. The garden was neglected, although there were signs that it had been hastily tidied. There were no neatly planned and well-tended herb beds as there were at his father's house, just straggles of half-wild sage and lurching clumps of rosemary. He supposed that although Giles probably used this place for bachelor pursuits when he was in the city, it seldom became a domestic household.

He glanced at the shuttered window above the hall where Giles was slowly bleeding his life away and told himself that the horse would have rolled on Giles whether he had struck out with the stool or not, but the feeling of guilt remained.

Giles's heir was a frail child whose lands would have to be administered by a guardian for many years, in whatever form that took. He suspected the Crown would sell the widow and her son by right of marriage to the highest bidder and entrust the buyer with the child's well-being and administration of his lands. From what he had seen, Giles de Montsorrel had been a poor husband and father but his successor would not necessarily be any more competent.

His ruminations were curtailed by Malcolm, a young Galwegian soldier in his troop who was sauntering on his own way to the latrine pit.

'Lady Montsorrel's got a visitor, sir.' His French carried a lilt of Lowland Scots. 'A paunchy wastrel from Leicester's household. Said he was a friend of the Montsorrels, but I misliked his manner so I took his sword before I let him go up.'

'What was his name?'

'Hubert de Beaumont, sir.'

Joscelin nodded. 'Paunchy wastrel about sums him up. You did right to confiscate his sword.' He slapped the young Lowlander's brawny arm and walked on to the house. He was on the verge of re-entering the hall and about to wash his hands and face at the laver, when Linnet de Montsorrel's distraught maid seized his sleeve, gibbered something about her mistress being murdered by the visitor, and pointed frantically at the stairs to the upper floor. Joscelin heeled about, drawing his sword as he ran, took the stairs two at a time, shouldered open the door and hurtled into the bedchamber.

On the bed, Giles de Montsorrel gurgled in a spreading stain of blood, fingers outstretched towards his scabbarded sword that was propped against the wall only just out of his reach. Joscelin leaped across the bed to the choking woman and the man panting over her. Grabbing a handful of Beaumont's hair, Joscelin wrenched him off his victim and threw the knight to the floor, levelling the sword-point at his windpipe.

'Christ's blood, what goes forth here!'

Linnet de Montsorrel clutched her bruised throat and drew great gulps of air, her breathing no less desperate than her husband's.

His complexion a deep wattle-crimson, Beaumont

glared along the sword at Joscelin. 'It's a private matter,' he snarled. 'None of your interfering business!'

Joscelin was heartily sick of being told what was and was not his business. 'Almost a private murder,' he retorted. 'You'll answer to the justiciar.'

'No, let him go,' Linnet choked. Her veil had been torn off in the struggle and her hair tumbled around her shoulders in two dishevelled fair-brown braids.

Joscelin stared at her in disbelief. Beaumont used the instant's loss of concentration to lunge sideways, past the bed and out of the door.

'Please, I beg you, let be!' Linnet implored as Joscelin made to run after him. 'Let him go!'

'But he would have killed you, my lady!' Joscelin said incredulously but, after a hesitation, sheathed his sword and helped her to her feet.

'And I thank you for your concern but, as he said, it was a private matter.'

Joscelin shook his head in disbelief. Red fingerprints blotched her throat and there was a long graze where Beaumont had tried to tear off the leather cord she was now clutching. Joscelin suspected the key to the Montsorrel strongbox was sequestered upon it beneath gown and chemise. 'My lady, I do not think it is,' he said curtly.

Avoiding his gaze, she hastened to the bedside, knelt and took her husband's hand. Her hoarse entreaties to the Virgin were drowned out by Giles's rasping struggle for air. He stiffened, exhaled on a choking bubble of blood and did not draw another breath. As his body sagged against the mattress, Linnet bowed her head. Against the shutters the rain spattered in lieu of the tears she would never cry. She was free, unanchored and driving towards the point where she would smash on the rocks of her own guilt.

Leaning over her, Joscelin de Gael gently closed Giles's staring eyes and told the maid to fetch the chaplain from his meal in the hall.

'I assume he wanted the contents of the strongbox?'

'Assume what you wish,' she said tonelessly, adding, 'He was Giles's friend, not mine.'

'Hubert de Beaumont is no one's friend.'

Linnet looked over her shoulder and saw that he had gone to the curtain behind which Robert was asleep on his small rope-framed bed. Drawing the fabric slightly to one side, he looked down on her sleeping, vulnerable son, his expression inscrutable. Then he gently let the curtain fall back into place and gave his attention back to her. 'I can see you object to my questions,' he said, 'but you will let me post a guard at the door and send word to the justiciar.'

His tone was courteous but it held authority and expectation of obedience. Since she had no reason to challenge him, she nodded. Her jaw started to chatter and suddenly she was frozen to the marrow.

He took her cloak from the back of a chair and draped it around her shoulders.

'You need someone to stay with you, another woman of your own rank to help where your maid cannot. Do you know anyone?'

Linnet shook her head. 'My husband did not permit me to meet with other men's wives and sisters except on formal occasions when he had no choice.' She grimaced. 'I suppose the Countess of Leicester is my kinswoman after a fashion, but I would rather not turn to her for succour.'

'No,' he agreed wryly, his tone revealing that his opinion of Petronilla of Leicester differed little from her own. 'I have an aunt in the city. She's a widow herself and of excellent character.'

'To be my jailer?'

His brows drew together. 'I don't blame you for being suspicious but it was truly an offer of comfort.'

The outer door swung open and the hissing sound of the rain followed the priest into the room. Linnet touched her bruised throat. She was as good as a prisoner already if a guard was to be set on the door. Another woman's company would make her fears less overwhelming; there would not be so much time for her to brood on them and magnify them out of proportion.

The priest was brushing rain from his robes and bending over the corpse. Giles demanded her attention. There were rituals to observe for the sake of his soul and his body had to be washed and prepared for its final resting.

'I apologize,' she said to Joscelin. 'Your aunt will be most welcome if she will come.'

His eyes remained guarded but his mouth softened a little. He bowed to her, crossed his breast to the priest and left. She heard his footsteps clattering down the stairs, as Giles's had done only yesterday and would never do again.

8

It was midmorning when Joscelin had the dream. He was riding through a forest of mature hazel and birch trees, dusty sunlight diffusing through the foliage, turning the world a luminous green-gold. He could hear birdsong, the drone of bees and the chock of a woodsman's axe muted by distance.

A woman was riding beside him. Breaca, he thought at first, but when she turned to speak to him her eyes were not brown but a quiet blue-grey and filled with a world of sad experience. Behind them his troop escorted a coffin on which there was neither lid nor pall. Open to the air, Giles de Montsorrel stared up at the green lacework of branches with dry, dead eyes. Initially Joscelin thought that the corpse was wearing a hauberk but then he realized, his scalp crawling, that Giles was clad in a mesh of silver pennies. The coins flashed and slithered and Joscelin felt a scream gathering in his throat as the corpse slowly started to sit up. The linen jaw bandage slipped from its anchoring and Giles's mouth laughed open.

The woman spoke anxiously to Joscelin. Struck dumb with horror, he couldn't respond. The birds ceased to sing and the flash of sun on steel in the trees ahead caught the corner of his eye. Too late he realized he had ridden into an ambush. Even while the thought staggered through his brain, the attack was launched. His shield was still on its long strap at his back, his sword still in its scabbard, when the bright blade of a hand axe took him square in the chest. He screamed his denial and woke shivering and drenched in cold sweat. Disoriented, he stared at the smoke-blackened rafters and the curtain screening his pallet from the main room. The clatter and bustle of a busy domestic household rang in his ears together with the fading echo of his cry.

Sitting up, he pressed his face into his palms and shuddered. The dream had been horribly real, and the fading images still held their colours and emotions. A blinding pain thumped behind his eyes.

The curtain parted and Stephen entered the tiny alcove, bearing a horn cup of watered wine. 'Justiciar de Luci is waiting to see you,' he announced as he presented the drink.

Joscelin took a tentative swallow and his stomach churned. He stifled a retch.

'Is something wrong, sir?'

Joscelin fumbled for his undergown and tunic. They were still creased and damp from last night's rain. His body ached with bruises from his fight with Ralf and the whip welt on his face was throbbing. 'I slept badly and I can do without my father and the justiciar this morning.' He caught his breath with pain as he raised his arm to don his shirt. Stephen made haste to help him but, even so, by the time he had finished dressing, Joscelin was pale and sweating. He pressed his hands over his eyes for a moment.

'Go and ask one of the maids for a willow bark potion before my skull splits in two,' he said, swallowing hard.

The youth left at a run. Joscelin's own gait was a slow shamble as he followed him into the hall. A hound scented the fear still lingering on his body and growled softly. He ignored the dog and the gossiping serving women who pretended to be busy while he passed and then returned to their chatter. Two priests and a clerk sat at a trestle, breaking their fast on bread and fat bacon. A scribe had set up his lectern on the dais and was writing steadily. Joscelin walked gingerly to the hearth, trying not to jolt his precarious stomach and even more precarious skull. Richard de Luci and his father were deep in conversation but, when they saw him approaching, they broke off and looked quickly at each other like a pair of conspirators.

'You wished to speak to me, my lord?' Joscelin said, hoping that de Luci was not going to procrastinate.

De Luci looked Joscelin up and down with concern. 'It has been a rough night,' he said.

Joscelin winced a reply and rubbed his aching forehead. He had not finished reporting to de Luci until after midnight, and by the time he had come off duty and arrived at his father's house the matins bells had been ringing in the dawn.

'Leicester's claiming the blood-right to be the warden of Montsorrel's heir,' de Luci said. 'He served me notice at first light and I told him that the Crown's right was greater and that either myself or the king would appoint the right man to the post in our own good time.'

Joscelin struggled to concentrate. His wits had not gone wool-gathering – they were the wool itself: grey, fuzzy and tangled. De Luci was looking at him expectantly. What was he supposed to say? 'What about the silver?' he asked.

'Ah, yes, the silver.' Smile creases deepened at the corners of de Luci's eyes. 'Lord Leicester was not slow to raise the subject either, nor the fact that when his representative went to the Montsorrel house last night to make enquiries he was summarily seen off the premises by one of my men. "A rustic trouble-causing oaf" you were described to me.'

Joscelin avoided de Luci's sparkling gaze and wished himself a hundred miles away and dreamlessly asleep. 'Hubert de Beaumont's business was not legitimate,' he said. 'The only reason I did not arrest him was that Lady de Montsorrel pleaded for leniency.'

'Oh, I applaud your diligence,' said the justiciar. 'That coin no more belongs to Leicester than does the boy's wardship and I have no intention of letting it go to Normandy.'

'Just how much is there?' Ironheart asked curiously. 'Have you had a chance to find out?'

'Indeed yes, Linnet de Montsorrel was very cooperative. Including the plate, I would say about two hundred marks.'

Ironheart whistled through his chipped teeth. 'That's as much as the inheritance relief on two baronies.'

'I confess I did not realize the extent of the sum myself until I opened the chest.' De Luci thoughtfully rubbed his chin. 'Joscelin, I want you and your troop to escort the widow and her household to the keep at Rushcliffe. You are to remain there as acting castellan and hold the place in the name of the king until you receive further orders. The strongbox will travel with you since it is the boy's inheritance and you'll need monies to run the place. You can cast accounts, can't you?' It was a rhetorical question, for de Luci was fully aware of Joscelin's abilities. 'I am told that the coffin will be ready the day after tomorrow.' There was an expectant silence. Joscelin knew the justiciar was waiting for him to reply decisively and with gratitude but in his mind's eye he was seeing the open coffin of his dream and feeling very sick indeed.

De Luci looked at him and frowned. 'Of course, if the commission is not to your taste, I can always find someone else.'

Joscelin struggled to focus. 'My lord, I'll be pleased to fulfill any commission that you lay to me,' he said sluggishly. 'Have I your leave to go and make preparations?'

De Luci stared at him in open amazement. 'What in God's name is wrong with you? Anyone would have thought I'd kicked you in the teeth, not offered your career a substantial hoist.'

'It's not that, my lord. Truly, I'm grateful . . .' Joscelin swallowed jerkily.

Ironheart said quickly, 'Let the boy go, Richard, before he's sick all over your boots. You'll get more sense out of him later, I promise.'

The justiciar frowned but allowed Ironheart his way. 'Very well,' he said and dismissed Joscelin with a curt nod. 'I will speak with you at dinner. Best get yourself pulled together by then.'

Hardly bothering to bow, the young man staggered from the room.

De Luci turned to Ironheart. 'If he's going to let me down, then I'll allot the task elsewhere,' he said grimly.

'He won't fail you,' Ironheart replied. 'What you saw now was an affliction he gets sometimes – like Becket used to. A sickness comes upon him and a headache worse than anything you'd get out of a flagon of bad wine. All he needs to do is sleep it off. His mother was the same.'

De Luci shook his head, not entirely convinced. 'Nevertheless, he seemed disturbed at the command.'

'That's because he's attracted to the widow and knows that if he abandoned his honour and the trust you have in him, he could have her out from beneath your nose and her fortune, too.'

'He told you this?' De Luci's nostrils flared.

William laughed sourly. 'Christ, my sons never tell me anything! But I have eyes in my head. Joscelin's not like Ralf to rut all over the town. He'll do without rather than take anything just for the sake of sheathing his sword. Your young widow appeals to him and she's only just beyond his reach. If he stole out on a limb, he might just touch her.'

De Luci stroked his chin. Clever and shrewd was William de Rocher and he loved his bastard son with an intensity he tried not to parade, and didn't always succeed. De Luci well knew his friend's vulnerability – and his ambition. He was aiming high for Joscelin, but not hopelessly so given de Luci's own opinion of the young man.

'This needs thinking about more deeply than I have time for just now, William,' he said to give himself a breathing space, then he smiled knowingly. 'You wouldn't have planted that notion in my mind unless you thought it had a chance of taking root.'

Ironheart returned the smile and did not attempt to press the matter further. 'I think we know each other well enough by now,' he said.

9

Stripped to the waist, Ralf worked at putting an edge on his sword: smoothing the oiled Lombardy steel over the grindstone, honing out the nicks, brightening the edge until it shone bluish silver like the underbelly of a fish. Honing a blade was something Ralf did well if he was in the mood to be patient and even a professional craftsman would not have bettered his work today.

He blotted his sweating brow on his forearm and paused to rest. The courtyard was bustling for the earl was preparing to leave London for Southampton tomorrow dawn. The girl Aelflin smiled intimately at him across the yard, her arms piled high with linens for the countess Petronilla. Ralf looked in the opposite direction, watching a wain that had become stuck in the muddy wheel ruts by the gateway. Pleasure he had had from her in the stables not an hour since but, as far as he was concerned, the silver penny he had given her was a release from obligation.

The sun disappeared into shadow as Hubert de Beaumont arrived to stand over him. 'May I?' he asked and, without waiting for Ralf's consent, took the bare sword from the latter's knee and hefted it, testing the balance and then the edge. 'Excellent,' he said, then grinned. 'You could make your fortune as a swordsmith.'

Ralf snorted. 'Do I look like an artisan?'

Beaumont eyed him up and down. 'I suppose not. You're too disreputable by far without half your clothes and sporting that purple eye.' He returned the sword.

Ralf applied more oil to the stone. He wondered why Beaumont had sought him out. The knight was a seasoned member of Leicester's mesnie and not given to applying the lard of friendship to newcomers unless he had wheels to grease.

'That half-brother of yours is fast on his feet for one so tall,' Beaumont remarked.

Ralf scowled and touched his tender eye socket. 'I'd have got the better of him if Brien of Ravenstow hadn't poked his nose where it didn't belong.'

'Doubtless you would, but I was thinking of my own tangle with him yesterday evening.'

Ralf laid the sword edge to the grindstone and rasped it across. He almost smiled because, while he might detest Joscelin, there was satisfaction in seeing the de Rocher blood triumph in a fight. 'What's your interest in him?'

Beaumont watched the steady rhythm of Ralf's arm. 'Lord Leicester wants the Montsorrel silver for our cause and your brother is its guardian.'

'Ah.'

'Is he open to bribery?'

The sword sparkled on the grindstone as Ralf choked on mirth. 'Good Christ, no!' he spluttered. 'Why do you think he's in such high favour with the justiciar? Whatever you offered him would not be enough to make him bend his precious honour. He knows that you are Leicester's man through and through.' He scabbarded the sword.

'The only way you'll get that silver out of Joscelin is over his dead body.'

Beaumont wrapped his fist around his own sword-hilt. 'That can be arranged,' he said, 'but he is my adversary and I need to know more.'

'You are taking a risk by asking me.'

'I don't think so. I saw the "brotherly love" you have for each other two nights ago. Look, come to the Peacock and we'll talk over a jug of wine.' Beaumont jingled the purse lying against his dagger sheathe.

'Is that by way of a bribe to me?' Ralf pushed his sweaty hair off his forehead. 'Do you think I am more easily bought than my brother?'

'You appear to have finished your work for the moment and you look thirsty.'

Suddenly Ralf smiled, revealing fine white teeth that no chirurgeon's pincers had ever been near. 'The Peacock, you said. It just so happens that I am indeed a very thirsty man.'

'Joscelin's always been my father's favourite,' Ralf said and drew the shape of a dragon in a puddle of spilled wine on the trestle. His other hand propped up his head, which felt far too heavy for his neck. The task of sharpening his sword in the hot yard had made him so dry that he had gulped the first two cups of wine without moderation. The third had followed more slowly, matching pace with Beaumont, and he was now more than halfway down his fourth. 'I know that if the Arnsby lands were not mine by right of legitimacy, he would give them to Joscelin – his precious do-no-wrong firstborn son.' A querulous frown appeared between his eyes.

'You said the other night his mother was a whore.'

'She was. My father picked her up among the loose women of the army camp during some battle campaign.

Supposedly she was a baron's daughter but no decent woman follows the troops for a livelihood.' Ralf lifted his cup and gulped. 'After she died in childbed, my father built a chapel to her memory and endowed a chantry of nuns to sing her praises forever. God's death, do you know how much it sticks in my craw to see him riding off to visit the place like a damned pilgrim? She wasn't a saint, she was a witch!'

Beaumont made sympathetic sounds and refilled Ralf's cup before tipping the final half-measure into his own. Then he took a contemplative swallow and set his enquiries back on their original course. 'So how did your brother come to be a mercenary? Surely your father could have found him an heiress with lands?'

'Originally Joscelin was going to be a priest,' Ralf said. 'He boarded with the monks at Lenton for three years until one of them tried to make him into his bum-boy and Joscelin knocked his teeth down his throat. My father decided that his true vocation lay with the sword and started his training.' Ralf resumed dabbling his finger in the spilled pool of wine.

'And?' said Beaumont, leaning forward. His curiosity was like the tip of a knife probing an open wound. Ralf began to feel nauseated.

'There's little more to tell.' He shrugged. 'When Joscelin was fifteen, he and my father quarrelled and Joscelin ran away. My father said he would be home within a month but we didn't see him again for seven years. When he returned, it was at the head of his own troop of merce-naries. He was treated like the prodigal son, put on a pedestal and held up to me as a shining example.' Ralf stared at his wine-stained fingertips. 'For seven years I had dared to dream that he was dead, out of my life for ever, amen.'

Beaumont folded his arms across his broad belly. 'And

you don't know what happened to him in those missing seven years?'

'He never spoke about it. I suppose he went to his mother's brother, Conan, and learned all that was necessary for a common mercenary to survive.' Ralf raised drink-fogged eyes to Beaumont. 'How are you intending to kill Joscelin?'

Beaumont pursed his lips. 'I can see a way of obtaining the Montsorrel silver without directly confronting your brother, a way that will be a far greater blow to his pride.'

'Are you afraid to face him?' Ralf's voice was contemptuous.

The knight reddened. 'I fear no one,' he growled. 'Fortunate for you that you're drunk or I'd break your arm for that remark. My first concern is recovering Lord Leicester's money. If you want to be rid of your brother, do it yourself.' Rising from the bench, he tossed a coin on the trestle to pay for the wine.

'Where are you going?' Remaining seated because he did not trust the steadiness of his legs, Ralf blinked up at him.

'To hire a boat to take me upriver. I fancy a little excursion.' Beaumont smiled at Ralf. 'I'd take you with me but you'd probably puke all that wine over the side.'

Ralf watched him stride from the alehouse. For a moment he stared bleakly at the recently limewashed walls, already streaked around the sconces with candle soot. A serving girl approached to take the money and the empty flagon. Ralf fumbled in his purse for another coin and commanded another jug. There was no point in being only half-drunk.

Beaumont's excursion consisted of paying a river Thames boatman three silver pennies to row him upriver from

Leicester's house until they were opposite the far more modest building that constituted the Montsorrel dwelling. From his bench on the prow of the boat, Beaumont studied the small shingle beach and wooden steps leading up to the unkempt garth. He heard a rooster crowing and saw hens pecking among the high grass and brambles. The buildings were of the old Saxon type – dung and plaster with thatched roofs. Only the main house was covered with the more expensive red tile. In the heat of the day, the window-shutters facing the river had been flung wide.

'Want me to beach her, my lord?' enquired the boatman, who was struggling to hold his craft steady on the tide.

Beaumont shook his head. 'No. I've seen enough. Row me over to the Southwark side. I've business there now.'

The boatman arched his brow but did as he was requested without demur. You got all sorts hiring Thames boats, especially these days when so many nobles were in the city seeking permission to join the war in Normandy. The Southwark side had been very popular recently. You could purchase anything you wanted there, from a good time to one that in future you would rather forget. Souls were easily bought and sold in the dark alleyways of the Southwark stews. The boatman eyed the fancy sword and long dagger on the knight's tooled belt, the well-fed gut hanging over it. 'Is it a bathhouse you're wanting, my lord? I can suggest several good ones. Nice clean country girls, no hags.'

Beaumont smiled. 'Later perhaps. First I want you to row me to the landing nearest the Maypole. You know it?'

'Yes, my lord.' The boatman tipped a forefinger against the broad felt brim of his hat. He knew the Maypole, all right. It was a dingy back-alley establishment that housed the worst den of thieves and cut-throats this side of Normandy. 'You won't be wanting me to wait for you.'

Beaumont produced another coin from his purse and held it up between forefinger and thumb where it glimmered like a fish scale. 'I've got business there,' he said. 'I won't be long, and it's full daylight. This will be yours if you're here when I come back.'

The boatman eyed the money and wondered if the Norman knew what the odds were against returning alive from the Maypole. 'I'll wait an hour, no longer,' he said grudgingly and began working his boat out into the river.

10

Cheapside, London's main marketplace, simmered with activity in the afternoon heat. From the fly-plagued butcher's shambles at the far west side through the prestigious stalls of the goldsmiths, the drapers and the spice-sellers in the centre, to the poultry, grain and fish markets leading down to Oystergate on the east side, shopkeepers stood by their booths enticing folk to buy their wares. And buy some of them certainly did, with much alacrity and no discrimination.

Clutching a casket of sugared plums, a cage containing two black coneys, a skein of scarlet wool and a box of peppercorns, Joscelin was still marvelling at the speed with which his aunt Maude had whisked him away from his essential duties to escort her and Linnet around the stalls of the Cheap.

'Poor girl, cooped up in that house with naught to do but worry and pray!' Maude had clucked at him as though it were his fault – which he supposed, in the most indirect of terms, it was. 'She needs a respite. I know that I do!'

Joscelin had opened his mouth to protest, but that was

as far as he got as Maude overrode him with a look that said, *I knew you when you were a squalling brat in tail clouts, so don't presume to know better.*

'There are things she needs to buy before she leaves – women's things, needles and thread and the like. A man wouldn't understand, not until his backside wore through his braies. And you need a freshening, too. Have you still got that megrim? Did you drink the betony tisane I sent down to you?'

Realizing it was impossible to swim against a flood tide, he had capitulated and now, for his inability to say no, was a sweltering packbeast for Maude's various impulse purchases, though he had managed to persuade her out of buying a smelly goatskin from a tanner's stall on the corner of the Jewry just because she liked the coloured pattern. By the time the women had reached the Soper's Lane haberdashery booths in their quest for a bargain, his head was throbbing and so were his feet. The women's stamina was prodigious and he wished he could take them on for garrison detail once he was back in the field.

Yawning widely, he leaned against a booth pole and watched them haggle. His aunt was as vociferous as a barnyard hen and the merchant parried her assaults with cheerful vigor. Linnet de Montsorrel, however, was a surprise. Instead of leaving Maude to do all the bargaining, she made offers herself and held firmly to them. When the merchant refused, Linnet's eyes grew large and tragic and her lower lip drooped. When he conceded defeat, she transfixed him with a shy, radiant smile. The gentle mixture of pathos and coaxing achieved far more success than Maude's blustering threats to take her custom elsewhere.

Linnet de Montsorrel looked soft and vulnerable, Joscelin thought, but there was a tough core, a will to survive. Breaca had been like that – quietly unremark-able until something kindled the flame and her spirit shone through.

Robert detached himself from Ella's hand and came to Joscelin to look at the coneys. Their usual colour was a greyish brown but these were dark, almost black, and lustrous as sables.

'Are you going to eat them?' he asked Joscelin solemnly.

'They're not mine, they belong to Lady Maude,' Joscelin replied, crouching to the child's level. 'I know for a fact that she doesn't like the taste of coney, so I expect she has another purpose in mind.'

Robert touched the soft fur through the wickerwork bars. 'I don't like coney to eat, either. Papa showed me how to kill one once but I couldn't copy him, so he beat me.'

Joscelin's mouth tightened. No one could live through November without seeing animals slaughtered for salting-down during the winter months but the age of three or four was overly young to be taught to kill for food, espe-cially using a coney. To a child's eye, the rabbits were pretty and soft, something to cuddle. And Robert would not have the strength to make a clean death.

'Papa's dead now,' Robert added. 'That means he's gone away and he won't come back.'

There was a hint of a question in the statement, a need for reassurance that constricted Joscelin's throat. 'No, he won't come back,' he said gently.

After the thread-seller had been bartered down to his lowest price, Linnet and Maude assaulted another stall-holder to purchase needles and then moved on to a draper's booth to buy necessary supplies of linen and trimmings. Maude's ankles started to swell. Robert, who had been very good all afternoon, was drooping with fatigue. Joscelin lifted him on to his shoulders and gave him custody of the sugared plums as finally they turned towards home.

Linnet returned to Joscelin the purse of silver he had given her at the outset. 'You will need to make a record for the justiciar of how much I have spent,' she said. 'I obtained the best bargains that I could.'

'So I noticed.'

She turned a delicate shade of pink but smiled.

Joscelin handed her the purse. 'Keep the coin. I've already set it down in the accounts for your personal use. "One mark to the lady Montsorrel for the purchase of household items." Not that I've been watching all you have bought but I reckon you've not spent more than ten shillings.'

Her colour deepened. 'You are generous, messire.'

He gave her a sharp look, unsure whether to take her remark at face value or read sarcasm into it. Her lids were downcast and she had turned her head a little to one side, ensuring that their eyes would not meet. He saw not so much anger as embarrassment, and was intrigued. However, the opportunity to question her was not forthcoming for, when they arrived at the Montsorrel house, the sight of smoke and flames rising in thick gouts from the kitchen building banished all other considerations from his mind. Men were passing leather buckets furiously from the water trough in the yard to the source of the fire, while others used long hooked poles to drag the burning thatch off the roof. Joscelin's troops were battling to prevent the fire from spreading to the stables. In the garth the grooms were trying to control the frightened horses, which had been removed there to safety.

'Dear Holy Virgin!' gasped Maude, a half-eaten sugarplum suspended on its way to her mouth.

Joscelin ran across the yard to the bucket chain. 'Milo,

what in God's name's happening?' he demanded of his senior serjeant who was toiling hard with the other men.

'Kitchen fire, sir!' Milo panted, and stepped out of line for a moment. He was long of body and ungainly like a heron. His linen robe was soaked with water from the buckets he had been helping to carry. 'Started not long after nones – a stray spark in the kindling for the bread-oven, so the cook thinks. He went to inspect the wares of an oystermonger and when he returned the kitchens were well ablaze.' He rubbed his long jaw, leaving behind a black smear. 'A good thing the main house is roofed with tile the way the wind's blowing, else we'd all be sleeping in the almshouse tonight.'

Kitchen fires were a common enough way for a blaze to start but Joscelin's scalp prickled. He looked along the row of men on the bucket chain and his unease deepened. 'You took Gilbert off guarding the strongbox?'

'Yes, sir,' Milo said, confident of his decision. 'I gave Walter the task instead. He'd have been no use on the buckets with that bad shoulder of his.'

'Leave that, come with me.' Joscelin stalked towards the main building.

Milo ran at his side. 'What's wrong, sir?'

'Nothing, I hope.' Joscelin mounted the external stairs to the upper chamber. The door at the top was closed, a good sign, but matters deteriorated the moment Joscelin set his hand to the latch. Although it yielded to his pressure, the door would not budge, as if there was something behind it, blocking entry.

'Walter, open up!' Milo bellowed. He thudded the door with his fist, receiving only the vibration of the blow in response. Together with Joscelin, he threw his weight at the door. It gave way the tiniest crack, not even enough to see through with one eye.

77

'I'll get an axe,' Milo said and pelted away down the stairs. Joscelin hurled himself at the door again, venting his frustration and anger, then took a grip on himself, breathing hard. Milo returned at the run, brandishing a Dane axe. Joscelin grabbed the weapon from him, swung it and sank the blade into the door, close to the hinges. Splinters leaped out of the wood like white javelins. Joscelin wrenched the axe-head free and launched it again with all the strength in his upper arms. A split opened in the oak and he worked on this. A couple more strokes north and south, and wood parted from metal. Milo thrust at the door with his shoulder and it fell inward, slamming down like a drawbridge upon the corpse that had been lying behind it.

'Christ on the cross!' Milo leaped over the door and, together with Joscelin, heaved it off the body. Walter's throat had been cut; the walls bore bright splashes of blood and the room reeked like a slaughterhouse. Making a mental inventory of the room, Joscelin saw that the strongbox was gone from its place beside the great bed. Other items had been taken, too – Giles's hauberk was no longer on its pole and the fine Flemish hangings had been stripped from the walls.

'Whoever it was can't have gone far,' he said, quickly assessing the span of time that had passed between now and the fire starting, and setting it against the sheer weight and bulk of the goods that had been taken.

'No one has gone out of the front entrance on to the street; I'd swear my life on it!' Milo's voice was hoarse with shock but he was a mercenary, a man who lived by the sword, and his thinking processes remained sharp. 'The only way to get such weight out in a hurry is by the river!'

'Fetch six men, take them off the bucket chain if you

have to, and meet me at the wharf,' Joscelin ordered. 'And post another one here; a servant will do, but tell him on no account to allow the women into the room, and especially not the child.'

'Yes, sir.'

Joscelin ran down the stairs, sprinted across the neglected garden and down through the small orchard to the wharf bordering the rear of the property. A set of slippery, weed-covered steps descended to the gravel shoreline where several small rowing boats in varying stages of decrepitude were beached.

The tide was out and, on the shingle, two men, their tunics drawn high through their belts, were striving to push a beached Thames shallow boat into deeper water. A third man sat aft of the boat upon the missing strongbox, urging them to greater effort. Before him were heaped several waxed linen sacks, probably containing the other missing items, which were easily worth their weight in silver. The rower's exhortations suddenly changed to a cry of warning as he noticed Joscelin's approach. The men on the beach looked over their shoulders and then began to push harder, trying to free the boat.

Joscelin half-ran, half-slithered down the weed-green stairs, only saved from falling by the firm grip of his boot soles. He thrust with his toes on the final step, sprinted across the shingle and launched himself upon the thief to his left. So hard and swift was the impact that the man had no chance of remaining upright and tumbled into the river with Joscelin on top of him. The chill water rapidly saturated their garments and hampered every movement. They thrashed and floundered. Joscelin, having landed uppermost, used the advantage to push his opponent's head under the water. He lost his grip and the thief broke the surface, choking, but by then Joscelin's

79

troops had arrived and the man was seized and dragged ashore.

The second thief had succeeded in pushing the boat free but had lost his footing as he tried to scramble into it and had been caught by Milo and another panting soldier. The rower worked frantically to scull his craft into deep water, away from the danger on the bank.

Stripping his sodden tunic and shirt, Joscelin plunged into the river and swam towards his quarry – it was quicker than trying to run, for he was armpit-deep by the time he laid his hands to the prow and hauled himself on board like a dripping merman. The small vessel yawed as the robber rose to a crouching stand and raised an oar to strike at Joscelin. Joscelin ducked and the oar missed his skull but landed a bruising blow across one shoulder. His attacker struck at him again and the boat see-sawed as if in a gale, water sloshing over the sides to form a deep puddle in the caulked bottom.

Joscelin lashed out with his feet and the oarsman staggered backward and landed hard against the side. Immediately Joscelin was upon him, using the oar between them to bear down and crush the man's thorax. Panic-stricken, the thief kicked frantically. Joscelin grunted in pain as his body absorbed the blows but he did not yield his inexorable pressure. The resistance slackened; the thief choked. Joscelin held him within a hair's breadth of death. One more push and the windpipe would collapse. His victim went limp as he lost consciousness. Joscelin threw the oar aside and unbuckling the belt around the man's waist, rolled him on to his stomach and lashed his hands firmly behind his back, jerking the latch viciously on to the last hole of the leather. The thief groaned as he started to recover his senses. His head moved feebly as he tried to avoid the water pooling in the bottom of the boat.

'Don't give me any trouble,' Joscelin said, lifting his victim's head by the hair and shoving Giles's hauberk beneath it to prevent him from drowning. 'I'm quite likely to throw you to the fish, and in that padded jerkin you'd sink like a chest full of silver, wouldn't you?' Patting the strongbox, he seated himself upon it, retrieved the oars and turned the boat for shore.

It was well past compline before Joscelin was sufficiently free of his responsibilities to sit down with the women and take a cup of wine and a cold venison pasty – one of a batch fetched by Stephen from a cook shop on King Street, the Montsorrel kitchens being little more than smouldering ruins.

A door had been improvised out of planks from one of the rowing boats on the shoreline and the floor had been laid with new rushes borrowed from a neighbour. All traces of blood had either been removed or covered up. Out of sight but not out of mind, Joscelin thought as he sat down on a stool and leaned his back against the wall. The stolen hanging had been replaced and it cushioned his spine from the scrubbed, damp patch on the plaster. Once he had eaten and reassured the women, he had to go and spend at least the small hours in vigil over Walter's body. His men were the outer ring of his family and to lose one hurt him. Walter had been a staunch companion, one of the first to join his banner the year that Juhel died.

'I have three men below in the hall, guarding the strongbox,' he said. 'And more within immediate reach should the necessity arise, although I do not believe we'll be troubled again in London. Leicester and his retinue are leaving at first light, so I gather.'

'Have you spoken to Richard de Luci yet?' asked Maude.

Joscelin dusted crumbs from his spare tunic. It was more threadbare than the one he had ruined in the river, and only just respectable. It was better for a mercenary to invest his coin in the best weapons and horses he could afford rather than in fine clothing. 'No, he wasn't at home. It can wait until morning now. His prisoners are securely confined, although I doubt he'll get much out of them before they swing.' He fell silent for a moment and stared into his half-empty cup. When he spoke again it was to Linnet, not his aunt.

'Perhaps you will tell me now about Hubert de Beaumont, about this "private quarrel" of yours. I think that perhaps it is not so private after all.'

Linnet raised her hand to the spectacular necklet of bruises at her throat. A red burn mark showed livid where Beaumont had tried to tear off the leather cord upon which the strongbox key had hung. Joscelin was its custodian now. 'If you had made an issue of it, there would have been a scandal and I would have been branded a harlot at the least. Hubert de Beaumont has a murky reputation and there have been several incidents involving other men's wives. You ride the tourney circuits, you know the type.'

Joscelin inwardly flinched. Being a tourney champion and an itinerant mercenary he was, by association, linked to such men. He did indeed know the type. Besides, he couldn't claim to be a lily-white innocent himself.

'He wanted the silver. It was Giles's wish, too, but I denied them both. I had to decide how to act in my own interests and my son's, since the strongbox belongs to him now. I'm not sure I have done the right thing. There is no surety that King Henry will emerge from this rebellion the victor. To lean too far in either direction seems dangerous to me.'

Joscelin had been taking a drink of wine and he almost choked at hearing her deliver these less than honourable sentiments in a thoughtful, pragmatic voice. 'Playing a double game is even more dangerous,' he croaked.

She dipped her head and smoothed her gown over her knees. All he could see was the curve of her cheek and her lowered lashes. After a moment, she drew a deep breath and lifted her gaze to his. 'And sometimes safer, I do believe. No, please, hear me out.' She lifted her hand quickly to stay his protest. 'I have a suggestion to put to you about tomorrow's journey.'

Joscelin looked at the hand she had stretched out to him. It was a quick and capable hand with short-clipped nails. A practical hand, not that of a languid noble lady. 'Yes?' he said cautiously.

'The strongbox is obviously a target. Leicester knows that if he takes his claim to court, he is likely to lose. He also knows that we are leaving for Rushcliffe tomorrow and that we will have to travel through lands where his influence is almost as powerful as the justiciar's.'

'Yes,' Joscelin said again, beginning to frown.

'What I suggest is that to protect my son's inheritance, we take—' She stopped speaking abruptly, her gaze darting to the makeshift door as it was heavily thumped by the fist of the guard outside.

'Come,' Joscelin commanded.

Malcolm the Scot poked his head around the door, his flaming hair standing up in spiky tufts. 'The justiciar and your lord father have arrived, sir, and want a word.'

Joscelin sighed and rose to his feet. 'All right, I'll be there directly.' He turned to Linnet. 'I'll be interested to hear what you have to say when I return,' he said, adding ruefully, 'If I can stay awake that long.'

* * *

Arriving in the main hall, Joscelin found his father and the justiciar waiting for him. Ironheart's expression was smug and Joscelin was immediately put on his guard. It was a relief to have the culprits under lock and key awaiting interrogation. Against that small triumph, though, a man had died and the kitchens and stables were naught but heaps of smoking cinders – nothing to foster a smug expression.

Joscelin made a concise report that bordered on the curt. He was tired, but the sharper he became the more his father's lips curved. De Luci, too, seemed to find it necessary to smile as he seated himself on a padded bench along the wall of the room. Beside him was a wicker cage lined with straw and inside it, curled at the back, Robert's two black rabbits slept nose-to-tail.

'Food for your journey?' de Luci asked, peering inside.

'They are a gift from my aunt to Robert de Montsorrel,' Joscelin answered neutrally.

Ironheart made a contemptuous sound. 'Maude's got more wool in her head than a downland sheep has fleece.'

'And more sense than most,' Joscelin snapped and then, aware that both men were staring at him, shrugged. 'I lost a good man today and got thoroughly belaboured by an oar when I went after the strongbox on the boat. Between one and the other, I'm not fit company.'

De Luci sobered. 'It is always a grief to lose a companion. I will pay for masses to be said for him once you are gone. We won't keep you long but I have a proposal to set before you, one that is very much to your advantage, and it has a direct bearing on the task I have set you.' His gaze flickered briefly to Ironheart and back to Joscelin.

It was a night for proposals, Joscelin thought. He saw that his father was openly grinning now.

De Luci steepled his fingers beneath his jaw. 'Originally

I wanted you to escort Linnet de Montsorrel and her son back to Rushcliffe and take up the position of castellan while I found a suitable warden for the boy. Well, it seems that it's my good fortune to have found one already.'

Joscelin eyed de Luci. How could that be of advantage to him unless de Luci was offering him a higher post, which he very much doubted? The qualifications for such a position were means, breeding and influence, and he possessed none of these. 'My lord?' he questioned, because it was required of him to play the game out.

'I am here to offer you the wardship of Robert de Montsorrel by right of marriage to the widow.'

The words entered Joscelin's consciousness but made little sense to his reeling mind. His eyes widened and his lips moved, silently repeating what the justiciar had said.

De Luci gave a self-satisfied smile. He enjoyed tossing surprises like snakes and then watching his victims juggle frantically. 'There will be a fine to pay to the Crown for the right to take the lady to wife, but you'll still have enough to live on while you set the lands to rights.' He chuckled softly. 'Don't look so stunned. If I did not believe you capable of donning baronial robes, I'd not have offered you Rushcliffe to administer. Of course, it will only be yours until the lad comes of age but there is still his mother's dower property and that's worth a decent sum. What do you say?'

Joscelin swallowed. His mind was so full of conflicting thoughts and emotions that he was at a loss. 'I do not know what to say, my lord.'

De Luci laughed. 'I have thought for some time that you should settle down and breed some sons to follow you in service to the Crown.'

'Women should be kept busy,' Ironheart agreed, exposing his chipped teeth and cavities in a broad grin.

'The bed, the distaff and the cradle: that's the way to run your household.'

Having seen what the bed, distaff and cradle had done for his father's wife, Joscelin wondered if Ironheart really believed what he was advocating or whether he spouted it blindly from force of habit. 'I would rather not season my dinner with wormwood,' he replied; and turned to de Luci. 'My lord, I will be pleased to accept what you offer me, providing the lady is willing.'

'She has no choice in the matter,' Ironheart growled.

'Then I am giving her one.' Joscelin looked defiantly at his father until Ironheart dropped his gaze and spat his disapproval into the rushes.

'Very well,' said de Luci with a grave face but a twinkle in his eye, 'only if the lady is willing but I expect you to persuade her on that score.' His own wife had had no say in the matter of their marriage but he remembered wanting her to agree to the match of her own volition. First and foremost, it was pride. De Luci did not believe there was the slightest possibility of Joscelin giving up an opportunity like this for the sake of a woman's word. He wagged an admonitory finger at Ironheart. 'It damages a man's esteem, William, to think he has to force his bride to marry him.'

'It never damaged mine,' Ironheart snapped. 'Good Christ, if anything, Agnes was forced on me, the sulky bitch.'

'And if you had had to force my mother?' Joscelin asked.

A shadow crossed William's face. 'Then perhaps she would still be alive,' he said bitterly. 'I warned her to be careful while she was with child but she went her own way, as usual, and I was idiot enough to let her.'

An uncomfortable silence seized the room. Joscelin

knew he had stepped upon forbidden territory but sometimes it was the only way of fighting back. The subject of his mother was seldom raised in conversation. For all that Ironheart believed in plain speaking and honesty, she was one subject that he kept locked away in his own personal hell. He blamed himself for her death and his guilt was a wound so deep that it was still bleeding.

Joscelin inhaled to speak, and thus break the stifling silence, but a draught from the door-curtain made him stop and glance round. His eyes widened in dismay for Linnet de Montsorrel was standing on the threshold. From the look on her face, it was plain she had heard every word of their discussion and was fully prepared to be as unwilling as a heifer smelling a slaughter shed.

Ironheart, a superb general, went straight into the attack. 'Is it your habit to eavesdrop?' he demanded with a glare that made it obvious what he thought of a woman's interruption of a man's domain.

Her face blanched of colour but she stood her ground. 'No, my lord,' she answered with dignity, a slight tremble in her voice. 'I came to fetch the coneys. My son had a nightmare about them being killed and I wanted him to see that they are safe. I heard you talking and, since it concerned me most intimately, I had no qualms about listening.'

Ironheart spluttered.

Linnet faced Joscelin. 'You want me to consent to be your wife?'

'I ask of you that honour, my lady,' he answered with a bow.

'Honour,' she said with weary scorn. 'What an overused word that is.'

Ironheart clenched one fist upon his belt buckle as if he were contemplating unlatching it to use upon her. De

Luci's face wore an expression of shock, as if a butterfly had just bitten him.

'My son has need of me,' she said and, taking the coney cage from the bench beside the justiciar, she raked the men with a look of utter contempt and walked out.

'By Christ, she needs her hide lifted with a whip!' Ironheart snarled.

'I don't want a wife like the lady Agnes who cowers every time you raise your voice,' Joscelin answered, staring at the swaying door-curtain.

'That is precisely the kind of wife you do want!' Ironheart retorted. Striding across the room to the nearest flagon, he sloshed a measure of wine into a cup and, raising it on high, toasted his son. 'To the lady's willingness!' he mocked, eyes bright with cruelty.

'William, enough!' de Luci admonished.

'I will gain her willingness.' Joscelin clung to his temper. 'And I won't have to beat her to do it.'

Ironheart grimaced. 'No, I know you. You will flay your own hide and offer it to her for a saddle blanket.'

'Perhaps I'll offer her yours instead,' Joscelin snapped. 'You don't know me at all!' And he stalked from the room before he committed patricide.

Reassured that no one had butchered his coneys, Robert had fallen asleep, one small hand lightly touching the cage. A lump grew in Linnet's throat. Quietly she rose from his bedside and went to the laver. Tilting the reservoir, she poured water into the pink-and-cream marble basin beneath and splashed her hot face. De Gael's words had been courtly, but they were dross. He was as calculating and ambitious as any other landless wolf. A castle, a comfortingly heavy strongbox, someone to mend his clothes, see to his food and pleasure his bed. Servants, herself included, to call him 'my lord' and fetch and carry at his whim. And she was supposed to be honoured? Say no, and the soft words would be replaced by a bludgeon. Feeling dizzy and sick she held her wrists in the cold water and tried to breathe more slowly.

'Whatever's the matter?' Maude advanced on Linnet from the other end of the room where a maid had been preparing her for bed. She wore a chemise and her grey hair lay in a frizzy plait on her bosom.

Linnet laughed bitterly. 'Giles is barely in his coffin and already I've been given a new "protector."' Her mouth twisted on the final word.

Maude's expression grew concerned. 'You mean de Luci has appointed a permanent ward to look after Robert's inheritance? What about Joscelin? Is he still taking you north tomorrow?'

Linnet stared through waterlogged lashes into the older woman's bemused, homely face. 'Joscelin,' she said stiffly, 'has been given full custody of everything by right of marriage. My son, myself and our lands. All he requires is my consent and even that can be obtained by a handful of silver to the right priest.'

Maude looked astonished. 'Richard de Luci has offered you in marriage to Joscelin?'

'Yes.'

'Well, well, well.' Maude folded her arms and assimilated the fact with pursed lips. 'What did Joscelin say?'

'That wedding me was an honour, that he desired my willingness,' Linnet said in a scornful voice. 'Of course, it's an excuse for him to take what he wants without a bleat from his conscience. He was paying lip service to honour, and I told him so.'

'You said that to Joscelin?' Maude's expression became guarded.

'I said it to all three of them,' Linnet answered, drying her hands on the rectangle of bleached linen hanging at the side of the laver. 'Giles believed in honour, too.' She yanked her gown and chemise to one side and showed Maude the livid mark of the bite on her neck, the yellow smudges encircling her throat, the friction graze of the leather key-cord. 'Here's the proof.'

Maude unfolded her arms and put them around Linnet in a warm embrace. 'Oh my love, not all men are so tainted,' she said in a voice tender with compassion. 'My husband never took his fist to me, nor did he reproach me because I was barren. We were very fond of each other. I still miss him terribly.'

Linnet refused to be diverted from her course. Such paragons might exist but they were a minority. 'And your nephew, how does he treat women?'

'Joscelin would not abuse you, I know he would not.'

'With his father for an example?'

Maude squeezed Linnet's shoulder. 'Once you know William, he's more bark than bite. I'm not saying he's an easy man; sometimes he can be so vile you want to murder him, but his bad temper is a shield to prevent him from being wounded. Joscelin has always had the strength of will to go his own way. That's one of the reasons he and William sometimes quarrel fit to fly the doors off their hinges.'

'Madam my aunt, I would be grateful for a moment alone with Lady Linnet,' said Joscelin.

Linnet pulled away from Maude's embrace. 'I have nothing to say to you,' she said curtly to him.

Maude stepped protectively in front of her. 'I think tomorrow would be better for us all,' she said.

'No, now.' The quiet determination in the words informed her that while she might badger him and win on trivial issues such as shopping trips, she would have no success on this matter. He sat down on the coffer where he had earlier eaten his pasty and leaned his back against the wall, indicating that he was not leaving.

Maude held her ground for a moment longer then capitulated with a deep shrug and an apologetic glance for Linnet. She retired to the far end of the room and would have left the partitioning curtain open but Joscelin signalled her to draw it across. After a silent battle of wills, she yielded with an exasperated twitch of her hand.

Feeling sick with apprehension, Linnet faced Joscelin.

He came straight to the point. 'If not me,' he said, 'it will be someone else and soon. You cannot remain a widow, you must know that.'

His tone was reasonable but she was not deceived. He was as tense as herself and filled with anger. She had seen the signs often enough in Giles.

'My husband has yet to be buried and you speak to me of marriage? Mother of God, you even pursue me here to my chamber to press your claim? You must be eager indeed!'

He looked wry. 'I would have discussed it in the hall but you showed no inclination to stay.'

'With the three of you staring at me like hucksters deliberating over a choice piece of ware?'

'I suppose it must have appeared like that to you,' he admitted, 'but the justiciar has not made me this offer out of pure generosity for services rendered in the past. He sees me as a choice piece of ware, too.'

'So he uses me and my son to buy your loyalty.'

'In Christ's name, woman, use your wits for a moment!' he snapped with exasperation. Then he slumped on the coffer and rubbed his eyes. 'I'm sorry. I'm tired and sore and my temper's frayed. I don't mean to frighten you.

Look, de Luci has offered me something that will never come within my grasp again. Most mercenaries die in the ditch. Those who don't might rise as high as the post of seneschal in a modest keep if they are fortunate. It's a glittering prize and I would be mad not to desire it with all my being. Surely you can see that?'

Linnet had flinched when he snapped at her but his apology gave her the courage to fight back. 'Rushcliffe is my son's by right. You make it sound like a choice morsel that has landed on your trencher for you to devour.'

Joscelin gave a judicious nod. 'It is true,' he said, 'that being the warden of a small child who is heir to wide estates is a lucrative post. I pay de Luci for the privilege and then make good my loss and hopefully a profit out of the estate's revenues. It would be dishonest of me to claim otherwise but unless I'm a competent steward those profits are going to be negligible, and in the end they will dry up.'

His words held the ring of common sense but Linnet was not yet ready to be mollified. And certainly she had no intention of trusting him. 'Giles was not averse to selling his own child's inheritance to the French,' she said coldly. 'Why should you as a stepfather be any more tender?'

'Because . . .' he began but stopped, the words unspoken. A haunted look filled his eyes. He indicated the right portion of the coffer and eased along slightly so that there was room enough for her to be seated without having to touch him. 'Please, sit down.'

Linnet did so, not for his asking but because she no longer trusted her legs to support her. She perched right on the edge, her hands clenched together in her lap.

'When your son comes of age and I have to yield the lands, there will still be your dower estates in Derbyshire and rights to a lead mine,' he resumed. 'If I serve the justiciar well, other rewards will come my way. Why jeopardize a comfortable future for the sake of a few years of extravagance?'

Yes, she thought, my lands, my rights, myself. Most surely Giles was turning in his coffin. 'And a life on the tourney circuits qualifies you for such a post?'

'I've lived on crumbs and I've lived on largesse, depending on my fortunes, but I have never been reduced to begging in the gutter. Early on I learned to pace my income and not live beyond it. You will find me well qualified to govern.'

The weight of his gaze was almost tangible. 'What advantage is there to me in becoming any man's wife when I can remain Giles's widow?'

'De Luci will still have to appoint a warden for your son. And your dower lands will cause men to seek you in marriage, perhaps by force.'

'Richard de Luci would never permit that to happen!'

He shook his head. 'Possession is nine-points of the law and money the other. If the justiciar decides you are difficult because you rejected my suit, he'll be far less inclined to sympathy on the next occasion – he might well choose to levy a fine and turn a blind eye.'

She stared at her hands, forcing them to be still so that her agitation would not be displayed to his miss-nothing stare. She studied the walls of her trap for a means of escape. There were doors in her cage but, as she examined them, she saw that they only led into other cages, smaller and meaner, without even the room to turn and chase her own tail.

She studied Joscelin from beneath her lashes. He had been kind to Robert and he had twice the patience of Giles but that by no means made him a saint. Like Giles, he was strong-willed, determined and ambitious; she had no reason to associate those traits with her own personal good, yet what was the alternative? The thought of men such as Hubert de Beaumont made her shudder.

'What would you have done had I not overheard you talking downstairs?' she asked curiously.

'Approached you in the morning.' A self-deprecating smile lifted his features and took her completely by surprise. 'Probably on the turf seat in the orchard after Mass with Stephen playing his lute behind the wall and me on my bended knees.'

She had to swallow a treacherous answering smile. 'Then I would have refused you indeed.'

'And do you refuse me now?'

Linnet glanced around the current setting – a bedchamber at night in shadowy rushlight, with a curious audience a mere curtain away, and the bed itself, the satin coverlet gleaming like horsehide, inviting the wild ride and the nightmare. How she hated it. Throughout her life it had been a symbol of betrayal, pain and death. She inhaled deeply. 'I do not refuse you,' she said.

A spark leaped in his eyes. 'And you are willing?'

'I give my consent.' Which was not the same thing. 'And I want to observe three months of mourning for Giles in the proper manner. I owe him that duty at least.' She uttered the last sentence softly, more than half to herself.

She saw him stiffen as he registered the tone and content of her reply. His own gaze on the bed, he said quietly, 'I doubt you owe him any kind of duty at all.' Then he looked at her and shrugged. 'It's as close as I'm going to get for the moment and the prize is worth the compromise.' He rose to his feet. 'Will you agree to plight troth in front of witnesses tomorrow before we leave the city?'

Linnet hesitated then mutely nodded assent.

'You'll have no cause for regret, I swear,' he said earnestly.

Her father-by-marriage Raymond de Montsorrel, had whispered those same words to her once and he had lied. Christ on the cross, how he had lied as he destroyed her.

Joscelin waited but when she did not respond and kept her face averted, he sighed and went to the door. On the threshold he stopped and turned round. 'You were going to suggest something about the security of the strongbox earlier, before all this cropped up?'

Linnet rose unsteadily from the coffer. She had been silently praying for him to leave but obviously she was not a good enough Christian. It would be easy to put him off by saying that it was nothing, that it could wait until the morning. She knew he would not argue, for there were tired shadows beneath his eyes and he still had his vigil to keep at the bier of the soldier who had died. But by the morning there would be too many other considerations to snatch at her time.

And so she told him and was rewarded by a look of admiration and a dark chuckle. 'I'll set it in motion straight away before I go to prayer,' he promised, and when he left her his tread was buoyant, as if he saw her willingness to cooperate with him where the silver was concerned as a willingness on other levels too.

11

In the warmth of a midsummer afternoon, Joscelin approached Rushcliffe by way of the Fosse road that ran through the undulating wolds to the east of the river Trent and the city of Nottingham, and then he struck on to a rutted byway that linked Rushcliffe to Southwell and Newark.

Leaning against his chest, tucked into his cloak, was Robert de Montsorrel. Joscelin had taken the child on to his saddle to give Linnet and her maid a respite and, besides, he now had a paternal responsibility to the little boy. Indeed, an empty space within him seemed a little less barren for the comfort of the warm weight lying against his ribs.

He smiled down at Robert's drowsy blond head, imagining Ironheart's response could he but witness the scene. His father would snort and say that he was storing up trouble, would say that people would consider him soft and afford him less respect. A child's place was with its mother and its mother's place was at the hearth if a man had any sense. Joscelin's smile grew wry and dark. He was obviously not a sensible man.

As he rounded a turn in the dusty road, the castle of Rushcliffe came into sight, filling his vision, and momentarily taking his breath. Limewashed to protect the timber and stone from the weather, it stood out in the landscape like a perfect white tooth, proclaiming the local power of its lord. Joscelin had served garrison duty in imposing castles such as Dover and Nottingham but as a small cog in the doings of influential men. But this keep before him was greater by far because the authority was now his own. A warm feeling of possession washed over him but he did his best to hold it down. Rushcliffe was only on loan to him until the child in his arms should come of age and it was unwise when faced with a banquet after years of privation to devour and gorge. For his own sake he had to consume sparingly.

A village had grown up in the security of the castle's shadow and, as they rode down the narrow main street and negotiated the market cross, folk emerged from their wattle-and-daub dwellings to watch the procession of soldiers and the funeral cortège. Poultry and children scampered from underfoot. Dogs barked. An enormous spotted sow held up their progress while she was persuaded to leave the middle of the road, where she had been lying in a puddle suckling her litter.

Women with children at their skirts and babies in their arms watched from their doorways. A carpenter stood outside his workshop, wood shavings curling from the plane in his hand. Joscelin was aware of cold eyes and unsmiling mouths. One or two people crossed themselves as the coffin filed past but most just stared. An old woman outside the alehouse was even bold enough to spit and shake her fist.

Joscelin guided his mount over to Linnet's roan mare. 'Giles was not popular,' he remarked.

'They hated him,' she said. 'He wanted their respect but never understood it was an entitlement he had to earn. He ruled them with a heavy hand – often with a whip in it.'

He gave her a searching look. 'Did you hate him, too?'

She lowered her gaze. 'He was my husband.'

'A fittingly dutiful answer.'

She flushed. 'Do you have a complaint?'

'Only that I would know your true thoughts, not what you think you ought to say.'

She gave him a startled look.

Joscelin shrugged. 'I'm used to the women of the barracks and the camps. Propriety never stands in their way and better so, I think.'

She considered this for a moment and he saw her hands clench on the reins. When she spoke, though, her voice was steady and dispassionate. 'By all means let us be candid but I do not want to talk about Giles.'

Joscelin was enough of a strategist to know when to withdraw. From the set of her jaw he judged that persistence on the subject would cultivate hostility. He looked down at the sleepy blond head pillowed against his body. 'Then let us talk about this young man's future. As soon as I have an opportunity, I'll find him a pony of his own.'

She nodded with alacrity and looked relieved. 'Indeed, I agree with you. It is past time he began his training.'

In murmured conversation, so as not to wake the child, they rode on, past the water mill and then through some coppiced woodland of birch and hazel. Beyond the woods lay rich meadowland on which grazed the castle's dairy herd and farther up the slope, closer to the keep, sheep and geese kept the grass nibbled to a springy turf.

Robert woke up and Joscelin returned him to his mother. The child straddled the saddle in front of her, small hands grasping the pommel. Dusty sunlight turned his hair to white gold and lightened his eyes to the palest grey-blue, making of him a radiant faery being.

From somewhere on their left at the far side of the coppice they heard the chunk of an axe on wood. The nape of Joscelin's neck began to prickle. The coppiced trees resembled deformed fists with fingers sprouting from the knuckle joints. He glanced over his shoulder at the pall-covered coffin. The wain on which it lay creaked and jarred over the ruts in the track and Joscelin had an irrational expectation that they were going to jolt into one rut too many and awaken the dead.

'What's the matter?' Linnet asked.

'Oblige me by riding in the centre of the men, my lady.' Unstrapping his helm from the side of the saddle, he donned it then brought his shield from its long strap on his back and slipped his left arm through the two shorter handgrips.

Linnet stared at him, her mouth open.

'Ware arms!' He turned in the saddle to alert his men. 'Malcolm, stay with my lady!'

'Yes, sir!' The young Galwegian took Linnet's bridle and guided the mare into the heart of the troop.

The path through the coppice remained innocent and sunlit but the soldiers took up their positions, weapons bared and shields raised.

'Did you see something, sir?' asked Milo de Selsey, riding abreast of Joscelin.

'Intuition,' Joscelin said. 'A soldier's gut, as my father always says. Have you noticed how still it is – no birdsong? Something is not right.'

De Selsey looked over his shoulder into the trees. He narrowed his eyes and nodded brusque acknowledgement of Joscelin's concern.

As they rode on, Joscelin strained his eyes and ears, every tiny hair on his body upright. Whitesocks pranced, responding to his master's mood. They approached the end of the coppice, the track bearing the imprint of foresters' carts and old hoof marks. The path divided like a snake's tongue but a fallen log blocked the wider route and the troop had to filter into the narrower one.

A glint of silver flashed among the trees, disappeared, then flashed again closer. Joscelin heard a shout and the thunder of hooves as a troop of horsemen moved to block the way out of the coppice. The leading knight whirled a mace around his head, the sunlight gleaming along its flanges. Then he caught it by the base of the haft and used it as a baton as he bellowed the command to attack.

Within moments the enemy troop was upon Joscelin's. The advantage of surprise had been lost, thus the first impetus of assault was not as devastating as it might have been. Nevertheless, the odds were against Joscelin, for he was outnumbered and, with two baggage wains and a coffin cart to protect, unable to manoeuvre.

Two of the enemy hacked their way through the guard surrounding Linnet and Robert. A bay destrier drew level with Linnet's roan and its rider seized the bridle to bring the small mare around. A screaming Robert was torn from her arms. She shrieked at the full pitch of her lungs for aid and looked desperately around. Malcolm struggled valiantly to respond but he was engaged in fierce battle with an opponent on either side of him and couldn't break free.

A powerful chestnut stallion surged into the midst of the attempted abduction. The downswing of Joscelin's sword took off one man's hand clean through the wrist, freeing the restraint on Linnet's bridle. Howling, the knight toppled from his saddle. Joscelin spurred Whitesocks around Linnet, thrust his shield into the swordstroke of the second knight who held Robert, heaved the blade off, and counterstruck. The knight doubled over, choking on blood. Joscelin caught Robert and hauled him to safety.

'Take him!' he gasped to Linnet.

She closed her arms convulsively around her child and then, seeing the blood, recoiled. Feverishly she dabbed at where it was thickest with a fold of her cloak, trying to gauge the extent of his injury.

'God's death, woman, it's not his!' Joscelin snarled. 'You'll have wounded aplenty to tend without fussing over trifles!'

She shot him a fulminating glare but he had gone, spurring Whitesocks towards one of the wains which the enemy had succeeded in capturing.

Joscelin's driver was sprawled facedown on the coppice floor and in his place one of the attacking knights was making a competent effort at turning the horses. He had set his shield down while he handled the wain. The device of a golden firedrake on a scarlet background was enough identification for Joscelin but, before he could reach his brother and deal with him, his sword was caught and turned by a hand axe wielded by a paunchy knight, powerfully muscled in arm and shoulder. Joscelin tightened his thigh against the saddle to hold his seat and turned his wrist to free his blade. In the moment that the weapons disengaged, he locked eyes with Hubert de Beaumont and knew that this time there would be no backing down.

Beaumont swung the axe. Joscelin ducked. The blade sang past his ear and struck his shoulder. The blow bit through the links of his hauberk and rocked him back against his cantle, but in the surge of battle he felt no pain. Beaumont attacked again but Joscelin had his shield up now and struck back forcefully. Taught to fight in the routier camps of Normandy and Flanders, he could stand hard and Beaumont, although strong and well muscled, was not in the same physical condition. Joscelin's sword-work was fast and inexorable. When he saw a gap he took it and the look of astonishment on Beaumont's features was his final expression as he tumbled from the horse, struck the ground and was still.

Panting with exertion, Joscelin watched the baggage wain containing the Montsorrel strongbox disappear down the track in the direction of the Nottingham road, escorted by a dozen hallooing, jubilant soldiers.

'Shall we ride after them, sir?' asked Milo de Selsey.

Joscelin shook his head. 'No, let them go. We're outnumbered and we've been fortunate to escape with the mauling we got.' His smile was brief and humour-less. 'Let Ralf savour his victory for the small time it is his. Safer, I think, to ride for Rushcliffe before he takes it into his head to look at his prize.' He stared round the battle site. 'Put our dead across horses. The men too badly wounded to ride can use the funeral wain.'

'Yes, sir.' Milo turned away and began shouting commands.

The uninjured men in his troop began the depressing task of tying their lifeless companions across spare horses like slaughtered deer at the end of a day's hunting. Four dead in all and four too badly injured to ride with compe-tence – almost a third of his troop. He picked his way among the men, talking, helping, until he came to Linnet who was bending beside one of the sorely wounded, comforting him while he waited his turn to be lifted onto the wain.

'Malcolm?' Joscelin crouched beside the young merce-nary and looked at the bloody spear gouge that had ripped open the milky, freckled skin from collarbone to bicep.

'I wasn't fast enough, sir . . .' Malcolm's teeth clenched in a rictus of pain. Tears oozed from his eyes and trickled into the red hair fluffing around his ears. 'There were two of them and I was stuck between them like a fox in a trap.' He stared from Joscelin to Linnet, who was holding his blood-soaked shirt in her hand. 'I'm going to die, aren't I?'

'Of course not!' Joscelin snapped.

'I'll admit it is a nasty tear—' Linnet's voice was firm as she bent over him 'but no worse than holes I've had to mend in my gowns. It can be darned and you'll live to fight another day. See, it's only of the flesh; no vital part has been touched.'

Beneath her calm authority, Malcolm's breathing eased. 'Ye must think I'm a bairn!' he lamented.

'No worse than any man,' she said. 'It's going to hurt when they lift you but, God willing, you'll soon be comfortable in a bed.'

As Malcolm was gently raised by two soldiers and taken to the wain, Joscelin laid his hand upon Linnet's sleeve. 'Thank you,' he said.

She shrugged. 'It was the truth. If he does not take the stiffening sickness and if the wound stays clean, he'll survive with barely a scar.'

Her pragmatic tone sat completely at odds with her earlier hysteria over her son but Joscelin knew only too well how fierce the bond between mother and child could be. A glance showed him Robert cuddled in the maid's arms, his eyes as huge as moons in his thin, pale face.

'I am sorry I shouted at you,' he said as he turned to mount up. 'In the heat of battle, everything happens so fast.'

She shook her head and smiled ruefully. 'You made me so angry that you killed my terror.'

He acknowledged their pax with a brief smile of his own but quickly sobered. 'Hubert de Beaumont was leading them, so they must have been acting on Leicester's orders.' He looked grim. 'My brother Ralf was with them, too.'

'I'm sorry, it must be a grief to you.'

He shook his head. 'I have never known Ralf as anything but my enemy. The grief is all my father's.'

'They took the strongbox.'

'Yes, they took it.' A look of understanding flashed between them. 'And also five casks of vinegar and two of scouring sand for cleaning mail. Nothing of value.' The hangings and tapestries, household goods and trinkets, were stored at Nottingham and would arrive later that week down the Trent by slow barge. Grimacing, he turned his stallion. 'Nothing of value,' he repeated bleakly, 'but the lives of four good men. The life of Hubert de Beaumont is scarcely adequate recompense.'

Waiting impatiently for the ferry on the wooded banks of the Trent, Ralf looked over his shoulder, ears straining for the sound of pursuit, but the horizon remained innocent. He returned his stare to the sullen sheet of grey water. The ferry was a dark wedge on the opposite side of the river, and the two ferrymen were taking their own good time about pulling their craft across.

Ralf chewed his thumbnail and cursed under his breath. He could still see Hubert de Beaumont's eyes wide open in disbelief as Joscelin's sword entered his body and the image within his mind's eye made him queasy. He glanced at the baggage wain. His instructions had been to capture Montsorrel's strongbox and deliver it to the

Earl of Leicester, its rightful owner. Success should have elated him but he was assailed by nagging doubts. Something stank like rotten fish. He eyed the strongbox where it stood, squat and stolid amid various casks and barrels. Joscelin had been entrusted with its safety and it was more than his hide was worth to lose it. So why had he not pursued?

The doubt became a sickening suspicion. Ralf drew his sword from his belt and went to the box. The iron bindings and oiled bolts gleamed almost like a smile. He could not bear the tension and struck at the hasps but they were stoutly made and held fast. Sparks flashed in the dim light and the sound of his blade on the iron was loud enough to waken a corpse. It brought the other men running, demanding to know what he was doing.

Sobbing with effort and frustration, Ralf took one last swing. The hasps shattered and a sliver of metal from his beautiful, lovingly honed sword flew from the blade and lodged in his brow-bone. Blood streamed from the wound, blinding him. It was one of the other soldiers who opened the violated strongbox and discovered that the scuffed leather money pouches within held not silver pennies but small, round stones, smelling pungently of river and weed.

12

Arnaud de Corbette, Rushcliffe's seneschal, folded his hands inside his silk-edged sleeves and rocked back and forth on his gilded leather boots. Heel and toe, heel and toe, restless with anxiety. Eyes narrowed against the wind, he stared over the wall walk towards the approaching troop. A messenger had brought him advance warning of the new lord's arrival, together with a parchment bearing the seal of the justiciar ordering him to yield the castle into the hands of Joscelin de Gael and offer him every cooperation.

Corbette focused upon the glossy liver-chestnut stallion and the man sitting confidently astride. William de Rocher's bastard, a man of repute in some circles and reputation in others, hand-picked by the justiciar. But this new position was a step up indeed. Obviously de Luci had selected de Gael for his ability, a thought that made Corbette ease his finger around the gilded neck band of his tunic.

Halfdan, the serjeant in command of the keep's garrison, jutted his jaw. 'Why can't we just keep the drawbridge up and tell 'em to piss off?' he demanded.

'If you want to end up in the forest as an outlaw you may do just that,' Corbette said irritably. 'If you had brains, you'd be dangerous. It is not just a piddling matter of someone's fetch-and-carry presenting a writ of authority at our gates. It is William de Rocher and Richard de Luci; it is the King himself!' He shook the parchment beneath Halfdan's nose like a curse. 'Don't you understand!'

Halfdan stared at him blankly. Corbette gave an exasperated growl. 'Just keep your mouth shut and stay out of the way. Let me do the talking.'

Halfdan shrugged and shambled off down the stairs. Corbette breathed deeply in and out. Old Lord Raymond had favoured Halfdan, whose muscles and fighting ability were as impressive as his intellectual capacity was lacking. Occasionally, for entertainment, Raymond had organized fights between Halfdan and other mercenaries, sometimes to the death, with money wagered upon the outcome. Corbette had found the man useful for keeping awkward castle retainers in line after Raymond's death but this change of master had rapidly altered that perspective.

Descending to the bailey, Corbette could feel sweat chilling his armpits. The next few moments were going to be uncomfortable.

As the liver-chestnut stallion paced over the drawbridge and entered the courtyard, Corbette hastened forward to bend the knee at the new master's stirrup. 'Welcome, my lord, and gladly so.' He made certain to emphasize the title.

De Gael drew rein. 'And who might you be?' he asked glacially.

'Arnaud de Corbette, my lord – I am the seneschal.'

The air grew more frigid still. 'Get up,' said de Gael and Corbette flinched, for the new lord's expression was carved from ice.

'Why did you permit armed men to lie up in the coppice on the Nottingham road?'

Corbette swallowed. He had known the question was coming – de Gael's messenger had told him what had happened – but finding an excuse was difficult. 'I did not know they were there, my lord. Some of our soldiers were in the village yesterday, but they made no mention of—'

De Gael cast him a look of utter contempt that boded ill, and stiffly dismounted. He swept the bailey with a disparaging gaze that took in its state of untidy filth and hurled it at Corbette's gilded leather feet. 'Your business is to know everything that pertains to the security of this keep, especially in times of rebellion and war.'

Corbette cleared his throat. 'Lord Raymond was a difficult master to serve in his last year and Lord Giles only came into the inheritance at Easter. I—'

'I am not interested in your excuses. The evidence before my eyes is enough to prove to me that you're as incompetent as your previous masters.'

'My lord, I'm not seeking to absolve—' Corbette began, and broke off with relief as a roan mare entered the bailey, pacing daintily beside a wain that bore a pall-covered coffin and several wounded soldiers. 'My lady,' he murmured, flourishing a bow and silently thanking God for the distraction.

'Messire Corbette,' she acknowledged with a cool nod.

'I am sorry to hear the news about my young lord, God rest his soul.' Corbette crossed himself. 'It is a shock to all of us.'

'I have no doubt it is,' de Gael interrupted curtly. 'I promise you that more than dust is going to fly in this place before I am finished and I will talk to you of what's to be done very soon. For now, I want a priest to minister to such of my men as are in need and food and rest for all.'

'My lord,' Corbette said, and gestured to a servant. De Gael was right. Something would have to be done, and very soon.

Linnet looked up from the row of pallets occupied by the men of Joscelin's troop too sorely wounded to return to their duties, and saw their commander standing in the doorway. It was late. Dusk had fallen and rush dips flickered in the gloom. The tallow in which they had been dipped was so coarse and salty that there was more sputter and smoke than flame and the room was filled with the stink of burning mutton fat.

'I thought you were not coming.' She turned away to pick up her shears.

He moved stiffly into the room and, unlatching his belt, laid it across a bench. 'I've been inspecting the keep. The structure is sound but the rest is little better than a butcher's shambles.'

'Giles's father had no wife to keep the place in order.' She turned the shears in her hands and studied the dull gleam of the tempered iron. 'After he and Giles quarrelled, we did not visit to see how he lived – not even when Raymond was on his deathbed.'

'What about Corbette's wife? I assume he has one?'

'Oh yes.' Linnet wrinkled her nose. 'The lady Mabel. She was always conspicuous by her absence whenever there was work to be done and I doubt she's changed. I haven't seen her in the sickroom once, nor her daughter, but the moment the dinner-horn sounds they'll be first at the trough.'

'In my troop, the men who don't work don't eat,' he said grimly, and went to the row of wounded men to address each one in turn and speak words of comfort.

Linnet could see from the manner with which he carried

himself that he was tired and in pain, but he did not skimp his duty. He lingered at Malcolm's pallet and she heard their low exchange of words and then wry laughter. Joscelin was still grinning broadly and shaking his head when he returned to her.

'Malcolm says I'm nae to fash myself, you've a touch like an angel,' he declared in appalling mimicry of a Lowland Scots accent and sat down on the padded cover of a clothing chest.

Linnet opened and closed the shears and smiled. 'Did you believe him?'

'He's a notorious fibber but I reckon you're bound to be gentler than Milo, who'd act the chirurgeon otherwise.' He started to remove his surcoat, but desisted with a gasp of pain.

Quickly Linnet moved to help him, easing the garment over his shoulders. The mail shirt proved more difficult for it was heavy and the sleeves fitted closely over the padded undergarment. The intimacy was disturbing; the heat of his body, the acrid smell of battle sweat. The proximity made her feel stifled and panicky. She had too many memories of this room and what had happened here, and it was with relief that she finally succeeded in divesting him of his mail and gambeson and was able to step away.

His head was bowed, his breathing harsh with pain. When it eased, he looked up at her through sweat-tangled hair. 'Is there any wine before we go further?'

She laid his garments on the coffer and fetched a pitcher and cup from a trestle by the embrasure. 'It's last year's,' she apologized, pouring him a cloudy measure. 'It tastes more like verjuice than wine but it's all we have according to Corbette's manservant. I will check myself when I have time.' She gave the cup to him and tried to conquer her feelings of oppression.

'It doesn't matter.' He took several fast swallows.

His shirt was glued to his shoulder-wound by dried blood. Linnet started to soak it away with firm, careful strokes, watching his face for indications that she was hurting him too much. 'You're fortunate it wasn't much worse,' she murmured. 'It looks as if you've only cut a surface flap of skin. The rest is bruising.'

'What did Giles and Raymond quarrel about?'

Linnet ceased bathing his wound and turned away to wring the pad out in a bowl of scented water. The droplets plinked over the surface and were absorbed into the shimmering whole. Her fingers started to hurt as she twisted the linen. Her womb, her lights, the center of pleasure in her loins, were twisting, too. By asking her a question to take his mind from pain, he had inadvertently touched her own wounds.

'Giles and his father were always disagreeing,' she said with careful neutrality as she resumed her ministrations. 'Giles could never do anything right. Raymond criticized him at every turn, told him how much better he could manage things and, of course, he could. Giles never had a chance. There, ease your shirt off now so I can take a proper look.'

'And?' he prompted.

Linnet drew the shirt over his head and pulled it off down his uninjured arm, avoiding the shrewd clarity of his stare. 'You come from these parts yourself. Did you know Raymond de Montsorrel?'

'Not well. Occasionally he and my father would go hunting together but they were uneasy neighbours. Raymond de Montsorrel had a high opinion of himself – born of the highest blood in Normandy, if you can call it that. He looked down on my father because my father's mother was English. Mind you,' Joscelin added wryly, 'he

111

was determined to improve the breeding stock of those less fortunate than himself; his lechery was a legend far and wide.'

Linnet drew a constricted breath and put his blood-stained shirt on the coffer, looking anywhere but at his face while memory and guilt assaulted her. Raymond de Montsorrel, here, almost where she stood now, touching her hair, his breath at her throat, hoarsely whispering. *If my son had any steel in his sword, I'd have a grandchild by now. You need a real man to quicken you.* And then the heat of his mouth on hers and his hand stroking between her thighs with delicate, perfect knowledge. It had been wrong, it had been shocking, but pinned against the wall by his suggestively thrusting hips, for the first time in her life she had felt exquisite twinges of pleasure stabbing through the other emotions.

A shudder ran down her spine. She was aware of Joscelin's scrutiny and sought frantically for a way across the pit that had opened up beneath her feet. 'Raymond baited Giles once too often and too far,' she said breath-lessly. 'Swords were drawn and Giles had to be dragged off by the guards. We left the same day and did not return until Raymond was dead.' She darted a glance at him and saw that he was frowning. Quickly she broke the wax seal on a pot of salve and dipped her forefinger. 'You have few scars to show for a man of your trade,' she said to change the subject. Men liked to talk about themselves and, by appealing to his vanity, she hoped to divert his attention from something she did not wish to discuss.

'You learn fast or you perish.' His pensive expression lingered as she daubed the ointment on his shoulder. 'And not all of the scars are visible. I – Ah!' He broke off and gripped the coffer edge.

'I'm sorry,' she said breathlessly. 'That's the worst part over now.'

He had clenched his lids against the pain but now he opened them and caught her gaze with his. 'I know what happens when you don't bury the past and let it go. My father has grown old on bitter grieving for my mother and I, too, have known my share of folly.' His expression grew bleak and he stared beyond her into the shadows behind the sputtering rush dips. 'The problem with burying the past is that you keep on stumbling over unquiet graves,' he added softly.

Linnet wiped the ointment from her fingers on a piece of softened linen and then used the material to bandage his shoulder. Not graves but corpses, she thought as she used a cloak pin to hold the dressing in place. The living dead.

Her fingertips touched his as he held the fabric and she secured the pin. Their eyes met and hunger leaped in his. A maid entered the room with a pile of linen sheets over her arm and he dropped his gaze. Linnet withdrew and Joscelin lowered his hand to pick up his half-finished wine.

'Do you remember your mother?' she asked.

He gave a one-sided shrug. 'Only in fragments. I was younger than Robert when she died. I know that she had long, dark hair and that she used to scent it with attar of roses.' He looked beyond her. 'I remember the ends of her braids hanging at my eye level when I stood at her side. She used to decorate them with ribbons and little jewelled fillets. Perhaps because she had lived such an uncertain life before she took up with my father, she was fond of frippery and fine clothes.' He swirled the drink in the cup. 'Truly, if I look into my childhood, my comfort wears the face of my aunt Maude. She had no children of her own, and since I had no mother, she decided that we could each fulfill the other's need.' He half-smiled. 'The wonder is that I'm not as fat as a bacon pig and that I still have all my teeth the way she used to stuff me with sweetmeats!' Then he added softly, 'Maude's care meant a great deal to me. It still does.' His gaze had been idly following the linen maid's progress towards the door but now it stopped and widened. Linnet had been about to say how much she liked Maude herself, but seeing the look on his face turned round instead.

A young woman had hesitated on the threshold of the room. The expensive dark-red wool of her gown encased a voluptuous figure that stopped just short of being plump. She had creamy skin and her glossy black hair was bound in two long braids. Her roving gaze lit upon Joscelin and she drew a deep breath that served to enhance her lush bosom. His eyes widened. Smiling, she ran her hands over her body as if to smooth her gown, although the motion was blatantly provocative. Then she undulated over to Joscelin and knelt at his feet.

Linnet stared with growing fury. The young woman's pose meant that Joscelin was being granted a more than generous view of cleavage down the unfastened neck-opening of the red gown. And he was taking full advantage.

After a moment he came to his senses sufficiently to lift the girl to her feet. She laid her hand over his, her long fingers enhanced by several fine gold rings and tipped by elegantly manicured nails. Lifting her head, she slanted him a look through eyes as hot and dark as coals. Her gaze was feral as it ranged over his naked chest and shoulders. She moistened her lips.

'Your shirt, messire.' Linnet thrust the garment at him then rounded on the girl. 'Where were you when you were needed earlier?'

'I'm . . . I'm sorry, madam. I was paying my respects to Gile – Lord Montsorrel in the chapel. His death was a terrible shock to us all, and so soon after Lord Raymond's, God rest their souls.' She crossed herself and looked pathetically at Joscelin, her moist lower lip drooping.

'I am sure it was a shock,' Linnet retorted, adding for Joscelin's benefit, 'This is Helwis de Corbette, our seneschal's daughter. She and her mother have been responsible for the housekeeping here these five years past.'

The girl shot Linnet a challenging look and moved closer to Joscelin. As she helped him don the shirt, her voice was low and intimate. 'My lord, I will strive to perform anything you desire of me to your satisfaction.' The final word was embellished with promise.

Linnet stifled a sound in the back of her throat. The words 'slut' and 'whore' burned the tip of her tongue. Joscelin's eyes were very bright and his complexion slightly congested. Lust was a tangible aura in the room.

'Then do this for me,' he grated, his voice suddenly a harsh echo of William Ironheart's. 'Get out of my sight now and return to your devotions. Since you were so concerned for your lord's soul as to avoid your duties here, you can spend from now until retiring in further vigil.' He stepped away from the greedy touch of her fingers.

Helwis de Corbette gaped at him as if he had spoken in a foreign language.

'Out!' he snarled.

She uttered a gasp, stared between him and Linnet, then whirled and fled the room.

'Giles's solace in the time he was lord here, and yours if you want her, judging from her behaviour just now,' Linnet said with bitter contempt.

115

'You think I'd follow my father's folly and take a mistress beneath my own wife's roof?' he growled and, before she could move or cry out, he put his arms around her waist, drew her hard against him and kissed her.

At first Linnet was too shocked to move. Images of herself and Raymond de Montsorrel embracing in this room were overlaid by the scratchy pressure of Joscelin's kiss, the heat of his touch, the pungent odour of his sweat. If she had felt stifled earlier, now she felt well and truly engulfed.

He swept his hand down her spine in a slow, powerful stroke until he cupped her buttocks and pressed her closer to him. Her back strained. Against her belly she felt the vigorous surge of his erection. Releasing her lips, he nibbled her earlobe and the angle of her jaw. Then he took her hand and slowly, slowly guided it downwards. As her fingers touched the bulge in his chausses, he swallowed a groan.

Linnet knew what to do. Raymond had shown her once, his hand over hers, his voice coaxing. Oh yes, she knew. The quicker the release, the sooner she would be free, but not here, witnessed by her conscience, four wounded knights, two maids and quite possibly her son should he wake from his slumber in the wall-chamber beyond.

She snatched her hand away as if he had burned her, and struggled to free herself from his grip. Succeeding in wriggling one arm free, she hit him on his freshly bandaged shoulder with as much force as her position would allow.

He cried out and his hold slackened. She tore from his embrace and faced him, panting and wild-eyed. Joscelin stared at her then cursed and sat down on the coffer, his breath hissing through clenched teeth, his good hand clutching his injured shoulder.

Linnet gnawed her lip and, still poised for flight, watched him with apprehension.

His breathing eased. He extended his hand in a gesture of apology. 'For what it's worth, I've been on too tight a rein recently and that girl . . .' He broke off and grimaced. 'I give you my word of honour it won't happen again.'

Linnet's stomach was turning over and over. She knew he could have beaten her for defying him and that the incident might have ended in rape upon the floor rather than retreat and apology. 'You frightened me,' she said, then added, 'I didn't mean to hurt you.'

'Nor I to frighten you. I don't want to live in a household like my father's.' He did not elaborate but, after a moment, sighed. The act of drawing and releasing a deep breath caused him to wrinkle his nose. 'Is there a bathtub in this place? I stink to high heaven.'

'There should be one in the laundry; I'll find out.' Linnet relaxed as their conversation started to flow over the difficult moment. 'What about the silver?'

His glance flickered to the great bed and the mattress that had recently been unloaded from beneath the coffin and thrown across the rope frame. Safe among the layers of goose down stuffing were nestled thirty leather bags, each containing five marks of silver.

'Leave it where it is for the nonce until I've had time to commission a new strongbox from the carpenter and the locksmith.'

'Will you not be sleeping on it?'

His smile was wry. 'And deprive a lady of her bed? No, Stephen's organizing something for me in the wall-chamber near the chapel.'

'And you trust me with the coin?' She was driven by a devil to challenge him.

'You would not cheat your own son. Yes, I trust you.'

117

His tone held mild rebuke as if he suspected her of deliberately needling him.

After he had gone, Linnet wandered to the bed and sat down upon it. It would have eased her conscience if he had taken the money into his own keeping or not stated his trust in her with so steady a gaze. No, she would not cheat Robert, he was all her life, but for his sake she had cheated Joscelin. She and Maude had sewn the thirty money bags into the mattress that night in London, but there had already been thirty marks stitched into one corner, money that she had sequestered from the strongbox in secret on the night Giles died. This was her security for the future, a secret hoard of her own.

She had made her bed and now she had to lie on it, lumps and all.

13

'For just how much is Corbette responsible in the keep and on the estate?' Joscelin asked Linnet at table that night. The main dish was mutton. It was tough as saddle leather and in places charred black, speaking of an inattentive hand at the spit. Joscelin swallowed a final mouthful by resorting to a liberal gulp of wine and abandoned the meat in favour of a dish of steamed mussels.

'I do not know. I haven't dwelt at Rushcliffe since . . . since the quarrel.' Linnet looked at him from the corner of her eye. He was acting as if nothing had happened between them a few hours ago but she could remember the taste of him too vividly to follow his lead.

He had made thorough use of the bathtub that had been found and he now exuded a scent of coarse laundry soap that stung her nostrils and made her want to sneeze. Time, she thought, and past time to set to work with the maids and manufacture something less caustic for personal use. Time would also have to be found to sew Joscelin some new tunics. The one he was wearing tonight was the brown wool from the horse fair and was beginning to look more than just hard-worn. Perhaps it would assuage her guilt about the thirty silver marks if she made him some good clothes, as befitted a dutiful wife.

He grimaced at the sourness of the sauce in which he had dipped a mussel and again reached to his cup. Then he said, 'Corbette appears to have wide-ranging authority. It seems that he is steward of Rushcliffe as well as seneschal. Every time I have wanted a key to a coffer or asked a question, I am informed that Corbette has it or knows the answer and that worries me. He has his own little kingdom here and everyone is subject to his yeasay.' Wiping his fingers on a napkin, he leaned back in the lord's chair and studied the man through narrowed lids. Linnet, too, looked at Corbette. He was deep in conversation with a stout man clad in a dark-red tunic that made his corpulent torso look like a ripe plum. As Corbette spoke to him, the other's pouchy gaze darted nervously in the direction of the high table.

'Who's that?' Joscelin asked.

'Fulbert, the senior scribe.'

'What's he like?'

She tilted her head and frowned as she sought to be impartial. 'He's pleasant and courteous and writes a fine fair hand, but he's as soft as unfired clay.'

Joscelin nodded consideringly.

The words between Corbette and the scribe were becoming heated. Fulbert shook his head, his glance flickering towards Joscelin with fear. A woman leaned between the two arguing men and spoke sharply. Rolls of fat strained at the seams of her blue brocade gown.

Despite her annoyance, Linnet's mouth twitched. 'Giles bought that blue cloth she's wearing because he wanted a new court tunic but, when we left at the time of the quarrel, it went missing. I don't think Giles could ever have graced the stuff the way it now graces Mabel de Corbette.'

'*That* is Corbette's wife?' Joscelin said in astonishment.

She watched him stare from Corbette's lean, aristocratic profile to the woman's blowsy overabundance and try without success to reconcile the two. 'I am told that she was once as beautiful as her daughter, Helwis,' Linnet added mischievously.

He gave an amused grunt. 'Is that a warning?'

'I would not presume so far, messire,' she said sweetly. 'Besides, I trust to your common sense.'

His lips curved with sour amusement and his regard travelled outwards again. 'That brocade will have to last her a lifetime. She'll find herself beggared of all but homespuns from this day forth.'

Linnet directed a servant to fill his empty cup but Joscelin swiftly set his palm over the top. 'Would you have me so gilded that I spend the night under the trestle in a stupor?'

'I thought that was your intent since you swallowed the last three with a swiller's skill.'

He made a face. 'I'd not have eaten my dinner else. We have enough tosspots in this hall already to drink an alehouse dry.' He stared at the serjeant Halfdan who was arm-wrestling with another guard, lighted candle stubs set to either side of their straining wrists. Halfdan was using his free hand to raise a cup to his lips, egged on by his cronies.

Abruptly Joscelin rose to his feet and, leaving the dais, set out to mingle with the people gathered in the hall. It was not a conventional move and earned him glances of suspicion and hostility as well as approval. Raymond and Giles de Montsorrel would have retired to the private rooms on the floor above long since. However, for the moment, the new lord was a gardener in diligent search of weeds to uproot and plants to nurture.

121

Joscelin passed close to Corbette. The seneschal had ceased his vehement conversation with the scribe and bowed in deference to his new lord. His wife curtseyed and batted her lashes at Joscelin but she had run to seed and her flirting did not have quite the same effect on him as her daughter's had done. Moving into the well of the hall, Joscelin sought the fletcher and immersed himself in a conversation about the possibility of making arrows to suit the Welsh bows he was thinking about introducing to the castle's armoury.

The shouts of the soldiers watching the arm-wrestling contest drowned out what the fletcher was saying. Frowning, Joscelin lifted his head and stared down the long trestle to the chanting men. Halfdan was about to press his victim's knuckles into the molten tallow of the burning candle-end. Fists pounded on the board in unison with the chanting. The wood vibrated. Cups leaped up and down. Halfdan applied a last burst of pressure and seared his opponent's wrist into the hot wax. Then he held him there as if branding a beast. The other soldier gasped through clenched teeth. A stronger stink of tallow smoke thickened the air as a grinning Halfdan released his victim and scooped up his winnings to unanimous cheers. No one wanted to be on the wrong side of such a man. Flexing his powerful shoulders, Halfdan stared round the ring of fixed smiles and saw, beyond them, an unsmiling Joscelin.

'Want to challenge me?' Halfdan extended a meaty paw. 'Or are you too frightened?'

A silence fell – as loud as the shouting that had preceded it. One by one the smiles fell away.

'You've more words than wits, man,' Joscelin said with quiet contempt. 'It's the drink in you talking; you'd not last a minute against me.' Rising from the trestle, he turned his back and started to walk away.

'Coward!' Halfdan shouted. 'Weakling!'

There was an audible gasp from the men at the board.

Joscelin paused, weighing up the risks. He could ignore the comment and by doing so display his scorn. That was the prudent thing to do. He was tired and sore, did not relish a confrontation tonight with a man of Halfdan's bulk; yet if he passed it over, those words would stick. Whatever he did, there were going to be repercussions. Slowly he turned round and, with a measured walk, returned to the trestle.

Halfdan gave a triumphant grin. His companions were notably more circumspect. One of them relit the candle stubs from a rushlight and then retreated, giving the adversaries room.

Joscelin seated himself opposite Halfdan. 'You have a death wish,' he said in a conversational tone of voice and held out his hand.

Halfdan wiped his hand down his chausses and fortified himself with another drink of ale, adding to the gallon he had already consumed. 'I am not the one who will die,' he answered. Planting his elbow solidly on the scuffed oak board, he clasped Joscelin's hand within his enormous fist.

Joscelin resisted as Halfdan started to push, and smiled into the soldier's face. He was no stranger to this game himself, for he and his uncle Conan had played it constantly on campaign, sometimes for stones when there was no money. There was a skill to it, brute force alone was not enough, and Joscelin knew that Halfdan's reactions must be impaired by the amount of ale in his belly.

Their forearms remained at the starting point. Halfdan's muscles tightened and bulged with strain but he moved Joscelin scarcely an inch towards the candle. Struggling, he held his breath and pushed with all the force of a woman in the last throes of childbirth. His efforts bore no fruit and, as he expended the last of his breath on a sob and drew more air, Joscelin began to apply slow, inexorable pressure of his own, bearing down smoothly. Halfdan grimaced, then he howled, his whole arm rigid and shaking with the effort of keeping his pride out of the molten wax. Flesh and flame made tenuous contact. It was too much for Halfdan to bear and, with a bellow of rage, he tore himself free of Joscelin's grip and towered to his feet.

'Bastard spawn of a whoring bitch!' he roared and, throwing himself across the trestle, seized Joscelin by the throat. Joscelin knew his death was seconds away. He jerked his knee hard into Halfdan's groin, freed the boot knife that no self-respecting mercenary was ever without and drove it upwards and forwards with all the strength in his body. Halfdan bucked and sagged forward, following the knife as Joscelin withdrew it. His hands lost their grip. He struck the trestle and rolled off it, landing with a thud amid the filthy floor rushes.

'My lord, are you all right?' Sword in hand, expression grim, Milo reached Joscelin.

Between coughs, Joscelin nodded brusquely. He might just have been half-strangled, his shoulder might be screaming with pain, but he was still alive and he had made a lasting impression on the boggle-eyed witnesses. They would not dare to challenge his authority now that their champion had been sacrificed across his own profane altar.

'Get rid of this,' he said huskily, gesturing to Halfdan's corpse. 'The men can dig a grave in the morning.' Pivoting on his heel, he returned to the dais, making sure to stalk disdainfully, although in truth he wanted to crawl. He sat down in the lord's chair, propped his dagger-boot on the edge of the table in fine vagabond style, and stared out over his domain. Conversation started again, raggedly at first but rapidly gaining volume. Halfdan's corpse was dragged from the hall by its heels like a carcass fit only for the hounds.

'They'll be searching his belongings already for what they can scrounge,' Joscelin said with weary distaste.

'You should not have ventured below,' Linnet remonstrated as he coughed again. 'You were almost killed.'

'There was need.' This time he did not refuse when she directed a servant to replenish his cup. 'To know Rushcliffe, I must know its backbone and root out the rot. If I am known as a man who does not stand on ceremony, I become more approachable and my task is made simpler.'

'You also become known as a man who carries a dagger in his boot,' she said.

'Indeed, and a man who plans for adversity and has the wit and will to overcome it.' His tone was light but the words themselves carried conviction. He gave her a twisted smiled and raised a toast. 'You're a woman of a similar breed yourself. Here's to our wedding bed, all hundred and fifty marks' worth.'

Linnet blushed as she lifted her own cup.

14

The first business of the morning was Giles's funeral, a short unpleasant affair. The weather was warm and, despite having been well salted and divested of internal organs, the corpse had defied attempts at preservation and was riper than an overhung pheasant. Perfumed smoke rippled from the censers in the chapel but did nothing to conceal the stench of rotting meat.

Helwis de Corbette fainted and had to be carried out. Linnet suspected that it was a deliberate ploy on her behalf to avoid the smell. Indeed, Linnet doubted that Helwis had been anywhere near Giles's coffin yesterday, despite her professions of piety.

The ceremony was hastily concluded by the ashen-faced priest, and the coffin was borne away to the crypt and placed beside the tomb of Raymond de Montsorrel. Father and son were together in death as they had never been in life, Linnet thought and shivered, feeling as if a bony finger had run down her spine. As soon as it was decently possible, she made her excuses and went to attend to her patients in the bower.

As she changed dressings and administered medicines,

she swore to herself that she would expunge every trace of Giles and his father from the living core of the castle. However, that involved pacifying the dead with a show of duty. Having reassured herself of the condition of her charges, she left them in the hands of her maids. Retiring to a corner of the bower near the window, she sent for Fulbert, the scribe. When he arrived with his quills, ink and sheets of vellum, she set about composing a letter to a noted Nottingham stonemason. She would have effigies carved and set upon the tombs. Let no one accuse her of a lack of respect. She would pay to have prayers said, too, so that all could rest – the dead and the living. Dear Holy Mary, let this be an end and a new beginning.

Joscelin studied the men drawn up before him in the court-yard. On first sight, they appeared to be a flabby collection of dregs and gutter sweepings: sullen, defensive and afraid. Watching them shuffle and mutter, he wondered whether he ought to dismiss them all and ride into Nottingham to recruit anew. But then, he reminded himself, even the best troop in the world could suffer from bad leadership and he could not spare the time to go picking through Nottingham's alleyways and alehouses for likely men.

Hands on hips, he delivered the gathered soldiers a brief lecture on what he expected of them, what they could expect of him in return and what would happen should they break the codes under which they would now be living.

'You have a month to prove yourselves,' he told them. 'After that, any man who has shown himself worthy will be guaranteed his wages for the rest of the year. Those who do not measure up will be dismissed. Any questions?'

When he left them in Milo's tender care, he knew that their eyes were pursuing him into the keep. He was aware that many of them would fail the test but there were others who just needed the fire rekindling and who, with some intensive training, would do well enough.

'When I'm talking, you pay attention!' Milo roared, striding forward to fill their vision, a spear brandished in his fist. 'Anyone know what this is? No, it's not for leaning on while you fall asleep or ogle a serving girl's tits! You, stop smirking and come here. Show me how you'd beat down a sword attack with one of these.'

Smothering a grin, Joscelin left his captain in full flow and went to the small chamber off the hall where the account rolls, tally sticks and exchequer cloth were stored. Taking the key that Corbette had reluctantly handed to him the previous evening, he unlocked an ironbound chest, removed the top layer of parchments, the tally bags and chequer cloth, and bade a young manservant bring him a waxed tablet and stylus.

'Shall I fetch Sir Arnaud to attend you, sire?' asked the man as Joscelin loosened the drawstring on the tally bag and tipped the notched sticks it contained onto the trestle.

'I'm quite capable of deciphering these without the seneschal's aid,' Joscelin replied, then gave the servant a wintry smile. 'A pitcher of ale would be useful, though. Doubtless there's a recent brewing if the state of the men in the hall last night was any indication.'

'Yes, sire.' The young man hurried out, his manner one of cheerful alacrity that was refreshing after the dull indifference that Joscelin had generally encountered thus far. He returned promptly with the requested articles and poured Joscelin a horn beaker full of golden-brown ale. 'You'll get none better between here and Newark, my lord,' he announced with pride. 'And I doesn't say that just because my aunt's the brewster.'

Joscelin took a deep swallow and savoured the complex,

malty bouquet. 'You're right,' he said with a smile and a toast of the horn. 'My compliments to your aunt. She's a skilled woman.' He smoothed out the chequer cloth.

The serving man, who had yet to be dismissed, eyed him quizzically. 'Do you really know how to use one of those, sire?' He indicated the cloth.

Joscelin shrugged. 'There is no mystery once you have learned the principle. I was taught by the monks at Lenton when I was a boy. We used to count the flocks when they came in for shearing.'

'But you're a fighting man, sire.' The servant looked perplexed.

'Does that mean I cannot have more than one string to my bow? It is useful to have someone else to do this for me but my knowledge of letters and ciphering means that I can check their honesty if the need arises. How else will I know if I am being cheated?'

The young man shifted uncomfortably from foot to foot as if the floor were hot. 'Sire, I know it ain't my place to speak, and I saw last night as you could look after yourself, but the seneschal's mighty vexed at what you're doing.'

This volunteering of information was precisely what Joscelin had been hoping for. 'He's going to be more vexed yet,' he replied and leaned against the carved chair back. 'What's your name?'

'Henry, sire.' Given encouragement, he was enthusiastic. 'I was born the year the king came to the throne and me mam had me christened to honour him.' He added with a note of pride, 'My da's head groom here and older brother's following him on. I serve in the hall with me mam and two sisters.'

'So you must see and hear a great deal of what goes forth?'

'I do, sire, more than some would like.' He glanced furtively over his shoulder. 'But I ain't a gossip. I know when to keep my mouth shut.'

Joscelin considered him with thoughtful amusement. 'I'm sure you do,' he said. 'But I also hope you know when to speak out.'

Henry was quick on the uptake. 'Yes, sire,' he said. 'I know where my duty lies.'

'Well, do it well by me and I will see you promoted. I promise you that, and I keep my promises.'

Henry's face shone with pleasure. 'Thank you, sire.'

Joscelin smiled wryly. 'Don't thank me just yet,' he said. 'Wait and see a while before you make judgement.'

'Yes, sire.' Henry continued to beam. 'Me mam said you'd be good for us, though, and she can always tell.'

'And which one is she?'

'She tends the big soup pot, sire, and airs the pallets by the fire.'

'Ah, yes.' He grinned as his mind filled with the image of a beady-eyed stick of a woman poking all two brawny yards of Milo away from her precious cauldron, armed with nothing more than her ladle and her razor-sharp tongue. That was the kind of spirit he had to nurture in order to obtain a harvest from his ambition.

After Henry had departed, jaunty as a young cockerel, Joscelin's grin faded and, with a sigh, he set to work. Gradually he began to frown. Several times he erased his own calculations and began again. As he moved counters on the chequer cloth, his frown deepened and his lips compressed.

Thirty hogsheads of wine delivered last week, so the accounts stated, and only eight left. The lord not being in residence, that left only a skeleton household of servants and retainers to maintain, half of whom would only drink ale or cider. Someone, it seemed, had found a fatted calf and stuck in the knife with a vengeance.

Leaving his calculations, Joscelin took a lighted lantern and descended into the vast, vaulted undercroft beneath the great hall, intent on checking matters for himself.

Near the door, standing against three casks of cider, he found the hogsheads of wine, the barrels stamped with the mark of their Angevin producer. There were seven of them. He had passed the eighth in the hall where one of Henry's sisters had been filling flagons from it for the high table. The evidence agreed with the tally. So what had happened to the others?

Holding the lantern on high, Joscelin prowled forward. There were barrels of salt beef and pork, herrings and cod. Cured sausages and hams dangled from the ceiling together with bunches of herbs and strings of onions and garlic. A dozen Easter buns had been hung up to dry so that, when required, pieces could be broken off and crumbled into drinks to cure the ague. There were crocks of honey, firkins of tallow, ash staves, hides, bundles of rushes and two broken cartwheels. Obviously Rushcliffe's wheelwright was not a master craftsman. Neither was its chatelaine, to judge by the chaotic state of the undercroft. Sins had been swept in here out of view and provisions used without the supervision of a diligent storemaster or mistress.

Staring around the arc of lantern light, Joscelin's stomach contracted as he realized that if this place were tidied up, and everything that was useless discarded, it would be nigh on empty.

A castle was built to hold supplies, to be self-sufficient for long stretches of time. As a mercenary, he knew just how vital the principle was. Run out of salt beef, stock fish and wine, and you ran out of morale. Run out of bread and you were finished. Cursing under his breath, he picked his way across coils of rope and a broken eel-trap to the stores of winnowed grain. It appeared to be plentiful and of a high quality. He examined all the bins, thrusting his arm well down into the golden harvest to make sure that it was not just a thin layer of wholegrain poured on top of chaff. All appeared to be well until he stepped back and realized that it in no way tallied with the written accounts. Standing there, staring at yet more evidence of not only mismanagement but outright thievery, he remembered the previous evening in the hall and Corbette's urgent conversation with Fulbert, the scribe. His temper ignited and he stormed from the under-croft and upstairs to the bower.

His wounded soldiers gaped at him in astonishment as he strode past them without a word.

'Someone's in for it,' muttered Malcolm. 'I've never seen him look sae fashed before.'

Joscelin strode across the bower to the corner where Linnet and Fulbert were working on a parchment. Jaw clenched, he flung the most damning of the evidence across Fulbert's lectern. The pot of goose quills flew across the room and smashed on the laver, and the ink tipped over, ruining the exquisitely formed letters on the parchment.

'What's wrong?' Linnet stared at Joscelin in astonishment.

'Ask this turd here!'

Fulbert's neck reddened against his fine linen shirt. 'I do not know what you mean, my lord,' he said, his gaze sliding off Joscelin's as though it were a sheer glass wall.

'These accounts are in your hand, I presume?'

Silence.

Joscelin slammed his good fist down on the lectern,

causing the remaining sheets of parchment to slide off on to the floor. 'Answer me!' he bellowed.

'I'm only a scribe, my lord!' Fulbert gibbered. 'I write what the seneschal tells me and the rest is none of my business!'

Joscelin clutched a fistful of Fulbert's thick mulberry-red tunic. 'Your clothes sing a different tune, scribe. You dress more finely than the king himself!'

Unleashing the power in his bunched arm, he shoved Fulbert away as if the man's deceit had physically soiled his hands.

The force of the thrust sent Fulbert to his knees. He did not rise, but stayed there, weeping. 'I had no choice, my lord. If I had protested, Corbette would have set Halfdan upon me and my family. Lord Raymond was not in his right wits at the end and no one could make him understand what was happening. And where Corbette's influence didn't run, his daughter's did, if you take my meaning.'

'In God's name, will you tell me what is happening?' Linnet demanded, rising to her feet.

'Thievery on a vast scale,' Joscelin said tersely. 'The undercroft's near-empty and, if I'm not mistaken about the grain tally, about to be emptier still.'

Her eyes met his, appalled, then settled on the weeping Fulbert.

Joscelin breathed out hard. As he looked down at Fulbert's pathetic snivelling form, his anger dampened into disgusted irritation. He remembered building castles of mud as a child and then pissing on them from a height to watch them collapse. 'I doubt marching you down to the cells is going to be of benefit to anyone, including myself,' he said in a more normal tone of voice. 'I'm very tempted to swing you from the battlements but there are things I need to know and perhaps you would like to barter your hide for the answers?'

Fulbert nodded. 'Ask of me what you will. I've a wife and four children, the youngest is only a babe in arms. They will starve if I hang.'

'You should have taken thought for that earlier,' Joscelin said icily. 'Where are the stolen goods sold?'

'Corbette has a relative in Nottingham who's a merchant. The goods go to him downriver or on pack ponies once a month. Please, messire, I beg you to be lenient. I'll serve you faithfully, I swear it!'

'As well as you served your two previous lords?' Narrowing his eyes, Joscelin scrutinized the spineless blob at his feet. He had every right to hang him. At the very least he ought to have the fool stripped, flogged and put in the stocks for a week without sustenance, but as he stared an idea came to him, one that might yet save the man from himself. 'You're of no use to me,' he said. 'For your own safety and my peace of mind, I cannot keep you in this household but I know that my father, William de Rocher, is in sore need of a scribe at Arnsby. He can read and write after a fashion but he's not fond of the quill and his eyesight is not what it was. You'll go to him under escort, giving him your full history and a letter of recommendation from me.'

Fulbert gave a wet sniff and looked at Joscelin in abject misery.

'It's either that or the gibbet. Make your choice quickly before my patience comes to an end.'

'Wh— When do I have to leave, my lord?'

'As soon as you can pack your belongings and gather your family.'

Fulbert sat up. He was still shivering but his tears had ceased.

'Serve William de Rocher honestly and you'll have nothing to fear,' Joscelin said. 'Go now and, as you value your reprieve, say nothing to anyone.'

Whey-faced, looking as if he were about to be sick, Fulbert bowed out of the room.

Joscelin exhaled through his teeth. He began collecting the scattered tally sticks and replacing them in their drawstring bag with an untoward gentleness that spoke of rigid control.

Linnet picked up the sheet of parchment Joscelin had thrust beneath Fulbert's nose. 'I still don't understand. What do you mean, the undercroft's empty?'

'Corbette's been diverting the keep's vital supplies elsewhere to his own profit and Fulbert's been falsifying the accounts to make everything seem normal at first glance. Come, I'll show you.'

On their way to the undercroft, Joscelin paused in the hall and spoke to two of his off-duty troops who were playing a game of merels. 'Leave that,' he said quietly. 'Go and find the seneschal and bring him to the solar. I want him kept there until I'm ready to deal with him.'

'What will you do to Corbette?' Linnet enquired as once more Joscelin kindled his lantern and together they descended the steps into the darkness of the undercroft.

'String him up,' Joscelin said. 'Village or bailey, I haven't decided yet. Village probably. His corpse will serve notice that I'm not to be duped and that my justice is swiftly meted.'

'And his wife and daughter?'

'They've aided and abetted him and I don't want them under my roof. Let them be put out of the keep to make their own way. There are enough troops in Nottingham to assure them of employment and the daughter certainly has talent. As long as I never see them again, I care not.'

They reached the foot of the stairs and he took her arm to guide her into the depths of the undercroft. He was aware of the closeness of her body and felt an echo of yesterday's havoc ripple through him. It was going to be hard to keep his distance for the required three months.

Raising the lantern on high, he showed her the storeroom: its state of disarray damning evidence of sloppy housekeeping. She clucked her tongue and walked ahead of him, staring round.

'What about supplies elsewhere?' she asked him.

'I've included them in my estimations but, even so, we're dangerously short.'

Drawing her between the pillars, he showed her the wine casks, the salted meats and the grain. 'See how the barrels are spread out? Close them together and you have next to nothing.'

Linnet lifted her gaze to his. Unspoken between them lay the knowledge that a war was at hand and they were woefully unprepared to face it. No supplies, a sparse demoralized garrison and villagers who were either hostile or indifferent.

Footsteps grated on the undercroft stairs and the light from a torch swirled around the walls. Joscelin turned. 'Who's there?' he demanded.

'Henry, sire. I knew you was down here; I saw you unlocking the door.' The servant rounded the corner of the newel post and peered anxiously down. 'There's a messenger arrived, says he's come from the ju—justiciar?' He stumbled over the last unfamiliar word. 'My sister's given him somat to drink and settled him by the fire.'

'Did he give his name?'

'Yes, sire – Brien FitzRenard.' Henry stared around the undercroft, absorbing every detail.

Joscelin nodded and moved towards the stairs. 'I trust

your discretion,' he said to Henry with an eloquent arch of his brow.

'I ain't seen or heard a thing, sire.' Henry answered blandly. 'We're always short o' supplies this time o' year.'

FitzRenard had left the bench where Henry's sister had served him hot wine, and was restlessly prowling the hall. His garments were powdered with dust and his mouth was tight, but when he saw Joscelin he relaxed enough to smile.

'I'm sorry to take you from your toil.' He nodded at Joscelin's tunic.

Glancing down, Joscelin brushed perfunctorily at the cobwebs and crumbs of old mortar festooning his tunic. 'I've been seeking rats in the undercroft – two-legged ones.'

'Ah.' FitzRenard nodded. 'Always a hazard when there hasn't been anyone capable of hunting them for a while. I wish you good fortune.'

'What brings you to Rushcliffe?' Joscelin took the cup of wine that Linnet handed to him.

FitzRenard sighed. 'You know Robert of Leicester was sailing for Normandy with an aid of money and men for the king? Well, he's done what we half-suspected he would and turned rebel. He's ridden straight for his own lands and declared for young Henry. The shore-watch has been alerted, the shire levies are being called up and every baron is required to swear his loyalty to the king. Those who do not are by default rebels and their estates forfeit. I'm riding north with the justiciar's writ commanding the oaths of fealty and serving notice to stand to arms.'

Joscelin nodded grimly. 'Anyone who trespasses on these lands will receive the greeting of my sword. Is my father still in London?'

FitzRenard shook his head. 'Actually we rode part of the way here together; he was escorting his womenfolk back to Arnsby.' Brien gave Joscelin a shrewd glance. 'Your brothers were not with him, apart from the little one, and it was more than my life was worth to enquire after them.'

'They've joined Leicester's rebellion,' Joscelin said, 'and you would indeed have risked life and limb asking my father about them.' He changed the subject. 'Are you resting here the night or are you bound elsewhere?'

'I've to go on to Newark but I was hoping for a bed and a fresh horse in the morning. My grey's got a leg strain. I can collect him and reimburse you on the return journey.' Brien sent a perusing glance around the great hall. 'I had no inkling of the size of this place. You have landed on your feet indeed.'

'I have landed', Joscelin retorted, 'up to my neck in dung.'

Undeceived, Brien smiled. Despite the complaint, he had heard the proprietorial note in Joscelin's voice and seen the glance the mercenary had cast at his bride-to-be.

A knight entered the hall from the forebuilding and strode up to their group.

'Corbette's gone, sir,' said Guy de Montauban, breathing hard. 'The gate guards say he and his family rode out an hour since.'

'And the guards did not see fit to stop them?'

'No, sir. They assumed you had ordered Corbette to leave, because all his belongings were loaded on three pack-ponies and all the men knew that there had been strong words between you already.'

Joscelin swore. He could not blame the guards for their action. He had given them no instructions to detain the seneschal until now and their reasoning was logical. 'All right, Guy. Tell the grooms to saddle up the horses. We should still be able to pick up their trail.'

'Yes, sir.' Montauban saluted and hurried away.

Brien cocked an enquiring brow. 'Trouble?'

Joscelin shook his head. 'The seneschal's been bleeding Rushcliffe white for the past year and a half at least. He knows I'm wise to him so he's run, doubtless with his pockets crammed at Rushcliffe's expense. I should have arrested him last night, not waited until I had evidence.'

'Lend me a horse and I'll come with you.' Brien put his cup down on the nearest trestle.

'Be welcome,' Joscelin said with a brisk nod then turned to Linnet, who was staring at him in dismay. 'What's the matter?'

'You're as battered and bruised as a tiltyard dummy!' she protested. 'What of your shoulder? If you are pulling yourself in and out of a saddle and controlling a war-horse, you'll tear the wound open again. Even now it should be in a sling.'

He gave her a lop-sided shrug. 'It will hold up for what needs to be done.'

'Let Milo go in your stead. He's unscathed.'

'No, the responsibility is mine. Some things I can delegate elsewhere but not this. I'll be careful.'

She set her jaw. 'Then let me at least add some more padding to your bandages – for my peace of mind if not yours.'

Joscelin drew breath to deny that he required any such tending but Linnet was quicker.

'You have to come to the bedchamber anyway to put on your hauberk and it won't take a moment.'

His lips closed and then slowly curved in a smile. He

inclined his head in amused capitulation. 'If you were a swordsman, you'd be deadly,' he said.

Linnet went pink and turned away to the stairs.

'You've seen some fighting already then?' asked Brien.

'A skirmish,' Joscelin said, down-playing yesterday's assault. His gaze followed the sway of Linnet's hips. 'I'll tell you about it while we ride.'

15

Finding Corbette's trail was a simple matter for a seasoned troop of mercenaries who, like wolves, were accustomed to hunting in a cooperative pack, their senses sharpened by the proximity of their prey.

Corbette could only have taken the one road and all that Joscelin had to decide was whether to pursue it to Newark or Nottingham. The latter led through the village and, since Corbette was heartily disliked there, Joscelin sent Guy de Montauban to question the people. Henry accompanied the soldier to reassure the occupants and translate as Guy had few words of English. A bag of silver went with them, too, to loosen reluctant tongues. Joscelin took his own suspicions towards Newark at a rapid trot.

Within two miles those suspicions were confirmed when they came across a lame pony grazing among a flock of sheep. It still wore a rope pack-bridle and there were sweaty cinch marks branded on its belly. When it saw the soldiers' horses, it nickered and limped eagerly to greet them. The pony bore a distinctive star marking on his forehead and Joscelin recognized it as one of the sturdy pack beasts that had carried supplies on the journey between London and Rushcliffe.

The wind ruffled the grass. A small shred of colour fluttered upon the spikes of a young hawthorn bush growing against a crumbled wall. Dismounting, Joscelin went to investigate and discovered a veil of blue silk and nearby a linen bolster stuffed with women's clothing.

'They've had to lighten their load,' Joscelin said to Brien with satisfaction. 'We're on the right track. Jean, return to the village and fetch Sir Guy.' Joscelin remounted and strapped the bundle to his crupper.

A mile farther on, a narrow cart track branched off the road to give access to one of the granges beholden to the castle. Thick woodland lay to one side of the track, open fields to the other. Huddled in the sheltered corner of a dip in the undulating wolds stood the farm buildings – a longhouse in the old Saxon style, together with a barn and outbuildings. The longhouse was on fire. As the breeze backed and eddied, the smell of smoke reached the riders. Ripples of heat zigzagged and shimmered, giving the burning building the illusion of being underwater.

'It doesn't look as if someone's just been careless with a cooking fire.' Brien unstrapped his helm from his saddle.

Joscelin heard the tension in Brien's voice. The thought of Leicester's rebellion was uppermost in everyone's mind but surely it was too soon for that kind of trouble – unless it was concerned with the skirmish on the road yesterday. Perhaps it was by way of revenge. Joscelin shook the reins and urged Whitesocks towards the farmstead. The eddies of smoke strengthened and the stallion pranced and plunged. Joscelin almost lost control of him when they came upon the body of a horse stretched across the track. It was a palfrey this time, a dainty black barb mare. Her foreleg was broken and someone had cut her throat. A thick cloud of flies buzzed around the blackening wound. Of harness there was no sign, although her hide still bore the impression of bridle and saddle.

His spine prickling, Joscelin steadied Whitesocks and rode on. The smell of burning was woven with the crackle of feeding flames. In places, all the flesh of the longhouse had been devoured and the wooden bones were enveloped in greedy tongues of scarlet fire. Beside the track, face-down in the grass, a body sprawled.

Arnaud de Corbette had been stripped of his fine garments and was clad in naught but his linen braies. Three diagonal slashes were carved across his corpse as if he were a fish on a griddle. One eye glared. The other was concealed against the bloodied earth. Joscelin dismounted and, holding the reins fast in one hand, crouched to examine Corbette's wounds.

Brien's face twisted. 'What are you doing?'

Joscelin looked up. 'Seeking answers. Look at these cuts. Whoever did this had a good sword and some useful weight behind his swing. An axe or a club would have left different marks.'

Brien's gaze was full of fastidious distaste. 'So why does it matter how he was killed?'

Joscelin stood up. 'It matters because only a man of wealth or professional fighting ability would own a sword and only a man who sells his services would strip a body like this. I've done it myself in winters past when an extra cloak means the difference between living and freezing.'

'So you think this is the work of mercenaries?'

'Very likely.' Joscelin remounted and rode towards the palisade surrounding the burning farm. A stifled sob close on the left made Whitesocks throw up his head and snort with alarm. Joscelin calmed the horse and stared at the reeds and sedge bordering the muddy ditch at the foot of the palisade slope. 'Come out where I can see you,' he commanded in English. 'You will not be harmed. I am Joscelin de Gael, appointed by the Crown to govern here.'

Two women, one young and very pregnant, the other older but still handsome, emerged from their hiding place in a clump of feather reeds. Their gown hems were mud-stained and heavy with water. The younger woman was sobbing and clutching her gravid belly. Her companion gripped a knife in her right hand and suspiciously eyed Joscelin and his troop.

'What has happened here?' he asked. 'Where are your menfolk?'

The older woman shook her head. 'Soldiers came with weapons,' she said. 'Their tongue was foreign but not French like they speak at the castle. We saw them coming, heard them too, the bastards, because they was chasing the seneschal, and he was screaming like a coney. Our menfolk are at the mill, else they'd be dead, too.' She put her arm around the younger woman, who continued to snuffle and sob. 'Me and Alfreda was outside feeding the poultry when we heard the commotion and we saw the seneschal and his family being attacked and robbed by soldiers. I made Alfreda drop everything and we hid in the ditch. We could hear them yelling and boasting.' She shuddered. 'The women were screaming and I was sure they'd discover us, they was so close, but we prayed to the blessed Saint Edmund and we was spared.' The woman's eyes glittered with angry, unshed tears. 'Although God knows what for. How are we supposed to live now with the rent due at Michaelmas and our house and half our stores gone?'

'You need not worry about that. I'll see to it that you're not destitute.' Joscelin tried to keep the impatience out of his voice. Their concerns were obviously vital of this moment to them. 'How many soldiers did you see?'

'I don't know, only got a couple o' glimpses.' She counted laboriously on her fingers. ''Bout a score, I suppose, but only half of them had horses. They took the seneschal's destrier and madam's palfrey. They'd have had our old cob, too, if Rob and Will hadn't taken him this morning.' She surveyed the burning building dismally. 'We'd heard rumours o' trouble, but we thought it was all ale-talk. King Henry won't stand for no nonsense from his sons, we said.' Her chin wobbled and she compressed her lips and glared at Joscelin.

'I am responsible for the king's justice on these lands,' Joscelin replied. 'If there are bands of routiers at large of whatever faction, I will deal with them and swiftly.'

'Yes, my lord.' She looked sceptical. And then her eyes widened and focused on a point beyond Joscelin. The younger woman shrieked and fell to her knees.

Turning in the saddle, Joscelin saw a motley assortment of horsemen and foot soldiers advancing towards them from the direction of the woods. The leading horse was the seneschal's handsome piebald stallion and the warrior astride it had the raddled face of a fallen angel. A scar running from left mouth corner to mutilated left ear tilted and creased his grin, transforming it into a leer as he drew rein before Joscelin.

'Greetings, nephew,' said Conan de Gael, performing a mocking salute with the hilt of his drawn sword.

'We heard in Nottingham that the Rushcliffe lands were yours.' Conan shook his head, the grin still in place, and reclined on one elbow in the grass. 'Lucky bastard – no offence intended.'

Joscelin was not deceived by his uncle's air of relaxed

145

affability. The hazel-green eyes were as hard as stones, and although Conan had removed his sword in token of goodwill he would still have a knife in his boot and another up his sleeve. 'I could be forgiven for disbelieving you,' he replied, nodding at the smoke still puthering from the longhouse. An ox that had been slaughtered in the earlier mayhem had been carved into chunks and was now roasting over a purpose-built fire pit. The two peasant women had retired to a distance but Joscelin could feel their hatred boring into his spine, together with their belief that he was a worse devil than the two previous lords of Rushcliffe put together.

'Ah, come now, Josce, that wasn't my fault.'

'Wasn't it?'

Conan drew his meat dagger from his belt and went to the fire pit to test a lump of meat to see if it was cooked. The women glared at him. Conan saluted them, the tip of his knife holding a sizzling, bloody chunk of their plough ox. 'We bumped into your seneschal and his family on the road. Course, I didn't know he was yours then and a man has to have the money to eat and clothe himself – you know that. If a fatted calf walks up to you dripping in wealth, it's just begging to be sacrificed. It was obvious he was on the run with his ill-gotten gains.' The mercenary tore a shred of meat off the edge of the beef portion and chewed vigorously. 'The women ran like headless chickens into the longhouse and barred the door against us. One of them must have caught her gown in the hearth because, next thing we knew, the place was on fire and the flames too fierce for any of us to get near enough to rescue anyone.'

Joscelin eyed Conan narrowly. 'I saw my seneschal's body,' he said. 'In the old days you'd not have mutilated the dead.'

Conan spat out a knurl of gristle. 'That was Godred's

work.' He jabbed his head in the direction of a young soldier sitting close to the fire pit, moodily prodding the glowing embers with a stick. 'He's not fond of Normans at the best of times and the way we were treated in Nottingham was bound to have repercussions.'

'What were you doing in Nottingham in the first place? I thought you were in Normandy.'

'We sailed just before Pentecost. Trouble was brewing and men of our trade have to sell our swords where we can – unless we land ourselves an heiress.' He flashed Joscelin a mocking glance. 'We took employment with Robert Ferrers, Earl of Derby and Lord of Nottingham.' He spat another piece of gristle into the grass. 'Ever worked for him, Josce?'

'No. He might have several fiefs in Nottingham but the castle itself belongs to the Crown. My employer has always been the king.'

Brien, who had been looking at Conan from the corner of his eye as if he did not quite believe in his existence, said, 'I have heard that Ferrers is a haphazard paymaster.'

'Haphazard? Hah! If we saw four shillings a week between us, we were fortunate. When I tackled him about it he threw us out, said that he could get Flemings for half as much as he was paying us and that we were lucky he hadn't slung us in his dungeon for presumption. Arrogant, soft-cocked wind-bladder! He's lucky I didn't slit his throat to silence him.' Conan wiped his bloody knife-blade on the grass.

'Instead you slit my seneschal's,' Joscelin said frostily.

'You didn't want him, did you? You ought to be grateful.'

Joscelin made a disgusted sound and shook his head.

'Did Ferrers hire you for any particular purpose?' Brien asked.

'No, just building up his troops in the area. When we were in Nottingham, we were billeted in some ramshackle houses of his near a stinking marsh with tanneries right next door. I've shat in better cesspits.'

'But he said he was going to replace you with Flemings?'

'Flemings, Brabanters, whoever he could get the cheapest,' Conan said with a shrug. 'Of course, like us, they'll have to cross the Narrow Sea. Be quite an invasion, eh? If you ask me, they'll come piecemeal, rounded up by those rebellious earls of yours and sent over here with promises of riches beyond their greediest imaginings. Most of 'em won't be professional soldiers – jobless weavers and dyers for the most part. Won't know the business end of a sword from the holes in their arses.'

'But you are not part of the vanguard?' queried Brien, persisting like a dog with a bone.

Conan half-closed his eyes. 'You want to know a mortal great deal, my lord.'

'Brien works for the justiciar,' Joscelin explained and was amused by the look of consternation that briefly flickered in Conan's eyes. 'It is his duty to discover as much as he can about the doings of the rebellious barons.'

'Well, don't look to me,' Conan growled. 'I can tell you more about the latrine habits of Nottingham tanners than I can about the doings of Robert Ferrers. All he said was that he was going to replace us with Flemings, and we're not part of anyone's vanguard, although there's hiring aplenty going on across the Narrow Sea.'

Joscelin regarded Conan with a mixture of exasperation and curiosity. 'Well, what are you really doing in England when Normandy is your true field?'

Conan sucked his teeth and eased a fingernail between the front two to loosen a tag of meat. 'I'm not getting any younger – eight and forty next Christmastide, although

I know I don't look it,' he added with a sour grin. 'One day, experience won't be enough to save me from some youngster's sword and I'll be glad to die. But before that happens, I've to attend to some personal family business.' He looked pointedly at Brien, who was swift to take a hint by rising to his feet to go and cut himself a portion of ox.

When he was out of earshot, Conan said, 'I'm here to make my peace with your father – and Morwenna. When I heard you'd got yourself lands in the area, I thought I'd muster your support first.'

'You might find making peace difficult,' Joscelin said wryly. 'My father never mentions her. If I bring up the subject, he looks at me as if I have deliberately stabbed him.'

Conan grunted. 'Tore him asunder when your mother died. He begot on her the child that killed her. He wasn't there to catch her when she tripped on her gown and fell down the stairs. You'll never reason it away from him. God knows I tried in the months after her death, and in the end he kicked me out because he wanted to wear his guilt like shackles for the rest of his life.'

'He has made a shrine of his guilt now,' Joscelin said. 'Near his hunting lodge in Arnsby woods he's had a chapel built to house her remains. He has masses said for her every day and candles to burn in perpetuity.'

Conan shook his head and stared numbly at Joscelin, as if unsure whether to be pleased or appalled.

'The first time I saw the white chapel, I wept,' Joscelin confessed. 'He had it built after I ran away to join you. In part I think it was a shrine for me, too. He never thought to see me again.' He looked at the ground and stirred the grass with the toe of his boot.

'He probably wouldn't have done either, if not for me!'

Conan declared, his voice loud and overhearty. 'You were greener than the grass stains on a whore's gown when you arrived in my camp!'

'I was, wasn't I?' Joscelin glanced sideways at his uncle, not in the least deceived. Conan was deeply affected by what he had just been told and, rather than flounder a reply, had taken refuge in coarse banter.

'You grew up fast, though.'

Joscelin arched his brow. 'I had no choice.'

Conan massaged his scar with two fingers. 'I don't suppose you did, nephew,' he said in a gentler tone. 'I saw your woman, Breaca, the month before we sailed. She gave me board and lodging in Falaise for two nights.'

'She's not my woman any more.' Joscelin returned to stirring the grass. He watched the shiny, stiff stems bend and spring upright. Then he glanced at Conan, driven to ask despite his determination not to. 'Is she happy?'

'Merry as a nesting sparrow with three fine fledglings to show to the world – two little wenches and a baby boy in the cradle. She told me to wish you well the next time I saw you and to say that you and Juhel are constantly in her prayers.'

Joscelin bit the inside of his mouth. After Juhel had died, he had been unable to hold Breaca. She had been at a crossroads age, craving a roof over her head and more security than he could provide. In the year of grieving determination it had taken him to become a competent, tough soldier, standing on his own merits and paid accordingly, she had ceased following the mercenary road from one war to the next and settled down with a hostel keeper from Falaise. 'She is in my thoughts and prayers too,' he said softly. 'And if she has found what she wants, then I'm glad for her.' He changed the subject. 'Are you seeking employment now?'

The older man eyed him suspiciously. 'Depends. Why do you ask?'

'I'm short of troops. I was thinking of riding into Nottingham to hire men but, since you've already lined your purse with Rushcliffe's silver, perhaps you and your men would like the position?'

Conan stared. He grasped the drawstring pouch at his belt and waggled it at Joscelin. 'What do you mean? See – empty as a hag's tit!'

'You're not going to tell me that my seneschal rode into your troop wearing nothing but his drawers?' Joscelin scoffed. 'You said yourself that he was "a fatted calf, dripping in wealth" and not his at that. It belongs to my five-year-old ward.'

Conan continued to stare. Despite his best effort his lips twitched and in a moment he was lost to a full grin. Joscelin himself was similarly afflicted, his hazel eyes bright with amusement.

'You are your father's son,' Conan growled by way of capitulation.

'And my uncle's nephew,' Joscelin retorted.

16

'Look, Mama. What are they doing?' Robert wriggled upright on the saddle to point at the cage of scaffolding confining Arnsby's tall, octagonal keep. Men stood on platforms or toiled on the ground, caparisoning the monstrous stone beast in white summer plumage.

'They're giving it a fresh coat of limewash to protect it from the weather,' Joscelin said over his shoulder and slowed his courser so that Linnet could join him. 'We've to do the same to Rushcliffe before the winter comes.'

'Why?'

'To protect the fabric from the bad weather and keep it strong.'

Robert sucked his underlip while he considered the reply. Linnet had watched her son gain rapidly in confidence during the weeks following Giles's death. Given space to breathe without being slapped, glared at or found lacking, Robert had begun to emerge from his shell – tentatively at first, with much drawing in of horns, but growing bolder by the day. Joscelin had put him on an ancient pack pony in the tiltyard and begun teaching him to ride. He had fashioned a small, blunt-tipped lance for him and a wooden sword. Conan de Gael, Joscelin's uncle, had played at knights and outlaws with Robert and conceded defeat with dramatic death throes, much to the boy's consternation and delight. And Robert, so silent and withdrawn before his father's death, had started asking questions. One after another they tumbled out of him, queuing up to trip off his busy tongue. Why is the sky blue? Why don't people have fur like coneys? How does Job the shepherd know when it's going to rain? Where does the sea go when the tide is out?

'Why are we here?'

'I told you; to visit Sir Joscelin's father.' Linnet kissed Robert's fair hair.

'Why?'

'Because I need to talk to him,' Joscelin said. 'Here, come and sit on my saddle and stop bedeviling your mother with questions. You can guide Whitesocks if you want.'

The words were no sooner spoken than accomplished. Robert scrambled with alacrity from his mother's arms into Joscelin's and settled there as if they had been his security since birth.

They approached the open gateway, the horses' hooves thudding on the solid drawbridge planks. The huge iron pulley chains were speckled with limewash and there were splashes of it, like enormous bird droppings, on the bridge itself. Robert's small hand pointed and he chirruped a question. Joscelin bent over him and responded with patient good humour. A pang cut through Linnet to see them thus: the familiar sensations of guilt and love and a deeper, primal twisting of heart and womb and loins.

'Ach,' said Conan softly as he joined her on the drawbridge. 'Give him a child and he turns to butter.'

There was a strange note in the mercenary's voice that

153

caused Linnet to look at him curiously. 'Certainly my son has taken to him,' she replied. 'And in London I met him in the company of his youngest brother.' She looked thoughtfully at Conan. He was wearing a garish tunic of Welsh plaid and riding Corbette's piebald stallion. Bracelets of copper and silver jangled in abundance on his forearms. The word *disreputable* came easily to mind. And yet he had helped ungrudgingly with his own war-scarred hands to rebuild the farmhouse that he and his men had burned. 'You must know Joscelin very well.'

Conan made a face. 'Yes and no, my lady. He came to me when he was fifteen, stubborn, proud and half-starved.' A sardonic grin curled his lips. 'I took him in and I took him on, taught him the bare-fist-and-teeth side of fighting, the kind that keeps you alive.'

'Like a knife down your boot?' she asked with a half-smile.

Conan chuckled. 'Never be without one.' He regarded Joscelin as he was swallowed by the darkness of the portcullis arch and emerged again into the bright sunshine of the courtyard. 'His own lad was about Robert's age when he died,' he added quietly. 'It's a hard life for a mother and child in a mercenary baggage train. It is a good thing that Joscelin has a place of his own to settle now and a family. There's as much hunger in his soul as there is in his damned father's.'

They entered the darkness themselves, emerged into light. Linnet was unaware of blinking in the brilliance, nor did she feel the warmth of the sun. 'You are telling me that he was married once?'

'They never had a priest say the words over them or witness borne to their handfasting but they were together for more than five years and she bore him a child. After the lad died, she wandered with us for a little longer but it was finished between her and Joscelin. She married a widower from Falaise and settled down with him to run a hostelry.'

Linnet was stunned. Conan leaned closer, taking her upper arm in his calloused, strong hand. 'I'd prefer you to keep it to yourself, lass. Not even his father knows the tale and Josce would kill me if he thought I'd been interfering in his private concerns. But I thought it was something you should know.' Releasing his grip, he leaped lightly from his mount and stood at her stirrup to help her down.

Linnet thought that he deserved murdering to spring something like this upon her at a moment when she needed all her social skills to be polite to her betrothed's dreadful father.

Robert's hand clasped in his, Joscelin appeared at her side. She saw his glance flicker to Conan's bland expression. 'What has he been saying to you?'

He spoke lightly and there was a smile on his face but she was still reminded of Giles, who had been suspicious of her every conversation with another man. 'I . . .' The words stuck in her throat and her mind went blank with panic.

'I was giving her some friendly advice on being a dutiful wife to my nephew,' Conan said smoothly. 'If she is lost for words, it is because she cannot repeat what I told her without being indelicate.' He winked at her, slapped Joscelin hard on the shoulder and turned to face the keep. 'Hasn't changed a stone in twenty years! I always liked this place – good and solid, a gem to defend against siege.'

Agnes de Rocher pushed the weft through the narrow shed of the wool braid she was weaving, knocked down the twisted threads into the pattern and stared at her work with dissatisfaction. The tension was uneven, dictated by her mood at the different times she had sat down to the work, and the braid snaked broad, thin and slantwise by turns, like the unruly river of her thoughts. The colours were supposed to be autumnal – gold, brown and soft green – but they looked sallow to her now, without enough contrast to make them interesting.

She laid down the horn weaving-tablets on the trestle and secured them with another piece of completed braid. Her hands were smooth and adorned with gold rings as befitted a baron's wife and the only thing of vanity left to her. She tended them assiduously, anointing them with scented white fat and trimming and buffing her nails until they gleamed. Not that William ever noticed. To him she was either invisible or an irritation that he bore with ill grace and the long-sufferance of obligation. It was all the fault of the whore.

Sometimes in the corner of her eye Agnes would catch a glimpse of Morwenna de Gael: her luxuriant dark hair rippling down her back, her green silk gown trailing the floor rushes and her body ripe with the new life that was never to come to fruition. Morwenna's scream as she fell on the stairs that twisted down to the great hall occasionally echoed in Agnes' ears. Morwenna the bitch and the whore. Morwenna, who, not content with sharing William's bed, had taken everything that he was and buried it in the faultless white tomb he had built for her, ensuring there was nothing left for his rightful wife.

Agnes' mind was less free to wander when her sister-in-law was in attendance. Maude's cheerful, inquisitive nature, her sheer garrulousness, left little space for Agnes to brood. But Maude was visiting a pensioned-off servant at a convent close to Newark and would not be back for two days at least. Agnes knew that Maude found her company a trial and was always eager for moments of escape. The feeling was frequently mutual.

A small sound in the doorway caused Agnes to jump and turn round. She screwed up her eyes the better to focus on the young woman and child standing in the threshold behind her maid. Surely she knew them, and recently so?

'Lady Linnet de Montsorrel,' the maid announced and ushered the visitors into Agnes's chamber. Agnes frowned, remembering. Maude had been asked to take care of Linnet de Montsorrel in the days immediately following the husband's death, caused by being rolled upon by a rogue horse at Smithfield Fair. That she was Giles de Montsorrel's widow was a matter of supreme indifference to Agnes. That she was betrothed to the whore's bastard and brought with her a marriage portion to elevate him at one stride from hired soldier to baron of the realm made her blood boil.

'This is indeed an unlooked-for pleasure,' she said with a stiff smile. 'Come, my lady, be seated.' A peremptory gesture sent another maid hurrying to plump the cushions of a barrel chair.

'Thank you, Lady Agnes.' Lady de Montsorrel smiled in return and approached the chair. The child hung back, looking over his shoulder at the door.

Agnes scrutinized her guest. Her veil of blue silk gave emphasis to the wide mist-blue eyes, as did the subtle blue and silver-grey hues of her gown and undergown. The hem of the former was trimmed with braid such as Agnes was making but the design was more complex and the weave beautifully even. Agnes's antipathy increased. It would have been easier to offer hospitality to Linnet de Montsorrel had she been plain and less

157

stylishly apparelled. Agnes had no cause to like or trust women of such looks.

'Have you come alone?'

The maid went to a sideboard and poured wine into two cups.

'No, my lady.' Linnet de Montsorrel hesitated then sat down and said, 'You must know that Joscelin is here to see his father.'

Agnes sniffed. 'I knew it would not be long before he came prowling to Arnsby like a starving wolf after a pen of sheep. And he was bound to bring you – his prize.'

'It was a matter of courtesy that he brought me,' Linnet replied, her smile fading. Her son clambered on to her knee and wrapped his arms tightly around her neck. 'I see now that it was a mistake.'

'Oh, no mistake on *his* part,' Agnes sneered. Her skirts swished upon the rushes as she turned. 'For thirty years I have lived with the humiliation. My sons count for nothing in William's eyes and yet he'd move heaven and earth for the bastard of his conniving whore. I well know why Joscelin is here.'

'I think you are overwrought, Lady Agnes,' Linnet was shocked by the older woman's bitterness. 'Joscelin is here to talk to his father about borrowing supplies for Rushcliffe.'

'Doubtless that is the excuse he would mouth to anyone gullible enough to believe such a lie. He has come because his brothers are involved in Leicester's rebellion and he thinks to secure Arnsby's inheritance for himself. Others may be taken in but I am no dupe.'

Linnet stiffened. 'You malign him, Lady Agnes. Even if Joscelin did desire Arnsby of his father, you still have another son at home and I know that he loves Martin dearly.'

'Martin is a child, not yet nine years old,' Agnes snapped. 'He's hardly a threat.'

'Even so, I know that Joscelin is not here with the intention of disinheriting his brothers,' Linnet defended. She thought, but didn't add, that they were quite capable of accomplishing that feat themselves. 'The only other reason we are here is that Joscelin has brought his uncle, Conan de Gael, to make his peace with Lord William.'

Agnes's face drained of colour. 'You dare to come here to my private chamber and utter the name of that hell-begotten, swindling whoremonger?' she hissed and took two threatening steps towards Linnet.

Linnet hastily rose from the chair, afraid that Agnes was going to assault her and Robert. The maid, who had been about to present Linnet with a cup of wine, quickly sidestepped to avoid spilling it. With Robert in her arms, Linnet headed towards the door. 'I think it best if I leave, my lady,' she said. 'You are obviously unwell.'

'No, you will hear me out first.' Agnes continued to advance on Linnet but the sole of her shoe caught in the hem of her undergown and sent her sprawling.

The maid, a look of horror on her face, set the cups aside and stooped to her mistress. Linnet hesitated on the threshold, desiring nothing more than to make her escape but prevented by her conscience. Supposing Agnes had broken a bone or was having a seizure?

She set Robert on his feet. 'Do you think you can go down to the hall and find Conan and Joscelin?'

Robert looked up at her. 'You come, too.' He tugged on her hand.

'I cannot. Lady Agnes needs help. Find Joscelin and stay with him until I come. Yes?'

Robert nodded, his underlip caught in his teeth.

159

'Good boy. Go on then, quickly.' Linnet hugged him and shooed him on his way. It was astonishing how Joscelin's name had become a talisman to the child. Mention it and a hundred doors opened where doors had not existed before. Here he was in a place he did not know, turning from the security of her skirts because Joscelin was the prize.

Giving brisk orders to the frightened maid, Linnet checked Agnes for broken bones. Thankfully there were none and she helped Agnes to rise and wobble to her bed. The sheets had a stale smell and there were smears and crumbs upon the coverlet. Linnet urged a cup of wine upon Agnes. Grey-faced, the woman sipped and gradually her colour began to return. Her eyes cleared and focused on Linnet. 'How I envy your innocence,' she said wearily. 'I, too, was innocent once. I can see it in your eyes; you think I am mad, don't you?'

'I certainly think you are ill,' Linnet said, pity softening her attitude.

Agnes looked bleakly at the wall where a plasterwork scene depicted two lovers seated at a merels board in a garden. 'William wants to lock me up in a nunnery. I'm past childbearing and naught but a burden to him, but I would have him carry his burden until it kills him and then may he rot in hell with his precious whore!'

When Linnet rose to leave, Agnes did not try again to stop her but rocked gently back and forth in her bed, cradling her cup, and muttering softly to herself.

It had been more than twenty years since the last encounter between William de Rocher and Conan de Gael. On that occasion, William had taken his sword and fought Conan from tower to tower, room to room, across the ward and out of Arnsby's gates. Then he had slammed

160

them in the mercenary's face and ordered him never to return on pain of hanging.

Now, face-to-face, eyes on a level, they confronted each other.

'Going to string me up, then?' Conan asked, lounging upon his sword hip.

'Don't tempt me,' William growled. His hands gripped his belt in lieu of Conan's throat. 'What are you doing here except to cause trouble?'

Conan looked reproachful. 'You do me an injustice, William, but that's nothing new. You've always believed my motives to be the worst in the world. Don't worry, I'm not staying long. I've about as much taste for your company as you have for mine.'

'Then why are you here at all?'

'He's working for me,' Joscelin said. 'I need seasoned men with the trouble that's brewing and Rushcliffe's garrison is as magnificent a collection of oafs and lack-wits as ever graced a fool's banquet.'

'You must be one of them if you're hiring him!' William snapped.

'Not so much that I would cut off my nose to spite my face.' Joscelin fixed his father with a hard stare. 'Would you rather he sold his sword to the rebellion?'

Ironheart ground such teeth as remained to him.

Conan smiled, the creases at the corners of his eyes deepening with sardonic humour. 'I think he would,' he said to Joscelin. 'I could keep my eyes open for Ralf and Ivo then, couldn't I?'

Joscelin cast his uncle a warning stare and made a chopping movement with his right hand. Unperturbed, Conan continued to smile, his scar turning his expression into a leer.

'Is he really your uncle?' asked Martin, who had

attached himself to the three men without being noticed. He looked upon Conan with the same bright curiosity he had given to the bear at Smithfield Fair.

Joscelin chuckled and tousled his younger brother's chestnut curls. 'I'm afraid he is but don't let his appearance deceive you.' He looked at Conan. 'Although he's a liability when there's no one to fight, there are few people I'd rather have at my back on the battlefield.'

Conan raised a mocking eyebrow. 'Kind of you to admit it,' he said but Joscelin could tell he was pleased.

'Why aren't you at sword practice?' William snapped at his youngest son.

Martin regarded his father without fear. 'Sir Alain sent me to get another sword. The old wooden one I was using broke.'

'And you are on your way now?'

'Yes, sir. But I thought it good manners to stop and greet our guests.'

Ironheart's lips twitched. 'I suspect that a long, inquisitive nose is nearer to the truth. Go, hurry now, before you find yourself answering to Sir Alain for your tardiness.' He gave the boy's shoulder a swift shake.

No sooner had Martin gone than Robert appeared at a run and flung himself at Joscelin, who swung him up into his arms.

'Where's your mother? Does she know that you are here?'

Robert nodded and burrowed his head against Joscelin's throat, his arms tightening. Joscelin could feel the rapid pitter-patter of the child's heartbeat beneath his fingers. 'She sent me to stay with you,' Robert said. 'The lady we went to see wasn't very nice. I didn't like her, but she fell over and Mama stayed to help her get up.'

Joscelin looked across Robert's fair head at his father.

'Agnes has been very difficult of late,' Ironheart said with an impatient shrug and a look of distaste. 'She spends all her time brooding about Ralf and Ivo and plotting ways to see them back into my favour.'

Joscelin cuddled Robert and said nothing.

'In the spring, once Martin has gone for fostering in de Luci's household, I'm going to buy her a corody and settle her with the nuns at Southwell,' William said.

'Should have done it years ago, man,' Conan said bluntly.

William's mouth twisted. 'She is my penance. I have worn her presence like a hair shirt for more than half my life.'

And she had worn his, too, for the sake of her sons, Joscelin thought, and was unlikely to agree to enter a nunnery while their future remained in doubt.

'I saw another lady on the stairs,' Robert piped up as his hero's attention strayed. 'A nice lady. She smelled like flowers.'

'Did she?' Joscelin said, not taking much notice.

'Her hair was longer than Mama's, nearly to her knees, and she was wearing a pretty green dress with dangly sleeves,' Robert babbled.

His words were like stones dropped in a pool. Ripples of silence expanded from them and drowned the men in shock. William's face turned the colour of ashes.

'Jesu!' Conan muttered and, crossing himself, stared at the child.

'Did she speak to you?' Involuntarily, Joscelin looked towards the dark entrance of the tower stairs, then raised his head to study the long walk of the gallery and the double row of oak rails. Sunlight from the tall windows above the dais gilded the spear tips that impaled the family banners above the hearth. They stirred in the updraught

163

from the flames. He could feel the erratic, hard thud of his own pulse against the pressure of the child's body.

Robert shook his head. 'No, but she smiled and walked down the stairs with me so I wouldn't be frightened of the dark. She's gone now.'

The men looked at one another, not daring to voice what their minds were shouting.

'Probably one of the maids,' Conan said, his heartiness too hollow for conviction. 'Or perhaps the lad has overheard something and embroidered it with his imagination.' His gaze went as Joscelin's had done to the dark tower mouth where they had found his sister unconscious, tangled in the folds of her green gown. He closed his eyes and did not open them again until he had turned to face William Ironheart. 'You asked why I was here. I never did pay my respects at Morwenna's tomb. You threw me out and said you would hang me like a common felon if I so much as set foot on Arnsby land. But that was a long time ago. We're old men now. I want to make peace with the past before it is too late for all of us.'

'There is no such thing as peace,' William replied hoarsely, his own eyes riveted on the tower entrance.

17

The chapel dedicated to Morwenna de Gael stood on the
edge of the forest, close to the village of Arnsby but separated from it by the mill stream, which was crossed by
means of a humpbacked stone bridge. In front of the
chapel sheep cropped the grass, keeping it nibbled to a
short turf dappled with daisies and pink clover.

Astride her mare, Linnet studied this shrine to Joscelin's
mother. The white Caen stone wore a golden reflection
of the afternoon sun. Windows eyebrowed with intricate
stone patterns viewed the world from dark irises of painted
glass. A solid wooden door, handsomely decorated with
barrings of wrought iron, was wedged open and a path
of sunlight beckoned the eye over the threshold and into
the nave. Beautiful and tranquil, she thought, so unlike
the restless spirit that walked Arnsby's corridors in the
minds of its occupants.

She glanced at Robert, whom Joscelin was lowering
from his saddle on to the turf. Joscelin had told her what
her son had said. 'He scared us half to death.' He had
looked wry. 'Conan says it was probably one of the maids
and we're all clinging to that belief, but . . .' Then he had

shrugged and spread his hands. 'It is strange all the same, very strange.'

Linnet watched Robert kneel in the grass and cup his hands around a ladybird. The sunlight made a nimbus of his hair and his face was open and bright with pleasure. Whatever he had seen or absorbed on that stair had done him no harm. Any darkness had settled on the adults long ago and was probably of their own making. She thought of Agnes de Rocher with mixed feelings of pity and revulsion.

Joscelin was waiting at her stirrup and he held up his arms to lift her down. 'Why the frown?' he queried.

Her brow cleared and she shook her head. 'Nothing. I was thinking of your father's wife, and there but for the grace of God . . .' She descended into his arms, twisting slightly to avoid hurting his wounded shoulder.

'She upset you, didn't she?' He set her on the ground but his hands remained lightly at her waist. She felt the pressure of his palms and fingers, and her loins softened. She was aware of the rise and fall of his chest and the brightness of his stare.

'More than a little,' she admitted breathlessly and tried to concentrate on what he had said rather than the effect of his closeness on her senses. 'She told me you had deliberately come to Arnsby to remind your father that he still had a loyal son of full age and also to show me off as a trophy of your success.'

He smiled and tilted his head to one side. His hand drew light circles in the small of her back. 'And is there anything wrong with either of those?'

'It was the way she spoke of your motives, as if you had come to take what advantage you could.'

'She doesn't know how close to the truth she was,' he

166

said with obvious double meaning and lowered his head to kiss her.

It was heady and sweet, tender and strong. Linnet clutched him for support and felt him move back on his heels to keep his balance as she swayed against him. In that moment Robert thrust between them, eager to show off his ladybird. Joscelin staggered and released her. Linnet stumbled one pace after him then steadied herself. Robert stared up at the adults out of light, shining eyes.

'Look, Mama!' he cried, holding out the ladybird on the palm of his hand. The beetle opened its glossy red wing-cases and whirred into the air. 'It's gone!' Robert dashed across the grass in pursuit.

Joscelin drew a slow, deep breath and clamped his hands around his belt, in unconscious imitation of his father. 'Sometimes,' he said, 'being honourable is very hard. Yes, I've considered laying claim to Arnsby. If it weren't for Martin, I might even have discarded my integrity to do it.' He smiled with more pain than humour. 'And if it weren't so important to you that this three months of mourning be observed, I'd have laid claim to your bed weeks ago.'

Linnet could feel her spine dissolving in the look he was giving her. She was sorely tempted to say that the three months of mourning were far less important than they had been but she held back. He knew that Giles had not trusted her and she did not want to give Joscelin cause to wonder if Giles had been right. Let him see that she could resist temptation. And, on a level far deeper and fraught with guilt, she had to prove it to herself.

'It is not that I am unwilling but I would rather make sure that I am not carrying Giles's seed,' she said. 'And because it is the "honourable" thing to do by the dead. Besides, people must see that you are the justiciar's true

167

representative, not some adventurer who has snatched me from across my husband's coffin and dragged me before the nearest priest.'

Joscelin sighed. 'People will see what they want to see,' he said. 'They always do,' but stood aside to let her walk up the path to the open chapel doorway.

She could feel his eyes burning upon her spine like a physical touch. Shivering, she forced herself neither to quicken her pace nor to look over her shoulder. She heard Robert cry to Joscelin that he had found another lady-bird, and Joscelin's distracted reply. And then the solid walls of the chapel interior cut off all sounds from outside and she was immersed in a tranquillity of pale stone arches rising in two tiers to a ceiling patterned with curves and lozenges of chiselled stone.

Linnet's breathing slowed as she absorbed the atmosphere of clarity and peace. She paced solemnly up the small flagged nave to the altar and, kneeling, crossed herself and honoured God before she rose and approached the tomb of Morwenna de Gael.

Diamonds of colour from the windows painted Linnet's shoulder and the drapes of stone clothing the plinth. She touched the smooth alabaster pleats of Morwenna's robe. White, with a hint of translucence, Ironheart's mistress lay in stone state above her mortal remains, her hands clasped in prayer. Tucked against her arm was the swaddled baby she had died bearing. Someone had recently crowned the folds of her veil with a chaplet of threaded marigolds and they cast an amber glow upon the smooth, white brow.

Ironheart and Conan had come to kneel side-by-side facing the altar. Tall candles, thick as a warrior's wrist, stood upon it like spears and between them rose a Byzantine cross of garnet and silver-gilt, a crusading

168

legacy of a former de Rocher. There was no sign of the priest or the nuns, although they must be nearby to tend the candles and the votive lights beside the tomb. For now, the two men were left to their silence and perhaps their healing.

Linnet quietly lit a votive candle of her own. Her lips moved in silent prayer for the soul of Morwenna de Gael. Then she said a prayer for herself, asking silently for courage and forgiveness. When she crossed herself and rose she noticed that William de Rocher's hands bore a golden dusting of pollen, as if he had been gathering flowers.

18

September 1173

It was raining outside and pitch-dark. Joscelin cursed as he surfaced from sleep and heard the water spattering against the shutters. He pushed down the sheepskins that had been cocooning him and, shivering, sat up. The night candle had gone out. Groping, he found the coffer, and, after a moment, the tinderbox on top of it. By the time he had managed to coax a light from the two flints and the small pieces of shaved wood, a yawning Henry had appeared with a sputtering taper in his hand.

'I'm sorry, my lord. You woke before I did,' he apologized, kindling a steadier flame from the night candle. 'My mam's boiling up some pottage for the men to eat before you ride out.'

Joscelin grimaced. There had been other times like this in his days as a mercenary – foul pre-dawn mornings when any sane man would bury his head beneath the covers and hibernate. Even packed in waxed linen for travelling, mail shirts, helms and weapons would be rusty within hours, and the chill of steady rainfall would seep through garments into flesh and permeate the bones. Unfortunately, with the Scots over the border in force and rapidly heading south, granted free passage by the treacherous Bishop of Durham, there was no alternative but to ride out and intercept their ravages. The command from de Luci had arrived yesterday noon with the instruction that Joscelin was to take his men and join a preliminary muster at Nottingham.

Henry's teeth chattered as the rain threw itself full force against the shutters. 'Can't say as I'm sorry to be staying here, my lord,' he said. 'Do you reckon they'll get as far as Derby?'

Joscelin donned his gambeson over his shirt and tunic. 'If we act now, I doubt it. But the Earl of Leicester is massing troops across the Narrow Sea for an invasion. It would be inconvenient if he were to strike at the same time as the Scots. That's why de Luci said we had to move as fast as possible.'

'I'll pray for your safekeeping and victory, my lord,' Henry said, crossing himself.

When Joscelin arrived in the great hall, his men and Conan's were crowded around the fire, sipping bowls of pottage, wrapping their leggings, fastening belts, yawning and scratching. Not particularly hungry, but knowing he must eat something if he was to survive a long wet day in the saddle, Joscelin went to claim his own breakfast from Henry's mother, Dame Winifred.

'God send you good fortune, my lord,' she said, presenting him with a steaming bowl. Her bright black eyes fixed on him until he had taken the first mouthful and assured her that it was good. The crone at the caldron Milo called her, but only because she guarded its contents jealously and would not permit him to go sampling them as and when he chose.

Joscelin moved among the men, speaking a brief word here and there. Conan eyed him sidelong, concealing a smile in his greying beard. 'Seems not a moment since I was giving you the orders,' he remarked.

'More than five years,' Joscelin said sharply.

Conan raised a defensive hand. 'Pax, you pay my wages. As long as your head doesn't swell so much that you can't fit it through your tunic neck, I'll not interfere.'

'And as long as you keep your tongue behind your teeth, I'll not be tempted to cut it out!' Joscelin retorted. 'When you've finished your pottage, you can give the order to mount up. I want to be on the road by first light.'

Conan pursed his lips. 'You always were a grouchy sod in the mornings,' he said, but attended to his food with increased speed.

Joscelin narrowed his eyes but let the comment pass. At a tug on his gambeson hem, he looked down to find Robert standing at his side. The child's hair was still sleep-ruffled and his tunic had been put on back-to-front and inside out. Juhel had often stood thus but his hair had been black and he had had the dark eyes of a faun.

Joscelin crouched. 'Shouldn't you still be in bed, young man?'

'I wanted to see you – to tell you not to go.'

Joscelin took Robert's icy hands in his, then drew the shivering little boy into the circle of his arms and perched him on his thigh. 'We spoke about this last night, didn't we?' he said gently. 'I have to leave for a short while at least. The man who asked me to take care of you and your mother needs my help.'

'But if you go to him, you won't be here to look after us.'

'Milo is staying. You know Milo; he won't let anything happen to you. And Malcolm will be here, too. His wound's almost better but not quite enough for a long ride. I won't be gone long, I promise.'

Robert was quiet for a moment, but not in acquies-cence. Joscelin could almost see his mind working, seeking reasons for Joscelin not to leave. 'Mama doesn't want you to go either,' he said.

'But she knows that I must.'

'She was crying last night. She thought I was asleep but I wasn't. She told Ella she did not know what she would do if you were killed.' Robert flung his arms around Joscelin's neck in a throttling grip. 'I don't want you to die.'

Joscelin swallowed and held him close. 'I'm not going to die. There's too much to live for.'

The boy trembled and shook his head. 'I don't want you to go,' he repeated.

Joscelin delved inside his various layers of clothing and pulled out a leather thong upon which was threaded a small wooden cross. 'I've had this since I was sixteen. It was given to me by someone very special and I've not taken it off once. It protects me in battle.' A lie, since Joscelin relied on nothing in battle except his own skill and the speed of his responses. But the child had need of magic and talismans. Breaca had given the token to him as they lay on sheepskins beneath the stars on the road to Falaise. His first time with a woman. A piece of the true cross, she had said, her mouth both scornful and tender.

Robert touched the dark, crudely carved wood and seemed to derive some comfort from it, for Joscelin felt him relax slightly. 'Does it really protect you?'

'I swear it,' Joscelin said solemnly. 'But it will help its power if you pray for me, too, every day after Mass.'

Robert nodded and wriggled, his attention wandering now that his fears were a little allayed.

'And when I return, I expect you to be able to canter your pony round the tiltyard all by yourself.'

'I can nearly do that now!'

'I know, but I won't be gone long. Now then, you had better go and find some warmer clothes if you're coming out to see us on the road.' He gave Robert a final hug and set him on his feet. Then he rose to his own as Linnet and her maid entered the hall. Ella immediately took Robert in hand, scolding him gently as she led him away to be properly dressed.

Joscelin tucked the old wooden cross back down inside his tunic and looked at Linnet. There were shadows beneath her eyes as if she had not slept well and she was very pale. He thought about what Robert had said and wondered how he should go about calming her fears. It was hardly politic to do as he had done with Robert and show her Breaca's cross.

The men were drifting from the comfort of the fire and their now-empty bowls. Joscelin was aware of time trickling all too rapidly through his hands. So much to say and the words all stuck in limbo.

'I've still got a knife in my boot,' he smiled, 'and Conan riding at my left shoulder.' Reaching out, he touched her face. 'In another week, the three months of your mourning will be over. When I come home, we'll hold a wedding celebration. Take some silver and make yourself a fine gown.'

She bit her lip and suddenly looked both guilty and afraid.

'Linnet?'

Her colour rose. She met his eyes and then looked quickly away. 'I already have some silver – thirty marks, to be precise.'

'What?' He had been about to set his arm around her waist but stopped in mid-motion. 'Where from?'

She drew a deep breath. 'The strongbox. No, wait,

hear me out. I took the money in London between the time when Giles died and Richard de Luci gave you custody of the coin. When you and he counted it, I had already removed the money. I did not know what was to become of myself and Robert. It was his inheritance and I wanted to secure some of it at least.'

Joscelin did not know whether to laugh or rail. Certainly he was unsettled.

'Why tell me?' he asked warily. 'You could have said nothing and I would never have suspected a thing.'

'I know you enough to trust you now.' She looked up at him through her lashes. 'You would not do anything to diminish Robert's inheritance.'

Joscelin laughed inside himself with admiration at the way she had disarmed him. Her timing was superb. He had no opportunity for indignation and by the time he returned the matter would be half-forgotten, its cutting edge blunted. 'I don't think I would dare,' he said wryly.

'Then you are not angry?'

'I didn't say that.' He drew her into his arms and kissed her long and thoroughly.

Behind them, Conan cleared his throat. 'Do you want me to instruct the men to bide awhile while you finish your breakfast?'

Joscelin lifted his head and looked round at his grinning uncle. 'No, tell them to mount up. I'm coming now.' He kissed Linnet again, as hard as the rain that was sweeping down outside.

'God keep you safe, my lord,' she gasped as he released her. Her eyes were very bright, holding the suspicion of unshed tears.

It was the first time she had ever afforded him that title and it was not yet his right. Perhaps it was a placebo aimed at smoothing his ruffled feathers but he did not think so. Her response to his kiss had been too spontaneous. 'If ever there was a reason to hasten home in one piece, I'm looking at it now,' he said before he swept on his cloak and headed towards the door.

19

'Christ's nails,' Ironheart wheezed before his voice was robbed from him by the innocuous-looking clear liquid in his cup. 'What is this stuff?'

'Don't tell me you've never sampled usquebaugh before!' scoffed Conan, sloshing a liberal amount into his own drinking horn and passing the flask to Joscelin. It was part of the meager spoils bludgeoned from a party of Galwegians earlier in the day as the Scots retreated over the Tees, pursued by de Luci's hastily mustered army.

Ironheart rubbed his throat. 'God, it's barbaric!'

Conan laughed. 'Give it time, my lord. Their usquebaugh's like their women – rough at first, but soon your blood's so hot that you don't notice.'

'That depends where you keep your brains.'

'Same place as yours.' Conan straddled a camp stool. 'I saw you eyeing up that laundry wench when we were setting up camp.'

Ironheart made a disparaging sound and took another tentative sip of the fiery pale-yellow brew. This time his throat did not burn quite so much. A warm glow was spreading from his stomach into his veins, comforting him against the evening chill. Autumn came earlier in the north. Up here on the Scots border, the leaves and bracken were already burnished gold. He stared into the heart of the fire until the heat made him blink and acknowledged that he was becoming too old to go on campaign. His body ached with the effort of keeping pace with younger men and his mood was tetchy. Knowing his limitations did not make accepting them any easier. Perhaps he ought to spread the laundry wench on his cloak and comfort himself with her softness, except that he had an aversion to the women of the camp, an aversion rooted in deep fear. He raised his cup to his lips, took a full swallow this time and told Joscelin to pass the flask.

His son darted a look at Conan but handed it over without comment.

'What's wrong, don't you believe I can handle my drink?' Ironheart snapped. 'Good God, the night you were whelped, Conan'll tell you I drank him under the trestle and walked away damned near sober.'

'Usquebaugh is not wine, sir. You'd not be able to stand up if you drank that flask to the dregs.'

Ironheart was tempted to prove the opposite but resisted. Joscelin had spoken with the conviction of experience. 'Where did you learn that, as if I didn't know?' He scowled at Conan.

Joscelin's eyelids tensed. 'In a disease-ridden camp on the road to Falaise,' he said. 'It bought me oblivion for a time.' Rising to his feet, he left the fire and went to check their horses. Ironheart watched him pause at a captured Galloway pony tethered beside the packhorses and destriers. It was a young but sweet-natured mare with a fox-chestnut hide and silver mane and tail. Ironheart knew that Joscelin intended her as a mount for Robert de Montsorrel, knew everything and more than he wanted to know about the woman and child because Joscelin talked of little else – a besotted fool. The usquebaugh burned in Ironheart's stomach like a hot stone – or perhaps it was bitter envy mixed with the corrosive lees of memory.

Sparks hoisted their way into the darkness on ropes of smoke. A soldier softly played the mournful tune of 'Bird on a Briar' on his bone flute. Conan took out his needle and thread and began mending a tear in his hose. Nearby, two soldiers played dice, gambling for quarter pennies. Joscelin returned to the fire, threw on a couple more branches, and sat down.

William drank, then raised one wavering forefinger at his son. 'It was on a night like this that I met your mother. Has Conan ever told you the tale?'

'You're drunk,' Conan said with a perturbed look in his eyes. 'Whatever you say now, you'll regret it in the morning.'

Ironheart answered the question himself. 'No, he hasn't.' His lip curled. 'But I wouldn't expect him to boast his part abroad.'

'So help me God, William, I've made my peace with you and her. I'll not have you drag it out of the tomb again because you cannot hold your drink!' Conan said sharply.

Ironheart hunched his shoulders and, ignoring Conan, faced Joscelin. 'I was sitting at a fire like this one, drinking some poison from Normandy that dared to call itself wine and eating bread with weevils in it, when a young Breton mercenary approached me and begged for employment. Begged,' he emphasized with a fierce look across the flames.

Conan sat very still. A groove of muscle tightened in the hollow of his cheek.

· 179

'Sir, if you want to speak about this, do it tomorrow when you're sober,' Joscelin said.

Ironheart looked down at the restraining hand Joscelin had laid on his sleeve. 'I won't want to talk when I'm sober. No, you sit here and listen; it's time that you knew.' He shook Joscelin off and raised his cup in toast to Conan. 'As it happened, I needed men and decided that if he was useful with a sword, I would hire him. In the meantime, soft fool that I was in those days, I let him sit at my fire and share my supper. Imagine that. I might as well have invited a wolf to dinner!'

'You were as glad of my company as I was of the warmth,' Conan said with quiet anger. 'And when I asked if you had employment for my sister, too, you immediately jumped to the conclusion that she was a whore.'

'It was the way you said it and the way she came to the fire with neither wimple nor veil to cover her hair.'

'She was a virgin; she didn't have to wear a head covering to be respectable.'

Ironheart's laugh was caustic. 'God's toes, I'm not stupid. No man in his right mind would allow his sister to walk around an army camp with her hair uncovered, especially if she was a virgin. It would be an incitement to rape if ever there was one. You knew what you were about, Conan. You thought you'd use Morwenna to make sure of your position in my retinue. A clean untouched lass would be certain to appeal to a man who was finicky about using the camp sluts and had been a long time from home. It's the truth, isn't it?'

Conan chewed the inside of his mouth. 'She *was* a virgin,' he said thickly. 'And it was her own idea to remove her veil, not mine. We had argued about it earlier. She said that she was sick of traipsing the mercenary route never knowing where the next meal was coming from and that she intended finding herself a provider. I came to you genuinely seeking employment, hoping we could settle somewhere for a while and that she could work as a seamstress or lady's attendant, but Morwenna saw you and wanted more.'

Ironheart gulped the last mouthful of usquebaugh. 'You didn't stop her when she loosened her braids and you didn't refuse the silver I paid you for her maidenhead.'

'No,' Conan bit out. 'You're right. I was enough of a whore myself to sell her to you. Would to God that I'd kept away from your banner that night.'

'Amen to that!' Ironheart snarled and looked at the son he had begotten on that long-ago campaign. Morwenna's clear, beautiful eyes watched him across the firelight. He remembered her laughter, her willfulness and her impudence that sat so at odds with his ideal of women. He remembered her hair in his hands, dark and heavy and cool, the predatory demands of her body that took his own by surprise, although she had indeed been a virgin. And suddenly all the usquebaugh in the world would not have been enough to grant him oblivion. His eyes burned and filled with moisture and his chest and throat tightened. 'I need a piss,' he said and, lurching to his feet, staggered off in the direction of the latrine pit.

Conan put his face in his hands for a moment, then lifted his head and looked at Joscelin. 'I should never have taken the usquebaugh from that Galwegian,' he said bleakly.

'Was that what really happened between him and my mother? I have never heard him speak of it before.'

'More or less. I knew she was determined to make his bed her haven. She told me that she would give her maidenhead while she had a choice. You know how hard it is on the women of the camp; their men are killed in battle and they become the spoils and chattels of the survivors. Morwenna saw her freedom in your father.' Conan rubbed his scar. 'I don't suppose it was a strange choice back then. He was a handsome man in his younger days and he had presence and a way of smiling that turned women to water. I could see she was set on him. The silver was incidental. I did not mean what I said about being whore enough to take it from him. As far as I was concerned, it was a bride price.'

Joscelin's mind filled with a faint but evocative recollection of his mother's thick dark hair and her hand touching his head. A glint of laughter. The memories must be painfully intense to the grown man who had possessed so much more and lost everything. 'Perhaps it was too high for him to pay,' he said softly, his eyes upon the tall shadow beyond the firelight.

20

Quivering with excitement, Robert stood at his mother's side in the dank autumn evening while Rushcliffe's courtyard filled with men, horses and laden baggage wains.

'Mama, there's Joscelin!' He pointed vigorously at the familiar liver-chestnut with its distinctive stocking marks.

Linnet's heart fluctuated between her throat and her stomach. For three weeks they had heard nothing, apart from occasional frightening rumours that came down the Humber and the Fosse road with Nottingham-bound traders. They had been told on different occasions that the Scots had reached Yorkshire and were marching on York itself, that the Scottish army was thirty thousand strong and every man a savage. Both Milo and Malcolm had scoffed at such exaggerations.

'Three thousand perhaps,' Malcolm had said as Linnet smeared soothing ointment on his scar to prevent it from itching. 'I'm no saying they won't be doughty warriors, and gey savage, but they'll be more lightly armed – out for what they can loot. They'll nae hold fast against mounted Normans.'

Linnet had taken what comfort she could from his

confidence and gone about her normal business as if Joscelin and his mesnie were out for the day hunting game and not hundreds of miles farther north engaging the Scots. To keep herself from brooding, she had taken up needlework with a vengeance. Not only was her wedding gown of sky-blue wool finished but she had also made Joscelin two shirts and a tunic of deep forest-green. Beside her, Robert was resplendent in a new tunic of that same green, his garment mirroring in miniature the one she had made for Joscelin. In Robert, the colour admirably set off the blond of his hair. In Joscelin, it would bring out the green flecks in his irises.

He was home to wear that tunic now but not for long. Earlier that day, Brien FitzRenard had arrived in a state of near exhaustion, craving food and lodging for the night and a fresh horse in the morning. He had staggered to the pallet she had hastily arranged for him in a wall-chamber and fallen asleep almost immediately, but not before telling her that he had orders for Joscelin the moment that he returned. Orders that she knew, with a heavy heart, would only send him somewhere else to fight.

She watched Joscelin light down from the saddle and noted with relief as he came towards her that he moved easily, without any impediment to suggest injury. Robert danced from one foot to the other like a hound straining on a leash. The man's lips twitched. Linnet stooped, murmured in her son's ear and gave him a gentle push. With a pang she watched him run to his hero.

'I prayed every day like you said and I can gallop my pony now and guess what, one of the coneys has had five babies and they've got no fur!' Robert gabbled out in one long breath, then shrieked with delight as Joscelin swept him up in his arms.

'And he has learned to write his name, too!' Linnet

184

added, laughing, and, coming into the curve of Joscelin's free arm, received a hard, scratchy kiss. 'I've set the laundry tubs boiling, so you'll be able to bathe, and there's mulled wine in the chamber.'

'You'll turn him soft, wench,' said a harsh voice and Linnet turned on Joscelin's arm, her eyes widening with a dismay she was not quite swift enough to conceal. William de Rocher's presence was a shock. Having had eyes only for Joscelin, she had not realized until he spoke that his father was with him.

'I doubt it, my lord.' An icy civility entered her tone. William de Rocher set her teeth on edge with his attitude. His look upon her was that of a merchant eyeing up a doubtful piece of ware. And he was soon to be her father-in-law. 'Surely it is the duty of any chatelaine to offer her lord such comforts on his return.'

Ironheart grunted, unimpressed. 'You've learned duty since midsummer then?' he said.

'And I didn't even have to beat her.' Joscelin put himself between his father and Linnet. 'Don't you want a goblet of mulled wine and a hot tub to take away the aches of the road? I know that I do. And if that's turning me soft then I can live with it.'

'Pah!' Ironheart snapped and, without being invited, stalked towards the hall, his gait marred by a noticeable limp.

'Pay no heed,' Joscelin said. 'The damp weather gives him joint ache and makes his temper worse than a mangy bear. If his pride wasn't so touchy, he'd accept everything you offered.' He shrugged and sighed. 'It has not been the easiest campaign. Conan and my father haven't really made their peace and I won't become embroiled in their battle to blame each other for what happened in the past.' He looked at the child in his arms and changed the subject.

'That's a fine new tunic to greet my return,' he admired.

'It was supposed to be kept for our wedding,' Linnet said, 'but he wanted to wear it and today is a day of celebration. Who knows when the next one will be.'

He gave her a sharp look. 'Why do you say that?'

'Brien FitzRenard rode in earlier with parchments for you, and they do not bode well, I think.'

Joscelin groaned softly and turned to walk into the hall. On the threshold, while they were still alone, he turned to Linnet. 'Marry me now,' he said. 'Today.'

His words sent a ripple of shock through her but the after-effect was one of pleasant warmth. 'If that is your wish, then it is mine too,' she said demurely, but knew from the eager look on his face that he was not deceived by her very proper response.

'The Earl of Leicester has landed an army on the east coast,' Brien FitzRenard grimly announced and drew his stool up to the edge of the large, oval bathtub. 'And Hugh Bigod of Norfolk is giving him all the aid he requires.'

'Bigod? He must be seventy if he's a day!' Joscelin rested his arms along the sides of the tub. The water contained crushed salt to ease the aches of hard riding and was deliciously hot, almost unbearable.

Brien tiredly pinched the bridge of his nose. 'He's a perennial rebel. If there's a brew of trouble, you'll find Hugh Bigod taking a turn at stirring it. I've got parchments in my baggage for you to read – and you, too, my lord de Rocher.' His glance went to Ironheart, who was sitting on a coffer, condescending with bad grace but a copious thirst to drink Linnet's mulled wine. 'Hugh de Bohun, the constable, is mustering an army to prevent Leicester from striking across the Midlands to join his allies. You are commanded to respond as soon as you can.'

186

Joscelin sipped the hot wine and watched Linnet and a maid warming towels at the hearth and laying out clean garments for him to wear. Linnet stopped in the act of unfolding a shirt and stared his way, a look of dismay on her face.

'The horses are in no fit shape,' Ironheart said tersely. 'We've pushed them up hill and down dale these past three weeks. What do you want, blood out of a stone?'

'If we don't stop them now, it will be worse later.' Brien's voice was laden with weariness. 'I need not remind you, my lord, that Arnsby and Rushcliffe will be prime targets for Leicester to attempt should he gain a solid footing in the region.'

Ironheart gulped down the wine and stalked across to the hearth to replenish his cup. Robert skipped nervously out of his way and ran to the side of the bathtub. Joscelin gently tousled the boy's thistledown hair. He could not remember the anarchy of King Stephen's reign, since he had only been a small boy himself when it had ended. He had, however, heard enough from his father and seen the lasting effect of its ravages to have a healthy fear of the like ever happening again.

'Give me a night and a day to get married and I'll put the troops on the road,' Joscelin sighed to Brien. 'As my father says, the horses need to be rested but I daresay I can commandeer some fresh mounts round and about.'

Brien looked from Joscelin to Linnet and spread his hands in a gesture of apology. 'I know it is a lot to ask but if we can break Leicester now then I do believe we have a chance of peace.'

When Brien had gone, Joscelin looked at his father. 'If you want to stay behind, I'll take your men,' he suggested.

'I'm not in my dotage yet!' Ironheart said indignantly. 'All right, I would rather not go chasing across the country but Ralf and Ivo are with Leicester and it is past time they weren't. I have given them free rein to no avail. Now let them feel the weight of my displeasure.'

Joscelin bit his tongue and attended to his ablutions, knowing that his words would only be wasted on his father's current mood. To Ralf and Ivo, the weight of Ironheart's displeasure would probably seem little different to the way he usually treated them.

Drying himself, Joscelin stepped from the tub and donned the new clothes that Linnet had laid out – a shirt of softened linen, an undertunic also of linen in a mustard colour and a tunic of dark-green wool. All were new, and while there had been no time for Linnet to do any embroidery they were embellished with braid and far finer than anything he had owned before.

'Fine feathers,' Ironheart said sourly.

'Very fine,' Joscelin smiled at Linnet.

With an impatient sound, Ironheart turned away and, shrugging off his cloak, began unlatching his belt. 'There's no point in wasting this bathwater, it's still hot enough to boil an egg. Lay me out some fresh towels, will you?'

Beside him, Joscelin felt Linnet stiffen. Her eyes narrowed. Oblivious, Ironheart continued to tug off his clothes and toss them on the floor. In a quiet, cold voice, she told her maid to see to the towels and find fresh clothes for Ironheart to wear. Then, on the pretext of checking that the dinner arrangements were in hand, she excused herself.

Ironheart scowled after her. 'She's a wayward wench,' he said.

Joscelin eyed his father with no small degree of irritation. 'I think she had had enough of you,' he said. 'To have played bath maid, as duty insists, would have been

188

too much. She might have drowned you. I know I certainly would.'

'Where's Mama gone?' Robert sidled nervously around Ironheart.

Joscelin picked him up. 'To talk to the cook. Do you want to come to the stables and see what I've brought you all the way from the north?'

Robert nodded vigorously.

Ironheart shook his head and, naked, went to the hearth to pour another cup of hot wine before stepping into the bath.

It had been October when Linnet had married Giles: fine, clear weather, scented with the pungent mulch from the harvest of cider apples and the trees all russet and golden in the beauty of their dying leaves. She had worn a chaplet woven with ears of grain as a fertility charm representing the ploughing of the virgin soil and the scattering of seed in hope of abundant harvest, and had felt dead inside.

It was October again: the cider harvest under way and the grain stacked in the barns. The weather this time was grey and damp, her bridal chaplet was a simple band of silver-woven braid and feelings were flowing through her, some of them with the same kind of discomfort that came to a cramped limb when unfolded.

On the high table, which was adorned with Rushcliffe's rescued silver plate, Linnet sipped from the handsome, engraved marriage cup. She had toasted her first union in its depths as now she was toasting this new one to Joscelin. Henry, resplendent in a new tunic of green fustian, leaned between herself and Joscelin to refill the loving cup from the flagon in his hand. When he drew back and moved on down the table, she was faced by the bright hunger in Joscelin's eyes. His look was like a hot handprint on her bare skin.

She swallowed, feeling afraid. Giles had been drunk and fumbling on their wedding night, full of terse instructions and curses. *Open your legs, damn you. Wider, higher. Don't just lie there like a cabbage. Stop screaming, it doesn't hurt.*

Joscelin placed his hand over hers and with the other lifted the refilled loving cup to drink from the place where she had set her own lips. It doesn't always hurt, she told herself. *There is pleasure in sin.*

She became aware that Conan was watching them with benign amusement. The mercenary raised his cup in toast and murmured something sidelong to Brien FitzRenard. The justiciar's man laughed and looked teasingly at bride and groom. Linnet wanted to snatch her hand from beneath Joscelin's but knew that it would only intensify the ribbing. It was, after all, their wedding night and Conan was doing his best to preserve the traditions. Now and then, Ironheart would raise his head from the stupor of wine fumes to mutter about duty.

'Use her well in bed,' he slurred, eyes focusing independently of each other. 'Girl children're what you want.' His head nodded as if too heavy for his neck. 'When they marry you can choose your sons. Won't be lum— lumbered with idiots.'

Joscelin cast an exasperated glance in his father's direction. 'God, how much longer before the drink poles him silent?' he muttered to Linnet.

Linnet grimaced as she watched her father-in-law's behaviour sinking further into boorishness with the diminishing level of wine in his cup. She laid her hand urgently along Joscelin's sleeve. 'I know that we are indebted to your father for the restocking of the keep,' she said quietly, 'but duty or not, I know I won't be able to strip myself

naked before him when it comes to the bedding ceremony.'

He shook his head. 'There is no need for us to stand
unclothed before witnesses.' He set his hand over hers.
'You have seen me naked before and have been able to
judge that you are not getting damaged goods, and I
would have to be mad to repudiate you because of some
unseen physical flaw. Besides,' he added with a rueful
glance at Conan, 'do you think I relish the thought of
being stripped and drunkenly commented upon? A man
has more to conceal than a woman. Stiff or limp, I'll be
cause for all manner of bawdy jests.'

Linnet felt a weak surge of relief and gave him a heartfelt thank you. She bit her lip. 'When I married Giles,
the bedding ceremony was as if I was being shut in a
cage with a wild animal and all the guests were grinning
onlookers.'

'You have nothing to fear from me.'

'Yes, I know.' She crumbled a sweet honey cake set on
the platter beside her trencher. 'It is not you I fear.'

He frowned in thought for a moment, then leaned
closer to speak softly.

'Look, there's only one more course to be served and
we've eaten ourselves stupid anyway. Make the excuse
that you're going to check that Robert has settled down
and go to our chamber. I'll sit here and make idle conversation for a while to disarm their suspicions, then I'll visit
the latrine. By the time they realize what has happened,
we'll have the door bolted in their faces.'

She nodded with alacrity and rose to her feet as the
final parade of food began arriving from the kitchens –
sweet frumenties and tarts, pressed cheeses, small pasties
and bowls of fresh green herbs. She was aware of the
salacious glances following her, of men imagining how

she would look unclothed, her hair loose. She heard the bawdy remarks shouted to Joscelin and his good-natured rejoinders. Her face flamed and her heart began to thump. Glancing over her shoulder as she reached the tower entrance, she saw that Joscelin was unconcernedly helping himself to a slice of nutmeg tart and bandying words with Conan, lulling him into a false sense of security. Gratefully, Linnet started up the concealing twist of the dimly lit stairs.

Joscelin dropped the bar across the door. 'They might rattle at the latch,' he said, 'but I doubt they'll go to the trouble of fetching an axe to see tradition upheld.'

Linnet sighed with relief. 'I could not have endured the bedding ceremony.'

'Once must be penance enough for anyone,' he said wryly and sat down in the chair before the hearth. He knew what he wanted. He also knew that to take it with the directness that was now his right would be a grave mistake.

'Was Robert asleep?' he asked as he unwound his leg-bindings.

'Indeed yes.' Her face brightened. 'Thoroughly exhausted by all the excitement. He's head over heels in love with that pony you brought.'

'I thought they would suit.' Joscelin felt a glow remembering the joy in Robert's small face when he set eyes on the little Galloway mare.

'Do you know what he's called her?'

Joscelin shook his head.

'Giles once said that Leicester's wife had the teeth and backside of a mare. Robert must have been listening. He's named her Petronilla after the countess.'

Joscelin choked. Petronilla de Beaumont did indeed

resemble a horse, although her colouring was more iron-grey than chestnut, and on balance he thought the Galloway pony the more attractive. 'I don't know whether the horse should be insulted, or the countess,' he said with a grin.

'Is it true that she girds herself like a man and rides into battle at her husband's side?'

'More or less. She's with him now for certain.' He looked at her from under his brows. 'Not thinking of following her example, are you?'

'Perhaps it would be easier than to sit here waiting,' she said and looked at him as she unbound her braids.

Leaving the chair, he took her wooden comb from her coffer and sat down beside her on the bed. 'Give me your hair,' he coaxed. 'You don't want to unbar the door to summon your maid and I've done this many times before.'

She had tensed at his approach but now she relaxed and gave him an inquisitive smile. 'Is that by way of reassurance or confession?' she asked mischievously.

'Which do you want?' he responded in a similar tone, and taking her hair in his hands started to brush out the twists of braid. The firelight caught the ripples that the plaiting had left behind, gilding the soft honey-brown with golden-red lights. The scent of rosemary and chamomile rose from the slow movement of the comb and delicately assaulted his senses. 'If you think I've led a debauched life of bedchambers and broken hearts, you are sadly mistaken.'

'And you a tourney champion?' Her voice was pitched low as her head yielded to the gentle passage of the comb. He watched the movement of the sinews in her slender throat, the soft hollow above her collarbone. The memory of Breaca hovered bittersweet in the shadows.

'I do confess to plucking the occasional ripe fruit from a tree overhanging someone else's orchard wall but, if not into my hand, it would have fallen elsewhere.' He worked in contemplative silence for a moment. Her hair crackled and glowed with light as if it were an extension of the fire. 'Besides,' he added, 'for a long time I had a woman of my own and no inclination to go filching forbidden apples. Breaca would have gelded me for certain.'

She turned her head. 'Conan has made mention of your past,' she said.

'I thought he might. Probably he believed you would feel sorry for me and your heart would melt.'

'He was watching you and Robert together. I think he spoke because he was pleased for you, and he said very little. Only that your son had died and that you and his mother had parted.'

How distant it sounded, spoken softly in this chamber resonant with his new beginning. 'Bloody flux,' he said. 'He was only four years old. Breaca nearly died, too. He is buried in a churchyard on the road to Falaise and it cost all the silver I had to bribe the priest to let Juhel lie in consecrated ground – a mercenary's unshriven bastard child.' He gathered her hair to one side and stroked the back of her neck with gentle fingers. 'It hit me hard. For a time I was wild, didn't care. The summer Juhel died was my most successful ever on the tourney route. I earned back all the silver I had paid to the priest and enough to employ my own troop of men instead of traipsing in Conan's wake.'

'Your son's name was Juhel.'

'It's Breton, the name of Breaca's father.' He felt her tremble beneath his touch or perhaps it was his hand that trembled with the effort of controlling all that was within him. 'He was small like his mother but quick and bright as a pin.' He shrugged. 'It's ten years ago now.'

Again she turned to look at him, her brows arching this time in startled question.

'I was a little short of seventeen when he was born.'

'And Breaca?'

'She was two and thirty – old enough to have been my mother,' he added with a hint of self-mockery.

'Why are you telling me this?'

'You think it would stay a secret long with Conan in the same household? He would let you have it piece by little piece and I would know from the way you looked at me which occasions he had chosen to enlighten you. Now it is told, it no longer lies between us.'

Her throat moved. Her lashes swept down, making feathery shadows on her cheekbones.

'Or does it?' Frowning, he tilted her chin on his fingertips.

'No,' she said huskily, 'it doesn't.' But other things did. She was not brave enough to give him the sword of her own past to break across his knees.

He brushed his fingers lightly over her face, traced her brow, her cheekbone, her mouth. She felt his urgency and his restraint and her breathing shuddered as she too fought for control. The tentative first intimacy yielded to a more sustained assault on her senses, but refined and delicate. They drank the last of the spiced wine from earlier and shed their garments slowly, layer by layer, until they were skin to skin. Gestures became bolder, more explicit, as pleasure and tension mounted and they lay down on the bed. Perspiration dampened Linnet's brow. She was no longer cold. The hot pressure of Joscelin's body pinned her to the feather mattress but it was a good feeling. Against his ribs she felt the driving thud of his heart. Her palms slid upon the textures of wet skin, smooth muscle and taut tendons. She tangled her fingers in his hair and sought his mouth at the same time arching her hips and opening herself to him. She felt him push inside her – no inexpert fumbling here but the surety of experience. The sound of pleasure he made caused her to gasp and tighten her arms around him.

Someone banged on the door with what sounded like one of her best silver-gilt cups. 'Joscelin, open up, you spoilsport!' Conan bellowed. 'You haven't been properly bedded yet!'

Linnet stifled a scream and stared over Joscelin's shoulder at the shuddering door, hoping that the bar would hold.

Joscelin muttered an oath and tensed.

'Joscelin!' The door quivered beneath the repeated hammering. Then there was a curse of pain. Milo de Selsey's voice came muffled through the thick oak and Henry's, too, trying to cajole Conan away from the barred door. 'Not fair! 'Tsnot tradish— tradishnal!' Conan complained.

Henry murmured enticingly that a new cask of wine was about to be broached. Footsteps staggered and scuffled. 'That's it, Sir Conan,' Linnet heard Henry say. 'It's much better down in the hall than up here on a draughty landing.'

'Spoilsport!' There was a final thump on the door. Sounds retreated and the silence resumed. Joscelin sighed and pressed his head into the curve of Linnet's throat. 'Conan in his cups is a fiend straight out of hell,' he muttered. 'It's because we've come out of one battle to go straight to another. Drink and women, the mercenary's sovereign remedy.'

She heard the self-mockery in his tone and touched his sweat-damp hair. 'Then lose yourself,' she whispered.

He was quiet for a moment, then he lifted his head and breathed soft laughter. 'Conan was right,' he told her. 'We haven't been properly bedded – yet.'

He was still within her, although somewhat diminished. Now she felt his surge of renewed eagerness.

'Do you think he'll come back?' she wrapped her legs around him.

'I'll kill him if he does!'

Linnet strained her ears, wondering if anyone was listening outside the door, but there was nothing, just the intimate sounds of lovemaking: the growing harshness of Joscelin's breathing, the movement of their bodies, the rustle of the bed clothes. Her voice catching in her throat. Her loins were stretching and filling with a pleasurable tension so huge that she knew she was going to burst.

Joscelin's lips were upon her breast, his head butting the angle of her jaw. She clenched her teeth, trying not to make a sound, but the cries came anyway. Against the curve of her breast, Joscelin groaned. His spine arched, his head came up. She closed her eyes and gripped him, absorbing his tremors through her own.

As his breathing eased, he lazily returned his attention to her breast, throat and jaw. Linnet shivered, savouring the sensations. The edge between this tender, feathery nibbling and Giles's sated wet fondling shone as keen and narrow as the edge of a blade. One slip and she would bleed to death. She did not want the memory of other occasions to mar this one and she pressed herself against Joscelin's body, hiding her face in his sweat-salty skin as if by doing so she could absorb even more of him into her than she had already taken.

197

21

Maude de Montsart shook out her crumpled riding gown of Flemish twill. 'Has there been any news, my dear?' she asked Linnet as a groom led away the placid bay ambler to be watered and rubbed down. The two soldiers who had escorted her from Arnsby were already on their way to the guardroom to wait out her stay before the comfort of a stoked brazier.

Linnet sighed and shook her head. 'Not since last Tuesday. Joscelin sent me some hides he'd bought at a bargain price from a tannery on Leenside and wrote that he was leaving Nottingham the day after, but that was all. What about you?' She drew Maude across the bailey and up the forebuilding stairs into the great hall.

'William sent a messenger to fetch his thick cloak and waxed linens. That must have been about the same time that Joscelin wrote to you. My brother never communicates well even at the best of times.'

'No,' Linnet said wryly, thinking of her wedding day. Maude looked at her curiously.

Linnet told her about Ironheart's ungracious behaviour. 'And then he had the gall to soak in the tub until the water was nearly cold!' she said indignantly. 'Nor did he object when I gave him Giles's old fur-lined bedrobe to wear afterwards while he was barbered, the hypocrite!' Then she laughed reluctantly. Recounting it now, she could see the humour in the situation.

Maude's eyelids creased with amusement. 'William has a reputation to maintain. He's not as hard as people think. That myth grew out of the time after Morwenna died when he was mad with grief and no one could approach him without getting their head bitten off.' She smiled at Linnet. 'Look at it this way, my dear, rather than riding to Arnsby, he chose to stay at Rushcliffe before leaving to rendezvous with the constable's troops.'

Linnet nodded. It was a dubious sign of favour, she thought, and one she could easily have foregone.

Maude lifted her eyes to the high windows. 'I cannot blame him either. This is a beautiful room.'

Linnet looked up too. The proportions of this, Raymond's lair, were surprisingly elegant. The strong, pure lines picked up and carried the Romanesque curves of windows and supporting arches like embroidery on a beautifully cut but austere gown. 'Giles's grandsire went on Crusade and captured an emir. He put all the ransom money into this place,' she said and led Maude up the stairs to the bower.

Panting somewhat from the climb, Maude surveyed the large, sun-flooded bower, its whitewashed walls decorated with Flemish hangings. 'Oh, it's lovely! Just look at the size of this fireplace, and a stone canopy too!'

Linnet was silent as Maude examined and enthused over the bower. At length the older woman plumped herself down on the padded settle. Something of Linnet's mood must have communicated itself to Maude for she cocked her head inquisitively.

'Do you not like living here, my dear?'

Linnet frowned as she studied the warm, bright room. 'It is the memories I do not like,' she said after a hesitation. 'My marriage to Giles and what came after.'

Maude nodded. 'But that is over now. You are a new wife and you have new memories to make. I trust Joscelin is treating you well?'

Linnet blushed and sat down on the other end of the settle. 'He has been very good to me.'

'More than that, to judge from the colour in your cheeks!' Maude smiled.

Linnet returned the expression but without her entire heart. Yes, he had been very good to her but perhaps he would cease to be if she told him about herself and Raymond de Montsorrel. She had almost said something as they lay entwined in the afterglow of a second mating but her first tentative words had been met by the indifferent mumble of a man already three-quarters asleep and her courage had failed her. Why tell him at all? It was in the past, finished. And all the time, at the back of her mind, a small voice was crying, *You would revile me if you knew what I had done.* Not even to a priest had she ever confessed her sin. She would go to hell when she died and assuredly meet Raymond there.

Maude's humour faded and, leaning over, she gently touched Linnet's knee. 'You are troubled, my dear?'

Linnet blinked moisture from her eyes and swallowed. 'No,' she lied. 'It is nothing.'

The curtain across the bower entrance billowed and then was flurried aside by a giggling Robert, who was running away from Ella.

'Just you come here this instant, young man, and wash those muddy hands!' the maid cried, and catching him, tickled him into a state of helpless submission before sweeping him across the room to the laver.

Distracted by the intrusion, Maude craned round to watch the child complain and grimace at being scrubbed. 'I never had infants of my own,' she said wistfully. 'William's brood has been my family.'

Linnet saw the sadness in Maude's face. Her lap was generous and made to nurse small children. 'Robert has no grandparents,' she said. 'I would be honoured if you became one to him.'

Maude stared at Linnet as if she had just been offered a place in heaven, and her eyes filled with emotion. 'There is nothing that would give me more pleasure,' she said in a shaky voice. 'Martin's leaving Arnsby after Christmas to join Richard de Luci's household and I'll miss having a child about the place. To know I can visit you and be special to Robert is a gift beyond price.' She embraced Linnet in a fervent hug.

'It is as much for my sake as yours!' Linnet responded, her own voice unsteady. 'My mother died when I was a baby. I've never had an older woman to talk to, except Richard de Luci's wife sometimes and the Countess Petronilla.'

'That's the name of my horse!' Overhearing, Robert skipped up to them, his demeanor as chirpy as a squirrel's. 'She's called Petra for short. Malcolm's been teaching me to jump her over logs.' He leaped in the air, demonstrating. 'Joscelin says that he's going to show me how to tilt at the quintain when he comes home and he's promised me some bridle bells, too. Joscelin's my papa now.'

'Yes, my love, so that makes you and me relatives,' Maude said and produced a small box containing squares of a sticky date sweetmeat, which she gave to the child.

'Don't eat too many at once; you'll make yourself sick and your mother will be cross with me.'

Robert was more taken with the carvings on the little box than he was with the contents. Maude helped him to eat one of the glistening dark pieces and enquired after his coneys.

'They're grazing in the garth,' Linnet said. 'I've had the carpenter fashion an enclosure to keep them from harm and prevent them escaping and eating the salad leaves.'

'The babies were all pink and blind at first but they've got black fur now,' Robert announced somewhat stickily. 'The messenger said he'd like a black coney-skin cloak but Malcolm told him my coneys were special pets.'

Linnet grasped Robert's arm. 'What messenger, sweetheart?'

'The one who arrived when we were unsaddling Petra. He was all covered in dust and his horse was foamy. Henry's sister gave the man a drink.'

Linnet stood up, her mouth dry and her heart pounding. She had taken only two steps towards the chamber door when she heard voices on the stairs and Malcolm appeared on her threshold with Milo. They flanked a travel-stained, dishevelled and obviously exhausted young soldier.

Linnet stood straight and still as she looked at the men. 'What news?' she demanded. 'Tell me.'

The messenger advanced and bent the knee. He was one of Conan's Bretons, a stocky young man scarcely out of adolescence with a downy beard fuzzing his square jaw. 'There is no need for fear, my lady, the news is good,' he said as she gestured him to rise and face her. 'Our troops met Leicester's near to Edmundsbury at a place called Fornham. All swampy, the land was, and no fit place to fight but we forced them to a battle nevertheless

202

and cut them to pieces. Them as we didn't get, the peasants did with pitchforks and spears. The earl himself has been taken prisoner and his countess with him.' Rummaging in his pouch, he withdrew a crumpled, water-stained packet. 'A letter from my lord. He says to expect him in three days' time, all being well.'

Colour flooded back into Linnet's face as she took the packet from the mercenary's blunt fingers. 'And is he whole? He has taken no injury?'

'No, my lady.' The young man grinned, revealing a recently lost front tooth. 'Mostly it was like spearing fish in a barrel. In the end we fetched up pitying the poor bastards that were left and let them run away into the marshes.' He shrugged his broad shoulders. 'Not as that'll do 'em any good. Like as not they'll drown or be picked off one by one by the eel fishers and fowlers round about.' His voice dried up and he began to cough.

Maude quickly poured him wine from the pitcher on the side table and brought it to him. 'Do you know what happened to your lord's half-brothers, Ralf and Ivo de Rocher?' she asked anxiously.

The mercenary took several gulps from his cup. 'No, my lady. All I can tell you is that they weren't taken with the earl and his wife. Sir William has offered a reward for their safe delivery into his custody and he's stayed behind at Fornham to see if anyone turns them in. Lord Joscelin says Sir William ought to come home, the damp's not good for him, but he won't be swayed. Says he doesn't care whether his sons are alive or corpses, they're still coming home.'

Linnet unfolded the vellum sheet and gazed upon her husband's firm brown ink strokes. Joscelin wrote almost as good a hand as a professional scribe, although the flow was a little too open and generous of vellum for a true craftsman. She imagined him seated at a table, one hand thrust into his hair, the other busy with a quill. It was a satisfying image and she deliberately enlarged upon it to banish the other one of him astride Whitesocks, brandishing a dripping sword.

'My heart bleeds for them,' Maude had said to her when the messenger had gone. 'William and my nephews both. What if Ralf and Ivo are dead? How will William live with the burden of knowing he might have killed them? They may look like grown men but really they are still jealous little boys.' And she had dabbed at her eyes with the trailing end of her sleeve.

Robert had taken Maude to the garth to look at his coneys, thus giving Linnet a moment alone to read her letter in peace. She sat down in the window embrasure. A puddle of late autumn sunshine warmed her feet through her soft leather shoes. The only sound was the muted conversation of two maids weaving braid by the hearth.

As a child, Linnet had received basic tuition in reading and writing from the household priest – enough so that she could understand but she was not particularly fluent. Painstakingly she picked up each word of Joscelin's and consigned it like a jewel from page to memory.

Joscelin de Gael to my lady and before God mine own beloved wife, greeting. As you will know by the time you read this, I am coming home to you unscathed from our army's meeting with the Earl of Leicester. A truce has been agreed with the rebels until spring.

We should reach Nottingham the day after tomorrow. I will lodge there the night at my father's town house, and ride to you as soon as I have concluded business with the constable.

Until then, I give you keeping of my heart.

Witness myself on the third day after the feast of Saint Luke.

The words warmed her as much as the splash of sunlight and foolish tears blurred her vision. Not since childhood had affection been hers to command except in Robert's eyes. Once she had made the mistake of believing that Raymond de Montsorrel was fond of her, that the gentle hands and persuasive voice were indicative of his concern, but it had all been a game to him, a bolster of his prideful boast that no woman, lady or whore, had ever refused him.

The sunlight blazed on the vellum as she folded it tenderly, her fingertips lingering on the strokes that bore the mark of Joscelin's hand. She went to her work basket, and taking her awl worked a hole through the folded corners. Then she threaded it onto the cord around her neck, which also held her cross. The cord lay between her breasts and the vellum lay on her skin; Joscelin's heart over hers.

22

'We're lost, aren't we?' Ivo snivelled.

Ralf clenched his fists on his wet reins and turned in the saddle to scowl at his brother. 'God's eyes, will you cease whining! You're still alive, aren't you?'

The rain had been falling steadily since dawn, making of the forest a permanent green twilight. Water sluiced down Ralf's helm and soaked through the twin layers of his cloak. His hauberk bled gritty rust and his thighs chafed against the saddle with each stride of his exhausted horse.

In heavy drizzle, Leicester's army had struck across the country towards the earl's Midland strongholds and had been met by their doom on the marshy ground near the village of Fornham. Earl Robert had relied too heavily on his Flemish recruits – weedy men and boys who were mostly unemployed weavers by trade – and Hugh de Bohun's knights had smashed them. Filled with rage and fear, Ralf had hacked his way to escape, dragging a terrified Ivo in his wake. Now the forests surrounding Edmunsbury and Thetford stretched for miles, punctuated by the occasional charcoal-burner's dwelling or verderer's hut. And outside of their gloomy green protection, for all Ralf knew, the Royalist army was waiting to finish anyone who had not died by the sword or drowned in the marshes.

'My horse is going lame,' Ivo complained. 'Do you think we'll find shelter soon?'

Ralf closed his eyes and swallowed. In a moment he was going to offer Ivo shelter – six feet deep with a cosy counterpane of leaf mould. The idiot was about as much use as a punctured waterskin. Couldn't fight, couldn't think. Ralf did not answer but urged his own horse to a faster pace.

The forest dripped around him like a giant open mouth waiting to swallow whatever was foolish enough to ride over the drawbridge of its mossy tongue. The smell of mildew and fungus was almost overpowering. Ralf's eyes stung and his vision became a green blur. He was a rebel, an outcast, shivering to death in a Lowland forest. The spark of rebellion that had led him in fellow sympathy to join young Henry's cause was extinguished. The desire to wound his father, and at the same time prove his own worth, still goaded him with a vengeance. He hungered for respect and admiration, and the more they eluded him the more desperate he grew.

'Ralf, wait!' Ivo's forlorn cry came muffled through the grey-green downpour.

Viciously, Ralf jabbed the stallion's flanks. The beast stumbled on a tree root then shied as a woodpecker dipped across the path. Ralf gripped the pommel to steady himself. One shoulder struck a tree branch and he cursed at the crunch of pain. He drew rein to recover and with resignation listened to the beat of approaching hooves as Ivo made up the ground between them.

'Ralf . . . ,' Ivo said miserably.

Ralf inhaled to snarl at his brother, but his breath solidified in his chest for Ivo was being held at spearpoint by a grinning English soldier who was one of a group of half a dozen armed men.

'If your hand is going to your sword, I hope it's only to surrender it,' said the soldier in thickly accented French. 'Give me one small excuse, Norman, and I'll have your guts to banner my spear.'

Ralf shuddered, more than half-tempted to give the soldier the very excuse he needed. It would be so simple. One thrust and everything would be finished. But was there any guarantee except a priest's prating assurance that the afterlife was any better? Slowly he grasped the hilt of his sword and drew it from its wool-lined scabbard.

'Ralf, for Jesu's sake, give it to him!' Ivo croaked, eyes huge with alarm. 'You'll find us worth the ransom,' he gabbled, eyes darting around the tightening circle of men. 'We're the sons of William de Rocher, known as Ironheart – his heirs, in fact.' He licked his lips.

Ralf sent Ivo a glare of utter scorn and threw the sword down into the thick leaf mould at his destrier's fore-hooves as if he were tossing a coin to a beggar.

The Englishman grinned. 'The sons of the great Ironheart, eh?' The relish in his tone scoured deep. 'I wonder how much your illustrious sire is willing to pay for the return of his two lost sheep. Better hope it's more than your true worth or I might be tempted not to go to the bother of ransoming you.'

'He'll pay anything you want,' Ivo assured the Englishman anxiously. 'He will, Ralf, won't he?'

Ralf narrowed his light-brown eyes. 'Oh yes,' he muttered. 'He'll pay.'

*　　*　　*

In the wet October afternoon, a bitter wind herded a fleece of clouds northwards and blew into the face of William de Rocher as he and his men drew rein outside the village alehouse to which their English guide had brought them.

'Is this the place?' A paradox of hope and sinking despair made Ironheart's voice harsh.

'Yes, my lord.' His guide looked at him sidelong. 'It might not seem much but there's a mighty stout apple-cellar under the main-room floor.'

A muscle flickered in Ironheart's jaw. 'My sons are in the apple cellar?'

'Safest place for 'em. If they weren't worth good silver, they'd be feeding the ravens of Hallows Wood by now.'

'Watch your mouth,' Ironheart warned as the soldier nimbly dismounted. 'Just because you have something I want, do not think you can take liberties with me.'

The soldier looked him up and down. 'I wasn't, my lord. I thought you were known as a man of plain speaking and I have told you nothing but the truth. Many of Leicester's troops have not lived to see their ransoms paid.'

William glared at him and felt a goutish envy for the lively arrogance and fluid grace of youth. Slowly he swung his stiff right leg over the cantle and dismounted. The ground was soggy underfoot with a mulch of dead leaves. They twirled from the elm trees across the green, like souls fleeing into the darkness, some of them falling by the wayside at his feet. Rain spattered into his face, forcing him to squint. Noisy laughter drifted from the alehouse and a raucous voice bellowed an English ballad about a virgin and a blacksmith.

'They're still celebrating their victory over Leicester's army,' said his guide with a tolerant smile as a well-lubricated villager staggered out of the doorway and towards a cluster of dwellings huddled around the green. 'It'll be the talk of the parish for generations to come – how Grandpa beat off hordes of Flemings with nowt but a pitchfork.'

'My sons,' said Ironheart icily. 'I want my sons. Now.'

The smile dropped from the soldier's face. 'Of course,' he said. 'This way, my lord.' He flourished towards the alehouse doorway like a servant ushering a great lord into a magnificent hall. It took all of Ironheart's control not to send him teeth over tail into the mud.

Ralf was dozing, the nearest he could come to sleep in his cramped, cold prison. They had handled him roughly, goaded by his lack of response and the contempt in his eyes. The places where they had kicked him had stiffened, and since there was virtually no room to move he had set.

In his shallow dream there was a witch who wore the face of a lovely dark-haired woman with shining green eyes that reflected the shade of her gown. But then she changed. The flesh began to melt from the face until it was a hideous skull. The hand reaching out to curse him was a white filigree of bone. The skull whispered, 'Look at me.' Terrified, but forced to obey, he raised his eyes to the cavernous orbits and saw the eyes of his mother staring out at him.

Ralf jerked awake, his breath ragged in his throat and his heart thundering against his ribs like a runaway horse. The sweet smell of apples cloyed the darkness, hinting that they would soon be overripe – rotting. Slumped against him, Ivo whimpered in his sleep. They had not abused Ivo as much for there had been no challenge in taunting such easy game.

Above their heads there was a continuous muffled

210

cacophony of footsteps, voices and raucous laughter. They were celebrating with a vengeance. Ralf thought about the mistakes he had made and how, when he got out of this pit, he would go about rectifying them. Groping in the darkness, he found the loaf they had lowered down earlier. 'Help yourself to apples,' his captors had said, laughing. He set his teeth in the coarse brown sawdust and thought of the soft, golden honey-bread that his aunt Maude would always bake on feast days. The thought of it brought moisture to his mouth and at least he was able to chew this current excuse for sustenance.

He swallowed hard then raised his head, suddenly attentive as the general noise subsided and the heavy trestle bench standing over the cellar trap was scraped to one side. He nudged his brother hard. Ivo woke with a start and a cry.

The bolt on the trap was drawn and the door flung back to reveal, by dingy rushlight, a rectangle of blackened ceiling-beam festooned with three coils of sausage and a bundle of besom twigs. These were almost immediately blotted out by the human shapes that bent over the entrance and peered down.

'Safe and sound like I told you,' declared the smug voice of the English soldier responsible for Ralf and Ivo's capture and their current ignominious situation. 'Snug as apples in a barrel.' A snort of amusement followed.

'Ralf, Ivo?' Ironheart's voice sounded as if his larynx were fashioned of rusty link mail. 'I've come for you. God knows neither of you are worth the ransom but at least I know the duty owed to my blood.'

Duty! Ralf almost gagged as he heard the word. How often it had been rammed down his throat like a medicine to cure all ills. By God, he would show his father duty!

'Sire?' he said and, inching gingerly to his feet, looked up through the trap. 'We were trying to reach you but these gutter sweepings took us for ransom and threw us down here.'

'Less of the gutter sweepings!' growled the soldier. 'We could have left your butchered bodies in the forest for the foxes and ravens to eat.'

'With your own for company!' Ralf retorted, fists clenched. Then he took a deep breath and steadied himself. 'Sire, you were right about the Earl of Leicester and young Henry. They're not worth the spit of any man's oath.'

Ivo struggled to rise and, even in the bad light, Ralf could see that his eyes were as round as candle cups. 'But you said— Oooff!' Ivo collapsed as Ralf's elbow found his midriff.

'What's the matter with him?' Ironheart demanded as a wooden ladder was slotted down through the trapdoor.

'Belly gripes,' Ralf said. 'He's been eating too many apples.'

Ivo groaned and retched. Ralf climbed gingerly up the ladder. His limbs felt like struts of rickety wood, and when his father stretched down his hand and pulled him out into the light he did not have to feign a grimace of pain. After the darkness of the apple cellar, the rushlit main room of the alehouse appeared as huge and bright as a palace, although the courtiers wore the appearance of reprobates and beggars. And his father was king of the beggars in his water-stained, shabby garments, grey hair showing wild wings of white and his flesh slack upon his gaunt bones.

Shock hit Ralf like a physical blow. Christ, he was looking at an old man, not the granite-hewed God of his childhood and adolescence.

'I knew you'd come to your senses, whelp,' Ironheart said with a disdainful curl of his upper lip. 'Pity it took so long and cost so much.'

'Yes, sire.' Ralf stared at the floor while he recovered himself.

'Don't think you can pull the wool over my eyes. It's no more in your nature to be meek than it is for a wolf to turn into a lap dog. Look at me!'

Ralf raised his head and stared his father in the eyes. Defiance flickered – there was nothing he could do to prevent it – but it brought a wintry smile to Ironheart's lips.

'That's more like the truth. I know you're not spine-less.' Ironheart turned his regard upon Ivo, who had emerged unaided from the cellar. 'If it had been your brother here, I could well have believed it.' He seized Ivo by the scruff and dragged him forward into the light. 'He's always had curd for guts!'

Hunched and shivering, Ivo stood like an ox outside a slaughter pen and made no defence. There was a tight-ness in Ralf's throat and rigors shook his jaw. He had never felt such hatred in his entire life but knew that it would transmute into an explosion of love and remorse if his father offered but one word or gesture of affection.

Hard-eyed, Ironheart said, 'Go outside and wait for me. There are saddled horses and an escort waiting.'

The alewife, a smirk on her face, handed over two meagre peasant cloaks. The fine fur-lined ones in which the brothers had arrived had been put away against her daughter's dowry.

'Are we under guard?' Ralf asked huskily.

'No,' Ironheart said.

'Then we are free to leave?'

'Where would you go? Take to a nomad life on the tourney circuits for the price of a crust? Walk out on me now, Ralf, and you might as well be dead. I'll not seek you out a second time. Why should I when I have a son at home and another whose loyalty I do not doubt?'

Ralf clenched his teeth and with a supreme effort prevented himself from either answering his father in the manner he deserved or storming out. He had learned all about cutting off his nose to spite his face. Taking the cloak from the woman, he swept it around his shoulders. The ragged hem hung drunkenly at knee level and the pin was fashioned out of a chicken bone. 'I know where I stand, Father,' he said, his voice quiet but filled with bitterness. 'I hope to God that you do.' And strode into the dark, rainy night to the waiting soldiers.

23

The weekday market in Nottingham was almost as busy as London's Cheapside, Joscelin thought as he threaded his way through the crowded butchers' shambles of Flesher Gate and Blowbladder Lane and headed up the hill to the shops and booths that thronged along the road to St Mary's Church and Hologate. Cheek by jowl, squashed together like herrings in a barrel, the stallholders cried aloud the merits of their wares or sat at their trade behind trestles cluttered with their tools.

At a haberdasher's booth Joscelin purchased a small set of bridle bells, thereby fulfilling his promise to Robert. They jingled merrily on their leather strap as he stowed them in his pouch. He remembered Juhel's dark eyes wistfully admiring such bright trinkets dangling from a trader's stall in Paris. In those days, money had provided the luxuries of bread and firewood and the gauds had remained a dream. He thought about a gift for Linnet. The coins in his pouch were not part of Robert's patrimony but his own property, courtesy of his prowess against Leicester's men. Withholding a death blow and claiming a ransom instead was by far the most profitable way of conducting warfare and he had indeed made an excellent profit.

There were gold and silver merchants aplenty to offer him cunningly worked rings and brooches, earrings and pendants. He knew that Linnet possessed little jewellery but what he saw upon the stalls did not appeal to him. It was too common-place. Every woman of means had a round brooch with a secret message carved on the reverse – *Amor vincit omnia* or *Vous et nul autre*. He had bought Breaca one in cheap bronze when she first became pregnant, and the memory was still so poignant that he had to avert his eyes from the wares at that particular stall. One stallholder offered him a reliquary cross in which, amid a confection of silver and rock crystal, was set a sliver of bone from the blessed Virgin herself, or so he was assured. Shavings of pig bone from the cesspit in the merchant's yard was the more likely source, Joscelin thought, and without difficulty declined the bargain.

What he did purchase finally was an exquisitely carved ivory comb and a mirror-case to match. The seller, Gamel, was a former mercenary who now made his living making such items as well as dice and trinkets for members of the garrison to which he had once belonged. A sword had sliced off his leg at the knee. He had survived the wound fever and now stumped around on a peg leg, ungainly but determined. Just now, the wooden limb was lying beside his bag of tools on the rushes of the Weekday alehouse as he thirstily accepted the piggin of ale that Joscelin had bought for him.

'How's the leg?' Joscelin joined him at the cramped trestle. A pang of nostalgia ran through him as he absorbed the smoky, noisy atmosphere of the little alehouse. He had not known Gamel when the man had two sound legs but the wound had only been a few months old when he first met him sitting in the guardroom at the castle, carving a rattle for a retainer's infant son.

'Not bad, not bad. Mustn't grumble or you'll not bother to keep me in ale.' Gamel wiped his mouth. 'Mind you, I had a close escape last month. The landlord's new hound took a fancy to chew up me old peg while I was resting here. Regular mess, he made of it – huge great teeth marks, you shoulda seen 'em.'

'I've seen the dog,' Joscelin said sympathetically. Chained in the yard was something that appeared to be a cross between a boar hound and a pony, and certainly looking more bite than bark.

'You'll not see it for much longer if I have me way,' Gamel muttered and took another drink of ale. Then he looked at Joscelin sidelong. 'We hear you're a man of means now.'

Joscelin smiled and spread his free hand wide. 'Who am I to deny rumours?'

Gamel ran his tongue round his teeth. 'They're fine, fair lands you've got yourself.'

'And a fine, fair wife.' Joscelin looked at the comb. He had wanted to give Linnet a personal gift and this, with its evocations of their wedding night, was perfect.

'God grant you many fine, fair children, too,' Gamel toasted, and when he had finished drinking, he lifted his empty cup on high and signalled to the serving woman. 'I carve the best infant rattles in three counties. Best walrus—' He broke off as four soldiers swaggered into the alehouse and made loud demands to be served. One of them apprehended the woman who was on her way to Gamel and Joscelin.

'C'mon, sweetheart, soldiers first, cripples c'n wait,' he sneered, grasping her arm.

Joscelin opened his mouth but Gamel quickly nudged

him silent. 'Leave be. It's best not to tangle with Robert Ferrers's men, 'specially when they're drunk.'

'You let them get away with it?' Joscelin eyed the raucous soldiers with disfavour. He knew the type. Put swords at their hips and they thought they had a licence to intimidate everyone they encountered. Give them ale to drink and the result was volatile. Looking at them, he judged they had already consumed a skinful elsewhere.

'Too many of 'em to do otherwise. Town's been overrun with 'em recently. There's no peace to be had in any alehouse this side o' Sneinton.'

Joscelin rubbed his jaw. Robert Ferrers, Earl of Derby, was a known ally of Leicester's. Had Leicester's army of Flemings reached the midlands, Ferrers would have leaped to join him, of that there was no doubt. Despite the fact that the Ferrers family owned substantial lands in Nottingham, the city had remained staunch to the Crown and showed no sign of wavering – a probable reason for the intimidation. With Leicester imprisoned and truces agreed until spring, there was bound to be a corked-up surplus of frustration and bad feeling.

Gamel shrugged. 'They'll not be here much longer. With all the king's men like yoursen arriving into the city, it won't be as easy for them to do their mischief.'

'Can't the garrison deal with the troublemakers?'

'Oh, aye, we've seen some rare old street battles and it goes quiet for a while, but then the trouble starts again. Earl Ferrers turns a deaf ear to all complaints. That's why the landlord's got hissen that dog in the yard.'

With set lips, the serving woman approached Joscelin and Gamel to replenish their cups. One of Ferrers's men tried to trip her but she avoided him with an adroit swish of her hips. Two tradesmen drank up and left. Joscelin decided to do the same.

'Strap on your leg,' he said to Gamel. 'I'll take you back to the castle.'

Gamel reached down for his peg, but before he could grasp it one of Ferrers's men darted forward and snatched it away. 'Look what I got, lads!' he crowed. 'A lump of firewood!' He approached the fire pit, tossing Gamel's stump from hand to hand.

Joscelin stood up. 'Return it now,' he said quietly.

'What if I don't?' The young soldier threw the leg in the air and deliberately refrained from catching it until it was almost too late. Joscelin looked at the rash of adolescent pustules on the young man's face, at the erratic individual hairs sprouting on his chin, and began to feel very angry indeed.

'You won't live to grow up.'

The young man flushed. Narrowing his eyes, he dropped Gamel's leg into the flames.

All hell let loose. Joscelin leaped upon the soldier, and his three companions leaped upon Joscelin. Gamel crawled across the floor to the fire pit to rescue his peg before it went up in flames. The serving woman ran outside screaming for help and encountered the landlord, who had just returned from an errand. He unchained his dog and, with his fist wrapped around the broad leather collar, plunged into the dark interior of the alehouse. Hard on his heels followed Conan, who was in search of Joscelin. For several frantic moments the pandemonium redoubled. The dog snarled and bit indiscriminately at anything it could get its teeth into. The landlord belaboured the soldiers with a quarterstaff until Conan seized it from him and, with his greater bulk and experience, wielded it to far better effect. Joscelin emerged from the heap of flailing arms and legs with his fist firmly upon the scruff of the youth who was spitting blood, teeth and curses.

219

He was the first of Derby's men to sprawl in the street and his companions quickly followed. Nor did they stay to hurl abuse. The dog made sure of that.

'Just like old times!' Conan panted with relish, leaning on the quarterstaff to regain his breath.

Gasping, clutching his bruised ribs, Joscelin gave him an eloquent look and turned to Gamel, who was blowing on his wooden leg and scrubbing at the worst of the charring with his sleeve. 'How bad is it? Can it be saved?'

'It'll do, until I can carve a new 'un.' Gamel shrugged. He did not seem particularly perturbed; indeed, a grin was slowly spreading across his leathery features. 'It were almost worth it, just to see them get their comeuppance, the turds.'

Joscelin sat down on a bench and gratefully took the cup of ale the landlord served him. Several inquisitive bystanders braved the Weekday now that the danger had gone and Gamel became an instant celebrity.

'Is everything ready to leave?' Joscelin finally asked Conan whom he had left in charge of loading the wain for the last stage of their journey home.

'That's what I was coming to tell you.' Conan rubbed the back of his neck. 'There's a bad axle on the front wheel. It might last until we reach Rushcliffe but, then again, it might break miles from anywhere. I've taken the cart down to Warser gate to get a wheelwright to patch it up but it won't be ready until noon at the earliest.'

Joscelin swore at the news and then swore again, cursing Rushcliffe's wheelwright for a cross-eyed, incompetent mash-wit.

'Does this mean another night in Nottingham?'

'It means travelling by moonlight if necessary,' Joscelin said. 'Come fire or flood, I'm sharing my wife's bed tonight.'

220

Conan flashed his brows 'A touch impatient, eh?' He grinned.

'More than that.' Joscelin gave his uncle a heartfelt look. 'These have been the longest days of my life.'

24

Matthew the peddler unfastened his pack and, spreading a cloth of madder-red wool on the floor rushes, proceeded to lay out his wares for the inspection of his potential customers. Every October and April for the past ten years, Rushcliffe had been a point on the circumference of his regular trade route between Nottingham and Newark. He was a sturdily built, red-cheeked man in his early thirties and usually enjoyed the rudest of health. Recently, however, he had caught a chill he could not shake off and today he felt like death warmed up. A tight band of pain was slicing across the top of his skull and his limbs felt as if they were made of hot lead. Shoulders jerking, he fought to subdue the spasms of a racking cough, knowing that it was extremely bad for business.

With shaking fingers, he reached inside a leather pouch and brought out a selection of ring and pin brooches, some plain bronze, some brightly enamelled. Another sack contained glass and ceramic beads for women to thread on waxed linen-string to make their own feast-day necklaces.

One of the keep's laundresses stopped by with her little

girl to watch him setting out his wares and started haggling with him over a small pair of sewing shears in a tooled leather case. Her astonishment was boundless when Matthew scarcely bothered to argue over the price of the shears and accepted her second offer with a wan smile. Emboldened, she also purchased half a dozen beads to make a necklace for her daughter.

'Lost your killer instinct, Matthew?' Henry asked as the laundress walked off with a gleam of triumph in her eyes, the little girl skipping excitedly at her side.

The peddler rumpled his hair and sniffed loudly. 'Bit of a chill in the bones,' he said. 'I'm all right.'

'I'll get me mam to make you some hot cider and honey,' Henry offered. 'Or Lady Linnet might have some mulled wine if I ask her nicely.'

Despite his savage headache, the peddler did not miss the proprietorial note in Henry's voice. The dapper cut of Henry's tunic and his new gilded belt had not gone unnoticed either. 'Taken a ride on fortune's wheel, have you?'

Henry smiled. 'I'm Lord Joscelin's understeward these days. It's my task to see that everything runs smoothly and that grumbles get aired rather than festering in dark corners. Lord Joscelin says it's no use having a head if there's no backbone to support it and legs to make it walk.'

'He's a better master than the last two, then?'

'Make up your own mind. He'll be home by compline tonight. You landed on your feet arriving when the men are due back in triumph from battle. They'll all have money in their pouches and women they'll want to spend it on. And there's to be a feast with marchpane subtleties and swan with chaudron sauce!'

Matthew gagged. Chaudron sauce was made from the bird's blood and entrails. It was considered a delicacy but at the moment even the mention of ordinary food was enough to make him heave. The image of the dark, almost black sauce was too much for his quailing stomach.

'Best go and lie down,' Henry said, his smile fading as he took a proper look at Matthew. 'Your customers aren't going to run away in a day.'

Matthew nodded, suddenly not having the strength to argue. Feeling as limp as a wrung-out dishcloth, he began clumsily replacing his wares in his pack. Henry stooped to help him, then spun round at an unholy whistling sound immediately behind him.

'Henry, look what cook gave me!' Robert waved a bone flute under the servant's nose. 'Father Gregory says he's going to teach me to play a tune!'

'Sooner rather than later, I hope.' Henry winced and decided a serious word with Saul the cook was long overdue, since the man's nature appeared to have taken an irresponsible and sadistic turn.

'Oh yes, before Papa comes home, then I'll be able to play it for him.' Robert gave the flute another excruciating twiddle then stopped, his head cocked on one side. 'What are you doing?'

'Matthew's too sick to sell his wares today; I'm helping him put them away.'

'Can I help, too?' Before Henry could answer, Robert had knelt down on the trade cloth and reached for a small heap of crosses carved of bone.

'Better, I think, if you leave me and Matthew to it, Master Robert,' said Henry as the child returned the crosses to their leather pouch, pulled the drawstring tight and handed them to the peddler. If Matthew was exuding evil vapours then this was the last place Robert ought to be. Although the child had grown in stature and girth this summer, he still looked as if a puff of wind would blow him away and his mother would roast anyone who put him in danger.

The peddler reached for the bag of beads but fumbled and knocked them over. Robert, attracted by the bright colours, ignored Henry and leaned over to pick them up. Matthew was taken with another bout of coughing. Spasms ripped through him, and although he covered his face with his cloak sputum still sprayed into the atmosphere.

'Go now,' Henry commanded Robert, his voice sharp with anxiety.

Robert jutted his small chin. Henry stared him out. The boy's eyes flickered away and landed on Matthew, who was loudly wiping his nose on his sleeve. Robert pulled a face. 'Don't want to stay anyway,' he said and scampered from the hall, the shrill notes of the bone flute alerting everyone to his passage.

It was very late and Joscelin had still not arrived. Linnet paced the bedchamber, beset by anxiety. The distance between Rushcliffe and Nottingham could easily be covered between dawn and dusk in the early autumn and he had said he would be here today. She went to the hearth and crouched shivering before the glowing logs as her imagination conjured up all manner of terrible things that might have happened to him on his way home to her.

The wind moaned in the chimney and the flames gusted upon the logs. Otherwise there was a suffocating silence. Below in the hall, the household was settling down for the night, the arrival hour of compline but a memory. The tables had been cleared of their fine linen cloths and glazed cups. The feast had been consumed by those with an appetite, but barely a morsel had passed her own lips and what she had eaten she had not tasted. Most of the swan had been polished off by the men of the garrison. Robert too had picked at his food and whined, demanding to know when Joscelin would be back. At length her patience had snapped and she had had her women put him to bed.

Rising from the fireside, she went to look at him. He was curled in a ball on his small truckle bed, his thumb in his mouth and his breathing easy and regular. She gently touched his cheek. It was flushed but he did not appear overly warm and she decided that it was just a residue of his earlier tantrum. Linnet felt like screaming herself and knew she was being foolish. It was only a night. If something disastrous had happened, Joscelin would have sent word. He might not think to do so for a minor delay, for men were like that, and what worried women did not worry them.

She undressed, washed her hands and face in the laver and went to bed. The sheets were cold as she drew them around herself. She thought of Joscelin's warm bulk and the comforting security of his arms and felt bereft. If he did not come tomorrow, she would send a messenger to Nottingham and find out where he was. The decision made her feel a little better and after a while, as the bedclothes grew warm from her solitary body heat, she fell asleep.

A dream came to her, shockingly erotic and vividly real. She was lying on top of the bed dressed in the red samite wedding gown of her first marriage. A man was teasing her, his hand beneath her skirts and his hot, slow kisses draining her.

'Does that feel good?' he whispered against her mouth.

'Joscelin,' she murmured, arching towards him. She raised her hands to bury them in his thick, dark hair. Instead she encountered thin wisps receding from a broad, bony forehead. Her eyes flew open and met the lustful gaze and cruel smile of Raymond de Montsorrel, and she screamed. Candlelight blossomed in her face and she shot bolt upright in bed, scrabbling backward in terror from the brightness.

The light flickered rapidly sideways as its bearer placed the candlestick on the coffer. She saw the glitter of raindrops on a wet cloak, the flash of metal on brooch and belt, dark hair curling around a cap. Her heart flopped over and over like a struggling, landed fish.

'I didn't mean to startle you,' Joscelin said.

She became aware that she was exposed to his stare and that it was both admiring and avid. Kneeling up among the bedclothes, she donned her chemise. 'I've not long retired and then to a nightmare. I have been so worried; where have you been?'

'We didn't leave Nottingham until after noon.' He tossed his hat and cloak over the coffer. 'I was using that old baggage wain of Giles's and another wheel broke.' He drew her against him and cupped her face for a long, exploratory kiss.

Linnet closed her eyes and melted against him. His lips and hands were cold but warmth spread through her from their touch. 'Do you want to eat?' she murmured between kisses.

'Only you.' He pushed aside the bedrobe to cup her breast. She uttered a small gasp that was silenced by another kiss. Her knees weakened.

'You're all wet!' she giggled as his lips followed the touch of his fingers and spikes of hair struck cold against her throat and chest.

'That's because it's filthy weather outside,' he answered in a muffled voice as they fell together across the bed. 'So are you, come to that.'

She revelled in his weight, the hard pressure of his hips upon hers. She found her way inside his braies and found him hot and hard, tight to bursting, and she could not bear it, she wanted him so much. 'Oh please, now!' she half-sobbed against his mouth in a fever of urgency, positioning herself to receive him and make herself whole.

The prickle of damp wool against her skin, the thrust of hot, smooth flesh, the grip of his cold hands lent exciting contrasts of texture and sensation to the experience and within moments she was thrashing on the crest of a wild climax as Joscelin surged to his own.

'God send me this kind of homecoming every time!' he said with a breathless laugh and, having kissed her tenderly on each eyelid, he sat up and removed the rest of his clothing. Linnet eyed his physique by the glow of the candle. He was not heavily muscled and broad like Conan. Indeed, he carried more than a hint of his father's wiriness. Here and there were minor scars, reminders of his life as a mercenary, but she could see no new ones to worry about.

'Now do you want to eat?' she asked. Coupling had always given Giles a voracious appetite and she knew that despite Joscelin's lean frame, he could put away vast amounts of food.

'Again? Give me time to rest, woman!'

'You know what I mean!' She nudged him, then smiled impishly.

He chuckled. 'Well, since I am ravenous on both counts, but have taken the edge off the most important, food would be welcome to replenish my strength for the subtlety to come.'

Linnet answered his pun with a laugh and went to rouse her women.

'We heard about the battle,' she said later as she watched Joscelin tuck into bread and thick slices of meat from one of the cold roasts. 'All sorts of rumours have arrived with merchants and peddlers. Will there be peace now, do you think?'

Joscelin swallowed and shook his head. 'Hard to tell. The king and his sons are still wrangling in Normandy. At least there's a truce until the spring. Once the grass stops growing, there is not enough provender for the destriers. I've known winter campaigns before but if they can be avoided, they usually are.' He cut another slice of meat and there was silence while he devoured it. Then he wiped his hands on a napkin and picked up his goblet. 'I know that the earls of Leicester and Chester are imprisoned but there are still plenty of troublemakers left – Norfolk for one, Ferrers for another. His men were all over Nottingham making nuisances of themselves.'

Linnet refilled his cup. She had met Robert Ferrers on occasion: a strikingly handsome young man, although short in stature and possessed of sharp-cornered aggression. He was one of Nottingham's greatest landholders and she knew it was a source of anger to him and jealous envy that he did not also own the castle, which was firmly in the hands of the Crown.

'That was another reason I was late,' Joscelin said. Rising, he dusted crumbs from the clean shirt he had slipped on and went to the bed where his hastily removed belt still lay, his knife and pouch hanging from it. He pulled open the drawstring of the pouch, removed something and returned to her. 'I went to the Weekday alehouse and met up with an old acquaintance from my garrison days.'

'You were late because you were gossiping in an alehouse?'

'Some of Ferrers' men were making fun of him and had to be dealt with. And then I saw Gamel safely home. He's a bone carver now, a skilled one. I bought this for you.' He placed an intricately carved comb and matching mirror case in her hand. 'I thought they were appropriate,' he said softly. 'A token of our wedding night.'

Linnet looked at his gifts, turned them over in her hands, and felt the pressure of tears at the back of her eyes. The carving on the mirror case was exquisite, depicting in miniature a man and a woman riding out with hawks and dogs. 'They are beautiful,' she said a little unsteadily. Giles had never given her anything. 'He's a member of the garrison, you said?'

'Used to be. He lost his leg in battle and had to find a different living. He has a small booth on the weekday market up near Hologate.' He smiled. 'Gamel even carves his own legs now.' Resuming his seat, he prepared to assault a dish of raisin honey-cakes. 'I've commissioned him to put the carving on two new chairs for the dais.'

Linnet was about to enquire if they could afford such luxuries, then remembered what the messenger had said about the battle at Fornham. 'Did you take many ransoms?'

He gave her a look of irritated amusement. 'Do you want me to show you a tally of the keep's accounts? I assure you I haggled a good bargain out of him – although not as good as yourself, I do admit, having seen you at work in London.'

She blushed but nevertheless held his gaze steadily. 'Well, did you?'

Joscelin sighed. 'Enough to keep Conan and his men until Easter. Enough to pay for two new chairs, a set of bridle bells for my stepson's pony and a gift for my beautiful wife.' He dusted crumbs from his fingers and finished the wine in his cup, adding a little pensively, 'And enough to repay my father for what he lent to us in the summer. He has need of coin and comfort now.' He frowned and shook his head. 'I never thought my prowess with the sword would lead me to contribute to my brothers' ransoms.'

Linnet ran her forefinger across the teeth of the comb. Although she disliked Joscelin's father, she was slowly coming to understand that his brusque arrogance was the blazon on a battered shield of pride behind which lay accumulated years of lonely pain. 'Will he find them, do you think?'

Joscelin shrugged. 'I expect so, unless they're at the bottom of a bog. The battle was chaos but we held the better ground and the spine of Leicester's army was made up of untried Flemings. Once they broke and ran, it was all over.' He pushed his hands through his hair. 'I helped my father search among the dead and the prisoners the next day but there was no sign of Ralf or Ivo. If they escaped the killing and there is any sense in their skulls, they'll try and make their way back to Norfolk's keep at Framlingham.' He turned to face her as she rose from the stool by the hearthside.

'If we have sons other than Robert, or indeed daughters, God forbid I should ever raise them the way my father raised us. I thought his face was going to crack beneath the strain of keeping it blank when we were looking at all the bodies laid out. Do you know, the only time I've ever seen him weep, the tears were made of usquebaugh.'

Linnet came to him across the dimness of firelight and wrapped her arms around him. 'You fear needlessly,' she said. 'Our sons and daughters, should God grant them to us, will know love and joy from the moment of their birth. Neither of us would have it otherwise because of what has gone before.' She stood on tiptoe to kiss the side of his mouth. 'It's very late my husband. Come to bed.'

25

Drawn by the sound of gleeful squeals, Linnet left her sewing and went to look out of the unscreened window into the area of greensward between inner and outer baileys. Joscelin and Robert were playing a chasing game, a romp of duck-and-dodge, catch-and-cuddle. Her heart filled with an ache of love that was almost too much to bear and tears prickled her eyes.

Beyond the keep walls, the forest was an ocean of gold and russet leaves tossed by a frisky wind and it was with delight that she watched the tints ruffle and surge. She had Joscelin to herself for the remains of the autumn and all the long winter. No campaigning, no dangerous separations, just time to gain fulfilling knowledge. She was not in the least dismayed by the thought of short, cold days and even colder long nights. Their chamber faced south to catch the best of the light, it had a fire and they could always pile furs upon the bed if their body heat was not enough. She smiled at the thought, warmth settling in her loins.

The sound of a throat being cleared made her jump and turn quickly round.

'I'm sorry to disturb you, madam,' said Henry from the doorway, 'but Matthew the peddler – the man you looked at last night – well, he's worse and I think Father Gregory ought to be fetched. Me mam gave him that willow-bark tisane like you told her but he just spewed it back up and his fever's greater than ever.'

'Is he so bad?' Linnet said anxiously.

'I fear so, my lady.' Henry tugged at one earlobe in a worried manner. 'When me mam looked at him there were red spots all over his chest and belly, the size of silver pieces. She reckons as it's probably spotted fever.'

'I'll come at once and yes, you had better send for Father Gregory.' She hastened to follow Henry down to the hall, her joy evaporating like morning mist.

On inspecting the sick peddler, Linnet's fears were both increased and diminished. Matthew did indeed appear to be close to death. His breathing was ragged and harsh, and the only colour on his face was provided by the two bright-red fever streaks on each cheekbone and the smudged caverns of his eye sockets. A glance at the spots Henry had mentioned, however, revealed that they were not pus-filled and angry as was usual in cases of the deadliest kind of spotted fever. If victims survived, they were nearly always left with scarred, pitted skin. These blemishes were pustule-free, more of a rash.

There was nothing to be done for him except to keep him lightly covered with a blanket, isolate him in a corner of the hall and try to make him drink brews of feverfew and willow bark to keep the fever down.

'Don't let Robert go near him,' she told Henry as she left the peddler to Father Gregory's spiritual care. 'He's plainly surrounded by evil vapours.'

Henry bit his lip and looked away. 'No, my lady,' he said.

*　　*　　*

The peddler's fever did not abate; his lungs continued to fill with fluid and he died at dawn the next morning. The words 'spotted fever' spread from mouth to mouth faster than plague itself. Women gathered herbs to burn to ward off the sickness. Rushcliffe's village wisewoman suddenly found herself inundated with worried customers. So did Father Gregory. Confessions poured into his ears by the bucket-load, quite gluing them up. Holy relics and badges competed for space on people's belts with nosegays and pomanders. Lurid stories of previous epidemics were related by sundry generations of survivors.

On the day that Matthew was buried in the church-yard, the laundress and her daughter complained of feeling ill, and by the evening of that same day, were both huddled upon their pallets with high fevers and blinding headaches. A report arrived via a pack-train from Newark that the spotted fever was raging there, too, and that several villages between the town and Rushcliffe had also been struck. The only good news was that most victims appeared to be recovering from the disease and that it was only dangerous to the old, the very young, the weak and the occasional unfortunates of whom Matthew seemed to be one.

Feeling tired and apprehensive, Linnet sent Ella away to bed and sat down on the couch in the bedchamber to finish sewing the hem of a new tunic she was making for Joscelin. He was in the antechamber talking business with Milo, Henry, Malcolm and Conan, the men who were fast becoming the nucleus of Rushcliffe's administration. Conan was present in a military capacity, being respon-sible for the garrison and patrols. Milo straddled a bridge between the duties of seneschal and steward, with Malcolm as his adjutant and Henry ensuring that all ran smoothly on a practical level.

The arrangement appeared to be working well. It was less than six months since Joscelin had taken up the reins of government but there was already a marked difference in people's attitudes. They had a sense of purpose and knew that if they took pride in their work their new lord would take pride in them and reward them accordingly.

The men left and Joscelin came into the bedchamber, arms stretched above his head to ease a stiff muscle. 'My brothers have been ransomed,' he told her. 'Apparently they were captured in the forest not far from the battlefield and held by some enterprising villagers in the apple cellar of the local alehouse.' Lowering his arms, he set them around her from behind and kissed her cheek.

'What happens now?'

'The usual,' he said and she felt his shrug before he released her and sat down on the great bed. 'They'll all snarl at each other but my father will snarl the loudest and Ralf will be forced to back down – for a while, at least. As soon as he sees my father's attention wandering, he'll up and cause mischief again and Ivo will follow him.'

Linnet yawned and, leaving her sewing, followed him to the bed. Her limbs felt heavy and she was a little cold, as if it were the time of her monthly flux, although that was not due for another week at least. Her mind upon the relationships between Joscelin, his father and his brothers, she asked, 'Why did you run away to Normandy when you were fifteen?'

He paused in the act of removing his boot. 'Because if I hadn't, either I would have killed Ralf or he would have killed me. Our father used to intervene – he put us in the dungeon once, in different cells, and left us there for three days. But that only made us hate him as well as each other. Running away was the only means of breaking the chain. When I came home, it was on my terms, not my father's, and I had outgrown Ralf.' He finished removing his boots and leaned his forearms upon his thighs. 'Ralf's still trying to break his chain but his struggles just bind him all the more tightly.'

'And if he breaks loose?' Linnet asked.

Joscelin's lips compressed. 'Then God help us all,' he said, then turned his head at a sound from the curtain that partitioned Robert's small truckle bed from theirs.

'Mama, my head hurts,' Robert whimpered, wandering into the main chamber like a little ghost. Linnet gasped and started forward, but Joscelin reached the child first and, picking him up, brought him to the bed.

'He's as hot as a furnace,' he said to Linnet, and they looked at each other in dawning horror.

'It's all right, sweetheart,' Linnet soothed, gathering his small body into her arms. 'Mama will give you something to make you better.'

Even as she spoke, Robert began to shudder with chills. 'I saw Papa, my old papa, in a dream and I was frightened.'

Linnet flickered a glance at Joscelin. 'Hush, there's nothing to worry about, dreams cannot hurt you.' She kissed her son's flushed brow. 'Sit here with Joscelin while I fetch you something to drink. It won't taste nice but it will help your poorly head.' Easing Robert back into Joscelin's arms, she left the bed and went quickly to the hearth.

Joscelin felt the rapid throb, throb of Robert's heartbeat against the fragile ribcage and heard the swift shallow breathing and knew, as he had known in the past, how terrifying it was to be helpless.

In the bleak darkness of the wet October dawn, Joscelin fitfully dozed in the box chair at the side of the great bed.

Beneath the covers, Linnet and Robert slept, the latter tossing and moaning in the grip of high fever. The rain drummed against the shutters, but in his mind the sound became the drumming of horse hooves on the hard-baked soil of a mercenary camp in the grip of burning midsummer heat. He sat astride a bay stallion, a horse past its prime with a spavined hind leg. The harness was scuffed and shabby, so was the scabbard housing his plain battle sword. With the eyes of a dreamer he looked upon his own face, seeing the burn of summer on cheekbones, nose and brow, the hard brightness of eye and the predatory leanness that showed an edge of hunger. He was very young.

A woman ran to his stirrup and looked up at him. She was slender and dark-eyed, her fine bones sharp with worry beneath lined, sallow skin. He tasted wine on his tongue and knew that he had been drinking, although he was not drunk.

Dismounting, he followed her urgings to a tent of waxed linen that bore more patches than original canvas. As he stooped through the opening, the fetid stench of fever and bowel-sickness hit him like a fist. Overwhelming love and fear drove him forward, instinct pegged him back.

The child on the pallet still breathed but he wore the face of a corpse: the dark eyes he had inherited from his mother sunken in their sockets, his mouth tinged with blue. He turned his head and looked at Joscelin. 'Papa,' he said through dry, blistered lips. The woman uttered a small, almost inaudible whimper and she, too, looked at Joscelin with dead eyes before slowly turning her back on him.

'No!' he roared and jerked awake to the sound of his own voice wrenching out a denial.

Linnet raised her head from the pillow and looked at him hazily.

'A bad dream,' he said, struggling to banish the image of Juhel's waxen face. 'How is he?'

Linnet leaned on one elbow to look at her child and set her palm against his neck. 'The willow bark has held the fever but not taken it away. He'll need another dose soon. I must try and get him to drink.' She sat up and pushed the hair out of her eyes, then pressed her hands into the small of her back.

'I'll fetch him something – apple juice from the press?' he suggested, knowing that the trees had been recently harvested and that cider brewing was under way.

'Yes.'

Joscelin hesitated, perturbed by the dull tone of her voice and unable to see her face behind the tangled screen of her hair. 'Linnet?'

She turned towards him and folded her arms across her breasts, not in modesty but in a gesture of shivering cold. 'It will be for the best if you give the apple juice to Ella and do not come back,' she said through chattering teeth. 'She has had the spotted fever before.'

Fear flashed through him like a sheet of fire and flared into terror. 'What are you saying?'

'I think you know.'

Stubborn anger joined Joscelin's other emotions. 'Then you will also know that you cannot command me to something like that.'

'Then I ask it.'

'No!' he said violently. 'You ask too much. Breaca sent me away when Juhel was dying. She said that it was a woman's domain, that I should be out earning silver to keep us in firewood. And when he died and she took sick with the bloody flux, she would not let me near her either.' His voice became ragged as old scars were torn open and became new wounds. 'Christ on the cross, I will not bear

238

it again!' Striding to the bed, he seized her in his arms and crushed his mouth down on hers in a long, hard kiss, absorbing her sweat and fever-heat.

'There!' He parted from her, gasping and darkly triumphant. 'I'm irrevocably committed now. I'll go and bring the apple juice and the willow-bark tisane and you won't gainsay me again!'

26

Left foot presented, Ralf leaned into his shield and hammered his sword-hilt lightly against the rawhide rim in a steady litany of challenge. The blade was fashioned of whalebone and his opponent was Hamo, one of his father's knights, who had agreed to a practice bout in a corner of the bailey.

All the pent-up anger and tension within Ralf came seeping to the surface. He found himself wishing that it were for real: that he could strike and see blood flow. From the perimeter of the battle circle, soldiers, knights and retainers shouted advice and encouragement. Ralf could smell their anticipation. A rapid glance upwards showed him that his mother and aunt were watching from the bower window. He would give them what they wanted, prove to them the kind of warrior he truly was. But desire for their admiration was not the spur that drove him. That particular goad was in the possession of the badger-haired man who had reined in his grey horse and, hand on hip, was watching Ralf thoughtfully.

Ralf started to circle Hamo, seeking a weakness, an

opening to exploit. He lunged. Hamo twisted and quickly parried with his shield.

'Come on, Ralf, get him!' shouted someone in the crowd. Two or three others added their voices and Ralf noted them with grim pleasure. For all that he had been in disgrace for joining Leicester's rebellion, he was still the heir. His father had pardoned him and accepted him back into the family fold. It was believed in some quarters that William Ironheart was beginning to fail and Ralf had done nothing to disabuse that notion. Only let them look to him as Ironheart's natural successor.

Hamo weaved and dodged and managed to strike the occasional good blow on Ralf's shield but the effort it cost him told in his scarlet complexion and whistling breath. Ralf remained on the balls of his feet – light, elegant and deadly.

'Get yourself out of that corner, Ham, or he'll have you!' a knight in the crowd yelled, his own sympathies with the older, heavier man.

Eyes blazing with exultation, Ralf sprang like a lion and made a triumphant killing blow. Hamo dropped sword and shield and knelt, conceding defeat. Ralf's roar of triumph rang around the bailey, raising hairs on scalps and spines. The whalebone sword lifted on high, he pivoted in a slow circle, acknowledging the adulation of the women in the window splay. Eyes hot with jubilation, he sought his father's gaze. But Ironheart's attention was not upon him. His father's back was turned and he was listening to the mercenary Conan de Gael, who had just dismounted from a foam-spattered courser and was talking rapidly.

Ralf's pleasure turned to bitter resentment. He spat over the side of his raised shield, then stalked over to his father and the mercenary.

'It is very important that you come—' Conan was saying but broke off and turned to look Ralf up and down. 'Learning to fight?' he said pleasantly.

Ralf wished that his practice sword had a true steel blade. He looked at his father but the old man's expression was so stiff with control that it might have been carved of rock. 'I already know how to fight – but if you want me to teach you a lesson?' he sneered and raised the whalebone sword suggestively.

Conan lifted his brows. He, too, glanced at Ironheart, but receiving the same stony response he shrugged his powerful shoulders. 'Why not?' he said. 'I've to wait while a fresh horse is saddled, and a man gets rusty without regular practice. Besides, it won't take long.' He went to Hamo. 'May I?' He took the whalebone sword from the knight and tested its balance.

Ralf quivered with rage at the mercenary's nonchalance. The man was near his father's age, with more scars than a raddled old tomcat. His blond hair was receding and the suggestion of a paunch bulged his quilted surcoat. It was obscene that Conan de Gael should even dare to take up the challenge.

A larger crowd was gathering now, drawn by the scent of drama. Martin pushed and wriggled his way to the forefront of the audience. Conan saw him and winked and grinned. Martin winked back and then cheekily stuck his tongue out at Ralf.

It was the final insult and Ralf attacked without warning, fast and hard. Conan was flung backwards by the flurry of blows but, after the first undignified leap, he kept Hamo's shield high to absorb the violence of Ralf's attack and played a defensive role until he had worn the edge off the younger man. Again and again Ralf came at him, full of vicious aggression, determined to make a kill. Conan parried and heard the shouts of derision from the watchers, the yells encouraging Ralf to finish him off.

'Come on, you whoreson, yield!' Ralf snarled as he pressed Conan to the edge of the circle.

Conan was panting hard and didn't reply – but the expression in his eyes was eloquent.

Ralf redoubled his efforts. Although he still moved with grace, his face was pink and streaked, and his chest was heaving rapidly. Conan watched and waited for his moment, then made a deliberate, almost clumsy feint at Ralf's legs. Ralf immediately lowered his shield to counter the intended blow, but Conan straightened and changed direction like a sudden dazzle of lightning and the blunt sword came down across the back of Ralf's unprotected neck.

'You're dead,' Conan gasped, lowering his guard and standing back.

A shocked silence descended, the onlookers not quite believing what they had seen. Ralf quivered, muscles tense to renew the attack. 'Don't make a fool of yourself,' Conan said softly out of the side of his mouth. 'Part of learning is knowing how to take defeat.'

'I don't need a lecture from vermin like you!' Ralf spat and, tossing down his sword, shoved his way out of the circle, making sure that his shoulder barged Conan's in passing.

Conan returned the whalebone sword and the shield to Hamo and watched Ralf stride towards the hall with thoughtful eyes. The spectators started to disperse.

'He let his hatred cloud his senses,' Conan said to Ironheart. 'Otherwise he's an accomplished young man.'

'You didn't exactly encourage him to be rational,' William answered as his courser was led out and a fresh horse was brought for the mercenary.

Conan set his foot in the stirrup. 'Neither would an enemy,' he retorted. 'He's wound up as tight as the pulley on a siege engine. Just make sure that when he lets fly you aren't standing in the way.'

Ironheart grunted. 'I don't need your advice on how to handle my own son. Ralf doesn't like you and I don't blame him.'

Conan sighed deeply. There was still a wide rift between himself and William de Rocher and he didn't think that, despite praying together at Morwenna's tomb, it was ever going to narrow beyond a brusque truce.

Ironheart glowered at him. 'Anyway,' he said shortly, 'why send for me? What makes you think I am going to be of any comfort to Joscelin?'

'If the woman and child die, he will need you. You have known the grief. I do not want to see him ruined as you and I were ruined. I've always had the lad's best interests at heart, whatever you think of me. He is my kin and the de Gaels were not always mercenaries and ne'er-do-wells. My grandfather had lands and a proud bloodline but he was brought low by taking the wrong side in a dispute. I want Joscelin to succeed. I want him to have a better life than either you or I have had.' Conan paused and sucked a breath through his teeth, his complexion dusky with high feeling. 'I have said more than I should but this is not the time for holding back.'

They rode out of the keep in silence: a normal state for William but not for Conan, who was usually as brash as a jay.

'The woman and child are mortally sick, then?' William asked after a long time.

'I do not know,' Conan said wearily. 'As few people as possible are going near them lest they breathe in the evil vapours – Lady Linnet's instructions. I only know that

244

Joscelin has scarcely eaten or slept since they took ill, and this morning he sent for Father Gregory.'

'Does he know you have come to fetch me?'

Conan shook his head. 'I do not think he knows anything but the mortal peril of his wife and stepson.'

William compressed his lips. 'He's only been wed to the wench since harvest time,' he growled. 'You're not telling me he's heartsick beyond all healing?' And, without waiting for Conan's contradiction, he rode on ahead, making it clear to the other man that he did not wish to communicate at all.

Joscelin eyed the congealing bowl of pottage that Stephen had brought to the bedchamber half an hour since. Small circles of fat were forming at the edges, encrusting the pieces of diced vegetables sticking out of the liquid. His stomach, normally robust enough to accept any form of sustenance without demur, clenched and recoiled. He abandoned the bowl on the hearthstones, an untouched loaf beside it, and reached for the flagon of wine that Stephen had brought with the meal. That at least he could swallow without retching.

With dragging feet he returned to the bed and sat down in the box chair that had become his prison and his prop during two lonely nights of vigil, or was it three? Time had lost all meaning as he watched the contagion invade and consume.

Father Gregory had visited mother and child, and used the opportunity to shrive them. A precaution and a comfort, he had said, but it had been no reassurance to Joscelin. To shrive them was to acknowledge that they might not recover.

His eyes felt raw with lack of sleep but he knew that if he closed them, if he relaxed his vigil for one moment,

245

death would come with swift stealth and take Robert and Linnet from him as it had taken Juhel. And even if death did stay away, he knew the dreams would not.

He stared at them both sleeping together in the great bed. Perhaps Robert was breathing more easily since the last dose of feverfew or perhaps it was just the fancy of his aching mind. Linnet tossed and moaned, her hair darkly damp, her face and throat marked with the red blotches of the fever. She pushed at the covers and began to mutter. Her body arched and bucked and she licked her dry, pale lips.

Joscelin leaned over her, grasping her hot hand in his, stroking her forehead.

Her glazed eyes flew open and she stared directly at him, but he knew she could not see him. 'Raymond,' she panted. 'Raymond, someone will come, please don't.'

'It's all right, Raymond's not here,' he soothed and turned briefly away to wring out a cloth in cold water and then lay it across her brow. 'You are but dreaming.'

'No.' She frowned, weakly fighting him. 'Not a dream.' Her body moved beneath the damp linen sheet, arching sinuously as if receiving a lover. 'No, please, it is too dangerous. I . . . ah!' A spasm caught her, leaving him in no doubt that her imaginary lover had entered her body. Prickles of cold shivered down Joscelin's spine. His gut churned as she twisted and cried out, for the sounds, despite the torment of fever, were of pleasure, not pain. Raymond de Montsorrel. He was being cuckolded by a phantom in his own bed.

'Linnet, in God's name, he's dead!' Joscelin cried, striving to hold her thrashing body. 'Christ, wake up!'

She fought him, her muscles rigid, her lips drawn back from her teeth in something that was part snarl, part sob, then she gasped and went limp.

246

Almost weeping himself, Joscelin slowly released her. 'Oh God,' he said, and put his head in his hands.

'It will be safer if you let me pleasure you in the other way,' she said in a hoarse, pleading whisper, her gaze darting upon the ceiling as if she could see moving pictures there. 'If Giles were to find out, he'd kill us both. I know you like it when I do this.'

The urge to crush his hand over her mouth and silence her almost overpowered him. He sprang to his feet and strode into the antechamber while he still retained the control to do so. Pressing his temple against the cold stone wall, he fought his gorge. He remembered the bawdy barrack-room gossip in Nottingham. Raymond de Montsorrel's appetite for sexual congress had been legend. The man himself had been nothing to look upon – balding, raddle-featured and with bowed legs from a life spent in the saddle – but that had never spoiled his attraction as far as women were concerned. His talents were all tucked inside his braies, so the gossip went. One of the garrison whores had boasted that Montsorrel had taken her up against the wall of St Mary's Church on Ascension Day and that the size of his manhood would have put a bull to shame. And Linnet had let him— Joscelin ground his fist against the wall, not feeling the pain, and tried to think with his head, not his lurching gut.

It was no different from himself and Breaca, he told his recoiling instincts. She had been twice his age, amused and experienced in the ways of lust, and he had had no sense of guilt or sin at the time. He had no right to cast stones but he was deeply chagrined to find them lying at his feet anyway. Filled with self-disgust, he turned round to go back to the bed and saw his father standing in the doorway.

247

'Conan told me,' Ironheart said and stepped over the threshold. 'For once he was right to open his stupid big mouth. Stand aside and stop glowering. Where are they − through here?'

Joscelin nodded. His head felt muzzy and he knew one of his incapacitating headaches was waiting on the periphery to attack. Damn Conan, he thought, and at the same time felt a tight swelling of relief in his throat and behind his eyes. Unsteadily he followed his father into the bedchamber.

Ironheart stood at the bedside. Joscelin heard the low mutter of Linnet's voice.

'What is she saying?' He hastened to his father's side, alarmed at what she might reveal in front of him.

Ironheart looked sidelong at Joscelin, his eyes bright with speculation. 'That you cannot lie with her any more because she is with child.'

'What?'

'Is it true?'

'I . . . I don't know. She didn't say anything before the fever struck.' Joscelin sat down on the chair at the bedside and clasped his hands. 'It is too soon, I think, and there have been very few opportunities.' How many opportunities had there been with Raymond de Montsorrel? His eyes flickered to the little boy. The fever flush had faded from his brow and he appeared to be sleeping deeply and calmly. He resembled his mother, scarcely any Montsorrel traits to be seen lest it be in the slant of cheekbone and jaw. Did it really matter which Montsorrel? An exquisite pain was beginning to throb through his skull, making rational thought impossible. Behind his closed lids, small specks of colour performed a wayward dance and he groaned softly.

'You need to sleep,' Ironheart said, giving him a sharp

look. 'There is nothing you can do that a maidservant cannot. Go to.'

Joscelin was horrified. The thought of what Linnet might gasp out to a maid or his father in her fever was enough to make him shake his head in vehement denial. And there was the memory of how he had lost Juhel and Breaca, one in the flesh, the other in spirit. 'I cannot!' he said hoarsely.

'You must.' Ironheart laid his hand on Joscelin's shoulder and stared him in the eye. 'I do not know how loyal your men are but, if necessary, I will give the order for you to be taken and bound. Milo and Conan for certain will not hesitate.'

'You would not dare!' Nauseous with exhaustion and pain, Joscelin returned his father's glare. For reply, Ironheart removed his hand from Joscelin's shoulder and headed towards the door, his breath indrawn to bellow.

'For Jesu's sake, you do not understand!' Joscelin cried after him, his voice breaking. The effort of forcing his shout through the tightness in his throat squeezed the band of pain across his forehead until he thought his skull was going to shatter. 'I had a woman and child once before and I lost them. I wasn't there when it mattered!'

Ironheart winced as if the raw anguish in Joscelin's voice was a physical blow. Turning, he took two paces back towards his son, then stopped. His fists opened and closed and his throat worked. When the words came they were heaved out with effort as if they were enormous stones. 'I wasn't there to protect your mother,' he said. 'When I arrived from their summons she was dead but still warm enough for me to believe she was yet alive – only sleeping.' He gave a choked laugh. 'They said I tried to kill myself for love of her but it wasn't true. It was for hatred of myself.' Clamping his hands around his belt,

249

he drew a shaken breath. 'The woman and child you mentioned, this happened during those missing seven years?'

Joscelin nodded, his pain too great for him to be amazed that his father had voluntarily spoken of his own hidden guilts and griefs. 'Breaca took me under her wing and then into her bed. She bore Juhel in the winter of 'sixty-one. Your grandson would have been twelve years old by now.'

'What happened?'

'Camp fever.' Joscelin bit his lip. 'He wasn't strong enough to survive it. When he died, so did the fire between his mother and me – or perhaps it was already out. I don't want to lose Linnet and Robert, too.' He bowed his head and closed his eyes. Even the candlelight was almost too much to bear as the headache invaded and wrecked his faculties.

'You won't lose them,' Ironheart said gruffly. 'The child looks to be over the worst, from what I saw just now, and the woman's got a stubborn core of steel.'

'No, I'm going to lose her, too,' Joscelin said bleakly. 'Everything has changed.'

'Don't talk such drivel. All that has changed is your ability to think.' Ironheart's harsh features suddenly softened and he gave a deep sigh. 'Conan thought I'd dredge up some wise words from somewhere to comfort you but I fear he overestimated my ability. All I can say is that I am here. You have to trust me. Give me the care of your wife and stepson for tonight and I promise I won't let anything happen.'

Joscelin wanted to deny his father, tell him it was impossible, but the pain that had been toying with him like a cat with a mouse now sheathed its claws in his skull and the world became a seething agony. He was only dimly aware that the words emerging from his mouth were not the ones he desired to say.

Ironheart went to the door and shouted for the servants.

Linnet felt something lying on top of her. Hot and smothering, it pinned her to the mattress, making it impossible to breathe. She struggled to push it off but it responded by tightening its grip. She thought she could feel cruel fingers digging into her flesh and the bowl of her pelvis cramped as if she had been invaded. Choking for air, she opened her eyes and at first saw only the darkness of the night illuminated by the one lonely flame of the night candle beside the bed. She could make out the figure of a man sitting in the chair. He started to rise and bend towards her, and as he did the weight on her chest grew leaden.

'Don't fight me,' whispered the voice of Raymond de Montsorrel. 'You cannot win.'

She tried to scream but there was no breath in her lungs. A whirling darkness engulfed her. Her eyes were blind but she could still hear voices. Raymond whispering in her ear with the darkness of lust, Giles raging, calling her a harlot. Joscelin . . . Joscelin saying, Christ, wake up, I don't want to listen to this. Another voice, closer, harder with frustration.

'Come on, woman, damn you. Fight. Or was I wrong about your spirit? Do you think I'm going to let you do this to my son? You will not die!'

The other voices faded and the darkness ceased to whirl. Her lungs shuddered, filling with cold air. Making a tremendous effort, she forced her lids apart. The figure was leaning over her now, eyes darkly gleaming in the candlelight, cadaverous features intense but very different from Raymond's. William de Rocher laid a calloused palm

251

on her brow in a surprisingly gentle manner. She tried to flinch but her weakness was too great. Indeed, her eyelids were too heavy to hold open, and after a brief struggle she had to let them flicker down.

'Hmph, still hot,' she heard Ironheart say, 'but steadying down. You, girl, see to your mistress.'

'Yes, sir.'

Linnet heard the trickle of water in a bowl, and in a moment a blessedly cool cloth was laid across her forehead. The bedside chair creaked as Ironheart sat down again. Why was he here? she wondered vaguely, and where were Joscelin and Robert? It was too difficult to think. Sleep was claiming her in a soft, deep blanket and she welcomed its embrace.

Ironheart watched Linnet sink into sleep as the maid lightly wiped her down. Dawn was still several hours away, late because of the encroaching winter, but he judged that the crisis had been reached and perhaps a corner turned.

After a while, as Linnet continued to breathe deeply and evenly without impediment, he left the maid in attendance and went stiffly into the antechamber, where Joscelin was sleeping with Robert on a makeshift pallet. The child was visibly improving. Probably by the morning he would be complaining he was hungry. Thin and small though he was, sapped to pallor and shadows, he also possessed the tenacity of a clinging vine.

Ironheart turned his attention to the man against whom Robert was curled. Even in sleep, the marks of pain were etched between Joscelin's dark brows. He remembered his son's earlier words. A woman and child in the mercenary camps. The thought, which had been held on the surface by other considerations, now began to seep into every level of his being. Ironheart stooped

252

to the hearth to pick up the flagon of usquebaugh-laden wine. Seven missing years in which, unaware, he had become a grandfather and then been bereaved. Joscelin was so much like him that he wondered if his bloodline was cursed.

27

Christmas, 1173

An inflated pig's bladder sailed through the air and struck the dais with a solid thump, dislodging a branch of evergreen and a pair of antlers pegging the foliage in place. The bladder bounced off the decorations and squelched into a dish of tripe on one of the lower tables. A diner fished it out and hurled it back the way it had come. Blazing a comet-trail of sticky lumps, the bladder curved across the dais and landed on the floor at Father Gregory's feet. A look of intense revulsion on his fine-cut features, the priest nudged the improvised ball away with the edge of his boot.

With considerably more enthusiasm, a gazehound surged from beneath the table to lick at the remnants of tripe still clinging to the bladder. When a servant approached with the intention of rescuing the missile, the dog wrinkled its muzzle and snarled, then secured the bladder firmly between its forepaws and bit at the knotted end. There was a bang. The remnants of the football shot into the air and landed on the dog's back. Ears flat, the hound scooted beneath the table and knocked Father Gregory off the bench.

Conan leaned down, flexed his forearm and hauled the unfortunate priest back on to his seat to howls of mirth and appreciation from the unruly crowd below the dais.

'Church always does take a tumble on Twelfth Night!' Conan laughed. 'Never fear, you've got all year to take your revenge in tithe payments, Peter's pence and penances. Isn't that right, Josce?'

'If you say so.' Joscelin, resplendent in a tunic of dark-red wool trimmed with gold silk braid, toasted his uncle in mead. The garment was a Christmas gift from Linnet. Robert had one exactly the same and could not be persuaded to wear anything else.

Conan made a rude face at Joscelin's indifferent tone of voice. 'God, you're getting to be as sour as your father!' he declared. 'Where's your Twelfth Night spirit?'

'Wearing thin,' Joscelin said as one of the cook's apprentices capered past the dais wearing a woman's gown, a wimple set askew on his yellow curls. Twelfth Night was never any different: short of murder, everyone was given licence to behave outrageously and the rules were always stretched to their limit. Usually Joscelin would have joined the merriment, if not with alacrity, then with a reasonable degree of grace, but tonight, although he knew he should be rejoicing, he did not have the will. The residue of yet another headache burned behind his eyes.

There had been no real peace since October's end – since Linnet had almost died of the spotted fever and shown him in her delirium what he did not wish to see. And she had no recollection of her illness beyond the first day of fever, did not know what she had said and what had changed. He had tried to behave in a normal manner while he battled his demons but, from the bewildered, almost hurt way she looked at him sometimes, he knew he was failing.

'Oh, come on, Josce! Don't be . . . don't be so miserable!' Conan's words were starting to slur under the powerful influence of the Welsh mead that Brien FitzRenard had sent to them as a Christmas gift in thanks for Joscelin's aid earlier in the year. 'Let's . . . let's have a game of hoodman-blind!' He pushed himself to his feet, took a step backward and then steadied himself. 'I'll wear the blindfold first, if you want. Henry, lend me your hood!'

Joscelin opened his mouth to say that he did not wish to play hoodman-blind, or any other boisterous, stupid game that his uncle had in mind, but the good humour surrounding him and the look of bright anticipation on Robert's face made him close it again and yield to Conan's jovial bullying.

A space was cleared in the well of the hall. Conan, blindfolded by Henry's hood, which he had donned back-to-front, was placed in the centre of the space, spun round several times to disorient him, then given a vigorous push. The object of the game was for the hoodman to try to capture someone to take his place, and for the others to poke and prod and tease him without being caught themselves.

Conan made several wild, bear-like swipes and embraced only thin air. He growled like a bear, too. Giggling, Robert ran in beneath the mercenary's clutching arms and struck him on the leg. Conan lunged, Robert evaded him and, shrieking with glee, ran to the safety of Joscelin's arms.

'Papa, did you see?'

Conan struck rapidly towards the sound of the child's excited voice. Joscelin spun Robert out of the way. Conan's fingertips touched the soft red wool of Joscelin's sleeve. Joscelin twisted sideways, grabbed hold of a laughing Milo and flung him straight into Conan's path. The mercenary's arms closed on his prey. Now all he had to do was guess whom he had caught.

'Not a wench,' Conan muttered, spreading his hand across the bearded face. 'Not unless she's standing on her head.'

'You'd be surprised what a wench will do on Twelfth Night, Sir Conan,' Milo said, affecting a falsetto voice that had an appreciative audience doubled up with laughter.

'Reckon I would. In fact, I'd be downright buggered!' Conan retorted, feeling lower across shoulders and chest until his fingers happened upon the ornate silver-gilt cross that Milo wore on a cord around his neck. 'I'd know this anywhere. It's bigger than anything Father Gregory's got! Has to be you, Milo de Selsey!' He pulled off the hood and gave a hoot of triumph.

The game progressed, becoming more boisterous. People swapped clothing to confuse the hoodman, although when Robert was captured by Henry and had to wear the hood, everyone gentled their performance and Joscelin allowed Robert to catch him, although not too quickly, for the sake of the child's pride.

As the hood was secured around his head, Joscelin discovered that he was actually enjoying the sport. It was like the tourney field where all thought was bent upon controlling the body in order to survive and no space was left for introversion and brooding.

'Now then.' He rubbed his hands, entering the bawdy spirit of the game. 'To catch me a coney!'

He felt a push low on his leg and heard Robert's squeal. The hood smelled of wool and sheep oil and very effectively blocked out the light from the sconces and candles. He tried to blot out the calls and countercalls, the disguised

257

voices. He ignored the pushes and buffets and gave his instinct free rein. He began to turn towards the nudges and blows before they were made; he began to know whose voice it was on the first word.

Twice he almost captured Milo, then Henry. He deliberately missed Robert, who spun away, shrieking with glee. Conan was very nearly his victim and only escaped by sheer brute strength. Joscelin staggered, unbalanced. A softness brushed against him, and a hint of summer herbs and rose petals invaded the smell of wool. Turning quickly, he grabbed and pulled, and suddenly there was a slender body in his arms and the summer scent was much stronger. Before he could begin a litany of bawdy suggestions and guesses, his victim snatched off the hood and stood on tiptoe to kiss him on the lips.

The audience cheered and whistled. Robert screwed up his face. Linnet and Joscelin looked at each other with a mutual combination of merriment and sparking lust, and kissed again.

Flushed, laughing, a little giddy with the mead she had drunk, Linnet hung against Joscelin, returning him kiss for kiss, then flopped onto their bed, her eyes soft with desire, with wanting, and the hope that tonight had broken the mould of the past two months.

Ever since she had almost died of the spotted fever, Joscelin had been different; not towards Robert – he still doted on the little boy. If anything, the bond between man and child had deepened; the change was in Joscelin's attitude to her. He treated her with the caution that had characterized the days in London when he had been a mercenary with a reluctant duty to perform and she had been a lady of high birth beyond his reach. Now and then she would find him looking at her, his expression

258

one of frowning, almost angry bewilderment but, when she asked him what was wrong, he would shake his head and smile and pretend that he had not been brooding. She had learned not to push the point.

But now he was neither brooding nor remote and his eyes were bright with laughter and desire. Whatever was troubling him had been banished for the moment and she intended it to remain that way. Reaching up, she unpinned her wimple and shook free her braids, then leaned forward, letting him inhale their herbal scent while their lips met and parted, met and parted. He buried his hands in her hair.

Below in the hall, where the yule celebrations still continued, the revellers danced to pagan tunes that wore only the barest dressing of Christian decency.

Naked, Linnet pressed herself against Joscelin, offering him her breasts, the willow slenderness of waist and flank. She parted her thighs and arched herself to welcome him, her eyes bright with anticipation. The pause extended and anticipation became impatience. A cold draught whispered between their bodies. Joscelin muttered a soft oath and, lifting himself off her, rolled on to his back.

She stared at him in worried astonishment. 'What's the matter?' Her gaze darted over him. He had been urgent and eager a moment ago but was rapidly becoming flaccid. The look on his face told her that he was well aware of the fact and was not best pleased.

'Nothing,' he said stiffly and moved to cover himself with the sheet. 'I'm tired and I've drunk too much mead.'

Linnet did not for one moment believe that the effects of drink and exhaustion had suddenly attacked him at the crucial moment. She tried to look into his eyes but he avoided the contact and stared silently up at the rafters.

Her body clenched with pain. 'Is it something I have

done or not done?' she asked, her throat tight. 'In God's name, tell me. I would rather you took your belt to me than treat me like this!'

The silence dragged out for so long that she thought he was not going to respond, that whatever was troubling him had eaten so deeply inwards that he was unable to bring it to the surface, but at last he turned his head on the pillow and opened his eyes. 'Raymond de Montsorrel,' he said wearily. 'In this very room, on this very bed.'

Linnet gasped as if he had indeed struck her. Her stomach heaved. 'Who told you?' she asked weakly.

'Who else knows, you mean? I assume it's a well-kept secret since I've heard no rumours within the keep itself.' His eyelids tensed with pain. 'You told me yourself while you were wild with fever. No, that's wrong,' he amended grimly, 'you acted out a scene before my eyes, begging him not to with your voice but wantonly offering your body at the same time. And then you said it was really too dangerous and suggested you satisfy him by other means, which you didn't specify but I could well guess at.'

Linnet gave a soft cry. She felt sick and anguished but even so there was relief – as at the bursting of a deep abscess. 'I thought it was finished – buried,' she said, her whole frame shuddering. 'If I could undo it, I swear I would.'

'So it is true?' His jaw clenched. 'I would have asked you before, but while I was ignorant at least I could cling to the hope that it was a delusion of your fever.'

'Yes, I lay with him.' Her breath caught on a sob. 'He was so kind compared to Giles. I – I thought he really cared for me but all he wanted to do was prove to Giles that he could better him in everything, that he could even have his wife just for the crooking of his little finger.'

Joscelin's nostrils flared. 'You lay with him because he was kind to you?'

Linnet swallowed. 'Yes. I mean, no – I don't really remember.' Panic surged through her as she saw the disgust flicker across Joscelin's face. This was horrible: far worse than the beatings she had endured at Giles's hands. 'Giles was away,' she said. 'Probably jousting in France. I don't remember the reason, only that he was not at Rushcliffe. Raymond was good to me, spent time with me and did not shout or become impatient. How was I to know he was baiting his trap? I was little more than a child. One evening he came to my chamber to talk about a feast he was planning for when Giles came home, so he said.' She paused to shudder. 'He brought a flagon of wine with him – not the ordinary household stuff, but something stronger and mixed with spices. I can still taste it now.' She heaved and almost retched. 'By the time I realized what he was about, it was too late and I was incapable of stopping him, nor did I wish to, God help me.

'When I woke in the morning he was not there beside me, but I knew what we had done.' Shivering, she risked a glance at Joscelin's face but his expression was as unreadable as stone. 'I had the maids prepare a tub and almost scrubbed my skin off, but it didn't do any good. I dared not confess my sin to Father Gregory, so I kept it to myself.' She rose from the bed and, pulling on her bedrobe, began to pace the room as if it were a cage. She rubbed her palms together and felt cold sweat between them. She would far rather have faced physical torture than have to reveal this shame to Joscelin. 'Raymond said if I didn't let him have his will whenever he wanted, he would tell Giles about what had happened in his absence and I knew that if he found out, Giles would kill me.'

A grimace crossed Joscelin's face. 'How long did you endure this?'

'A little over a year – until my pregnancy started to show. He left me alone then. Corbette's daughter Helwis was becoming a woman and he had started to notice. He had a new innocence to corrupt then.'

The question, unspoken, loomed between them. 'I am almost certain that Robert is Giles's,' she said. 'Raymond was away much of the month when I conceived, and the times he did pester me I managed to persuade him that other ways could be just as rewarding.'

Joscelin grimaced again.

'I was trapped, don't you understand!' she cried, rounding on him in frustration. 'If it had not been a mortal sin, I would have thrown myself off the battlements! How dare you sit there and judge me when you know nothing of what I suffered because I was helpless. How dare you!'

He shook his head. 'I know you were Raymond de Montsorrel's victim. The lack is within me. I keep seeing you with the vile lecher. I tell myself it doesn't matter, the past should be buried. I don't have to look further than my own father for proof of that.'

Linnet bowed her head. 'Then where do we go from here, if you loathe me,' she said, her voice cracking.

Joscelin's heart wrenched as she began to weep. Unable to bear the anguish – his or hers – he pulled her against him and enfolded her in his arms. He could not tell her that it did not matter – it did. He was as susceptible as Giles to the torments of jealousy, suspicion and pride. But holding her now, he vowed that they were not going to ruin his life or Linnet's. 'No,' he said. 'I love you and that's why it hurts. My heart was lost that first day on the road when you faced down Giles and myself for the sake of your child and I saw your courage.' His lips tightened with determination. 'I'll be damned if Raymond de Montsorrel is going to defeat us from beyond the grave. Tomorrow I'll burn this bed and all that has gone before and commission a new one that will be ours alone.'

Linnet raised her tear-streaked face, and upon it he saw the mingling of desperate hope and abject doubt.

'For tonight you can sleep like a true mercenary's woman,' he added, 'on skins by the fire.' Without more ado, he tugged the fur coverlet from the bed and his cloak from his clothing pole. Catching her hand in his, he pulled her to the banked hearth. It was the work of a moment to spread his cloak upon the floor, lay her down upon it and cover them both with the coney-skin canopy.

She pressed against him, seeking reassurance and comfort. He curved his arm around her waist. The warmth of her breath fluttered at his throat. Beneath his hand, her skin was like silk and he felt the welcome renewed stir of desire. He blotted Raymond de Montsorrel from his mind by thinking of a summer night beneath the stars, of the champing of destriers at the horse lines and the mournful sound of a soldier's bone flute. His hands moved in slow tandem with his thoughts. Linnet's breath quickened but she remained very still. He could feel her tension, the inner coiling of her body in response to his touch. He parted her thighs, kneeling up as he entered her, teasing her with his thumb until her reticence was broken and, arching, she cried out. Her pleasure became his and, with a soft groan, he thrust fully home, claiming her for ever from Raymond de Montsorrel.

28

Raising his head, the buck sifted the wind, ears and eyes alert, jaws moving rhythmically on a mouthful of birch bark strips. Something had disturbed the deep forest but he was unsure yet as to what it was and whether it was dangerous. His breath vaporized in the frozen February air and beneath his dainty cloven hooves the ground wore a dusting of snow. Tiny flakes, needle-sharp, fell from a flat blanket of grey cloud, making it difficult for the buck to absorb any scent. He remained nervous, facing the east where the light was brightest and from which direction he sensed the disturbance came. The other bucks in the herd had stopped eating too and were staring eastwards with flickering ears and switching scuts. Faint but clear and true on the breeze, threading through the particles of snow, the buck heard the call of a hunting horn and scented the rank, terrifying odour of dogs and men. Within seconds, the clearing was empty as the deer bounded into Sherwood's dark heart, but their spoor remained and the snow was falling too softly to cover it.

*   *   *

Chest heaving with the exertion of the chase, eyes bright with the lust of having witnessed the death of the magnificent buck, it took Ralf a moment to realize he was being addressed by Robert Ferrers, Earl of Derby.

'I'm sorry, my lord, I was still caught up in the chase.'

'So I see,' Ferrers said with amusement. 'I asked how your lord father was these days.'

'He is well, sire,' Ralf answered, suddenly on his guard. Robert Ferrers was not the kind who made small talk with relative strangers who were only here on the hunt because they happened to be friends with one of his knights.

Ferrers nodded and toyed with a loose thread on his saddle cloth. 'He seems to have emerged from last year's troubles gilded with honour.'

Ralf shot Ferrers a puzzled look, wondering whether he was being baited or courted here.

The kennel keepers were whipping the dogs to heel and two bearers were tying the buck upside down to a carrying pole. 'Ride with me awhile,' Ferrers commanded, and reined his horse out of the ring of trees where they had brought the stag to bay. The snow had all been trampled away, leaving churned soil and bloody leaf mould. When his squires made to follow, he gestured them to stay back.

The forest closed around them, the light a luminous grey filled with small, stinging barbs of ice. The heat of the chase began to seep from Ralf's veins, leaving him aware of the numbing cold. Weather like this always cursed the borders of spring.

Ferrers regarded him with pursed lips. 'You and Sir William are reconciled, so I am led to believe?'

'Yes, my lord,' Ralf said warily.

'And your half-brother, the one who married into such good fortune, are you and he on speaking terms?'

Ralf swallowed. Beneath him his horse paced smoothly, hoofbeats thud-thudding like his heart. 'I haven't seen him since we met in London last summer.'

Robert Ferrers grunted. 'It is a pity your father did not try to obtain Linnet de Montsorrel for you instead of him,' he said, watching Ralf closely. 'I would have thought it was the natural thing to do, you being the heir.'

Ralf said nothing. He might hate Joscelin and feel scalding resentment for the way their father favoured his precious bastard over his legitimate sons, but his rebellion had taught him caution. Hearts and hatreds were not to be worn on the sleeve, and he could play as cagey a game as Ferrers.

'Perhaps your father has a wife in mind for you, also?'

'I do not know, my lord.' Good God, was he going to be offered a wife of Ferrers's blood? His gut churned.

Ferrers sighed down his thin, sharp nose. The snow was falling with determination now, the flakes penny-sized and dry, the kind that would settle and remain on the ground for weeks unless it thawed. 'I can understand your suspicion,' he said. 'I suppose being locked in an apple cellar for two days and nights by a horde of ignorant peasants must have knocked some of the stuffing out of you, but there is no need to be on tenterhooks with me.'

There was every need, Ralf thought, but his curiosity must have shown on his face because Ferrers smiled and leaned intimately across his saddle. 'The winter truces end soon. Robert of Leicester might be in prison but he was only one wave on a flood tide. What will King Henry do when France, Flanders and Scotland take up arms against him in the spring? What was won can soon be lost.'

Ralf looked into the gleaming, predatory eyes. *What was won can soon be lost?* He looked over his shoulder. Men were riding along the path behind them, fellow guests, equerries, beaters and foresters, keeping their distance but obviously concerned by the increasing heaviness of the snow. 'What do you want of me, my lord?'

Ferrers smoothed the corners of his mouth between forefinger and thumb. 'I believe we might be useful to each other in the future. Running to my banner as you ran to Leicester's would be downright foolish and a waste of time to us both but if you were lord of Arnsby, matters might be different.'

Ralf's voice was suddenly hoarse. 'You mean if my father were to die?' What was Ferrers suggesting? In his mind's eye he saw a vision of himself waiting in a dark stairwell with a dagger in his hand or tipping a vial of poison into a flagon of wine.

Ferrers saw him baulk and laid a hand quickly on his sleeve. 'In the fullness of time, of course,' he soothed, but his eyes told a different story.

Ralf looked at Ferrers, both drawn and repelled by what he was intimating. It was like the times he had committed rape: the excitement of the struggle, the subjugation, the final tremendous thrust and then the revulsion and self-disgust.

'We'll talk again later,' Ferrers said, and turned his horse around to join his companions. Ralf sat where he was until the bearers came past him with the body of the deer. Snow fell, making new spots on its fallow hide, and was melted away by the residual body heat. Blood dripped in slow, black clots from its muzzle and stained the forest floor. Ralf gasped and spurred away from the sight of death to join his fellow huntsmen, seeking their company, their loud, trivial banter, to take the darkness from his mind.

* * *

'A nunnery!' Agnes said furiously to Ralf. 'I'll see him in hell first!' Her tone was pitched low, making the hatred with which it smouldered all the more intense. Her maid, who had become accustomed to the low muttering these past few days, did not respond to it except to make herself as inconspicuous as possible.

Agnes left the window splay where she had been sitting to watch William and his entourage ride away in the direction of the Nottingham road. 'He cannot force me. I'll not be put aside like a worn-out rag.' She faced her son, who was in her chamber to be fitted for a new tunic. He was standing somewhat impatiently for the seamstress, who was taking note of his measurements by making knots in lengths of string.

'No, Mama,' Ralf said, a glazed look in his eye, and stretched his arm horizontally to be measured from armpit to wrist.

Agnes regarded his broad, handsome strength and the gleam of light on his red-gold hair. William wanted to obtain a wife for Ralf and was looking around for a suitable girl. Agnes feared that she understood his reasoning. Martin would soon be squiring in Richard de Luci's household and her nest would be empty of chicks. She was of no more use to him. He would replace her in the household with Ralf's young wife. Jealousy and fear gnawed at her. If she were placed in a nunnery, she would not be able to keep an eye on the girl – as she had kept an eye on Morwenna.

With an irritated sound, she grabbed the string from the seamstress and waved her away. 'I'll do it myself!' she snapped. 'Go and look in the coffers to see what fabric we have.'

'Yes, madam.' The woman curtseyed, her eyes downcast.

Agnes moved in closer to Ralf's pungent, masculine warmth. She knew he had been out in the village last night, gaming in the alehouse and wenching. A residue of his indulgences still lingered in his pores. 'You would not put me away in a nunnery if you were master here, would you?' she wheedled.

His nostrils flared. 'Of course not, Mama!'

Agnes smiled and kissed his cheek, feeling the prickle of beard stubble under her lips where once his skin had been smooth like a petal. 'I knew you would say that, you're a good son.'

A slight shudder ran through him. At first, dismayed, she thought it was because she had touched him but then he said abruptly, 'Nottingham is going to be ravaged by Robert Ferrers.'

Her hands fumbled with the string and she stared up at him, a red flush creeping from her throat into her face. 'When?'

Ralf shrugged. 'Today, tomorrow, the day after. I don't know exactly but it will be while my father is there. One of Ferrers' own men brought me a warning last night. That's why I went to the alehouse. I've been in contact with the rebels since I went to Ferrers' Candlemas hunt. They are going to raze the town and, if all goes well, take the castle.' He folded his arms and leaned against a decorated stone pillar, his eyes golden with hunger. 'There is an understanding that were I suddenly to become master of Arnsby, there would be a handsome reward for the person who put me in that position.'

Agnes's wits were dull, but she possessed an innate craftiness and it did not take a scholar to unravel what Ralf was implying. 'You've employed someone to kill your father?' she whispered with a mingling of fear and exultation.

'It's more of an unspoken understanding. If I had wanted, I could have stopped him from riding out just now but why should I?' He gave her a moody stare. 'He has never taken the time to stop for me lest it be to bawl his disapproval. Arnsby is mine now, every stick and stone and beast in the field.' He ran a possessive hand over the blood-red chevrons decorating the pillar.

Agnes bit her lip and ran the knotted string through her fingers. 'What if your father returns unharmed?'

'Who's to know? Will you tell him?'

'What reason would I have after the way he has treated me all these years? You have my support and always will. One thing I will say to you: do not mention this to Ivo. He is a weak reed and not to be trusted.'

'I can deal with Ivo,' he said softly.

'What about the bastard and his wife?' she asked after a moment. 'I heard William say that he was meeting them in Nottingham?'

Ralf's mouth twisted in a dark smile. 'I also let it be known that the custodian of Rushcliffe is a thorn in my side that I would pay handsomely to have plucked out. The woman and child won't be harmed,' he added magnanimously. 'I've no grudge against them. They will make valuable pawns since I will be kin to the deceased with an interest in what happens to the lands.'

Agnes had never heard him speak like this before, in so controlled and calculating a manner. She did not doubt that he would deal with Ivo, and anyone else who stood in his way, and her admiration for him increased a hundred fold. He would prove a worthy lord for Arnsby, far more so than the father he was intending to usurp.

29

William Ironheart owned three houses in Nottingham on the hill that meandered down from the Derby road towards the merchant dwellings on Long Row and the poultry market. Two of the houses were leased to wine merchants. The third, his own, was maintained by Jonas and Gytha, a couple in late middle-age. While Jonas kept the house in repair, Gytha took in laundry from the merchants farther down the row and there was often a tub full of linens and steaming lye suds in the backyard.

From the doorway, Linnet watched the pungent steam billowing skyward and felt queasy. Inside the house it was no better, the air being humid with the odour of boiled cabbages and onions from the cauldron that bubbled over the fire pit in the main room. These last three days her stomach had been unsettled. Indeed, only this morning before they set out she had almost been sick when Stephen had placed a dish of smoked herrings in front of her. Usually she enjoyed such fare but she had scarcely been able to swallow a morsel of bread without retching.

She had begun to toy with the suspicion that she was with child but, since it was indeed no more than a suspicion, she had said nothing to Joscelin. Her flux was scarcely more than a week late and in her previous marriage she had been slow to conceive. She smiled through the nausea, thinking of their new bed with its coverings of plain linen, sheepskin and blankets of plaid. All ostentation had been consigned to the pyre in the bailey where together she and Joscelin had watched the burning of the Montsorrel family bed until it was naught but ashes, blowing away in the wind.

Joscelin was up at the castle visiting acquaintances from his garrison days and she did not expect him home until late afternoon. Robert had fretted at not being allowed to go with his hero, but Joscelin's promise to take him round the market booths on the morrow had mollified him a little. He was playing in a corner of the yard with a young tabby cat that Gytha had bought at the Weekday market to deal with the local rat and mouse problem.

Linnet watched her son and felt a deep tenderness well up within her. She still feared for his future as a natural part of her maternal instinct, but there was hope now too – bright and steady as a clean-burning candle. She could dare to believe that all would be well. Now she had Joscelin, she could dare to believe anything.

She had just turned to go back inside the house when Ironheart arrived back from his errand to a wool factor who lived close by the city wall.

'Daughter,' he greeted her with a gruff nod.

Linnet inclined her head in response and going into the house, dutifully offered him wine. Since her illness in the autumn, their relationship had subtly altered. She knew that Ironheart had been present at the crisis of her fever for Joscelin's sake and that he had remained at Rushcliffe until it was certain that she would recover, his support silent but solid as rock. She no longer thought of him as a threat, nor did she have to stiffen her spine in his presence to control her fear. Yes, he had his flaws, some of them deep and ugly, but beyond them was the rock and to that she trusted.

For his part, Joscelin's father had tempered his aggression towards her and in rare moments displayed a clumsy tenderness in his dealings. He had ceased speaking darkly to Joscelin of beating and bedding, and while she and Ironheart seldom held prolonged conversations at least they could communicate with each other without bristling up like cat and dog.

'Joscelin not back yet?' Ironheart asked. His long nose wrinkled in the direction of the cauldron. 'You can never tell whether it's her washing or the dinner you can smell when you come in the door,' he commented.

'No, he said he might be late.'

'Gossiping with his old cronies, I daresay.'

'Yes.' She gave him a wan smile.

Ironheart eyed her from beneath his brows. 'You're as green as a new cheese,' he said abruptly. 'Is something the matter?'

'No, Father.' Linnet moved away from the bubbling cauldron. 'A mild stomach upset, nothing more.'

'Hah!' He continued to eye her, not in the face but up and down. Linnet blushed and quickly put her hand to her belly, the gesture giving her away. Ironheart, however, did not press the point. 'You need to go and rest, then,' he said mildly. 'Dry bread and sweet wine are good for such an ailment.' He jerked his head. 'Go on, get you to the loft for an hour. I'll watch the boy.'

Linnet hesitated for a moment, but another pungent waft of steam from the cooking pot caused her stomach to lurch and she accepted the offer with a grateful smile.

*   *   *

273

'I don't like it,' said Ranulf FitzRanulf, garrison commander of Nottingham, as he stared out of the high tower window. Spread before his view was Nottingham's immediate southern hinterland: the rivers Leen and Trent holding between them the broad green floodplain of the Meadows and beyond them the villages of Briggford, Wilford and Cliftun. 'There are too many of Ferrers's men in the city and they are bent upon mischief.'

Standing beside his former paymaster, Joscelin, too, looked out on the scene of pastoral tranquillity. The trees lining the riverbank wore new mantles of tender green and the meadowland was a lush carpet of flower-starred grass dotted by grazing cattle. Smoke twirled from the roofs of the tanneries on the banks of the Leen and a supply barge was wending its way upriver towards the castle's wharf. 'I noticed a lot of Ferrers' soldiers when I was here in the autumn,' he said.

'Around the time of the battle of Fornham?' FitzRanulf turned to look at Joscelin out of watery, light-blue eyes. The left one had a slight cast so that FitzRanulf never seemed to be looking directly, even when he was. It was an illusion for FitzRanulf was the most direct of men. 'They were vultures waiting their moment to strike but it never came. When news of Leicester's defeat arrived, they melted away.'

'And now they are back.'

'The winter truces are at an end. I have men enough to defend the castle but not the town. Ferrers has too much influence there. If there is trouble, the citizens will have to fend for themselves. How long are you staying?'

'We're only here to buy supplies. Two, three days at the most, although my father will probably leave guards at his house since it's so close to Ferrers'.'

'Your father's here, too?'

'On different errands and likely to be here a couple of days more than myself. I know he intends calling on you.'

FitzRanulf nodded, then he gave a humour-filled scowl. 'It was the worst turn the justiciar ever did me when he gave you Linnet de Montsorrel to wife,' he grumbled. 'I lost the best men in my pay. Still, at least I can rely on Rushcliffe's loyalty now. When the Montsorrels had possession, getting them to cooperate on anything was like trying to turn water into wine. Old Raymond could be as difficult as they come.'

'Yes, I know.'

FitzRanulf cocked his head, his expression curious, but Joscelin had no intention of divulging the particular 'difficulties' that Raymond de Montsorrel had bequeathed to him. 'I have to return to Rushcliffe,' he diverted, 'but I can leave some of my men here if you want – trained up and in full battle kit.'

'At whose expense?' enquired FitzRanulf, revealing that he was as shrewd about money as he was about everything else.

'They have a contract with me until midsummer. All you need do is feed and house them and see that they receive a fair share of the booty, should the situation arise.'

'Fair enough.' FitzRanulf nodded. 'I know a golden goose when it waddles over my foot. If there's anything I can do for you in the future, let me know.'

Following his visit to FitzRanulf, Joscelin repaired to the guardroom to pay his respects there and was furnished with a piggin of the castle's justly famous ale and some bread and new cheese. One of the guards, Odinel le Gros, so named because of his enormous gut, nudged Joscelin, his eyes gleaming with relish. 'Josce, is it all really true about Raymond de Montsorrel, then?'

Joselin's mouthful of bread and cheese suddenly seemed

too enormous to swallow. He chewed, took a drink of ale and shrugged, affecting indifference.

'Come on, stop teasing. You know what I mean. They say he tupped every woman on the estate between the ages of thirteen and fifty. I bet everywhere you ride, you see little bastards made in the old man's image!' Odinel chuckled. 'Do you remember that wench we had who claimed he futtered her against St Mary's wall? She said his pizzle were the biggest she'd ever seen! I reckon it should've been preserved when he died, just like they do with saints' bones.'

Joscelin heard the laughter of the other soldiers but it was fuzzy, as if it were coming from a far distance. A red mist was before his eyes and sweat sprang on his body. However, he did not leap at Odinel and rip his voice from his throat, for to have done so would be to acknowledge that Raymond's ghost still had a hold on him. As far as Joscelin was concerned, the burning of the bed had been the final exorcism.

'You have a high imagination,' he said when he could trust himself to speak. 'Raymond de Montsorrel was a common lecher and whores will always tell exaggerated tales of any highborn client who passes between their thighs. It gives them a feeling of importance and makes people listen to them,' he added pointedly.

Odinel blinked uncertainly. There was a brief, uncomfortable silence. Joscelin wondered what on earth he was truly doing here in the guardroom. His title was a barrier as tangible as the fine braid hemming on his tunic and the beryl and amber brooch pinned high on the shoulder of his fur-lined cloak. Although he had not deliberately willed it, the situation had changed and he had become an outsider, one of 'them' and, because of his past status, viewed with both admiration and resentment. In his

276

absence they would talk about him as they talked about Raymond de Montsorrel. And it was not fair to stay.

He took his leave of them quickly, with relief on both sides. As the guardroom door closed behind him, the soldiers breathed out and relaxed as if they had been standing to attention all the time he had been in the room. And on the other side of the door, Joscelin closed his eyes and inhaled deeply like a prisoner released. His only dilemma, as he started down the hill towards the Saturday market, was where to go. Not back to Linnet, not yet, not with Odinel's words still sliding their slime trail across his mind.

In the end, he turned his feet in Conan's direction, which he knew of old would be the Weckday alehouse. He wound his way through narrow streets and alleys into the dip of Broad Marsh, then up the other side. The stream running down the middle of Byard Lane was blocked again, this time by a dead dog, and various residents of the cut-through were conducting a lively argument as to who was responsible for clearing the obstruction. Joscelin picked his way through the sludge at the side of the lane, easing past dark doorways that gave entrance to cramped dwellings with central fire pits and smoke holes in the roof. At one point, near the top of the hill, there were steps cut down to a series of dwellings carved out of the soft sandstone rock upon which the city was built.

A cordwainer sat outside his home, a small trestle set up to hold his tools and the cut pieces of leather he was making into shoes. Next door to him stood a small dyehouse, and as Joscelin walked past its proprietor ceased pummelling a cloth in a cauldron of dark-red water to watch him. Beside the dye shop stood a booth belonging to Rothgar the swordsmith and Joscelin paused here to examine a long dagger.

'Best Lombardy steel, sir,' said the proprietor, laying down his tools and coming forward.

Joscelin had known Rothgar since childhood when Ironheart had brought him in wide-eyed delight to this very same booth. Rothgar's wife had fed him sugared figs and made a fuss of him, and Rothgar had let him handle the weapons.

The dagger he was handling today had a nine-inch blade, sharp on both edges, and a haft of plain, natural buckskin that felt good in his hands. His own dagger, which had served him since his early days as a mercenary, was wearing out. It had already been fitted with several new grips and the blade was thin.

'How much?'

'Five shillings,' Rothgar immediately responded and wiped his wrist across his full moustache. 'The materials alone cost me two and there's my time and skill on top.'

'I'll give you two and a half,' Joscelin said, testing the sharpened edge against the ball of this thumb. 'That's how much I'd pay on the road in Normandy.'

Rothgar shook his head. 'Normandy's closer to the Lombards and the steel costs less because of it. It's a mortal long way to go for a bargain. Tell you what, being as you and your father are good customers here, I'll let you have it for four and a half.'

'Three,' said Joscelin, well accustomed to the etiquette of haggling, 'and I'll commission a blunt sword for my stepson while I'm here.'

Rothgar tugged at his beard. 'You drive a hard bargain, my lord. Call it three and a half and commission that sword for your stepson with half a shilling down, and we'll call it fair.'

'On the nail,' Joscelin reached in his purse and put the

278

required coins on top of the squat, flat-topped post Rothgar used for that purpose.

Rothgar counted the silver and swept it into his cupped palm. 'You'll need to bring the lad into the shop so I can see the size of him.'

'Later this afternoon?'

'Aye, that'll do.' Rothgar started to unlatch the toggle on his belt bag but paused and lifted his head. 'What's that rumpus?'

Joscelin ducked out into the street, the new dagger in hand. From the direction of the Hologate road he could hear shouting and the clash of weapons. Then louder shrieks of terror and dismay and the bright blossoming of flame.

'God's eyes, what's happening?' Rothgar peered over Joscelin's shoulder, his forging hammer in his fist.

'I can't tell, except that it's trouble. Best shut up shop and make yourself and any valuables scarce. As a weapons-smith, you're a prime target. I'm going to the Weekday; my mercenary captain should be there.'

Rothgar nodded and hastened back into his shop, bellowing for his apprentice.

Joscelin moved quickly across the narrow, muddy street and started up the hill towards the alehouse. Folk were emerging from their shops and houses, exclaiming, looking anxious, demanding to know what was happening. Other townsfolk were pouring down the hill away from the marketplace, fleeing in panic.

'Soldiers!' A panting merchant paused to cry warning. Tucked under his arm, a goose wildly paddled its orange feet. 'Derby's men. Save yourselves!'

Joscelin thrust himself against the tide of panicking humanity, shouldering through them until he reached the Weekday. The evergreen bush that was usually suspended on a horizontal pole from the gable, advertising the place as an alehouse, was trampled down outside the door, and smoke billowed in thick clouds from the interior. The empty yard showed no sign of the landlord's guard dog, only its kennel and the length of bear chain that usually leashed it.

People streamed away from the marketplace, heading for the sanctuary of the churches. Smoke belched from a row of merchants' houses on the King's road leading to St Mary's. Fire crowned the thatch in sudden licks of flame but no one stopped to organize a bucket chain. With life and limb at stake, houses could burn.

Joscelin was buffeted like a rock in the midst of a turbulent sea by the crowds milling around him. Then he saw the soldiers. Reflected fire from the torches they held glinted on their helms and mail. In and out of houses and shops they darted, setting alight thatch and straw, kicking apart hearths, scattering embers to consume homes and shops in the fury of flame.

He came across two bodies sprawled in the street. One of them was a whore, her gaudy yellow gown splashed with blood. The other, his arm still across her body, was Gamel. His carpentry tools were scattered across the street and his wooden leg stuck out at an awkward angle. Appalled, Joscelin crouched and made the sign of the cross over the bodies, closed Gamel's staring eyes and rose to his feet. Fear and anger surged through him. Where in God's name was Conan?

Church bells clamoured from all quarters. His thoughts flashed to Linnet and Robert. With his father absent on business and just a few servants in the house, they were vulnerable. His father's townhouses stood almost on top of Derby's. That might protect the dwellings from fire but it also meant there would be a high concentration of Derby's men in the area.

280

He began to force his way along the narrow street, pushing himself against the tide of humanity striving towards the sanctuary of St Peter's church. The ground underfoot was muddy and he slipped and skidded. Behind him there was panic as a barrel of pitch in a carpenter's workshop exploded, showering the crowd with flaming debris. A globule landed on his hand and sizzled into his flesh before he was able to brush it off. He was pushed and jostled, almost forced by the surge of the crowd to enter St Peter's, but managed to thrust his way out of the press and across the street to a narrow passageway that progressed in a crooked dogleg to the backs of the houses lining the Saturday market square.

Here, too, there was chaos, and Joscelin realized with a renewed leap of fear that the assault on the city was widespread. Surrounded by the sounds of looting and burning, he crouched for a moment in the garden of one of the houses to recover his breath. He wondered if the constable would send soldiers into the city or just hold fast to the castle and hope that Ferrers's attack was more an act of spite and bile than an attempt to subjugate city and castle to his will.

Brandishing his new dagger, Joscelin straightened and moved up through the garden. Suddenly, an enormous black sow galloped around the corner of the building and almost bowled him over. He leaped aside and found himself confronted by two foot soldiers, their own knives to hand for the purposes of pig-sticking. The sow snorted away down the garth, wallowed across the damaged wattle fence at the foot and disappeared into the noisome alley beyond. The foot soldiers and Joscelin appraised each other over their poised weapons.

'I have no quarrel with you,' Joscelin said. 'Let me go my way in peace and I will let you go yours.'

The men exchanged swift glances and returned their scrutiny to Joscelin. He was suddenly very aware of the gold braid edging his tunic, the quality of his cloak and its ornate clasp – temptations far greater than a prospective haunch of roast pork that was already halfway to Broadmarsh by now.

'We wouldn't rightly want to quarrel with you either,' said the older of the two men, 'but we'd like you better if you was to hand over that cloak and clasp as a sign of goodwill.'

'Your purse and belt, too,' added the second, whose quick crafty gaze had not missed the promising roundness of Joscelin's money pouch and the gilding on the tooled leather belt.

One soldier moved right, the other left. Joscelin ran at the latter, dagger lifted to strike. His attack was blocked as the man grasped his knife hand. Joscelin responded in a similar manner by grasping his opponent's wrist and used their grip on each other as leverage to hurl the man hard to the right, fouling the other soldier's path. Having broken free, Joscelin ran. He heard the sound of rapid footfalls in pursuit but he had a start on them and, being faster into the bargain, reached the market square well in front. Across it, Joscelin saw soldiers rolling wine barrels out of a vintner's cellar while the vintner and his family watched in helpless shock. A hauberk-clad soldier sat astride his war-horse conducting operations, a long whip dangling from his fist.

Behind Joscelin, there was a triumphant cry. 'There he is, the whoreson, get him!'

Flashing a glance over his shoulder, Joscelin saw the two soldiers he had just evaded running out of the doorway of a house on Cuckstool Row. Joscelin took to his heels, knowing that if they caught him they would kill him.

The marketplace was a shambles of overturned booths and stalls, the looters picking among them like scavengers at the scene of a larger animal's kill. Joscelin sought the shelter of these booths, dodging in and out between them, weaving from one to the other across the square towards Organ Lane. Near the low wall that separated the corn market from the rest of the stalls, a looter threatened him with a short knife but backed off the moment he saw the gleam of Joscelin's dagger and went in search of easier prey. Joscelin was preoccupied in watching the looter and did not see the body sprawled behind one of the raided booths until too late. He measured his length across the corpse and lay upon it, momentarily too winded to move. When he drew his first breath he almost choked, for the stench emanating from the dead man's garments proclaimed him an employee of one of the numerous tanneries down by the Leen bridge. Essence of excrement mingled with that of putrefaction, rancid mutton fat and the metallic tang of tannin. The stink was so powerful that Joscelin retched. In the background he could hear his pursuers approaching and knew that in a moment they would be upon him.

In haste, Joscelin tore off his mantle and gilded tunic. Stuffing them beneath the trestle in the booth, he rolled the corpse over, dragged off its cloak and stained tunic and dressed himself in the foulsome rags. A greasy, louse-infested hood and a knobbled quarterstaff completed the ensemble – and not a moment too soon. As Joscelin started to walk away from the corpse, his two pursuers ran panting round the side of the booth.

His fall had been greatly to his advantage. Still winded, Joscelin did not stride out as he might have otherwise done, which would have given him away immediately. Instead he moved with a shuffling walk more reminiscent of a peasant.

'Ho!' cried one of the soldiers. 'You there, have you seen a noble running this way? Tall, wearing a dark-red cloak?'

Joscelin shook his head and mumbled a reply in the rustic Anglo-Dane of the countryside. At the same time, he gestured with his arm so that the dreadful stench of his garments wafted towards the men. Neither of them, he hazarded, would want to move in as close as it would take to kill him.

'Ah God, he stinks as if he's been dead a week!' declared the other soldier. 'Can you tell what he's saying?'

His companion shook his head, equally baffled. 'His accent's too heavy. Come on, we're wasting our time. Let's search round the other side.'

Cold sweat clasping his body, Joscelin watched them walk rapidly away. He breathed out hard, then in again. The smell from his garments was not as bad now that he had grown accustomed and it had quite probably saved his life. Turning, he cut his way across the marketplace and up towards the town gate near Derby Road. The looted houses of Long Row bordered the marketplace with a ragged line of fire. As he hurried up the muddy thoroughfare, Joscelin hoped desperately that his father's houses were close enough to Derby's not to have been torched.

From a dark alleyway, a band of hurrying soldiers emerged like wine running from an open flask. They spilled over Joscelin before he could avoid them and then they drew back, exclaiming at the stench of him.

Joscelin's hand relaxed on the grip of his dagger. 'Where in God's name have you been!' he roared at Conan.

His uncle set his hands on his hips and stared Joscelin up and down. 'I might ask the same of you.' His scarred lip curved lopsidedly towards his left nostril. 'Christ's buttocks, but you stink worse than a three-week-old battle-field!'

'I had to exchange clothes with a tanner's corpse to keep myself from being skewered by two routiers,' Joscelin said shortly. 'I thought you'd be in the Weekday.'

'And so we would, except that Godred's uncle has an alehouse on Cherry Tree Lane. We were paying our respects there when a brawl of Derby men came by and started causing trouble. We got rid of them soon enough, then realized it was more serious than our little disagreement. We're on our way back to your father even now.'

'There's no time to waste.' Joscelin began hurrying up the hill again. 'I don't think Derby's men will harm Linnet and Robert – they're too valuable – but I don't want them taken into his care.'

'Surely your father's knights will protect the place?' Conan trotted beside him, his nose still wrinkled in response to the stench of Joscelin's garments.

'My father had business with a wool factor up Organ Lane and he gave most of his men leave to go round the town, the same as I gave leave to you,' Joscelin answered. 'As far as I'm aware, only the servants are there.'

They arrived at Ironheart's three houses to find them standing ominously silent and tranquil. A cookshop across the road was on fire but otherwise this quarter of the town had seen less damage. But it was still obvious that all was not well. The front door of the first house hung drunkenly on one hinge and on the floor in the passage were the plundered bodies of Ironheart's squire and Gytha's husband, Jonas. The rooms were all empty. Everything of value had been stripped and no one answered Joscelin's shout. He strode into the yard. Gytha's laundry tub lay overturned, a mess of torn, crumpled linens, spilling across the ground. Ears flat to its small skull, Gytha's kitten hissed and spat at him from beneath a wooden trestle. A bowl of water containing some strips of softened rawhide stood on the bench beside some of his father's weapon-mending tools. His father's red and gold shield lay on the ground, a great split running from a damaged section of rawhide right through to the centre boss. There were blood smears on the ground.

He picked up a pair of blacksmith's pincers and squeezed the grip until the pressure brought pain. He could not be too late. It was impossible; he would not allow it to happen.

And then he heard the sound of shouting from the gardens backing on to the other side of the narrow alley and a woman's scream.

Dropping the pincers, he grabbed his father's shield by the short hand-straps and began to run.

30

As soon as Linnet had retired to the sleeping loft on the
second floor of the house, Ironheart fetched his tools and
his shield and brought them outside to the bench by the
yard wall.

Bracing the shield against his leg, he took up a pair of
blacksmith's pincers and began to pull out the tacks that
held the shield's rawhide rim in position. A section near
the top was damaged and needed replacing. It was something he had meant to do in the winter but had kept
putting off. Now the truces had all come to an end and
there was no time left.

Robert ceased playing with the kitten and ambled across
the yard to watch Ironheart at work.

'What are you doing?'

'I'm going . . . ,' said Ironheart between grunts of effort
as he pulled the tacks out of the wood, 'to replace . . .
this damaged section at the top . . . with a new piece of
rawhide. See?' He pointed with a calloused forefinger.
'That's the mark of a Scottish short sword. Nearly got
me, the whoreson.'

Robert nodded, grey eyes large and impressed. 'Can I help?'

'I don't see why not,' Ironheart said gruffly. 'You see that jar over there? Bring it here, will you? I've had a piece of rawhide soaking in it overnight, so it should be soft enough to cut and nail by now.' He watched Robert carefully lift the yellow glazed jar and bring it to him, a look of intense concentration on his small face. A pang went through the old man, so warm and sweet that it made a mockery of the barriers he had erected against the world a quarter-century ago. Thus had Jocelin learned the art of caring for his weapons, a small child against Ironheart's knee. Those had been the springtime years. Now, in the cold approach to winter, he could smell the spring again and wanted to weep because he had missed the summertime completely and was aware of the last leaves of autumn drifting from the tree.

'Now what do we do?' asked Robert, bringing him firmly back to earth.

'Take the hide out of the jar and squeeze it as hard as you can.'

'Like this?' Robert screwed up his face in disgust as the wet rawhide bulged between his fingers. 'It's all slimy and it stinks!'

A chuckle rumbled up from the depths of Ironheart's chest. 'You can't nail it on when it's hard,' he said and looked at the child's tendons standing out on the bony wrist. There was nothing on him – he was like a skinned coney – but there was a powerful underlying tenacity. Still chuckling, Ironheart rummaged among his tools and discovered that his shears were missing.

'Leave that now. You've squeezed out most of the water. Go inside to Gytha and ask her for a pair of shears.'

Robert scampered off. Picking up the crumpled piece

of rawhide, Ironheart gave it a final wringing with his own powerful, scarred hands. Gytha's shriek and Robert's even louder scream brought him abruptly to his feet.

The little boy shot out into the backyard, the shears clutched in his hands, his eyes huge with terror. Gytha raced after him, followed by Ella, stumbling on her skirts. 'Soldiers, sire!' she gasped. 'Soldiers with swords coming this way from Ferrers' house! They mean mischief, I know they do!'

'What's happening?' asked Linnet in bewilderment. She stood at the foot of the loft stairs, her face flushed with sleep and her lustrous golden-brown braids bared.

Ironheart opened his mouth, but before he could speak the front entrance of the house was darkened by three men clad in the leather armour of regular troops. Two brandished long knives, the other wielded a hand axe.

Linnet screamed, then cut the sound off rapidly against the palm of her hand. Ironheart seized his sword and shield from the bench and faced the intruders.

'Get out of my house or, by God, I'll kill you!' he snarled.

One of the soldiers laughed. 'You're a foolish old man,' he said, advancing with a heavy, deliberate step. 'And God's asleep.'

Linnet backed away. Never taking his eyes off the soldiers, Ironheart sidestepped so that Linnet could squeeze past him. 'Hide in the cellars next door,' he muttered from the side of his mouth. 'Gytha has the keys.'

Linnet cast a frightened glance over her shoulder then ran into the backyard. Grabbing Robert's hand, she pulled him across the yard at a run and out of the back gate into the communal narrow entry running behind the houses. Gytha and Ella panted behind her. She reached for the iron ring on the gate of the house adjoining

Ironheart's and twisted. The door did not move. She thrust her shoulder against it until her flesh bruised and her bones hurt. The door's hinges had dropped at some time and its base dragged the dusty ground. Gytha and Ella joined her, kicking and pushing, fear lending them strength. Finally, reluctantly, the door scraped open enough for the women and boy to squeeze through into the yard of the vintner's house.

Wheezing, Gytha unfastened the hoop of household keys from the belt at her thick waist and found the one to the solid rear door of the building.

'Lord William said we should hide in the cellars.' Linnet panted, staring round the empty backyard with wide eyes and thinking that at any moment they would be caught. From the direction of Ironheart's house they heard a loud bellow and the shriek of steel meeting steel. Then someone screaming in pain. Gytha fumbled the key into the lock and twisted and pushed.

The house was dim and had the musty odour of places left unoccupied for a time. The walls were bare, for the merchant had taken all his portable goods with him and only the plainest of furniture remained. An empty cauldron stood over the fire pit, which had been cleaned of rubbish and new kindling laid to hand.

'The cellar's this way,' Gytha gasped and disappeared behind a wooden screen into the storeroom. Bunches of herbs and smoked hams hung from hooks hammered into strong wooden beams that supported the floor of the sleeping loft above. Two buckets stood on the floor beside an old pair of pattens and several cooking pots were laid out on a trestle. There was a candle lantern standing on the trestle, too. Gytha pounced on this and, with shaking hands, kindled a flame from the tinderbox laid beside it. Holding the light aloft, she hastened to a low doorway at the end of the room and told Ella to pull back the heavy iron bolts. Linnet ran to help the maid. Fortunately, the bolts, although stout, had been kept well oiled and were easy to draw back. The oak door swung open and the candle flame danced, making huge shadows on the rough-cut sandstone stairs that led down into a throat of darkness.

Robert hung back. 'I don't want to go down there,' he whimpered and clung tightly to his mother. 'I don't like the dark. Monsters might get me!'

'You cannot stay up here.' Crouching, Linnet cuddled him. 'And there are no monsters. Sir William wouldn't allow them to live in his cellar, would he?' Over Robert's shoulder, she gestured the other women to continue down the stairs. Gytha gave her the hoop of keys, holding out to her the cellar one, and started downwards to the dark horseshoe arch where the first room opened out. Linnet smoothed Robert's hair. 'Look, I'll carry you and you can hide your face against my shoulder.'

Robert still resisted, a whine of fear escaping between his teeth, but Linnet scooped him up in her arms. She did not have the time to cozen him further and could only hope that he would not begin to scream.

A scraping sound came from the direction of the yard entrance and almost simultaneously the women heard the thump of weapons upon the street door.

'Quickly, my lady!' Gytha hissed, beckoning from the foot of the stairs, her eye-whites gleaming.

Linnet started down the steps, Robert clinging to her like a limpet. She began to close the cellar door with the hand not supporting him but stopped as Ironheart staggered into the storeroom, his mouth twisted in a grimace of effort and pain. She widened the door again. He was too breathless to speak but gestured her down the stairs.

Wordless herself from the sight of blood glistening on his shoulder, she gave him the key and hastened down after the other women. As she reached the cave, she heard the front door crash down and the iron key grate in the cellar lock.

The dampness closed around them like a tomb, musty and cold. Gytha brought over the lantern to light Ironheart's way down the steps. He leaned heavily on the rope supports hammered into one side of the wall, and when he reached the bottom collapsed against a row of casks, his breathing harsh.

'I haven't given you away,' he panted. 'We killed the first three, me and Jonas . . . and the two who came after . . .' His eyes squeezed shut and he put his hand to the wetness at his shoulder.

'Where is Jonas?' Gytha asked. Her hand trembled as she set down the candle lantern.

Ironheart swallowed. 'I'm sorry, Gytha, there was nothing I could do. There were two of them at me and I could not reach him. I tried, God knows I did. Then one of the bastards ran into this yard after you and I gave chase. I got him – but he got me. You think you're safe enough in your own house not to bother with mail.'

'Let me have a look.' Kneeling, Linnet reached to examine the wide split in his leather jerkin, tunic and shirt.

'No time,' he gasped. 'They will be looking for loot, and in a vintner's house that means the cellar.'

Linnet withdrew and looked at him askance. 'Then why tell us to come here in the first place?'

'The cave runs the length of all the houses and then some more. There is a passage branching off beneath the entry where there used to be a meat store. We had a dispute with the old basket-weaver across the alleyway – he cut a room for his workshop and broke through into my cellars. As far as I know, the hole has only been boarded over. It should be possible to crawl through. Give me your arm, girl.'

Linnet was almost dragged to the floor by Ironheart's weight as he levered himself to his feet and leaned briefly against the casks.

'Here, boy,' he commanded Robert, who was holding tightly to Linnet's skirts. 'Carry my sword for me, be my squire.' He held out the weapon. The candlelight flashed upon the blade edge and up the tendons of the man's rigid hand.

Tentatively Robert did as he was bid, his own small hand inadequate on the braided grip.

At the top of the stairs, the door suddenly rattled vigorously on its hinges. 'Locked,' said a gruff voice. 'Use the axe, Greg.'

'This way,' Ironheart whispered hoarsely and began weaving a path through the casks. The cellar door shook beneath the blows of an axe and they all heard the sound of splintering wood.

Linnet did not like the way Ironheart was breathing and from the size of the wound, as she had briefly seen it, she was sure that it would need attention very soon if he was not to bleed to death.

They rounded a corner and had to stoop as the roof of the cave suddenly dipped and seemed to reach an end. The lantern light illuminated the chisel marks on the walls where the cave had been cut. To their left the shadows seemed blacker than elsewhere and it was towards these that Ironheart headed. In a moment, the shadows resolved themselves into a narrow, dark connecting passageway. Gazing over her shoulder, Linnet saw only

293

blackness but the hammering sounds went on and there was a cry of triumph as the soldiers split through the door.

'I want Joscelin,' Robert whimpered as they crouched along the passage and into the storage cave of the house next door. 'Will he come and save us, Mama?' He, too, looked back with the wide eyes of a hunted animal. The weight of the sword was making his wrist droop.

'If he is able to, I know he will,' Linnet said. She knew he had gone to the castle. Probably the alarm had not even been raised there yet, and by the time it was it might well be too late. 'But for now, sweeting, we have to use our own wits.'

'Mama, why can't we—?'

'Hush,' she admonished quickly, 'they will hear us!'

They could not see the soldiers' torchlight but suddenly they could hear their voices in the first cellar and the grate of footsteps on the sandy cave floor.

''E don't have much wine stored down here to say he's such a busy merchant,' complained a rough voice. 'Hold the light closer, Greg, I want to see the mark on this barrel. Hah, Rhenish!' A glint of greedy pleasure entered the voice and there were various unidentifiable clinking, scraping sounds, followed by the trickle of wine into some sort of vessel. All in the tunnel held their breath. Gytha shielded the light of the lantern beneath her cloak and turned away from the first cellar. Ironheart silently removed his sword from Robert's hand.

'You reckon there's anything upstairs worth a look?' asked one of the looters between swallows.

'We'll investigate in a minute. By Christ's toes, this is good stuff.'

Footsteps scuffed in the direction of the passageway

and Ironheart tightened his hand around the grip of the sword.

'Hoi, Thomas, look at this. There's a passage here; bring the torch!'

In the moment while the refugees deliberated between fight and flight, another voice, angry and imperative, filled the first cave.

'I might have expected you two tosspots to find the wine!' There came the sound of a blow and a pot smashing on the cave floor. 'Get upstairs now. The men I sent to de Rocher's house are all dead and there's no sign of the old fox or the woman and child. I want them found, is that understood?'

'Yes, sir. We was only investigating the cave. They could be down here for all we know!'

'Oh, aye,' said their captain sarcastically. 'I presume you were drinking all the barrels dry to make sure they weren't hiding in them. You must think I was born yesterday and blind. Go on, get out of here and find Simon; he's coordinating the search parties.'

'Yes, sir.'

The sound of running footsteps retreated and the captain's voice, softly cursing, followed them, boots crunching upon the shards of broken pottery.

Linnet released her breath and sucked air into her starving lungs. Ironheart groaned and slipped slowly down the wall. His grip loosened on the sword and it clattered sideways. A single blue spark flashed along the edge of the blade and was quenched in semi-darkness. Linnet crouched beside her father-in-law. His eyelids flickered.

'Go on,' he croaked. 'I won't be able to keep pace with you.' A wry smile barely curved his lips. 'I doubt I'm even able to stand up. Fetch help if you can. If not . . . guard yourself. Take my sword. I still have my dagger.'

Linnet bit her lip, considered briefly, then nodded. 'Give me the lantern,' she said to Gytha, and when the older woman handed it across she set it down beside the wounded man.

'Leave me,' he growled. 'You have no time.'

'Time enough to make you comfortable,' she retorted. 'I won't be gainsaid. You saved me once. At least let me redress the balance a little.'

Ironheart snorted. 'I didn't save you to indulge in this kind of folly,' he said but, after a brief attempt to push her hand away, allowed her to have her will.

Linnet raised her skirt and undergown to reach the good linen of her shift. Taking the hem in both hands at the side seam, she tore it upwards and then hard across. The fibres resisted and she had to use her belt knife to finish tearing off a long, wide strip. This she used as wadding and bandage to cover Ironheart's wound, securing it with her own braid belt. Ironheart's tougher leather belt she took and bound around her waist, setting her knife in the empty dagger sheath.

'It will cause you pain but you must press down hard on the bandage to staunch the bleeding,' she told him. 'I don't think you are losing as much blood as you were.' She picked up the lantern from his side and returned to the first cave, picking her way over the shards of broken pottery and the dark glimmer of splattered wine. There was a small ledge carved into the wall and on it stood two more pitchers of a similar design to the one that lay in pieces on the floor. Lifting one down, she filled it from the broached keg and brought it to Ironheart, setting it down at his good side.

He regarded her with grim amusement. 'What's this for, to drown my sorrows?'

'To dull the pain and replace the blood you have lost,' she replied, her tone sharp.

Ironheart hefted the pitcher and took a shaky gulp of the wine from the cracked rim. '*Waes hael*,' he toasted with irony. 'Go on, wench, get you gone. There's nothing to be gained in watching a drunkard die.'

Linnet blinked hard. 'Get as drunk as you want,' she said, 'but don't you dare die!' Bending over him, she kissed his cheek fiercely then straightened and gestured brusquely at Gytha to lead on.

Ironheart watched their small light disappear in the direction of the third cellar and raised the pitcher to his lips again. He was indeed inordinately thirsty. He was tired, too, and could feel the chill of the cave floor seeping up through his bones. How long did it take to die? He closed his eyes, then remembered he was supposed to drink the wine. The pitcher was so heavy. He raised it, swallowed, choked, swallowed, lowered his aching arm.

The meat store in the fourth cellar had a fatty, strong aroma, and this despite the cool temperature of the sandstone vaulting. Linnet's stomach churned and fluid filled her mouth so that she had to turn aside to spit. Gytha's wavering candle illuminated the boarded-up hole, the source of the dispute between Ironheart and his neighbours.

'We need something to prise off these planks,' said Gytha. 'It ain't safe down here. They'll be down after us soon enough, the scavenging vultures. My poor Jonas . . .' Her double chins quivered.

'Gytha, I'm sorry—' Linnet began, knowing that whatever she said would be inadequate, but the older woman cut her off short.

'Nay, Mistress Linnet, it is kind of you to offer comfort, but it ain't much use. It'll not bring him back, will it?'

Gytha compressed her lips. 'He's dead. It's our own lives we must save.'

Linnet bit her lip and nodded, recognizing the older woman's brusqueness as a bulwark against the onset of grief. On a stone slab jutting from the wall lay the carcasses of two skinned sheep and she had to swallow several times before she could speak. 'We could try the sword,' she suggested.

'You will break the blade, my lady.'

'I don't think so, not if we put the hilt under like this.' She lodged the pommel, which was shaped like a flattened fist, beneath one of the wooden planks and pushed downwards. For a moment nothing happened. Linnet raised her foot and braced it against another strut for more leverage. With a loud creak and then a sudden splintering sound, one of the holding nails flew out of the wood and tinkled on the ground. Gytha took hold of the loosened plank in her strong laundry pummeler's hands and ripped it away from the hole.

'It's mortal narrow,' she pronounced, peering dubiously through and running her hands over her ample curves.

Linnet loosened some more boards and Gytha and Ella pulled them free. The women held the lantern up to the hole and saw that it led through into a dusty cellar full of bundles of rushes and withies, woven baskets and trugs, some completed, some half-finished and beyond them, stairs leading up to a shadowed doorway.

'Old Andrew's workshop,' Gytha said. 'The door comes out in his garth, under his grapevines.' Her plump face wrinkled. 'There's no telling it's going to be any safer there, save that his cellar door's well hidden beneath all the greenery and he's not a rich man – nowt worth looting.'

But it was not loot alone they were after, Linnet thought,

remembering the exchange of words between the soldiers in the first cellar. She, Robert and Ironheart were sought, and God alone knew for what purpose. Anger at their helplessness flashed through her like fire and renewed her courage.

'Hold up the lantern,' she commanded Gytha. 'I'll go first and you can pass Robert through. Here, sweetheart, take the sword for me.'

The gap was like a lightless window set in the middle of the wall and she had to drag her skirts through her belt so that she could clamber through the aperture. The air on this side was thick with the chaffy residue of old Andrew's trade and made her sneeze. She stifled the sound against her hand but it still seemed to echo resoundingly.

'Pass me through the sword,' she called to Robert. 'Hilt-first; it's very dark in here and I don't want to cut my fingers.'

There was a scraping, grating noise. Using the haphazard gleams of Gytha's lantern, Linnet located the grip and pulled the sword through into the new cave. Robert followed it through, agile as a small ape. As she helped him down, she could feel him trembling, but he neither spoke nor whimpered.

Then, without warning, without time to run or hide, Andrew's cellar door was flung open and bright daylight flooded down the dozen stairs, blinding Linnet and Robert.

'I told you, I ain't got no valuables hidden away!' whined an elderly, cracked voice. 'See for yourselves. This here's me workshop!'

'Nothing valuable? Oh, come now, I wouldn't say that. Looks to me as if you've got two little birds nesting in your straw.'

Linnet's eyesight began to adjust and she saw a broad-shouldered, leather-clad soldier standing at the head of the stairs grinning down at them. An old, scrawny man dangled from the soldier's fist by the ripped edge of his hood.

'I nivver seed 'em before!' the old man squeaked with an incongruous mixture of fear and indignation. 'They're nowt to do wi' me.'

'Good, then you won't be wanting a share in the reward for finding them,' the soldier said cheerfully, and dropped him. Turning, he shouted, 'Lads, come and look at what I've found!' Grinning broadly, he started down the stairs. Linnet saw his look intensify as his eyes settled on the dark hole in the wall behind her and Robert. She licked her lips, knowing he would investigate and soon discover the two serving women and Ironheart. It was too late to distract him from what he had seen and deduced.

Robert was shuddering, his eyes growing wider with each footfall of the approaching soldier.

'My lady,' the man said. 'You will yield yourself and the child into my keeping.' His left foot scraped the bottom step. He made a beckoning gesture.

Linnet wrapped both hands around the sword grip and attacked him. The blade swung in an arc and hit his lower bicep and elbow. Although the blade did not bite flesh; he was knocked off balance. Cursing her, he began to straighten up and reach for his own sword but Linnet struck again and this time caught his throat between the edge of his gambeson tunic and his jawline.

He choked and clutched at the wound, blood spurting between his fingers. Linnet dropped the sword, picked up Robert and thrust him at the wall. 'Go back!' she commanded. 'Stay with Gytha and Ella until I come for you.' As the women took him, Linnet began feverishly

300

piling up baskets and stacking rushes against the hole to concealing it, while in front of her the man died, his eyes full of frightened disbelief.

More soldiers arrived at the top of the stairs. 'Found some treasure, have you, Rob?' one shouted. The laughter left his voice and his eyes widened as he took in the scene below. 'Rob?' he croaked. 'Christ, you bitch, what have you done to him?'

Linnet backed away from the men, sidestepping the body so that their eyes followed her to the far wall, not the one that concealed the opening behind the precariously balanced trugs and baskets. 'I am the lady Linnet de Gael, daughter-in-law of William Ironheart,' she said as they advanced down the steps, clubs and swords at the ready. 'It will go ill with you if I am harmed.'

She saw the looks they exchanged. The soldier who had spoken reached the foot of the stairs and crouched beside his dead compatriot to check him for signs of life. His fingers came away bloody and he looked at her across the corpse, his face twisted with revulsion. Linnet returned his stare. 'Soldiers killed my father-in-law,' she said. 'I took his sword to defend myself.'

He jerked to his feet and, crossing to her in two swift strides, struck her across the face. 'You whore!' he snarled. 'Rob would never have attacked you. Soft as mutton fat he was with women!' He raised his hand to strike her again but one of the others caught him back.

'Steady, Alex. Lord Ferrers said he'd pay good money for her and the brat. And he can be mighty peculiar. It's nothing to him to thrash a woman to death but if we bring her to him in any kind o' state, he'll have us on the gibbet for sure – and that'll be all of us dead because of her, and no profit.'

Alex resisted the hand clamped on his wrist for a

moment longer, then shrugged free and pushed his way out of the cave.

'Where's the boy?' demanded the soldier who had intervened. His face was stone-hard and without compassion.

'At the castle with his stepfather,' she lied, looking straight in his eyes. 'You'll not get your hands on him.'

He scowled. 'Get her out of here,' he snapped to his two companions. 'Take her to Lord Ferrers' house. Alex and I will follow with Rob's body.'

Linnet was seized by the elbows and dragged up the stairs into the full daylight of the basket-maker's backyard. They tied her hands with a strip of leather and knotted a rope leash through her belt with which to pull her along. Linnet put up a token struggle, enough for them to jerk her roughly a couple of times, but she did not engage in spirited resistance. The sooner they were away from the cellar, the better.

As Ferrers' hirelings pulled Linnet out of the yard, more men came running up the alleyway from the direction of Ironheart's house, their swords drawn. Linnet dug in her heels and stared. Her heart pounded in swift hammer strokes. 'Joscelin!' she screamed. 'Joscelin, Conan, help me!'

The soldier holding the rope swore and turned to strike her with his sword-hilt. Linnet dodged the blow and kicked him as hard as she could in the testicles. Unbalanced by her tied hands and the rope at her waist, the force of her effort toppled her and sent her sprawling in the alley's filth. The soldier grunted and hunched over, for while she was only wearing soft indoor slippers, his gambeson was on the short side and at least part of the blow had connected. Before he could straighten and turn, Joscelin was upon him with a single killing blow. Linnet screamed and rolled away as the body struck the ground at her side. She struggled to her knees. Joscelin pulled her to her feet and freed her wrists, untied the the rope at her waist, then pulled her fiercely into his arms.

She clung to him, shaking. One man had fled up the alley towards Organ Lane, the others lay dead. Linnet could smell their lifelessness as though they were already putrefying. The stench invaded her nostrils and descended to her stomach, bringing on a lurching nausea. Then she realized that Joscelin's garments were the source of the stink and that they were naught but infested rags.

'Are you all right?' He held her a little away to study her face. His hand gently touched the swollen mark where the soldier had hit her. 'Where are the others? Once they've done looting and burning, they'll turn on anything that moves and even the size of Conan's troop might not deter them. We have to reach the castle as quickly as we can.'

Linnet nodded jerkily. She was far from being all right but for the nonce she could cope because she had to. She compressed her lips as the stench of his garments continued to agitate her stomach. 'We hid in the house cellars. The others are still there.' She swallowed and swallowed again, then pushed out of his arms. 'Your father's been wounded – badly, I think. It was very hard to tell in the dark. We had to leave him in the passageway between the caves – he could go no further. I bandaged him as best I could and left him a pitcher of wine to ease his thirst and his pain. He gave me his sword, and I—' She shook her head and refused to think in that direction. She needed all of her faculties until they were safe. Averting her gaze from the corpse at her feet, she stumbled towards the vintner's backyard. 'I will take you to him,' she said.

Pausing only to give Conan orders and send a soldier in search of a hand cart to carry the wounded Ironheart, Joscelin hastened after her.

303

31

'If I'm going to die,' Ironheart grumbled, 'I'm going to do it at Arnsby in the bed where I was conceived and born, not on some poxy borrowed pallet in this godforsaken place!'

Linnet eyed him with exasperation as she cleaned the razor with which she had just finished shaving him and went to empty the laver bowl of scummy water down the waste shaft. 'This godforsaken place' was a comfortable private room in the tower of the castle and had been vacated by a senior officer at some considerable inconvenience. The bed, far from being poxy or a pallet, was a sumptuous affair, large enough to hold six people, and boasted crisp linen sheets and the finest Flemish coverings. In the three days since he had been placed there, Ironheart had gone from grey-faced docility to his current state of febrile crabbiness in which he was impossible to please.

'You're too lively to think of dying, Father,' she said briskly. 'If you would only keep still and cease complaining, the wound would pain you less.'

'It's the pain that tells me I'm still alive!' he retorted, shifting irritably against the pillows. His left arm was caged in a leather sling and beneath it he was padded with swathes of bandage. The constable had sent his own physician to attend Ironheart. According to the good doctor, who had stitched the tear, Ironheart was suffering from an excess of choler and the wound had only served to further unbalance his humours. Linnet had had to bite her tongue on the comment that her father-in-law's humours had always been out of balance. Fortunately, the physician had owned the good sense not to suggest bleeding as a remedy, otherwise she would have been bound to speak up since, in her opinion, Ironheart's wound had already bled him white.

The doctor had applied a token leech or two to Ironheart's arms and prescribed an infusion of Black Alder and agrimony to soothe the choler and help balance the humours. He had drawn up a strict diet for the wounded man, consisting of broth made from oxblood and dark bread soaked in milk, sprinkled with iron filings from a sword blade. It was small wonder that the invalid baulked every time he saw her or her maid approaching him with a bowl and spoon.

'I have a bad feeling,' he complained as Linnet returned to his bedside. 'I need to go home to Arnsby.'

'A bad feeling about what?'

'If I could put my finger on it, I'd not be so frustrated. All I know is that I have to go home.'

'Joscelin could go in your stead,' she suggested.

Ironheart shook his head and the two vertical frown lines between his brows deepened with anxiety and pain. 'It is not something Joscelin can do. I'm sick of lying here staring at the wall and swallowing that piss-faced chirurgeon's poisonous brews. One more day and, even if I have to crawl out of here on my hands and knees, I'm leaving.' He paused, out of breath, his skin shiny with the sweat of effort. Linnet wiped his brow, murmured soothing words until his lids drooped, and went in search of Joscelin.

She found him in a corner of the great hall sitting on an upturned half-barrel, patiently working the nicks out of his father's sword with a small, hand-held grindstone.

'Go and talk some sense into your father,' she said. 'He's threatening to leave his sickbed and ride home to Arnsby.'

Joscelin laid the sword carefully down and wiped his hands on a linen rag. 'I know. He spoke to me late last night.' Seeing her pinched expression, he added, 'Does the sight of this bother you?'

She glanced briefly at the sword, its edges bright now and unstained. 'I can look at it without feeling sick any more, if that is what you mean,' she said, 'but the sight will always bother me.'

'Once you have felt the killing force, it always does.'

A shudder rippled down her spine. They looked at each other, the weapon between them gleaming with dull, quiescent power. Joscelin rose from the barrel and, taking her by the hand, led her out of the hall into the courtyard.

'Where's Robert?'

'With Conan. He's taken him to see the hawks in the mews.' His expression was rueful. 'Much as I love the boy, I need some respite.'

'He kept asking for you when we were hiding in the cellars,' she said. 'And when you came, he thought you were a god to have answered his cry.'

They walked across the baileys to the small herb garden, which was set in a quiet corner near one of the auxiliary kitchen buildings. 'But I'm not,' Joscelin said grimly. 'My feet are as much clay as any man's, and if he believes otherwise he is going to be terribly let down one day. He clings to me so hard that sometimes it is like being eaten alive. I need to escape for a while.'

'And now I come to you to eat you alive with my burdens, too,' she said. They entered the small garden and were assaulted by the scent of the various herbs basking in the sunshine.

Joscelin squeezed her hand. 'Burden me with anything you want.' He drew her down on to a turf seat situated under a rose vine. The flowers were just coming into bloom, the petals as pink as baby toes. Bees from the castle's hives hummed industriously among the blossoms.

She looked at him sidelong. In the cramped confines of the castle, beset by demands from every quarter, there had been no opportunity until now for them to talk in privacy. 'Even with another mouth to feed?' she asked, smiling.

At first he did not understand, but she saw the moment of comprehension brighten in his eyes and then slowly spread, lighting up his whole face. He kissed her – hard first and then very tenderly. 'You bring me not a burden but a wonderful gift,' he said, hugging her against him. 'How long have you known?'

'A few days only. I had a suspicion when we were preparing to travel to Nottingham and it has grown ever stronger. I do not believe my flux will come now.' She laughed and squeezed him back. 'The baby will be born in midwinter, I think, between Christmastide and Candlemas. I haven't told anyone else but your father suspects. He has a very sharp eye for all he claims never to take notice of women.' She sighed with exasperation. 'I did wonder about using it as a lever to keep him in his bed – the opportunity to live to see his grandchild – but I think he would just bellow at me and rupture his stitches. He's a stubborn old ox.'

'The news might sweeten him a little,' Joscelin said

307

thoughtfully, 'but then again, if he already suspects, he'll have spent time mulling over the prospect and it won't keep him occupied for long.'

'What if we told him the child was to be given his name?'

'He would say that it was his due but be secretly flattered. I doubt it would have any deep hold on him.' Joscelin shook his head. 'If he wants to go home to Arnsby, then so be it. I may just be able to persuade him to be borne on a litter for most of the journey. It will be more than his pride can stomach to enter the place flat on his back, so we'll have to provide a quiet horse for the final mile.'

'He is very weak,' Linnet objected. 'He lost a great deal of blood and he hasn't the strength to fight off the fever if it sets in. A day's jolting in a litter would be dangerous. He says he wants to die at home in his own bed. That is surely what he will do, doubtless with his wife gloating over him.'

Joscelin sighed. 'It is his choice. I believe he is dying anyway and if I can fulfill his wish to do so at home, then I will.'

'So you are not going to stop him?'

'I will talk to him but I will not gainsay his final decision.'

Linnet rose and walked to a small sundial standing as a hub in the midst of a wheel of fragrant herbs. The sun was almost directly overhead and no shadow touched the surface. She laid her palm on the warm stone. One life beginning, one drawing to a close, she thought, feeling the connection, and in between a lifetime's wheel of light and shadow.

Joscelin came up behind her and she turned in to his arms, knowing that, for her and Joscelin, their time was now and every moment too precious to be wasted.

32

Leaning on his elbow in the hay of the stable loft at Arnsby, Ralf watched Hulda, a kitchen maid, tidy her hair and brush ineffectually at the stalks of straw caught in her gown. She slid him a look through her lashes. Her eyes were a bright, winter-blue and, apart from her lush white breasts, her best feature. Her nose was lumpy, her lips thin and she had crooked teeth. Still, she was athletic and accommodating, tight and moist where it mattered.

Hulda was frequently sought out by the castle soldiers because, not only was she willing to lie with them for a pittance, she had the added attraction of being barren. No man was going to plant his seed and then find a woman whining at his tunic hem, demanding financial support for her growing belly. This being the case, the lady Agnes turned a blind eye to Hulda's copulatory industriousness and only groused if it interfered with her work in the kitchens.

'I heard Cook say your father's gone into Nottingham to find you a bride,' she fished as she secured her braid with a leather cord.

Ralf said nothing and stretched. Tufts of red-gold hair sprouted in his armpits.

'Is it true?' Hulda pursued. 'Are you really going to take a wife?'

Her eyes were avid and made him smile and bite the inside of his mouth. To lie with the lord's son was a source of power in itself but to have snippets of information straight from his own lips was even more useful.

'When the time comes,' he said with a shrug and picked his shirt off the straw. 'Here's a penny for you to spend next time the new packman comes calling.'

She took the coin willingly enough, but he saw the sulky droop of her lower lip. His own mouth tightened. The slut need not think he was going to pay her with information.

'Go on, back to the kitchens; you've been away from them long enough!' He gave her rump a stinging slap.

She squealed and, rubbing her buttock, said reproachfully, 'You was the one who took me from my duties and kept me here so long.'

Ralf laughed. 'If you'd wanted a short ride, you should have let Ivo mount you!'

'P'rhaps I will.' She set her foot upon the top rung of the ladder. There was a loud commotion in the stable below, and after briefly looking down, she tossed her head at Ralf. 'I'll ask him now, shall I?'

In the stable, a hard-ridden horse was blowing loudly as the groom unsaddled it. Hulda descended to the bottom step and stood aside, hands behind her back, eyes coyly weighing up Ivo who had just dismounted.

'Where's Ralf?' he snapped at her. She rolled her eyes towards the loft hatch. Ivo brushed her aside and shouted up. 'Ralf, in Jesu's name, come down. There's news!'

Alerted by Ivo's flushed face and his breathing, which

310

was louder than that of his hard-ridden courser, Ralf came to the trap and stood fastening his braies. 'Oh yes?'

Ivo peered up at him, chestnut hair sweat-dark on his brow. 'I met one of our messengers on the road. He'll be here soon, but his horse was tiring and mine was still fresh. It's Papa, Ralf – he's been wounded in a fight and they're bringing him home.'

Ralf's complexion flooded with colour and his brown eyes turned to liquid gold. 'Who is "they"?' he demanded. 'Move out of the way, let me come down.'

'Joscelin and that wife of his.' Ivo was almost leaping up and down with excitement. 'They stopped off at Rushcliffe on their way to leave the brat and his nurse, so the messenger says. Joscelin's wife's insisted on attending Papa all the way to Arnsby because he's in such a bad state. What's more, they're on their way here from the whore's chapel. Papa wanted to be taken there. He's dying, Ralf.'

Ralf descended the ladder and strode from the stables towards the keep. Elation surged through him. Ivo, shorter in the leg, had to run to keep up. 'Ferrers attacked Nottingham. Apparently our houses were sacked but Papa escaped with the women into the cellars of the house next door.'

'How was he wounded, then?'

'In a sword fight defending them – a deep cut to the left shoulder.'

Ralf grunted. If it was not all that he had hoped for, then it was still excellent news. Joscelin was bringing the old man home to die. They would ride through Arnsby's gates and never leave again. He glanced sharply at his scurrying brother. 'You didn't ride back along the road to greet them yourself, then?'

'No, I came straight to tell you.'

Ralf nodded with satisfaction. As a younger son, Ivo's inheritance was slim and likely to stay so unless he married well. He was dependent on the goodwill of the head of the household and obviously he had decided which way the wind was blowing.

'Go and give Mama the tidings, will you?' Ralf said. 'She will need to prepare the bedchamber if our father is as bad as you say.' And strew it with wormwood, gall and deadly nightshade, he thought. Maude was absent on one of her frequent visits to friends in convents and not expected home until the end of the week. His mother was always worse without Maude's presence to lend an absorbent ear.

Ivo glowered. 'What are you going to be doing?' he asked in a disgruntled voice.

Ralf parted his lips in a narrow, white grin. 'Preparing a welcoming committee, what else?'

33

'Blast you, woman, leave me alone, I'm all right, I tell you!' Ironheart snapped at Linnet.

'I haven't said a word!' she protested.

'It's the way you keep looking at me. God's arse, I could ride before I was out of napkins. I've lived in the saddle all my life, and if I die in one I'll be a damned sight more happy than lying on a litter like an old woman!'

Linnet pressed her lips together and somehow kept silent. Ironheart looked dreadful. His eyes were sunken and their dangerous glitter was as much fever as rage. She had managed to get him to swallow a cup of willow-bark tisane when they were at Morwenna's chapel, but he had refused to the point of apoplexy to be borne in a litter and had forced his will beyond his broken, dying body in order to mount his grey stallion at the block by the chapel door. As she had watched him wrestle with the horse, a lump had ached in her throat and she had had to fight hard to suppress tearful words at his stupidity. Joscelin had said nothing, just held the horse steady while his father dragged his shaking body into the saddle.

Linnet glanced at her husband now. He was riding on

his father's other side, affecting indifference but close enough to grab him if he fell. She might have thought Joscelin cold had she not witnessed his anguish in the privacy of their own chamber. 'He hates sentiment and fuss,' he had said, staring bleakly out of the narrow lance of window into Rushcliffe's bailey. 'He's dying. Nothing can change that. I won't break his pride.'

And for the sake of that pride, William de Rocher approached the keep his father had built to protect the lands that the de Rochers had seized at the time of the great Conquest. Like the first William de Rocher, he came astride a war-horse, a polished sword at his hip, his gaze glittering and hungry. But his ancestor had had thirty more years of life before him to build his stronghold, marry a thegn's daughter and beget the next generation. Ironheart's own time was measured in hours.

Scaffolding stood against Arnsby's walls, although on a different section from last year, and the same builders, masons and painters were busy about the task of maintenance. The castle gates stood open and the road was a sunlit white ribbon disappearing into the bailey.

The grey stallion, scenting familiarity, plunged and strained at the bit and Ironheart almost lost control of him, for only one arm had any strength left in it to pull back and that was pared of flesh and fever-weakened.

Quickly Joscelin leaned over and grabbed the bridle. 'Whoa, steady,' he said. The stallion's ears flickered and the skin twitched upon its sweating hide, but its pace slackened.

'Let go, I can manage,' Ironheart said in a hoarse, death-rattle voice. His face was grey apart from two scarlet flashes of fever upon each cheekbone.

'Papa—'

'Let go, I tell you!'

314

Joscelin released the bridle and, setting his jaw, looked away. Linnet's heart ached for both men. She saw the glimmer of unshed tears in Joscelin's eyes and the rapid movement of his throat. It was almost more than she could bear and she had to turn her own head.

In the bailey, the messenger's arrival had ensured they were expected and there were people to greet them. Two serving men stood to attention beside a stretcher fashioned of latticed rope. Lady Agnes was present, attired in her best red gown and silk wimple. At her side, Martin shifted from foot to foot, his hair damp and his face freshly scrubbed. Ivo, a frown on his face, had one hand on the child's shoulder, the other on his sword hilt, as he watched the company approach. But it was Ralf who stepped forward to take his father's bridle; Ralf resplendent in a tunic of grass-green silk with gold braid trimmings. Ironheart's spare sword belt – the one he never wore because he said it looked as if it ought to belong to a court whore – was buckled around Ralf's lean hips.

Breath bubbling, Ironheart stared down at his heir. 'Why are you trapped out like a marchpane fancy?' he wheezed.

'To honour your homecoming, sire,' Ralf responded, his brown eyes reflecting golden glints from his costume. 'To accord you the respect that is your due.'

'You call this respect?' Spittle appeared on the old man's lips and his shoulders trembled with more than just the thud of his fever-driven heart. He stared round the silent group of his family and met his wife's bitter, triumphant eyes. 'When I am dead, then you can dance upon my grave,' he ground out, 'but by God, you'll not mock me while there's still breath in my body!' He wheeled the grey around and dug in his spurs. The horse neighed and gave a startled leap forward before breaking into a gallop.

315

'Papa!' Joscelin tried to turn Whitesocks but his way was blocked by other mounts and he could only watch helplessly as the grey bolted towards the gateway.

It was sealed. The port culis was down and the massive oak doors had been closed behind the party and the bar drawn across. The grey reared to a halt. Too weak to hold on any longer, Ironheart was pitched from the saddle and hit the ground like a child's doll made of rags and straw.

Linnet reined her mare aside and Joscelin was finally able to turn Whitesocks and gallop down to the gateway. The grey milled round the bailey, head high, eyes rolling, avoiding the efforts of the groom to capture it. Joscelin flung down from the saddle and knelt at his father's side. Ironheart still breathed, his willpower holding him yet to life and consciousness.

'Tell the guards to open the gates,' he forced out, then stopped to cough. 'Tell them I command it.'

The two menservants approached with the litter, Ralf pacing beside them.

Joscelin glanced at the four men on gate duty. They returned his stare with a blankness that penetrated his gut. He had never seen them before and, from the way their hands hovered over their weapons, he did not believe that they would respond to any command but Ralf's.

'The fever has overset his wits.' Ralf shook his head sadly and glanced over his shoulder. 'Mama, you had best take him to your chamber and care for him there. Obviously he has been neglected to the point of death.'

Ironheart made a choking sound. Joscelin jerked to his feet and faced Ralf's gleaming smile. 'How long have you been planning this?'

'Planning what?' Ralf gave a laconic shrug. 'I'm a dutiful son. Ever since I came home in the autumn, I haven't set a foot wrong. The gates are closed for a good reason.'

Ironheart groaned as he was lifted on to the rope stretcher and Agnes de Rocher smiled at the sound.

Joscelin stared at Ralf. 'What reason?'

Ralf shrugged. 'My father is too weak and sick to go anywhere and in such dangerous times it behoves me to keep those gates shut. The Scots are over the border again, did you know? And the Flemish will be sailing any day for Norfolk.'

'The gates were wide open when we arrived,' Joscelin said icily.

'Indeed and how better to defend myself than by capturing my enemies? I have the proof of what you have done to my poor father. In the name of King Henry the Younger, I arrest you for treason and attempted parricide.'

Joscelin began to shake. 'You stinking, conniving, treacherous *nithing*!' he spat and leaped, bearing Ralf to the bailey floor. He succeeded in making of his brother's nose a scarlet squelch before the gate guards managed to drag him off. Joscelin's soldiers were prevented from joining the affray by more of Ralf's hired men. The ordinary castle guards who had always owed their loyalty to Ironheart looked on and did nothing. Ralf might be overstepping his authority, and Joscelin might be Ironheart's favourite son, but their lord was dying and in the future they would look to Ralf to pay their wages.

Ralf regained his feet. Blood dribbled from his nose, masking his mouth and chin and dripping ruinously onto the green silk. Joscelin struggled in the rough embrace of the gate guards. 'You have no authority!' he spat.

'I have all the authority I need,' Ralf retorted nasally. 'And to prove it, at noon tomorrow, I am going to hang you from the battlements. Then I'm going to have you flayed and your hide nailed to Arnsby's gates.' He flicked a brusque gesture at the guards. 'Take him away and put him in the oubliette. Mama, I leave you to make arrangements for my father and Lady de Montsorrel.' He dabbed his bloody nose with his sleeve.

Agnes stared at Ralf as if he had descended from the heavens in a cloud of light. Slowly she folded him a deep curtsey. Open-mouthed, Ivo gaped at her, then at his brother. Beneath his frozen hand, Martin's shoulder quivered.

'I won't let you hang, Joscelin, I won't!' the child burst out. 'He hasn't done anything, you just want him out of the way because he's better than you are!' He flung himself at Ralf, screaming and pummelling.

'Hold your tongue, brat!' Ralf sent Martin reeling with a clout to the side of his head. 'It's not your place to speak of matters you know nothing about. Ivo, get him out of my sight!'

Looking dazed, Ivo took Martin by the scruff and dragged him away, still kicking and shrieking. The guards stripped Joscelin of sword, dagger and purse. Then they manhandled him towards the keep, jabbing him roughly with their spear butts to make him move.

Linnet screamed his name and rode her mare at the guards but she was intercepted, the bridle was grasped, and she was pulled down off the horse. Agnes de Rocher seized her arm in a vicious grip. 'You don't want to go where he's going, my dear,' she hissed. 'The oubliette's no place for a lady of gentle breeding.' Her voice oozed venom. 'Come with me to the bower and learn from me how a sick man should truly be nursed.' Her gaze gloated upon Ironheart.

Linnet struggled to wrench herself free but Agnes held fast. Hanged and then flayed. Burning nausea rose in Linnet's throat. Straining away from Agnes, she was sick.

Agnes did not for one second relent of her fierce grip, but her brown eyes roved quickly over Linnet's figure and then narrowed.

'You're not really going to hang him tomorrow, are you?' Ivo looked nervously at Ralf and ignored the steaming, skewered small birds on the trencher in front of him.

Shrugging, Ralf took a loaf from the dish that the squire had just placed in front of him. He sat in his father's chair on the high dais, a white linen cloth covering the trestle. The best tableware had been set before him: silver-gilt goblets and expensive golden wine glowing through the incised rock crystal of a Byzantine flagon. He had exchanged his bloodstained tunic for one chequered in two shades of blue. The effect was not as opulent as the green but it still flaunted his rank and displayed to advantage his strong bone structure and thick, red-blond hair.

'What else should I do with him?' Ralf broke the bread and bit into the fragrant, soft interior.

'He's our brother, too.'

Ralf swallowed. His gaze narrowed. 'Surely you're not squeamish?'

Ivo grimaced. 'I don't like Joscelin,' he said, taking one of the loaves, 'but I don't hate him like you do. It doesn't matter who his mother was, he's still of our blood.'

Ralf continued to eat. 'I have never noticed yours being thicker than water before,' he said.

'You have never taken it this far before.' Ivo crumbled the bread between his fingers and then blinked at the mess on his wooden trencher. 'Papa heard everything you said in the bailey. I saw his face.'

Ralf's expression darkened. He threw down his own bread and lifted a knife from the table to drag one of the

319

small birds off the spit. Amber fat dripped on to the cloth. 'I intended him to hear every word,' he said. 'Let him have his first taste of hell even before he gets there.'

Ivo drank his wine and wondered how long it would take to get drunk.

'Of course,' Ralf added softly, his voice still nasal from the dried blood clogging his nostrils, 'if you don't approve of what I do, you can always take to the tourney road and hold Joscelin's memory sacred by selling your own sword – although God knows who would want to buy it! I warn you, if you're not prepared to work in my interests then get out now.'

Ivo bit his lip. 'And if I am prepared?'

'You have always coveted our father's manor house near Melton. You can have that and the hunting lodge and I'll find you a rich young wife to go with it. But only for your obedience. I don't want you running here and there in your usual weasel fashion, carrying tales and blowing hot and cold.'

Taking his cup, Ivo left the table and went to stand before the deep fire pit around which the eating trestles were grouped. Red heat simmered over him. The manor house had only been built six years ago and boasted a proper stone fireplace and a private room where the lord could withdraw to his pleasures, whatever they happened to be. The windows in the solar were fitted with real glass and the ceiling had a French design of gold knots upon a rich green background. Their father did not care for luxury but recognized that sometimes important guests had to be entertained and it was useful to have somewhere opulent to do so. A manor house was far less expensive to furbish than a castle.

Ivo swung round to find Ralf still watching him. 'All right,' he said. 'You have my obedience.' And at the

320

back of his mind he saw the image of a man swinging from the castle battlements in the wind.

Ralf smiled. A moist white sliver of meat dangled between his forefinger and thumb. 'And you will do me homage for what I give you before witnesses. Tomorrow, in the bailey.'

Suddenly the image of the hanging man came sharply into focus and Ivo saw with foreboding that it was his own body that dangled on the end of Ralf's rope, suffused and choking.

'Go and get the scribe,' Ralf said, wiping his fingers on a napkin. 'I've got messages to send.'

34

In Maude's chamber a single candle burned at the dying man's bedside. The priest finished his ministrations and started to put away the vial of holy oil and Communion wafers in a small cedarwood pyx.

Linnet watched the proceedings from a low stool in the corner where she sat with Ella and Martin. Agnes lurked near the priest and Linnet fancied that she was like a demon, awaiting her moment to dart in and snatch Ironheart's soul. This was her dark domain. The rooms belonging to Ironheart had been seized by Ralf to underline his authority, and so Agnes had insisted on nursing him here.

Nursing him! Standing over him smiling like a gargoyle, Linnet thought with a shudder. The nightmare, she knew, had only just begun and she couldn't let it progress any further. Yet, trapped like this, how was she to prevent it?

The priest turned to leave, murmuring that now was the time for the grieving relatives to pay their last respects. Linnet rose from the stool and quietly apprehended the cleric as he approached the door.

'Father, I beg you to intercede with Lord Ralf, make him see that what he is about to do is godless.'

The priest looked down at the hand she had laid upon his sleeve with ill-concealed distaste and she quickly removed it.

'Daughter, what will be, will be, and I cannot change it,' he replied. 'Lord Ralf is not acting without just cause.'

Linnet wiped her hand on her gown, wishing now that she had not touched him. 'Just cause!' she choked. 'You call murdering his own brother a just cause!'

'Daughter, your loyalty commends you but it is misplaced. You must search your heart for the obedience to God's will.'

'To God's will I am ever obedient, Father,' she retorted. 'But perhaps you should search your own heart, too, if you can find it beneath the fear for your purse.'

The priest drew himself up but, full of disgust, she faced him and refused to let his haughty stare beat her down. Finally, he turned on his heel and stalked out.

Linnet released her breath and her shoulders drooped. When she turned round, she discovered that Agnes de Rocher was watching her with a smile. 'There is no way out,' she said softly, and a cold ripple ran down Linnet's spine. Thank Jesu that she had owned the foresight not to bring Robert to Arnsby. But if Joscelin was hanged, how long would her little boy be safe?

Ironheart groaned and Agnes's head rotated to the sound. She hastened to the bedside and leaned over her grey-faced husband who was propped up on several goose-down bolsters. Everything about him was sunken, as if all his vital juices had been sucked out, leaving naught but a skeleton clad in skin. Against all adversity, a spark of life still glinted in the bruised eyes and it was directed not at his gloating wife but at Linnet and his youngest offspring. With a tremendous effort, his hand wavered up and he beckoned.

Linnet approached the bed and stood at the opposite side from the glowering Agnes. Her flesh crawled. Martin hesitated, then came to stand beside her. He refused to look at his mother and Linnet felt his shoulders trembling as she put her arm around them.

Ironheart stretched out his hand to her and his youngest son. Linnet took it and felt through its thinness the blaze of fever.

'You were right,' he whispered. 'I should have died in Nottingham.'

Linnet blinked and swallowed. Within her, a rage of bitterness demanded that she agree with him but she held it down, knowing it would serve no useful purpose. Nor would she show him anything but love and duty in front of Martin and his rejoicing, mad wife. She looked at the scarred, shiny hand within her own two smooth ones. 'For that matter, we should have kept you at Rushcliffe.'

Agnes snorted and Linnet glared at her through a veil of tears.

Ironheart closed his eyes and Linnet saw him struggle, summoning what strength remained in his emaciated body for the effort of speech. 'The scribe . . .' he said. 'I have made my will known to him.' His eyes opened again and met hers, pushing a message at her. 'The scribe,' he repeated, as if rambling, but his gaze was lucid.

At first Linnet was bewildered and then she remembered that Ironheart's scribe these days was Fulbert, whom Joscelin had sent here rather than hang. Fulbert might owe Joscelin a life, but he was as spineless as a lump of blancmange. It was a slim thread of a chance at the most but, nevertheless, it was hope and the spark of it filled her with new energy.

Agnes snorted again. 'Do not look so eager, girl,' she sneered. 'There's nothing in his will for you. The fool has made grants to the Church and freed some serfs. Of course,' she added with a sly smile, 'the bequest to the nunnery won't be necessary now, will it?'

Ironheart's lips curved cynically. 'Do not be so sure of that, wife. Ralf won't keep you here unless it's under lock and key.'

'Ralf and I have a perfect understanding,' Agnes said coldly.

'Yours or his?'

Agnes drew herself up but he turned his head away from her and addressed Linnet. 'Have a care to yourself, whatever happens,' he whispered. 'And my blessing upon you and Joscelin. Give it to him if you can. There is so much I wanted to tell him . . . so much.'

Linnet leaned over Ironheart and kissed him on his dry, hot lips. The presence of death was so close that it was tangible. Once, she would have recoiled in horror from the very thought of doing this but she was free of her fetters now. And she wanted him to know that he was not alone, that she at least would stand on the edge of the river and bid him farewell with sorrow.

Then it was Martin's turn. He knelt at his father's bedside and Ironheart laid his hand on his youngest son's bright-brown hair. Martin flinched but once, then held his ground, his lips pressed together. Linnet could see that Ironheart was beyond speech and that the boy's composure was more than precarious as he struggled with his revulsion.

'If you die,' he suddenly burst out, 'Ralf will kill Joscelin!'

Ironheart's lids tensed and squeezed. He drew in a wheezing breath and let it out, shuddering with dry anguish. Linnet quickly drew Martin away from the bedside, gesturing the maids to come and take the boy, but he twisted in her arms and made the sign of the cross over himself. 'And then I swear by Jesus Christ that I will kill Ralf!'

'Martin!' Agnes marched around the foot of the bed and slapped her youngest son across the face.

'I will do it!' he yelled. 'I swear I will!' His chin jutted in defiance. The handprint on his cheek slowly turned from white to red.

His mother quivered. From the bed there came a sound that might almost have been grim laughter and Agnes whirled, her hands closing and unclosing, her face scarlet with pent-up fury.

'You think it amusing, do you?' she hissed at Ironheart, leaning over him. 'Then let me make you laugh some more. Let me tell you about your whore, your precious Morwenna, about how she died. You would like to know, wouldn't you?'

Horror froze Linnet to the spot as Agnes bent over her husband, her lips tauntingly close to his in the parody of a lover's. She saw the man try to turn aside but Agnes turned with him, her head moving like a snake.

'For all these years you thought she tripped on her gown and fell down the stairs. I saw her, you know, I was behind her at the time. She was so big with child that her balance wasn't good. One push was all it took, one small push and down she went, belly first, then head over heels.' Agnes spoke slowly, relishing each word, her eyes never leaving his face. 'She was still conscious when she reached the bottom of the stairs, so I dropped a loom weight on her head to make sure she was silenced. She never recovered her wits and I saw you put in the hell you deserved.' Her voice sank to a whisper. 'Jesu, but it was worth it.'

Ironheart's right hand whipped up and clamped around her throat.

326

'Poisonous bitch!' he wheezed. 'I'll show you what hell truly is!'

Agnes clawed and struggled, but the man whose physical strength had once denied the bite of an iron sword blade only tightened his death grip. The tendons stood out like ropes on his taut forearm.

Agnes collapsed to her knees at the bedside, her face the colour of ripe plums. Linnet recovered the use of her limbs and ran to the bed to pull Ironheart and his wife apart. She wedged hip and shoulder against the strangling Agnes and grasped Ironheart's arm at the juncture of wrist and palm. Through her own hand she felt the violent shuddering of his fury. And then, as she strove to break his grip, crying at him to stop, his eyes suddenly widened. 'Morwenna,' he gasped, staring beyond the women at something only he could see. His fingers relaxed and his arm fell limply to his side. He did not draw another breath.

Wheezing, gulping for air, Agnes fell to the floor. Linnet left her to the maids, and taking Martin's arm, pulled him away.

He was trembling and pale, and the eyes he raised to her were numb with misery and shock. Linnet squeezed his thin shoulders – too thin to carry the burdens with which they were being laden.

'We must save Joscelin,' she said, drawing him towards the door. 'Now is our one chance while your mother and the maids are distracted. Take me to the chapel and then go and bring Fulbert the scribe to me.'

He looked at her uncertainly.

'Fulbert owes Joscelin his life. I am calling in the debt. It is the only way of sending a message outside. Does Ralf read and write?'

'A little – only his name. He uses a scribe normally.' The words emerged stiffly, his lips barely moving.

327

'Good. Quickly now.' She urged him towards the door. A swift glance over her shoulder reassured her that for the moment Agnes was too taken up by her struggle to breathe to notice their exit and the maids were all fussing round her.

Once out of the room with its death smell and dreadful images, Martin rallied. A guard had been posted at the foot of the stairs but he let them pass when the boy told him in an authoritative tone that his mother had bid him take Lady Linnet to the chapel to light a candle and say prayers. Linnet, the image of distressed modesty, kept her eyes lowered and shrank from the guard's scrutiny. Let him believe she had no spirit.

A cold draught twisted round the newel post and fingered past her. She caught the familiar smell of dank stone, but there was an underlying, elusive scent. The guard must have noticed it too, for he turned and looked at the stairs behind him and even mounted them to peer around the newel post. Linnet shivered, thinking of Morwenna de Gael, and remembering Robert's tale of a lady in a green gown he had encountered here. 'If you can hear me,' she entreated Morwenna's spirit, 'help me save your son and your unborn grandchild!'

She was answered only by the echo of her own whisper and the heavy fluttering of the torches in the sconces.

In the cold, functional chapel, Linnet lit a candle and genuflected to the altar, then bowed her head to pray, seeking the strength to stay calm throughout the following hours. Martin dutifully crossed himself and then slipped away in search of Fulbert.

As Linnet eased her position on the hard stone flags, she heard a sound from one of the niches in the chapel wall. Heart pounding, she looked round, half expecting to see the luminous figure of Morwenna de Gael but it was a man's form that rose from the shadows and began edging towards the rear of the chapel.

'Who's there?' she demanded, standing up. The man did not reply but she knew he had heard her speak, for he hesitated. A brief gleam of light caught the side of his face before he went out and she wondered for who or what Ivo de Rocher had been praying. Was his soul troubled at the prospect of fratricide? She wondered if she dared approach him for succour.

Hesitant footsteps pattered outside the chapel door, stopped, were silent for the space of several heartbeats, and then advanced.

'My lady?' The scribe's whisper was hoarse with anxiety. 'It is not safe here. I just saw Lord Ivo. What if he says something?'

'He won't,' Linnet said with more confidence than she felt and came to draw the scribe farther into the church, before the altar so that the cross cast a long shadow between them.

Fulbert licked his lips and gave a worried look over his shoulder. 'I cannot stay long. I'm supposed to be visiting the privy.'

'I suppose I should be grateful that you have come at all,' Linnet said, her nostrils flaring with anger. 'Lord Joscelin spared your miserable neck once. Is it too much to expect that you should repay the favour?'

Fulbert ceased licking his lips and began to chew them instead. 'Of course I will help if I can, mistress, but I fail to see what I can do.'

She swallowed and controlled both her temper and her patience. 'It is obvious what you must do. Write to the constable in Nottingham and Conan at Rushcliffe, telling them to come at once. You are responsible for giving

329

sealed parchments to messengers and Ralf will have had much to send out today. It will not be hard to include another two.'

Fulbert gulped.

Linnet watched him wring his fat hands and wondered how he managed to create such wonderful, delicate script. Somewhere there had to be a hidden wellspring. 'Yes or no?' she said fiercely as he continued to mumble and scrutinize his feet.

'Mistress, I will do my best.' He darted her a look from beneath his brows and sidled towards the door.

Linnet's heart plummeted. The man was a coward; she could read his intention clearly in his eyes. 'God grant you forgiveness, for I will not!' she hissed, her voice shaking and then, hearing herself, she compressed her lips. Jesu, I sound like Agnes de Rocher, she thought. What if I become like her? And she knew that at noon tomorrow, if Joscelin died, she would not care what she became.

35

Torch in hand, Ralf wound his way down into the bowels of the keep. The guards he encountered saluted him, their eyes shifting. The authority to command them was now his, but while his father still clung to life it was incomplete. And what he intended to do tomorrow did not meet with unanimous approval.

Ralf responded to the sidelong looks with an air of supreme indifference but, behind his mask, he was irritated by their uncertainty. Indeed, they made him feel tense, for their attitude unsettled his own view of himself as being utterly in control. Once his father and Joscelin were out of the way, he told himself, everything would come right. The black bitterness would leave him and he would be healed.

He moved through the undercroft, the heat from the torch searing his face as he passed barrels, casks and bins of supplies, until he came to the cells. Behind stoutly barred doors set with small iron grilles for observation of the prisoners, Joscelin's men were being held captive together with those of his father's soldiers who had objected to his taking command of Arnsby. Keeping guard were two Flemish mercenaries he had borrowed from Robert Ferrers. Although unmannerly and rough, they at least seemed to know how to use their weapons, which half of their countrymen didn't, and they did as they were instructed without demur.

Finally, at the very end of the undercroft where the shadows were deepest, Ralf came to the bolted trap covering the mouth of the oubliette. He stood upon the door with its wrought-iron bandings, his legs planted wide, and imagined Joscelin twenty feet below him, staring up into the pitch blackness. The oubliette was a deep, windowless pit. Originally it had been constructed with the dual purpose of storing roots and confining difficult prisoners in hope of demoralizing them into submission. Underground seepage, however, meant that there was always six inches of murky sludge lying in the bottom of the pit and the roots were far better stored in the main undercroft. It was still, however, used occasionally for prisoners. A couple of days standing ankle-deep in cold water without food usually subdued the most stubborn captives – if they did not die of the lung fever first.

Ralf quivered. He could feel Joscelin's presence as if the two of them were bound together by an umbilical cord. The temptation to open the trap and peer inside was almost unbearable. What was Joscelin doing? What was he feeling, knowing that in the morning he was going to die?

Ralf's mind wandered back to a hot summer's day when he was on the brink of adolescence. Joscelin had been fifteen then, big-boned and gawky with a voice like a cracked cup. Ralf remembered baiting him, taunting and teasing, following him round, refusing to leave him alone. In the end, Joscelin's temper had snapped and he had turned upon his tormentor. Ralf had been injured but he had made far more of a fuss than his wounds warranted. Enough for their father to administer Joscelin a sound thrashing. Ralf could still taste the triumph of that day. At the time, he had thought it worth every bruise.

Of course, it had not lasted. Joscelin had run away, their father had blamed Ralf for it and the deception had come home to roost with a vengeance. Old fool. The torch sputtered and resin hissed at Ralf's feet. He considered tomorrow's revenge and through the triumph felt a disturbing frisson as he imagined Joscelin kicking at the end of a rope. A desperate need to see the thing accomplished warred with a feeling of utter revulsion. A small voice inside him was crying that he would never be free of Joscelin, whatever he did.

The torch was growing heavy and making his arm tremble. 'Damn you!' he snarled into the darkness and, turning on his heel, strode back towards light and company.

In the hall, he noticed that the scribe had returned from his visit to the latrine and was busy with his quill once more. He set his torch in an empty wall sconce and went over to the man.

'How soon will you be finished?' He braced his thin fingers on the trestle and leaned over the parchments.

'Soon, my lord, v-very soon.'

Ralf eyed Fulbert's trembling hand and then the script. That at least appeared neat and flowing even if its creator was a gibbering wreck. Well, he needed the man for now but he could soon and easily replace him. Scribes were ten a half-penny in Nottingham. 'Make haste,' he said. 'And have the messengers ride out immediately you have finished.'

'Yes, lord.' Fulbert swallowed bulbously. Then his gaze settled beyond Ralf's shoulder. Turning, Ralf saw Father Hubert standing to one side, his expression grim and his hands toying with a silver cross hanging on a cord from his belt.

'Sir William is dead,' announced the priest. 'I think you should come to your mother's chamber, my lord. He had some sort of seizure in his last moments and assaulted the lady Agnes. She is asking for you.'

Ralf looked down and gently opened the fists he had clenched on hearing Father Hubert's news. So now he was indeed 'my lord' and no one in the keep to gainsay his will. 'Tell her I will come as soon as I can,' he said, and felt a black desolation overshadowing his triumph.

Stomach rolling with fear, Fulbert finished working on the missives that Ralf had commanded him to write, sealing them in hot wax with the ring the young man had pulled from his father's finger in the courtyard. His hands shook as he set all except two to one side. He paused to try and think but was horribly aware of time slipping away with each moment he procrastinated. He had a choice to make and make it now he must. He imagined Judgement Day with his sins on one side of the scales and his good deeds on the other. He remembered Lady Linnet's accusing grey eyes. Then he thought of the fires of hell and came face-to-face with his own cowardice.

In trembling haste his hands went to the leaves of clean vellum at his left-hand side. He folded deftly, attached seals, scrawled salutations, but the pages were entirely blank. These he gave out to the messengers who were to ride to Robert Ferrers of Derby and the men of Leicester's and Norfolk's mesnie. The two letters most recently written, he gave to the men with the best horses. Fortunately for his quaking knees, Fulbert was not questioned. It was only polite custom that the king's representative in Nottingham be informed of a baronial death, and if Lord Ralf wanted letters delivered to Rushcliffe then that was his own business.

When the last horseman had clattered out of the postern gate onto the road, Fulbert returned to his lectern, and screwing up the letters he had written on Ralf's behalf summoning the rebels to Arnsby he tossed them in the great hearth. As soon as he was sure that they had been consumed by the flames, he went to rouse his wife and children and pack his belongings for another move.

36

In his prison, Joscelin stared upward and listened to the footsteps recede. Not even a glint of light betrayed the whereabouts of the trapdoor but he had felt Ralf's presence above him. He had almost cried out, wanting to reason with his brother, but the thought of Ralf's mocking smile had kept him silent. He knew no amount of reasoning would alter his brother's decision. Ralf had thought it out this time, had taken rapid advantage of the situation and manipulated it well.

Joscelin had witnessed enough hangings to know what would happen. If the angle was right and the rope did not snag against the keep wall, death would be instantaneous as the force of the fall snapped his neck. If not, it would be a slow, strangling fight for air, flesh swelling and discolouring, bowels and bladder voiding their contents. Either way, there was only death and indignity at the end.

He wondered if Ralf would force Linnet to watch. The thought ripped through him like a knife and he wrenched himself around in the darkness and splashed through the cold mud until the wall brought him up short and he struck it with bruising force, then slumped with a groan of frustration. Every breath he took was invaded by the smell of mould and damp – like earth clinging to a corpse. Shaking with cold, he considered taking his own life so that when Ralf came to drag him out to the gallows tomorrow, he would be cheated of his final victory. He could dash himself against the wall until he knocked himself unconscious and drowned in the sludge at his feet. Or he could cut the veins in his wrists with the sharp notch on his belt. His breathing calmed while he considered the enormity of such a move. Ralf would still have won but not on the terms he desired.

Joscelin knew he would be damned forever if he took his own life, but then he could spend eternity in pursuit of Ralf. Slowly he put his hand upon his belt and unlatched it, rubbing his thumb over the notch of the buckle. Above him, at the trapdoor, he heard movement again, the gritty scuffling of footsteps and the sound of something heavy being dropped on the trap. He ran the leather through his hands, to and fro, and stared aloft, licking his lips. The heavy bolts on top of the trap were being stealthily drawn back. Was it morning already? His gut churned. Surely not. Perhaps Ralf was easing his conscience by offering him the comfort of a priest before they took him out to the gibbet.

The trap opened. Joscelin saw the dull glimmer of a small candle and the dark bulk of a lone human figure. It made no sound, save to grunt as it worked busily at something above. And then a thick hempen rope snaked down towards him and dangled to a halt at his collarbone.

For one horrible moment Joscelin thought that they had come to hang him here and now in the oubliette – swiftly in the dark, without witnesses – but his common sense soon reasserted itself. If they were going to hang him now they would have brought a ladder and more lights. And there would have been guards to restrain him while the noose was placed around his neck. Whoever had cast down the rope meant him well.

Breathing lightly, gazing upwards, he listened hard and thought he heard soft footfalls walking away. The trap remained open, and the rope ceased to quiver and hung straight down before his face. All was silent except for the drip-drip of water down the walls. In the faint light from above he could see the gleam of wet stone and the pale vapour of his breath. He latched the belt around his waist again and rubbed his palms upon his tunic, for they were suddenly slick with cold sweat. It was a long climb to the top of the oubliette, and if he fell from a height his body would be broken, for there was not enough water in the base of the pit to absorb his fall. But since the alternative was death, what did it matter?

He crossed himself, murmured a plea to God, then he leaped, setting his hands upon the rope and winding his feet around it. The tough hemp fibres burned his hands as he struggled upwards like a caterpillar on a stem. Hot pain lanced up his arms as, hand over hand, knees and thighs inching and gripping, he progressed towards the dull light of the trapdoor, knowing that at any moment he might be discovered.

By the time he hauled himself over the edge, his palms were blistered raw. Every muscle was screaming and there was a red mist before his eyes. He was horribly aware that he was making too much noise in his efforts to breathe, that he was easy, conspicuous prey. He crawled to his knees, panting hard, trying to keep quiet.

When his vision cleared, he saw that whoever had dropped the rope had left a candle burning on a pricket

338

to give him light and beside it was an old scramaseax – a common Englishman's weapon, midway between a sword and a knife. However, it was good and sharp and made light work of severing the rope from the barrel of sand around which his rescuer had double-looped it to bear Joscelin's weight. He cast the rope back down into the oubliette, and after what seemed an eternity, heard it splash in the water below. His heart was still pounding like a runaway horse but his breathing was easier now and the fiery ache was leaving his muscles.

Tucking the scramaseax in his belt, he closed the trapdoor over the oubliette and refastened the iron double bolts so that, to the casual observer, all would seem normal. Who, he wondered, could have given him the grace of this chance to avoid death? He was certain that his first visitor had been Ralf. He had felt him, blood and bone and dark bitter hatred. But the second time? There were several people in the keep who might have sprung the trap for him – he was Ironheart's favoured son and well known to the family retainers – but he doubted they would have been permitted past Ralf's Flemish guards.

It was a mystery, and likely to remain so, for his rescuer appeared to desire anonymity – nor could he blame him. Joscelin picked up the candle and snuffed it out. Thus might his life have been quenched on the morrow. Thus might it still happen unless he succeeded in making his escape and freeing his men from the cells.

He moved tentatively through the undercroft, feeling his way past barrels and sheaves, laundry tubs and sacks. Each footstep had to be carefully negotiated for the darkness was almost complete, and if he knocked anything over he knew Ralf's guards would hasten to investigate.

He found one of the stone columns that rose in an

arch supporting the undercroft roof. Carefully he measured his paces between it and the next one. Ten. And another ten to the one after that. He knew that the dimensions of the undercroft roughly corresponded to those of the hall above, and that if he followed the pillars they would lead him eventually to the stairs.

Another ten paces, another column, and beneath his fingertips he felt lines cut in the sandstone. Investigation revealed that someone had carved out a gaming board. There was the outlining square, the two inner squares and the peg holes at intervals. Every sense stood on edge as Joscelin realized he must be very close to the cells now. The carving would have been made by one of the guards at some time to stave off the boredom of a long stint of duty.

Joscelin moved to the next column, took another five steps and came up against some barrels. Wine for the hall, he thought. That was always close to the entrance because of frequent use. Besides, he could see the dim outline of the casks. Beyond the next pillar two candle lanterns were hung from pegs in the wall and radiated a diffuse golden light. He caught the sound of voices, the rattle of dice in a cup.

He crept sideways along the row of casks until a short trestle table came into view between the pillars. Seated at either end was a guard. There was more light now, for a half-burned candle stood in the centre of the trestle. A mutilated loaf stood on a wooden trencher and there was a pitcher beside it. The men were not drinking at the moment because one of the cups was being used as a shaker for their dice.

He could see that each man wore a sword and that their spears were propped against the cell walls. The cells themselves were barred from the outside with stout oak planks and had small iron grilles at the top. Guy de Montauban was looking out of one of them, watching the game.

'How long until dawn?' Montauban asked the guards.

'An hour, less perhaps,' answered one of them in a strong Flemish accent. 'Eager to see the hanging and flaying, are you?'

'It will be cold-blooded murder. If you are a party to it, you will have signed your own death warrant.'

The Fleming laughed, shook the dice and rattled them across the trestle. 'At least you'll keep warm on all the hot air coming from your mouth,' he said and rubbed his hands. 'Seven again, Joachim, that's your belt you owe me.'

The other guard groaned and, removing his scabbard, unlatched the handsome tooled belt from around his waist.

Joscelin rose silently from behind the barrels. Guy de Montauban saw him and his eyes widened in surprise. Then he began to shout and howl and scream as if possessed. The guard who had been rolling the dice leaped to his feet and went to the cell to see what was happening. Joscelin ran round the barrels and attacked the other Fleming. The man had no time to defend himself. Belt still in hand, mouth open in astonishment, he turned to face Joscelin. Joscelin aimed not at his mail-clad torso but at his legs, which were only covered by woollen chausses and leggings. The scramaseax was sharp and the Fleming fell as Joscelin hamstrung him in a single swipe. His companion drew his sword and flung round to face Joscelin.

Casting aside the scramaseax because the Fleming's sword would far outreach it, Joscelin leaped over the bleeding soldier and grabbed one of the propped spears. Then he moved in again to the attack, jabbing and thrusting with the sharp iron point while, behind him, the other guard screamed and thrashed on the floor.

The Fleming parried a couple of times, cast a rapid glance over his shoulder at the distance to the stairs and cried, 'I yield, I yield!' and dropped his weapon.

Joscelin did not lower the spear. 'Unbar the cells,' he commanded, jerking the point.

The Fleming did as he was told, fumbling in his haste to lift the heavy wooden beams out of their slots.

'Now attend to your friend before he dies,' Joscelin said as the prisoners within pushed open their doors and burst out to freedom. 'Use that belt you so prized to strap off the bleeding.'

'Lord Joscelin!' Guy de Montauban's eyes were glowing with exultation and an excess of wild anger. 'How did you manage to escape?'

'Someone opened the oubliette trap and dropped down a rope. I don't know who; he did not wait to make himself known. Did you see anyone go past?'

'Ralf came before midnight, walking as if he owned the world, the whoreson,' Montauban spat, as if mention of the name had fouled his mouth.

'No one else?'

'I don't know. I think I must have slept some of the time. The rattle of their dice woke me up. What about you, Alain?' Montauban turned to a bowlegged, sandy-haired man. 'Did you see anyone?'

'Someone did come.' Alain rubbed the side of his nose. 'But I didn't see his face. He was wearing a cloak and a short hood – a blue one, I remember. The guards knew him and weren't bothered.'

'Ivo!' Joscelin said with surprise. 'I always thought he was Ralf's minion.' But then, perhaps Ivo was no longer prepared to follow where Ralf chose to lead. 'How many

342

of us are there?' He took a swift headcount. Six of his father's men, six of his own and himself. Thirteen, the unlucky number of the last supper. He grimaced.

'We have two swords, two daggers, two spears, a scram and a pair of mail shirts,' said Montauban, casting his eyes over the weaponry.

'There are spare lance shafts stowed over there; they can be used as quarterstaffs.' Joscelin pointed to a stack of shaped ash staves leaning against a wall. 'We won't have to tackle every soldier in the keep, only the mercenaries loyal to Ralf and, even then, their resistance is likely to be half-hearted.' He cast a look over his shoulder at the two Flemings. 'Ralf is the target. Down him and the resistance dies.'

'You want him dead?' Montauban licked his lips.

Joscelin drew a harsh breath through his teeth. Every nerve and desire directed him to answer yes, but he held back, afraid of the blackness at his core, as deep and dark as the oubliette in which Ralf had cast him. 'Hold back unless there is no other way,' he replied. 'Better if he is taken alive and dealt with by the justiciar.' His expression became bleak. 'Otherwise I am no better than he.'

37

Linnet watched Agnes de Rocher raise a coffer lid, take from it a pile of garments and bring them over to the bed where Ironheart lay. His hands were crossed upon his breast and his badger-grey hair was parted in the middle, combed and oiled as Linnet had never seen it in life. It had always been swept back from his forehead in leonine disorder and very seldom had he used a comb to tame it.

Death had softened some of the harsh lines graven into his face but, without flesh or colour, he was already a cadaver, bearing little resemblance to the living man she wanted to remember. And Agnes was revelling in her moment of glory. She was like an eager bride, her face radiant and her eyes sparkling as she went about her death-chamber duties.

Linnet had been escorted back from the chapel by two of Ralf's Flemish guards and informed that if she wandered off again, she would be tied up. Agnes had recovered from her near-choking, although her voice was nothing more than a harsh whisper, and she had exchanged the light silk wimple of earlier for a fuller one of linen that swathed her throat and shoulders, concealing all marks.

Linnet had been forced to sit on a stool and watch Agnes prepare her husband to be taken down to the chapel to lie in state; to watch the woman wash his body as tenderly as a lover, dwelling upon the ravaged, calloused flesh with obscene, possessive joy. It had made Linnet sick. Twice she had had to run to the waste pit in the corner of the room, although there had been nothing to bring up but bile. And each time she returned, it was to see Agnes crooning to her husband, smiling and stroking.

'You are mine now,' Agnes whispered, running the rose-water cloth over the body in long, smooth strokes. 'You cannot gainsay my will.'

Linnet shuddered at her tone. She wondered if Agnes, in her madness, would cast off her clothes and leap into bed with the body.

'Of course, when it comes your turn to do this, your own husband will not be so presentable,' Agnes continued as she shook out the garments, hurling small, brittle pieces of bay leaf and sage from the folds. 'I saw a human hide once, nailed on the gates of a house in Newark. You couldn't really tell it was human, it was all yellow and shrivelled; they mustn't have tanned it properly.'

Linnet was overcome with nausea again, her reaction so swift and strong to Agnes' words that she had no time to reach the garderobe and had to use her wimple.

Agnes clucked her tongue. 'You are suffering, my dear, aren't you?' she said, a parody of concern in her damaged voice. 'When is the babe due?'

'It is you who is making me sick,' Linnet gasped, removing her spoiled wimple. Jesu and his mother, help me, she thought, knowing she could not endure much more.

'Your heart is too tender, as indeed mine was once.

Perhaps you see yourself in me?' Agnes cocked her head to one side, eyeing Linnet with a terrible shrewdness. 'But you *are* pregnant, aren't you? I have carried enough infants in my womb to know the signs.'

Linnet removed her stained wimple. 'It is no concern of yours,' she said in what she hoped was a cold tone speaking of strength, not trembling terror.

'Oh, but it is,' Agnes said. 'In your belly grows the seed of Morwenna de Gael's grandchild. We shall have to do something about that unless you lose it of your own accord. It is no use looking at the door. There is a guard on the stairs and he has instructions not to let you pass unless in my company. Come.' She gestured. 'Help me dress my husband for the chapel. He cannot go before the altar in his shirt. It would not be seemly.'

Sickened to her soul, Linnet backed away from Agnes' beckoning finger, backed away until her spine struck the wall and she could go no farther. Agnes smiled and shrugged and turned to the body.

Linnet slipped down the wall until a low, dust-covered oak coffer caught the back of her knees. She slumped upon it, fighting to stay conscious, terrified of the danger to herself and her unborn child. As if from a great distance she heard Agnes directing her maid to lift and lower, pull and push, as they dressed William Ironheart in his court robes, decking him out in the finery that he had shunned in life.

'Neither will it be seemly for you to accompany me to the chapel with your hair uncovered,' Agnes croaked over to Linnet. 'You will find a wimple in that coffer. Put it on and make yourself decent for the priest.'

Spots of light danced before Linnet's eyes and the room was spinning. She wanted to snarl defiance at Agnes but knew that her only chance of escape lay in leaving this room, in persuading Ralf that she would be better guarded elsewhere if he wanted to preserve her to use as a bargaining counter.

Gingerly she turned round, knelt on the floor, and raised the lid of the coffer on which she had been sitting. The scent of faded herbs drifted to her nostrils as she looked upon folded chemises and summer linen under-gowns. Unable to find a wimple, she burrowed deeper, at last uncovering a rectangle of blue-green silk and another larger one of pale blue linen. A small securing brooch in the shape of a bronze horse was still pinned in the latter's folds.

It was this second one that Linnet chose, but as she drew the cloth from the chest the brooch pin caught on the garment folded beneath. She lifted both out in order to untangle them and found herself looking at the gown that had been lying in the bottom of the coffer. It was made of green samite with a trim of tarnished silver thread and, when she held it up, she saw that it was cut in the style fashionable when she had been a little girl and that it had been adapted to fit a woman big with child.

'Dear God,' she whispered and looked over her shoulder at Agnes. The older woman was busily adorning Ironheart's body and showed no sign that she had intended for Linnet to discover the gown. Linnet wondered if this coffer had been Morwenna's. Had she ever worn the blue wimple and horse brooch? Was the green silk wimple the one that belonged with the gown in the bottom of the chest? With shaking hands, Linnet covered her hair with the blue linen and brought an edge across to pin beneath her throat.

Agnes turned round. Her small eyes widened as she looked at the open coffer. 'Not that one,' she snapped,

347

'the one next to it.' She pointed at another, larger chest standing against the wall. Then she made a gesture of dismissal. 'It doesn't matter. Maude never uses it anyway.'

'It belongs to Maude?'

Agnes shrugged. 'I told you, it does not matter.'

Linnet drew the green gown from the coffer, shook it out and held it up. 'So this is hers?'

If Agnes had been capable of screaming, she would have done so. Mouth open, she stared at the creased green robe with its knotted hanging sleeves and rich silver borders. Her colour faded to the hue of ashes and she dragged air into her lungs with painful effort. 'I gave orders that it should be burned!' she wheezed. 'The stupid, sentimental bitch. I should never have let her stay here to comfort William and the brat after the whore died. Give it to me!' Hands extended to snatch, she stepped towards Linnet.

'You destroyed yourself when you killed Morwenna, didn't you?' Linnet sidestepped to avoid Agnes. Armoured with the green gown, she was no longer afraid. 'You kept her fresh and young for ever in your husband's mind.'

'Give me that gown, you harlot!' Agnes lunged. Linnet dodged. The tarnished silver braid glittered and the green silk glowed with absorbed and reflected light as Linnet swept out of Agnes' reach. Agnes stumbled against the larger chest. Standing on it was a small, open basket containing her tablet-weaving materials. From among the hanks of wool, she grasped her sewing shears and gripped them like a weapon. 'You whore!' Agnes whispered, her broken voice saturated with hatred. 'You'll not take him from me this time!'

Linnet jumped backwards, trying to avoid the shears as Agnes lunged. Moving sideways, dodging, Linnet tried to reach the bed in order to keep its bulk between herself and Agnes, but Agnes was too quick for her and Linnet's direction only incensed the older woman further. 'Keep away from him!' Agnes hissed, striking at Linnet with the shears. The pointed blades ripped into the old green silk, shredding the front from breast to hip.

Linnet narrowly missed being gouged. The force of Agnes' assault almost dragged the gown from her hands but she held on to it. As the shears stabbed at her again, she raised the gown on high. 'Have it!' she cried, tossing it over Agnes's head, and ran to the door. She wrestled with the heavy latch, knowing that at any moment Agnes would win free of the gown and come at her again.

Sobbing with panic, she rammed the heel of her hand down on the latch and felt it give. She wrenched the door open, intending to flee down the stairs to the guard but bounced off Ralf instead.

'Going somewhere?' he said softly and, seizing her upper arm in a grip of steel, turned her round and pulled her back into the room. He was not alone. Ivo, four knights and the priest followed him into the chamber.

'Your mother's trying to kill me!' Linnet panted, struggling against his imprisoning fingers to no avail. 'She thinks I'm Morwenna de Gael!'

Agnes had fought free of the green gown and was glaring wildly at Linnet, the shears still tilted at a wicked angle in her hand.

'She's a whore!' Agnes spat, 'and she's carrying a child. I'll have no spawn of a de Gael under my roof!'

Ralf lifted his brows. 'Mama, she is useful to us for the moment. She holds the key to the Rushcliffe estates. There is no profit to be had in killing her.'

Agnes' complexion darkened. She compressed her lips and her fingers tightened around her shears.

Ralf gestured towards her work basket. 'Put them

down,' he said reasonably. 'We can discuss matters later, after the hanging. My father bought you a nun's pension before he died. Mayhap we can use it to endow a young widow instead?'

Agnes' lips remained tight but she obeyed Ralf and replaced the shears among the hanks of wool. 'I only have your good at heart,' she said.

'I know that, Mama,' Ralf said gently, his tone imbued with a rare warmth. Releasing Linnet's arm, he crossed the room and looked down at his father's body, at the wine-red court gown and the battle-hardened hands clasped in an attitude of prayer.

'It doesn't look like him,' he said and rubbed his hand over his lower face in a nervous gesture. Linnet could see that his composure was brittle. There were dark shadows beneath his eyes and downward tucks at the corners of his mouth.

'It isn't him,' Linnet said coldly. 'He might as well be a dressed carcass on a butcher's slab.'

Ralf glared round at her. 'You will keep a civil tongue in your head or I will lock you up in the undercroft,' he snapped.

'Is that what you are going to do to everyone who contradicts your will?' Linnet retorted. 'Lock them away, strike them silent – murder them?'

Ralf's fists clenched. He swivelled and took two strides towards her.

'Ralf, don't,' said Ivo in a wavering voice. 'Not in here, with Papa . . .' He gestured towards the bed.

Ralf stopped. A pulse thundered in his throat and his eyes were narrow and wolf-golden. Linnet refused to be intimidated. She gave him back stare for stare, knowing that her own gaze was no less wild.

Abruptly he turned his back on her. His fists remained

clenched and his voice was raw with anger as he addressed Agnes. 'Is my father prepared for the chapel?'

'Yes, my heart,' Agnes said. 'See, I have dressed him fittingly in his court robes and set rings on his fingers.'

Ralf shrugged. 'If you were to have dressed him fittingly, it would not have been like this but in his oldest tunic and cloak,' he said.

Agnes stared at him, uncomprehending. Ralf shook his head. 'No matter,' he said. 'You have done your best.' He kissed her cheek.

Agnes started to speak, but broke off abruptly as the sound of sword on sword and a choked-off scream twisted up the stairs from the guard post at the foot of the tower.

Drawing his own blade, Ralf strode to the door and gestured one of his knights to go down and investigate. The man hurried out. Almost immediately the occupants of the room heard the clash of weapons and another cry. Ralf's man backed up the stairs and staggered into the room, blood pouring from his shoulder.

'Bar the door!' he gasped at Ralf. 'Your brother and his men are loose and they're armed!' As he uttered the warning, he kicked the door shut and leaned against it.

White with shock, Ralf stooped to pick up the draw-bar leaning against the wall. Seeing the hope of freedom, and then that hope about to be lost, Linnet ran to stop him from pushing the plank through the iron brackets. She blocked his way with her body, her arms outstretched. Ralf shoved her violently away. She landed heavily on her side, bruising hip and shoulder, but rolled over on the straw and grasped a handful of his long tunic. Ralf raised the plank and struck her on the side of the head with its corner.

Black stars burst in front of Linnet's eyes. Her grip weakened and Ralf tore free. Through swimming eyes she saw him lift the draw bar to slot it into position just

351

as the door was smashed wide by Joscelin and Guy de Montauban.

The wounded knight was thrown to the floor and rolled back and forth, clutching his shoulder. Ralf dropped the wood and leaped backwards with the speed of a bounding deer. The sword he had sheathed while he manipulated the draw bar he now snatched from his scabbard in a rapid flash of steel as he turned in a battle-crouch to face Joscelin.

The run upstairs had winded Joscelin and he was close to the limit of his endurance. He saw Linnet near the door. She struggled to sit up, her mouth working as if she wanted to cry out to him but no sound emerged and she sagged back to the floor. Blood masked one side of her face, staining her wimple and gown. Joscelin's rage boiled over and, with a howl, he flung himself at Ralf. The blow was made of white-hot fury, mistimed and without control. Ralf parried easily and made a smooth counterstrike, his own breathing calm and deep. The sword edge shrieked upon the ill-fitting mail shirt that Joscelin had purloined from one of the Flemings in the undercroft. He had the Fleming's sword, too, the hilt worn and slippery in his grasp.

The room filled with the clash and glitter of weapons. The priest sidled quickly out of the door, delicately stepping over Linnet. Ivo allowed himself to be made Guy de Montauban's prisoner without even a token show of protest.

Ralf's strength forced Joscelin backward and Ralf pressed his advantage, using his sword two-handed, swinging it almost as though it were a battle-axe. 'Side by side in the chapel,' Ralf panted as he fought Joscelin into a corner. 'You and our sainted father – wouldn't that be fitting!'

Joscelin stumbled against a coffer and knew that it must be his last move on earth, but Ralf lost his own footing upon a puddle of green silk that was bunched on the floor and his blow went awry, slicing the coffer instead of Joscelin's skull. The impetus brought Ralf to his knees, his sword lodged in the wood. Before he could recover and free the blade, Joscelin leaped upon him, bearing him to the ground beneath his weight. The air burst out of Ralf's lungs. His head struck the rushes, but he succeeded in landing a knee in Joscelin's groin, and as Joscelin recoiled Ralf was able to twist free and grasp his sword once more. Both hands to the leather grip, he went all out to take Joscelin.

His sword rang out great hammer blows on Joscelin's blade as he beat at it, striving to win past the slender bar of steel and cut out Joscelin's heart. And Joscelin, on the edge of exhaustion, could barely hold him off; his body had taken too much punishment this past night and day to serve him through another bout. His vision started to blur and hot pain seared through his limbs as he parried and defended.

Sensing Joscelin's weakness, Ralf gathered himself for a final, killing flurry and, in that moment, poised on the brink of his triumph, Martin burst into the room followed by Fulbert the scribe, who was wheezing like a set of bagpipes with the unaccustomed exertion.

'Soldiers!' Fulbert gasped out, clutching his side, his face purple. 'Demanding entry. The seneschal's just raising the bridge!'

Martin shot between his two brothers. 'Stop, you have to stop!' he shrieked, his face white. 'You can't kill each other!'

'Get out of the way, whelp,' Ralf snarled, his eyes never leaving Joscelin. 'You heard the scribe,' he spat. 'My allies have come. Either we finish this now or you swing on a gibbet for their entertainment. Which is it to be?'

Joscelin stared dully at Ralf. Every nerve and fibre of his body was sodden with exhaustion; there was nothing he wanted to do more than let the weight of his sword hit the floor, but he knew that he would rather die by the grim mercy of a blade, here and now, than by throttling on a rope before a host of witnesses.

'It will never be finished,' he said hoarsely and braced his trembling sword arm.

'Leave me alone!' Martin yelled, wrenching himself free of his mother as she tried to drag him away from the two men.

Fulbert was twitching with terror but he stepped resolutely forward. 'You do not understand,' he wheezed at Ralf. 'It is the constable of Nottingham who is here and Brien FitzRenard bearing the justiciar's authority. They are in the bailey even now.'

Ralf's face changed. He stared at the scribe in utter disbelief and Fulbert avoided his gaze, backing hastily away.

'What trickery is this?' Ralf snarled.

Ivo brushed aside Montauban's sword and went to the window. Throwing the shutters wide, he stood on tiptoe to look out on the bailey. 'It's true,' he said. 'It's the constable and FitzRenard.' He looked over his shoulder into the room, his expression half-afraid and half-relieved.

Uttering a roar of incandescent rage, Ralf swept Martin aside as if he were no more than a feather and attacked Joscelin, his sword a hacking, slashing blur. Joscelin parried and ducked, was forced backward, pushed and manipulated by Ralf's superior stamina until the dark tower stairway was at his back and he could retreat no farther.

'I'll send you to hell, you whoreson!' Ralf's lips were

drawn back from his teeth in a feral snarl as he brought up the sword.

Joscelin feinted one way, dived the other, and as he hit the floor he yanked at the length of green silk upon which Ralf had been standing. He felt the impact of a heavy blow upon his mail and a searing pain, and saw Ralf struggling to hold his balance on the very edge of the top step. Joscelin scrambled to his knees and clawed for Ralf's tunic to try and pull him back into the chamber. The friction of flesh on fabric burned his knuckles and Ralf's weight ripped back his fingernails. As Ralf fell, Joscelin was brought down the first stone steps with him, only preventing himself from falling the rest of the way by jamming his feet against the newel post and his spine against the wall.

Time thickened and slowed. Sounds caught in it were distorted and hollow. The scrape of armour grinding on stone, the thud, thump of a body rolling over and over. The scent of flowers. Silence.

Joscelin moved gingerly, his limbs feeling as if they were made of hot lead. There was pain across his shoulder and back. He could not feel the trickle of blood, but he knew that the sword must have split the hauberk from the very strength of the impact. He would have heavy bruising at the least and probably a couple of cracked bones. And Ralf?

Like an old man he inched down the stairs to his brother. The red-gold hair gleamed in the torchlight. When he turned him, so did the blood as it trickled from ears and nostrils. Ralf's eyes were open, but there was only the thinnest ring of gold-flecked brown to be seen. The rest of the iris showed only the blackness of a lost soul.

'Christ Jesu,' Joscelin whispered and bowed his head. And behind him, he heard Agnes' hoarse scream.

355

38

Linnet felt cold moisture on her brow and heard Maude's comforting murmur. There was the softness of a bracken mattress beneath her and feather bolsters supporting her head. Farther into the room, she thought she could hear the low rumble of masculine conversation.

She dared to open her eyes. Pain throbbed hard at one temple and the rest of her skull ached in dull sympathy. Through blurred eyes she stared around and wondered where she was. These were not her own chambers at Rushcliffe but neither were they Agnes' rooms. The walls were austere, whitewashed stone that hurt her eyes. For a moment she wondered if she was in a monastery, but there was not even the adornment of a crucifix to relieve the barrenness. Beneath her fingers was a thick blanket of the plaid weave common to the Scots border, the kind that she and Joscelin had on their own bed.

'Where am I?' she whispered and discovered that her mouth was sticky and dry.

Maude leaned over her. 'You're awake at last,' she said with relief. 'I was beginning to worry. A day and a night you've been asleep. You're at Arnsby, in my brother's rooms.'

Linnet tried to swallow but started to cough. 'Thirsty,' she managed to croak out, the pain rippling through her head with a vengeance. Maude helped her to sit and held a cup of watered wine to her lips.

'Slowly, my dear, slowly,' she soothed.

Linnet sipped and lay back against the bolsters. Her vision continued to clear and blur. She put her hand to the pain at her temple and touched gingerly. Her fingers encountered clipped hair and the thick hardness of dried blood.

'The leech said it was best to let it heal in the open air.' Maude said.

Linnet frowned. 'I remember now; Ralf hit me with the door-bar when I tried to stop him from closing the door.' Her eyes flew wide and she pulled herself to a full sitting position. 'And then he and Joscelin were fighting and Joscelin was losing. I tried to move but I couldn't. I don't remember anything except Ralf and Joscelin and that open doorway . . .' She pressed her fingers to her lips, feeling sick.

'It's all right, my love, don't you worry.' Maude enfolded Linnet in one of her smothering embraces, but not before Linnet had seen the grief brimming in the woman's eyes. Struggling, she fought herself out of Maude's arms.

'What happened? Tell me!'

Maude dashed one pudgy hand across her eyes. 'Joscelin is safe,' she said in a quivering voice. 'Never think that he isn't. Indeed, I will fetch him to tell you himself. I am upset for my brother, that is all . . . for the tragedy.' She gave a loud sniff. 'William and Ralf both. I know that he deserved it but he was still my nephew. And Agnes has not spoken a word since, just lies on her bed, her face all twisted to one side. She had a seizure, you know, the poor soul.'

'Ralf is dead?' Linnet's head spun.

'He fell down the stairs while they were fighting and cracked open his skull. We arrived moments after it happened. William's seneschal opened the gates to us when he saw the justiciar's writ – he had no choice. I almost feel sorry for the poor man. Conan and Brien FitzRenard were the first into the keep and they found Ralf dead and Joscelin collapsed on the stairs to Agnes' rooms.'

Linnet bit her lip, trying to remember. Her mind was like an autumn scene with areas of drifting fog changing the landscape from moment to moment. 'But how did you know to come?'

'I was on my way here and decided to stop at Rushcliffe for the night. That young red-haired Scotsman of yours, Malcolm, told me that William was dreadfully ill with a deep sword wound and that you and Joscelin had taken him to Arnsby. Then the messenger came with your cry for help, so we set off straight away. Apparently William's scribe used to be yours and took his life in his hands to send out the messages.'

Linnet gave a tremulous smile. 'I thought I had failed with him. I asked him to help me, but he would not meet my eyes when he said he would see what he could do. I will have to go to him and be humble now.'

'He is rather basking in his glory,' Maude admitted. She patted Linnet's hand and then looked round and rose to her feet as Joscelin approached the bedside. His eyes were all for Linnet and Maude tactfully made her excuses and left. The kiss she bestowed on her nephew's stubbled cheek before she departed was affectionate and under-standing, her embrace for Linnet tender.

When she had gone, Linnet and Joscelin looked at each other then, in a sudden simultaneous move, were in each other's arms, kissing, holding tight. 'Holy Virgin,' Linnet sobbed, 'I truly thought you were going to die!'

'So did I,' he muttered into the hair on her good side. 'If it had not been for Ivo, I would have done.'

'Ivo!'

He drew back and showed her the blistered weals on his hands. 'Ivo threw a rope down into the oubliette so that I could climb out. He says that it was the only rope on which he wanted to see me swing.'

'I thought he hated you.'

'Not as much as he loves the mortal state of his soul. Fraternal rivalry is one matter. Cold-blooded murder is another.'

Linnet shivered and pressed her cheek against his tunic, savouring a closeness she thought she had lost. 'And now Ivo is lord of Arnsby?'

'Not for long.'

She raised her head and looked quickly into his tired, unshaven face. 'You do not mean to dispute with him?'

'No. He says that he intends taking the cross and that, providing he can have Papa's hunting lodge and manor house near Melton, he'll pass over his right in Martin's favour.' He stroked her hair. 'It's not as strange as it sounds. Ivo's always trotted around in someone else's shadow. He does not know how to stand in the light.' He sighed heavily. 'I want to go home to Rushcliffe, I want to see Robert and sleep with you at my side for a week.' He paused, his hand clasped over hers, and added quietly, 'I want to forget. Why do we always want the impossible?'

Without speaking, for her throat was tight, she took his calloused hand and placed it against her womb, upon the hidden promise of new life.

359

EPILOGUE

Spring 1175

The white chapel held two effigies, side by side, one a woman wearing a crown of saffron crocuses upon her pale stone brow. Her companion wore mail and a surcoat, his sword carved at rest beside him and his hands clasped, not in an attitude of prayer, but holding a shield bearing the comet blazon of his family line.

'It looks like Papa,' Martin said judiciously and ran his forefinger over the stone ripples and folds. 'He'll be happy here, I know he will.'

Robert copied him by setting his own smaller hand upon the effigy's spurs.

Joscelin lightly touched Martin's shoulder and considered Ironheart's tomb. He had had to search hard among Nottingham's fraternity of alabaster craftsmen to find one who could carve the effigy as he wanted. No pious positioning of the hands or rigid garments confining the essence. He wanted Ironheart the restless, brusque warrior, not Ironheart the saint. By and large the man had succeeded, although his father's hair had never succumbed to a comb the way it had succumbed in stone to the craftsman's chisel. Ralf had a tomb, too, in the chapel at

360

Arnsby, and that was rigidly conventional and blessedly resembled his brother not in the slightest. The same went for Agnes' memorial, although that was not yet finished for she had only died the week before Candlemas of yet another seizure.

He would not dwell on the past. Linnet would rebuke him if she thought he was brooding, although she allowed him his moments of solitude and introspection. He heard her footfall now and turned to watch her walk up the nave towards him. She was wearing her thick winter cloak for, despite the sunshine, there was still a sharpness in the air and she had her burden to protect, but she walked gracefully, and he felt his heart and gut swoop together, producing a feeling of elation.

The others would be coming soon to fill the church and attend this Mass that was to be said for the souls of William de Rocher and Morwenna de Gael, but Joscelin had allowed a space of time for the solitude of his own immediate family, for the peace and breathing space to stand before the tombs of his mother and father and present to them their three-month-old granddaughter, dark of hair, green of eye – Morwenna.